CW01302301

A Study in Curses

Jessica Martinet

A Study in Curses

Mist & Magic

MISTANDMAGIC.COM

Copyright © 2024 by Jessica Martinet

All rights reserved.

No part of this book may be used, reproduced, distributed, or transmitted in any form or by any means, including photocopying, recording, or other electronic or mechanical methods, without the written consent of the copyright owner.

This novel is a work of fiction. Characters, places, events, and names are fictitious. Any resemblance to other events, other locations, or other persons, living or dead, is coincidental.

Book Cover and Illustrations by Virginie Martinet

First Edition : September 2024

ISBN 978-1-0687191-0-3 (hardcover)

ISBN 978-1-0687191-1-0 (paperback)

ISBN 978-1-0687191-2-7 (ebook)

Published by Mist and Magic Press

PO Box 26354, Crieff PH7 9BB

email: press@mistandmagic.com

www.jessicamartinet.com

Printed and bound in Great Britain by ImprintDigital

*To Virginie,
you're more than my sister,
you're the other half of my soul.*

CHAPTER ONE

September 18, 1936
York, United Kingdom

OLIVIA STOPPED TO ADMIRE the shiny, newly installed gold plaque that adorned the wooden door of the office. She had wanted to buy one for a long time now — her business was well into its third year — but had never got around to it. It had taken a heated exchange with a centuries-old cursed portrait that had exploded out of its containment wards a few weeks back, as well as one very broken door, for her to finally order the thing.

The Knight Curse-Breaking Agency.

She had to admit, that was one catchy name. She still felt the same twinge in her heart as when she'd first filed her business with the York City Register. A quick swipe of her sleeve made the metal gleam even brighter in the fading evening light.

With one last proud look, Olivia placed her hand on the handle and let out a heavy sigh. After spending all day with potential clients, she'd hoped for a quiet evening to catch up on some overdue paperwork, but if the grunts and other loud thumps coming from the other side of the door were any indication, she could kiss her hopes goodbye.

Indeed, as soon as she entered the office, Olivia realised that her earlier instincts hadn't failed her, and that the Grimoire they'd gone to retrieve the day before had *clearly* behaved with a calmness that was highly suspicious.

Godwyn was on his knees in the middle of the room, wrestling the stubborn book into one of their silverstone cages. But the great volume was having none of it and kept trying to escape out the window. Despite Godwyn pushing with all his might, the Grimoire only hovered over the cage's opening, refusing to go in, and lifting him off the floor with each jolt.

They must have been at it for a while now, because Olivia had rarely seen the dapper and elegant Baron Godwyn de Mowbray looking so dishevelled. His usually flawless dark hair was tousled every which way, and his crisp shirt was long undone. Olivia even noticed his expensive tie lying discarded on the corner of a desk.

Meanwhile, their newest employee, Cornelius, sat on the floor not far away, channeling his magic into the arcane circle around them, no doubt in an attempt to weaken the artifact. The lines drawn in chalk on the hardwood floor radiated a strong light, while an ethereal duplicate of the circle hovered in the air. He was chanting too, but the deafening rattling of the book drowned out his voice.

In addition to trying to make a break for it, the artifact despaired to reveal its musty, crumpled pages full of dangerous writings and words of power. Being bound by thick steel chains greatly hampered its efforts, but the stubborn book compensated by shaking violently and making an absolute racket.

Perfectly confident that her employees had the situation well in hand, Olivia carefully stepped around them to get to the back. Her French assistant, Adeline, sat at her desk, calmly sipping a cup of tea and enjoying the wrestling match happening before her.

As always, she was impeccably dressed, with a fitted pencil skirt and an elegant silk blouse that accentuated her curves, a string of pearls around her neck and a cascade of auburn curls falling gracefully over one shoulder. Her striking grey eyes missed nothing, a familiar wicked gleam in their depths. No doubt she was mentally scoring Godwyn's performance so that she could relay her observations to him later.

"What do you have for me?" Olivia asked her.

Adeline drummed her fingers on her teacup. "Some bad news, some intriguing ones, and a paper you're surely not going to like."

"You spoil me."

Her assistant's red-painted lips curled into a grin. "Which one would you like first?"

CHAPTER 1

Olivia held out her hand. "Give me that dreaded paper."

"I've finished the inventory. We're out of meridian stones, spectral lures, and we could really use some more feyroot. I know we're already over budget for the month, but I was thinking I could talk to Bowen, see if I can get us a good deal."

Olivia scanned the neat report her assistant had produced. "What? Those lures are utterly useless. And overpriced. Four times out of five, they do the opposite of what you want them to do. You know Bowen sells them at a huge markup because he's the only one in the country who can produce them in bulk. We don't need that rubbish, I can make much better ones."

"Ah. But can you make ones that don't smell like swamp water or explode if you so much as stare at them too hard?" Her assistant's tone was pointed.

Olivia loved tinkering with their supplies. Her creations had already shown some very promising results out in the field, but they were still experimental, and well . . . The last one had unfortunately met a tragic end, spraying Adeline with a bright orange liquid that had stained her hair. To say that she hadn't been pleased would be an understatement.

"I can certainly try my best?"

"Hmm."

Olivia decided it might be wise to change the subject. "And about this intriguing news?"

"An official from the Ministry dropped by this afternoon. Since you weren't here, he said he'd be back around six. Left his card." Adeline raised a hand, a white card tucked between two long and elegant fingers. The card simply read : Ryder Isaksson, Dark Artifacts Department, Scottish Arcane Ministry, Edinburgh, Scotland.

Olivia's lips thinned. She reached into her pocket for a cleaning cloth and removed her glasses. Today's choice had been her favourite, her lucky dragon glasses — tortoiseshell, with golden branches that ended in little claws where they met the glass. They obviously hadn't worked so far because surprise visits from Ministry officials meant one thing and one thing only : security inspections and other delightful unannounced audits.

"Isaksson . . ." Olivia cocked her head in thought. "That's odd, I've never heard that name before, and I know just about everyone who works at the Department. Do you know him?"

Behind her, Godwyn unleashed an impressive string of curses for a noble heir, before shouting at Cornelius to come help him contain that *"demonic mule of a book."*

"No, I've never met him before," Adeline told her. "When he came in, I was actually surprised to learn he worked for the Ministry, from the way he was dressed. He looked more like a private detective than anything else. Maybe even a bounty hunter."

Olivia slipped her glasses back on. "Keep your fingers crossed for a simple assessment and not a full security inspection. I've still got a ton of paperwork to do, and I don't want to add another five thousand pages to the pile."

"If that's the case, I'll distract him while you make a run for it," Adeline promised with a wink.

Knowing her, this wasn't a joke. With her charm and her sharp wit, her assistant could have a very successful career as a spy if she ever left the agency.

"Do you think you could find out more about him?" Olivia asked her. "I'd like to know exactly which service he belongs to. If he's here for an assessment, I'll have to lock Jerry in the upstairs cupboard again. He won't like it, but the last official still swears it was an attempt at coercion and we tried to strangle him so we could pass the evaluation."

Adeline scoffed. "As if we needed Jerry for that."

"By the way, have you managed to hear from Ravenscroft? All the papers are in order and ready to go, we just need his signature." Olivia patted the bag on her hip with a satisfied grin. "I finished the plans last night."

Her assistant grimaced. "And now for the bad news. I finally got through to his assistant. He's decided not to use our services after all."

"*Again*? What is going on with them?" Olivia blew out an exasperated breath. "Did his assistant tell you who they're going to hire?"

Adeline shook her head. "I haven't given you the bad news yet, *this* is : they're not hiring anyone."

"What." Olivia's features froze into a hard mask. "I spent an hour and a half explaining to him how unstable his curse is. I had to pull out the Chart. I left him with detailed instructions on what to do if it became active again. And you're telling me he's not going to do anything about it?"

"Apparently, he went to play golf with Lord Dryden, who convinced him that you were exaggerating the threat and that the artifact could wait until they had their Committee party."

It was good to know that golf trumped common sense.

"Oh yes, what a splendid idea," Olivia ground out. "Throw all of York's banking bigwigs together so they can be blown up to smithereens between canapes."

Olivia snatched the phone off Adeline's desk and marched to their supply room, the cord trailing behind her. It was the only place in the office that would muffle the sounds of the Grimoire's epic battle. "I'm calling Skelton."

Her assistant tried to stop her. "Oh no, no. That's really not a good idea, Liv. Remember what happened last time . . ."

The last time Olivia had had the Head of the Dark Artifacts Department on the phone, she'd yelled at him for the way he'd handled a case. No doubt the man dreamed of throwing her into a containment cage like one of his artifacts.

"It was a while ago," she stated. "He's forgotten."

Adeline gave her a flat stare, but Olivia ignored it, instead pointing a warning finger behind her. "Make sure those two don't destroy the whole building, will you?"

"No promises."

Olivia closed the door to the small room behind her just as a loud and triumphant shout rang through the entire office.

"So you see, the resonance pattern is very clear. This artifact is on the verge of activation. I made sure to explain this to Mr Ravenscroft in great detail, but he has chosen to ignore the situation. Worse, he is preparing for a gathering at his house as we speak. If his artifact does indeed decide to detonate, I cannot imagine what that would do—"

"Yes, I've heard all about this."

Olivia could clearly hear the annoyance lacing the voice on the other end of the line. "You've heard about this . . ." she repeated.

"I got a call early this morning," Skelton drawled. "While I was preparing for a report at the Halls of Law. From a very distraught Lord Protector who wanted to express his dismay at a member of his House being threatened by a private curse-breaker. I don't need to explain why I immediately knew who he was talking about."

Olivia's hand clenched on the receiver. While she'd been finishing up the plans to contain his artifact, Ravenscroft had been blabbing and whining. That deceitful toad.

"I can assure you that I remained professional and sympathetic to his circumstances. All I did was politely remind him that being aware of such a dangerous situation and failing to take appropriate action was considered a crime, not to mention a grave dereliction of the responsibilities of his title, and I would be duty-bound to report it to the authorities."

Skelton scoffed. "Will you stop exaggerating everything, Olivia? I've been in this Department for years and I have only ever seen these bloody things blow up a handful of times."

That may be true. But when they did, people died.

"Mr Ravenscroft is a civilian, he doesn't understand the danger. It is my professional opinion that his—"

"Ravenscroft is an extremely wealthy man with eccentric tastes," Skelton went on as if he hadn't heard her. "He probably believes his artifact to be nothing more than a novelty. We cannot simply invade his home and summarily confiscate everything that makes us uncomfortable."

Olivia swallowed her reply at great personal cost. Instead, she tucked the telephone receiver into the crook of her neck, grabbed a couple of clean jars and began filling them with her latest experimental concoction, hoping the careful movements would help her remain calm.

Either that, or she was about to repaint the walls of this room.

"All the signs are here. If you would just send a team, I promise you would find the same readings I did."

"Look, I have more pressing matters to attend to. I trust Ravenscroft's judgment on this. Besides, I simply cannot waste the Department's resources on every overzealous curse-breaker who thinks the sky is about to fall. Drop it and move on to the next job."

"With all due respect, I don't work for you any more." As soon as the words left her lips, Olivia winced. That hadn't been the right thing to say. "What I meant was that I have a moral and professional obligation—"

"You're quite right, Ms Knight, you do not work for my Department any more. Because if you did, you would know to keep your place. And I wouldn't have to . . ." Skelton bit off his next words and let out an exasperated hiss instead. "Let us be honest here. What happened with Lord Hadley was one thing, but threatening a member of one of the most powerful House? Ravenscroft is a highly respected arcanist, that is unacceptable. Not to mention unbecoming. You're tarnishing the reputation of the entire Ministry."

Godwyn's raised voice, coming from behind the door, cut through Skelton's lecture. "Look out! The lock is breaking!"

Olivia barely had time to blink before pandemonium ensued once again. She started to rise, but when she heard a volley of shouted orders, shrugged and decided to leave the crisis in the capable hands of her staff. She had a crisis of her own to deal with in here.

"Knight? Knight!"

A *thump* sounded as if he'd just slammed his hand down on his desk. "I swear, Knight, if you ignore me, I'll—"

"No, no, I'm here! The line is, ah . . . cutting off."

There was a furious pause before Skelton squeezed past gritted teeth, "Perhaps I should remind you that the accreditation that allows your agency to function comes from my Department. It would be most unwise for you to remain a thorn in my side, Knight."

Olivia's hand clenched on the jar. "We want the same thing here. No harm to befall the Ravenscrofts. Because if the worse were to happen, it wouldn't go the way it did last time."

A dangerous silence filled the line.

"Are you threatening me now?"

"I thought we were having an *honest* conversation, here," Olivia replied. "And I can *honestly* say that I may have taken the blame once, but I learn from my mistakes, Mr Skelton. If a tragedy were to happen, I would make sure everyone knew it was you who refused to get the Department involved. Perhaps you should weigh the consequences of that against the cost of sending a team over. Now, if you'll excuse me, I have work to do."

Olivia slammed the receiver down with a hard clank.

"Positions!" someone called from the next room.

She raised a hand to rub her forehead, but then her arm froze in mid-air.

She'd clearly recognised Godwyn's voice just now, which meant . . . the person giving orders earlier hadn't been him.

Olivia took off, managing by some miracle not to send her mixtures flying. She flung open the door and skidded to a halt, her eyes wide.

A huge beast of a man, with tousled blond hair and broad shoulders, was standing on one of their desks. He looked even taller than Godwyn, which meant Olivia would be lucky if her head even reached the top of his shoulders.

Standing somewhere nearby, Cornelius yelled "Ready!" and that spurred the giant into action. He bent his knees and leapt into the air to tackle the flying Grimoire. The force of his momentum threw them both wildly to the side, but the book held on, lifting them even higher until they reached the ceiling.

Godwyn and Cornelius each had a death grip on one of the chains attached to it. They groaned and cursed, trying to bring both book and stranger back down. Meanwhile, Adeline stared from across the room, mouth agape, clutching a long black jacket to her chest.

The book made a solid effort to knock the stranger off, swinging them from side to side like a dog guarding its bone.

"Come on, gentlemen, just a little more!" the mysterious man bellowed. His voice matched him, deep and slightly raspy, with a distinct Scandinavian accent.

His battle cry snapped Olivia out of her shock. She ran to their group, grabbed a free length of chain and began pulling with all her might.

Inch by agonising inch, they managed to lower the Grimoire to the ground. When the stranger's feet reached the floor, he wrestled the book the rest of the way into the open steel cage, his arm muscles bulging from the effort. Cornelius hurried to latch the thick lock.

As they all tried to catch their breath, Godwyn leaned his body against the nearest wall and slid to the floor, exhausted. Olivia wiped the sweat from her brow, looking around.

The office was in complete chaos. It was as if a small tornado had been unleashed inside. Papers that had been flying all around them were slowly falling back down, and after the infernal roar of the book, the sudden silence was deafening.

The stranger sprang to his feet with surprising agility for a man of his size and grinned, only the slightest flush to his cheeks. "That was one feisty old book, wasn't it?" His blue eyes were gleaming.

They all stared at him in disbelief.

The madman wasn't even winded when he turned to Olivia. "Ah, Ms Knight! I believe we have an appointment." He held out an arm towards her private office. "Shall we?"

CHAPTER TWO

"My apologies for what happened back there, Mr Isaksson. I'm sorry you had to intervene." Olivia closed the door behind her and gestured for him to take a seat in one of the leather chairs, but her mysterious guest ignored her. Shrugging, she made her way to her desk, tucking a few stray raven strands back into the neat braid down her back.

The thick carpet she'd recently added to her annoyingly squeaky floor absorbed the sound of Isaksson's footsteps as he began to explore, but Olivia still noticed that he moved incredibly quietly for someone of his stature.

Thick stubble covered a strong jaw, not quite a beard but still more than most city men allowed. It made him look rugged, a little wild. He had a square forehead, a nose that looked like it had been broken once, and intense blue eyes that scrutinised everything around him with unabashed curiosity.

His simple cream-coloured shirt hugged his abdomen, showing off wide shoulders and a heavily muscled frame. As he absentmindedly scratched his forearm, the bottom of his sleeve lifted to reveal the edges of an intricate runic tattoo.

Isaksson gave the impression that he did not quite belong in this urban environment and should be roaming the wilderness instead. Olivia had a sudden vision of him at the helm of a drakkar, one strong arm brandishing an axe in the air, in pursuit of some forgotten treasure.

He wasn't a mere Ministry employee, that was for sure. No, Olivia was quite certain there was a Viking in her office. And if he was here for a simple security inspection, she would swallow her glasses.

Even though his back was turned, Olivia swore she heard him chuckle. He'd stopped in front of the impressive wall at the back of her room, a trio of giant oak cabinets that spanned the entire length and reached all the way to the ceiling. This was where she kept all the artifacts from current or past cases, safely locked away.

Isaksson was currently laughing under his breath at the amount of warning signs nailed on there. "Danger, Cursed", "Do Not Approach" and "Hazardous Storage" were just a few. The biggest one read "Positively Cursed, Do Not Open" in bold red letters.

In truth, her Wall of Doom, as nicknamed by Godwyn, was something of a running joke in the office. Her employees liked to sneak in from time to time to nail up a new sign, before betting on how long it would take her to notice. Only she would always manage to know exactly what their bets were, and would purposefully wait to say anything until she was right in between two wagers, thus preventing any of them from ever winning. To this day, no one had caught on, her employees being far too smug to notice she had outsmarted them all.

Isaksson glanced over his shoulder and grinned, with a mischievous twinkle in his eyes Olivia was quickly learning was something of a trademark. "Don't apologise. That was by far the most fun I've had in weeks."

A small laugh escaped her. Oh yes, definitely a Viking.

Leaning down, he squinted and tapped his finger on a wooden plaque resting atop a set of drawers. "What is that?"

The light from an old lamp nearby reflected off the copper letters and symbols, making them appear aflame. The spinning hand in the centre twitched ever so slightly towards the right.

Strange.

Olivia guessed it must have been spooked by the Grimoire's antics earlier. Normally it could be found spinning around like crazy all damn day.

"That's an American spirit board from the early 1900s," she told him. "Used to contact and communicate with spirits."

Next to the board was a glass dome, partly covered with a cloth. She stopped Isaksson just as he'd raised a hand to tap on it too. "Please don't. He's sleeping."

His arm froze in mid-air.

Olivia only offered an enigmatic smile in response to his stunned expression. "So, Mr Isaksson. Welcome to the Knight Curse-Breaking Agency. What can I do for you?"

Glancing at all the other objects he hadn't been able to inspect, her guest finally agreed to settle into one of the seats in front of her. "The Dark Artifacts Department would like to hire you on a case. We need a duplicate of a certain object, and I have been told it is your speciality."

Olivia gave a professional nod, but inwardly pumped her fist in the air with a triumphant yell. Her lucky glasses *had* worked after all.

And she also thanked her lucky stars that Skelton seemed too preoccupied with his political games to oversee every case handled by his Department, otherwise he would have surely forbidden Isaksson from hiring her.

Even if this case didn't sound like the exciting job she'd been hoping for, it was still better than nothing. Isaksson had just asked for the same thing as most of her clients — back when she had clients, that is. A *Disposal and Geminus*, where she would take the cursed item off their hands and replace it with a fake. That way, they could pretend to have kept their great-grand-aunt's portrait in its ancestral home without being woken up in the middle of the night by its screams.

"That's right, we specialise in creating highly realistic replicas. Well, that seems straightforward enough, here is the form I—"

"I wouldn't say that," he cut her off.

Olivia's hand halted just as she was about to reach for a stack of papers. She raised an eyebrow. "Why not?"

Isaksson leaned back in his seat and clasped his hands, his large frame dwarfing the chair. Surprisingly, his voice turned amused, almost *daring*. His bright blue gaze held an undertone she couldn't place. "You might find my case, how can I put it . . . challenging. You're going to have many questions, but I won't be able to answer."

"Ah. Because you cannot or you will not?"

"Both, I'm afraid."

It was her turn to recline in her seat as she pondered him. Challenging, huh? Was she about to get her exciting new case after all?

"That shouldn't be a problem," she replied confidently. "Did you bring the artifact with you?"

"No. It can't be moved."

"Alright. Then when can we arrange a visit?"

"It isn't available for visits."

Ah. Now she understood what he'd meant by *challenging*. And it wasn't exactly what she'd had in mind.

Her index finger absentmindedly tapped the edge of her desk. "So, no seeing the artifact in person . . . Wait a second, you said it couldn't be moved. How am I supposed to retrieve it then?"

"Ah. I think you misunderstood me. I just need a replica of the cursed item, that is all."

Olivia swallowed her frustration. They'd finally landed a new case after *weeks*, and it wasn't even a real curse-breaking job. No retrieval, no containment, just the crafting of a fake. Turned out her glasses had completely abandoned her.

"In that case, what *can* you tell me about it?" Her voice was resigned.

Isaksson reached for a brown leather briefcase at his feet and pulled out a few faded snapshots that he handed to her.

She waited for him to say more. "That's it?"

"This is all I'm allowed to show you. By the way, I'll just warn you right now, they came out a little blurry."

Olivia simply sighed.

On the first photograph, a black wand rested atop a carved pedestal. A vibrant green glow emanated from it, along with tendrils of what looked like swirling smoke draped over the thick stone. The light came from the centre of the wand, where the black wood was twisted to reveal its glowing core. The handle was riddled with hairline cracks that let her peek at the energy within.

Squinting, Olivia cursed her terrible eyesight under her breath for the millionth time. She finally gave in and grabbed a magnifying glass, but there was a layer of white spots on all the pictures that made it extremely difficult to discern any details.

Almost all curses reacted negatively to photography and showed these marks on top of the artifacts, rendering pictures practically useless. That was why she always insisted on examining them in person.

"This is clearly an Eastern European wand," she began. "But one with a very unusual design. 14th, maybe 15th century. The runes, though, those are a very classical choice. Reminds me very much of a set of ceremonial swords from the Hunyadi family, in the old kingdom of Hungary. The wood certainly looks like ebony, although I cannot be sure. The way it shines . . . It could be something else." She pulled the reading lamp closer. "The exposed core at the centre of the blade is quite unusual for this period. It's often seen in later centuries for aesthetic purposes, but not until at least the 1650s. This makes me believe that whatever was used as the core may have been too strong to be completely contained by the outer shaft and so the wandmaker tried to let it 'breathe', if you will. Look at the handle, that would explain those fractures. After many years, the wood has begun to crack and split under the pressure of the core. This means that this wand is highly unstable. The cracks don't seem overly deep yet, but they will require conservative measures as soon as possible."

One of the most fundamental laws of wandcraft was the need to choose strong enough materials to withstand the manipulation of magic occurring inside. Otherwise, the wand could literally burst at any moment, releasing an incredibly powerful wave of pure energy. Throughout history, many lives had been lost because of poorly made wands.

"In this condition, your wand is particularly dangerous," she repeated.

Isaksson waved his hand. "Nothing to worry about. It will be taken care of as soon as the job is done."

"Hmm." Olivia pressed her lips together.

How original, she thought sarcastically. A Ministry employee who didn't take unstable artifacts seriously. Isaksson had better be telling the truth and deal with this. If that wand exploded, he was in for a really bad time.

She pointed to the green wisps of magic coming out of it. "This energy seeping out also worries me. Is this a new phenomenon? You must have had your fair share of incidents."

Something like a snort escaped Isaksson. "You could say that." Then he asked, "What else can you tell me about it?"

"Well, not much since I cannot *see* anything." Olivia put down the magnifying glass. "*Challenging* might be putting it mildly, Mr Isaksson. If a viewing is out of the question, do you at least have a component analysis? Since I can't examine it in person, I'll need the most detailed reports you can provide. But at least an elemental analysis, a capability and risk assessment and a trace appraisal. The Wilson-Corbyn evaluation chart would be best. The more I learn about this wand, the closer the replica will be to the original." Olivia opened a drawer and started rummaging through it. "I could give you a reference for a good appraisal lab, if you don't know anyone—"

"I'm only authorised to show you the photographs, nothing more," Isaksson interrupted. He winced as he reached for the business card between her fingers. "Sorry."

Olivia clenched her jaw, smothering a frustrated sigh. It was like talking to a brick wall. "So to be clear, you want me to recreate a magically charged object based solely on three blurry photographs. The replicas I offer here are true twins of the original, Mr Isaksson. They have the same aura, the same energy. Everything except the curse that was placed upon them." She leaned back in her seat and took off her glasses to rub her temples. "May I at least know what you intend to use it for? Do you want some sort of display piece? Because if you do, I suggest you find yourself a talented woodworker instead, who could craft you a perfectly inert fake."

And stop wasting my time, she wisely didn't add.

But Isaksson shook his head. "What I want is the most convincing replica you can make. It must be able to pass for the real thing in front of experts. It doesn't have to be able to perform any magic by itself, but it needs to feel like it could."

Olivia tried to hold back her annoyance. She was just barely successful. "And how am I supposed to achieve this if I can't examine the artifact in question, and you won't give me any reports? I don't have any special tool to divine the mystical abilities of this wand from your blurry pictures, Mr Isaksson."

That finally seemed to make him pause. He scratched the stubble on his jaw as he thought about it. "I can describe what it feels like to be next to it, if that helps."

Olivia had to close her eyes for a second. Was it too late to opt for the security inspection instead?

There had not been an ounce of sarcasm in his voice, the man was deadly serious. What did he think she did? Waved her hands around cursed artifacts like a fortune-teller with a crystal ball?

She needed concrete facts, data, measurements. A complete arcane analysis. And yet, so far, all she had to work with were a few blurry photographs and one particularly uncooperative Viking.

Just then a soft knock sounded. Adeline appeared, a tray between her hands.

"Sorry to disturb you," she said. "I just thought you might enjoy something to drink after all the excitement earlier."

Olivia welcomed the interruption. She needed a moment to compose herself after the absurdity Isaksson had just thrown in her face.

Her assistant came over to place the tray on an empty corner of the desk and leaned over to her, whispering quickly in her ear.

Ah.

Now, *that* explained it.

Isaksson thanked Adeline before she left the room, throwing her a wink. When he turned back to Olivia, he tried to keep the charming expression on his face, but she narrowed her eyes at him, unimpressed.

"If all this secrecy is because you are worried about my discretion," she said, "I can assure you that I maintain the utmost confidentiality in this office. Nothing you say in here will be repeated unless I were ordered to do so by a court of law."

"I appreciate you saying that, Ms Knight. But I have no choice in this. I am dealing with a confidential mission for the Ministry, you understand."

Olivia's lips curved into a small smile. She understood, all right.

"Tea? Coffee?"

"Coffee, please. Black."

As she poured the drinks, Olivia considered what Adeline had just whispered in her ear.

Not one to disappoint, her truly incredible assistant-spy had just filled her in on the latest gossip about the mysterious Mr Isaksson, who'd arrived straight from Stockholm a few months ago. Including his new occupation as the Cellars Warden.

The Cellars were a sort of Ministry-controlled prison where the darkest and most dangerous artifacts were locked away, safe from prying eyes. Located on a tiny island off the coast of Edinburgh, the Cellars formed a labyrinthine underground system filled with everything the Ministry didn't know what to do with.

The fact that Isaksson was the new Warden might explain his ridiculous demands, but not his absolute mule headedness in keeping the details of this artifact to himself. That, she still didn't understand. She'd worked on a few cases involving the Cellars before for previous Wardens, and she'd never had to deal with such a cloak-and-dagger meeting.

No, Olivia was sure Isaksson was hiding something. Or at the very least, something highly unusual was going on with his wand. She, therefore, was determined to find out everything about it.

This infuriating Warden had just made one *very* big mistake.

"May I interest you in a friendly wager?"

Isaksson's eyebrows jolted up in surprise. "A wager?"

"If I can prove to you that I already know some of the things you won't tell me," she replied, "then you'll share the rest."

He looked taken aback for a moment, but then a slow grin blossomed on his face. Clearly, he was amused by her idea. He reached a hand across the desk, blue eyes twinkling. "You have yourself a deal."

Olivia shook it. It was obvious that Isaksson was just humouring her, that he didn't really think she knew anything.

Oh, how she was going to enjoy this next part.

"I believe you have been instructed to remove a dangerous artifact from the Cellars and are looking for a perfect duplicate to put in its place. One that could fool any expert coming to investigate. The only thing I don't know is why."

Isaksson's cup froze halfway to his mouth.

Ah! Definitely not amused any more.

"To be perfectly honest, it wasn't that hard to deduce." Olivia continued, calmly sipping her tea under the weight of his stare. "As the new Cellars Warden, your job is to keep the artifacts inside safe and locked away. So why would you want a duplicate? I first thought that you wanted to move the real wand to a more secure location. However, I cannot think of a single place more secure than the Cellars. Then I realised you might be trying to transfer your artifact back to its homeland. There's certainly been a lot of that going on in recent years. My first guess was that the Ministry, for some mysterious reason, wanted to lie about it and send a fake instead. Especially since you said that *experts* shouldn't be able to tell the difference, which means the duplicate is meant to pass for the real thing, and you expect people to interact with it. That theory seems highly unlikely, however, and would certainly lead to an incident of epic proportions should they ever discover the truth. I know my replicas are good, but I wouldn't want the good health of international relations to depend on them.

"Moreover, you have been so adamant about not revealing *anything* about the artifact — not even so I could properly do my job — that I think you might actually be protecting it. Why all this secrecy if the wand is to remain safe and sound in its cell, right? Which finally tells me that it's not the replica that will leave the Cellars, but the real one."

Isaksson regarded her for a long moment, his face impassive. "And how would you know I am the new Cellars Warden?"

A smug smile curled Olivia's lips. "The curse-breaking community is a small group, Mr Isaksson. Very inquisitive and quite fond of gossip. I just asked around."

Between one blink and the next, his icy expression vanished. He leaned back in his chair, throwing one long leg over the other, and stroked the thick stubble covering his jaw. He laughed. "Ms Knight, I had a feeling you were going to surprise me. I have to say you didn't disappoint."

His sudden change of mood took her by surprise. She was the one who was supposed to have got the better of him, and yet Olivia had the distinct impression she'd just passed some sort of test. Could this day get any stranger? "A deal's a deal. Tell me more about your cursed wand."

Reaching inside his briefcase again, this time he pulled out a thick kraft folder marked with the Ministry's departmental insignia.

Olivia leaned forward. Like a shark spotting a school of fish, her eyes zeroed in at once on the big *Confidential* stamped in the corner.

"The wand has been difficult to contain for years," Isaksson began. "But it's only got worse over the past few months. As you guessed, the Ministry has decided to move it elsewhere. And they insist on putting a replica in its place, to pretend that nothing has been done." He handed her the folder.

Well, that sounded a bit unusual, but his explanation didn't exactly surprise Olivia. The Ministry was not known for its grace in accepting failure. If there was a way to pretend that something had never happened, they would take it.

"And where do you plan on taking this artifact?" she asked as she leafed through the pages. "Back to its homeland, I suppose?"

Many relics reacted negatively to being far from their birthplace, so bringing cursed artifacts home usually mellowed them.

Isaksson tapped the curse detector on her desk with the tip of his finger. He tilted his head, trying to read the inscriptions etched on the attached gold discs. "I guess I might as well tell you," he replied in a dry voice. "Yes, the wand is going home. To Romania."

That was when something occurred to Olivia that made her pause. She slowly raised her head. "Romania?"

"To the Romanian Institute of Dark Arts, to be exact. A certain Constantin Mitrea is taking custody of it, he's the High Commissioner. You may have heard of him."

Had she ever?

Constantin Mitrea was only one of the most influential figures in the international community dedicated to the preservation and handling of ancient artifacts. Everyone in the curse-breaking world knew his name.

"And when will this transfer take place?" she asked carefully.

"Friday."

Olivia did a quick calculation in her head. No, she couldn't possibly be right. He couldn't be planning to . . .

Today was the eighteenth of September, so that would make the transfer happen four days from now, on the twenty-second, the day before the autumnal equinox, or the celebration of Mabon. And in the curse-breaking community, autumnal equinoxes were quite a special date . . .

Olivia planted both her palms on her desk and slowly stood, her face darkening with outrage. "Mr Isaksson, if you tell me this wand is one of the items to be sold at the Institute's auction, I swear you're not leaving this office."

CHAPTER THREE

Isaksson's eyebrows rose to his hairline and an astonished laugh escaped him. "Are you really threatening me with that?" He gestured at her outstretched arm. "What are you going to do, throw it at my head?"

Olivia followed his gaze, only now realising that she was brandishing her rolled-up copy of the *Cursed Herald* magazine with a white-knuckled grip. Really not the best choice of weapon, to be honest. But no time to back down now.

"Yes. Yes, I am." She shook it at him menacingly. "So you better answer me. Quickly."

That only made Isaksson laugh again. He didn't seem overly concerned by her threat, which made her angrier.

"Ms Knight, I give you my word that the wand will not be auctioned at the Institute." He reached across the desk and snatched the rolled up magazine from her clenched hand. He smoothed it out and inspected the cover, lips twitching when he noticed the scribbles she'd made on it. "Next time you might want to grab that brass bust over there," he said while leafing through the pages. He poked his chin somewhere to her right without looking up. "I bet it would do some impressive damage to my skull. All right, I'm curious." Isaksson turned the magazine towards her, open to the portrait of her despicable fellow curse-breaker Crowley, and all the changes she'd made to his face. "Who is that, and why did you turn him into a *rat*?"

Olivia ignored his question.

Besides, it was a ferret, not a rat.

"If it's not part of the auction, explain to me why it's going there at the same time."

Isaksson rolled up the magazine again and crossed his muscular arms. He said nothing, but glanced repeatedly at her abandoned chair.

Deciding to give him the benefit of the doubt — *for now* — Olivia sat back down.

"About four years ago, an international programme was created to return artifacts to their countries of origin," the Warden finally deigned to answer. "The Repatriation of . . . ah, of Historical something."

"The Historical Heritage Repatriation Programme," Olivia corrected him.

"Yes. Since the Ministry was desperate to get rid of the wand, they decided to ship it back to Romania, as it originates from Transylvania. They have something similar to the Cellars for their most powerful artifacts. In an old gold mine, of all places."

"And the auction?"

"The Department has a few mild artifacts that are making the journey for that. With the wand getting harder and harder to contain, it seemed the perfect time to move them all together. The wand will stay in the Institute's vaults for safekeeping until it can be transferred again to its permanent home."

"Hmm."

The Romanian Institute of Dark Arts was known throughout the world, especially for its annual auction of rare magical artifacts. Every September, the richest and most avid collectors of unique items waited with bated breath for the incredibly selective invitation. The objects up for auction ranged from unique collector's pieces, all the way to once-in-a-lifetime opportunities.

Olivia loathed this auction with every fibre of her being.

Come September, her team was very careful not to mention anything about it, lest it send her into an hour-long rant. To her, it represented everything wrong with the curse-breaking community: highly volatile artifacts being treated as mere ornaments, the sale of priceless relics used for political gain, and the circulation of dark magical entities with absolutely no control whatsoever.

Olivia swallowed the wave of consternation building up inside her and returned to the Department folder, but a frustrated groan passed her lips. "It's practically all redacted."

Isaksson had the good grace to wince. "Yes. Sorry about that. The Ministry isn't very happy about it all and doesn't want to cooperate. Believe me, I tried."

That, she could believe. She'd had her fair share of run-ins with the Ministry, over some questionable artifacts in their possession, and well . . . Let's just say she'd quickly learned to look elsewhere for answers.

This entire folder was shockingly sparse to begin with, and of the few reports it contained, about half were redacted. The component analysis, for example, was completely useless. So was the risk assessment. The abilities part had even been left completely blank.

Surprisingly, however, the next few pages were very detailed. Incident reports were neatly transcribed, with dates ranging from three months to a few weeks ago. But Isaksson had said that the wand had been misbehaving for years . . . So where were the rest of the reports?

"And why does the Ministry want to get rid of it so badly?" she asked. "What's wrong with this wand?"

Isaksson heaved a long and weary sigh. "That, is going to take a while."

Olivia looked up, puzzled. That hadn't sounded ominous *at all* . . .

"Let's start with these incidents," she said. "What exactly happened?"

Isaksson's lips pressed into a hard line. He gulped down the last of his coffee. "Where should I start?"

Olivia had a feeling she was not going to like what came next. "From the beginning, please."

In response, Isaksson stood and began pacing her office. "I've only been the Warden for a few months, but I was told the problems started long before that. It was not much at first. Strange noises mostly. Voices. Guards said they could hear the sounds of a forest — branches cracking in the wind, leaves rustling . . . Others swore they could see someone walking the corridors at night. As I said, it wasn't much. I might have even thought it was all in their heads if it hadn't been for what came later."

Isaksson's voice had become grave and serious. Olivia found it strange to see him so sombre all of a sudden. "What happened later?"

"First, we tried to find out which artifact was behind it all. And, believe it or not, that took us a while. That wand is not the only thing down in the Cellars that likes to misbehave. And yet, every time I went down to investigate, I wouldn't see or hear anything. It would all be perfectly normal. In fact, I spent weeks thinking the culprit was a cursed mirror. That . . ." his voice turned into a growl, "that *lilla skit* was toying with me."

Olivia's eyes widened. She didn't know what *lilla skit* meant, but she had a feeling it was nothing good.

Isaksson continued his back and forth, determined to pace a hole in her floor. "As soon as we found out it was all coming from the wand, everything changed. It was as if it was done pretending. Immediately, the sounds, the strange vibrations, the visions . . . Everything got worse. Then the wand, it . . . I guess there's no other word for it. It started driving the guards mad."

"*Mad*? What do you mean?"

"Lapses in their memories, mostly, as if they went into some kind of trance. They would be in the middle of their security rounds, for example, and then suddenly come to, just as they were about to unlock cell doors. We tried everything to reinforce the wards in its cell. Nothing worked."

Isaksson pivoted towards her. His brows were furrowed and his jaw clenched in anger. "The worst incident we had was Burton. After his shift, he became absolutely convinced he was a medieval knight about to go to war. When we talked to him, he would eventually remember who he really was. But as soon as you left him alone for just five minutes, he would be looking for his sword and shield to join his king on the battlefield." Isaksson ran a hand through his already dishevelled hair. "He's a lot better now. It took him about a week at home and far away from the Cellars, but he's feeling normal again."

"Good. I'm glad to hear that," Olivia breathed.

"So now you understand why that wand has to go. No one wants to work in that section any more. Besides, there's something else."

Olivia's breath caught. There was *more*?

"As of three days ago, that wretched wand has started making the *other* artifacts act out."

Wow.

After a few more angry strides, Isaksson came and sat down again. "I know we've only just met, but I get the feeling that you being speechless doesn't bode well. Is it that bad?"

"Well . . ." Olivia decided to answer honestly. "I won't lie, in all my years as a curse-breaker, I've never heard of an artifact quite like this."

Sure, the display of the wand's power was impressive, especially since mental abilities in cursed artifacts were rather rare. But what really amazed her was how it had acted. And especially *why*.

"What's so different about this wand?" Isaksson asked her.

Olivia absent-mindedly began to gather loose papers on her desk and put them into piles, thinking about her answer. "In curse-breaking, we have a theory we call the passive and active state. At the very beginning, cursing an object means sharing some of one's magic, one's life energy with it. It is also about imbuing it with a will, a strong desire. Sometimes even complex emotions. Because of this, the cursed object has now acquired an aura of its own. A halo of energy, if you will.

"This aura can be faint and subtle. For example, if you are in close proximity to a cursed object, you might pick up the feelings that the conjurer felt when he cursed it many years ago: fear, jealousy, sadness . . . Like an echo of the past. And with very old artifacts, this aura is much more pronounced and can express itself physically. You saw an example of this not long ago with the Grimoire. Screaming, hurtling through the air, shacking . . . I've seen it all."

"And this is the passive state."

"Precisely. Now, the active state is when the object exacts the will that the conjurer placed upon it. When Sir Farebrother of Arundel felt he was about to be betrayed by the other members of his brotherhood, he cursed the Book of Mysteries, which had been his life's work and contained all his most secret spells and rituals. He didn't want anyone to be able to use his knowledge, but refused to destroy it either. So he imbued the Book with a sense of impending betrayal and a desire for secrecy. After his murder, his former brothers did indeed find his Book and tried to use its power for their own gain. But anyone who dared touch its pages was drained of their life force. Slowly, over a period of many days, until all that remained were barely alive, desiccated skeletons."

"Charming," Isaksson muttered.

"This is an artifact in an active state of cursing. It's exacting a simple command implanted in it by the conjurer — to keep the Book secret. Your wand, on the other hand, is not doing that at all." Olivia leaned forward, trying to keep the excitement out of her voice. She'd only ever theorised that cursed artifacts were capable of behaving this way. This wand could prove that all her theories were right . . . and more.

"See, the hallucinations, the memory loss, the trances . . . all of it sounds terrible. But it would make sense coming from a powerful object with mental abilities, right? We could say the wand is simply trying to protect itself in the only way it knows how. It certainly looks impressive, but that's not what I find so extraordinary, it's the intent behind it all. You said that one of the guards had been compelled to open cell doors. Not just one cell, not the cell to the wand, but *several*. If it was trying to escape, why would it do that? You also told me that it has now begun to affect *other* artifacts, making them act up. Why?"

Olivia shook her head. "This is not an object doing a conjurer's will. No, it rather sounds like the wand is doing whatever it wants, that it has a mind of its own. Which is to cause utter mayhem in your Cellars."

"Like when it pretended some other artifact was doing all of this," Isaksson remarked quietly.

"Yes. You said it yourself, the wand has been toying with you. This is nowhere near the normal behaviour of a cursed object. To be honest, I'm not sure *what* this is."

That wand had been playing hide-and-seek with him, for gods' sakes.

Olivia was surprised to feel goose bumps on her arms. After working on countless cases, she'd thought nothing had the ability to shock her any more. But this wand definitely did. The way it acted reminded her more of an animal playing with its food than an inanimate object.

She couldn't wait to share this with her team. Well, Cornelius in particular. She had a feeling that both Godwyn and Adeline would deeply despise this wand. They were, rightly so, very wary of dark artifacts, especially if they possessed mental abilities. Whereas Cornelius shared her strange fascination with the worst of them... And the darker, the better.

Case in point: the Book of Mysteries. Almost everyone reacted as Isaksson had when she told them the story, with disgust and fear. While Olivia found it the most fascinating thing ever.

To the Warden and his employees, however, this wand was nothing but a source of fear and endless frustration. So she schooled her features into a mask of concern and displayed none of her true feelings. "Thank you for agreeing to share all this information, Mr Isaksson. I now understand why you might want to get rid of this artifact as quickly as possible."

Isaksson rolled his eyes. "Don't even bother, I know you loved it."

Olivia thought she'd done a good job of hiding her enthusiasm, but she obviously hadn't tried hard enough.

She cleared her throat, uncomfortable. "I didn't *love* it. It's just that in my line of work, you don't often come across such interesting artifacts, so when it happens, we tend to get a tad more... *excited* than what is considered socially acceptable. But I really am sorry you're having so much trouble with this wand and that your employees are being attacked."

Isaksson waved off her apology. "I get it. I guess you wouldn't have become a curse-breaker if you didn't like curses, right?" Then a smile creased his cheeks, all seriousness gone from his face. "Were you really going to attack me if the wand was to be sold at the auction?"

Olivia decided not to take offence at his utter disbelief. Underestimating her meant he would never see her coming...

"From what you've told me, that wand is extremely dangerous. In the wrong hands it could become a weapon of incredible power, so of course I was."

"Do I need to remind you that I work for the Ministry? I could have you arrested for that." His words were serious, but the mad gleam was back in his eyes. The Viking was loving this.

"Well you could . . ." Olivia shrugged. "*If* your memories were still intact by the time you'd have left my office."

Isaksson inclined his head. "I'll have to remember that."

"You should, indeed."

Olivia couldn't believe the words coming out of her mouth. She was usually the picture of professionalism . . .

Well, now. Maybe that was a bit of an exaggeration. But she certainly didn't go around threatening clients with a rolled up magazine. Not even when they were getting on her nerves, as this Isaksson liked to do.

And then why, in the names of all hells, did she enjoy bantering with him so much?

Olivia cleared her throat. "Getting back to the transfer, you'll need to be really careful here. Creating a containment plan for an artifact that can manipulate its magic like this will be difficult. What system will you be using? Can I see the plans?"

A strange expression came upon Isaksson's face. It was gone so quickly that she didn't have time to understand it, but Olivia was sure she'd caught something unusual.

The Warden crossed his long legs, his intertwined fingers resting on his knee. "Plans?"

The nonchalance in his voice made her wary. "Plans, yes. For the containment cage."

"Well . . . I was told we were going to make a three-point null field. Or five. Throw the wand into a wooden crate lined with silverstone."

Olivia's mouth had hung open when he first began to speak, then dropped lower with each new sentence.

"A *null field*?" she finally managed to squeak out. Her voice was a good octave higher than usual. "But . . . But nobody uses null fields to contain artifacts, it's far too dangerous! You have to know exactly the power level of the item you're trapping, otherwise maintaining the field will kill you! Besides, you cannot travel with them, they're stationary constructs!"

Null fields were areas that magic couldn't cross, spaces devoid of arcane energy. Many rituals and spells created null fields as a byproduct, but sometimes they were specifically constructed to seal off escaping magic, or to protect from accidental releases. A group of arcanists would channel their magic into tethers, that would "nullify" it, creating a deserted zone around them. The more magic was poured into it, the larger the anti-magic field would spread. But maintaining a null field was very demanding, and many people drowned in it, letting it suck all the arcane energy out of them until it was too late.

"I certainly hope you're joking."

"You know, I've used quite a few null fields at the Cellars, they're very effective."

Olivia forced herself to take a breath, to lower her voice. "I don't doubt it, but that is not the point. Null fields are only effective if they are stronger than the object you're trying to contain."

"Surely, a five-point field is enough. You can't think the wand is more powerful than five arcanists putting their magic together."

Olivia gritted her teeth. "It could be a hundred points and my answer would still be the same. Null fields are only used in emergencies, to deal with sudden spikes of energy. Your wand would only need *one* second, Warden. Just *one* tiny gap in your field and it could convince one of you to let go. Stronger isn't always better. You have to be smart here. As cunning and devious as your wand."

Isaksson smiled at her indulgently. "I know you're passionate about these artifacts, Ms Knight, but this is still just a wand. It does not have the ability to form complex thoughts."

"With all due respect, I'm surprised a Warden would be so nonchalant about the abilities of the artifacts under his care."

Isaksson shrugged. "I don't need to know what I'm guarding to guard it well."

Olivia kept the retort on the tip of her tongue by sheer force of will. This was still a potential client, she reminded herself. Even if he was acting like an ignorant dunderhead— How the Cellars were still standing and not a pile of smoking rumbles by now was beyond her.

"Aren't all cursed things the same, anyway?" he asked.

"The *same*?"

"Yes. Cursed."

Olivia glanced at the brass bust on her shelf. She was severely tempted to throw it at his head to test just how much damage it could do to his thick skull. "Don't they teach you anything in Warden school?"

"Oh, lots of things actually. Like for example, how to keep demonic grimoires from flying out the window." He threw her a wink.

Her fingers actually twitched with the need to grab that bust. "Yes, I suppose big muscles *do* have some use from time to time," she squeezed past gritted teeth. "If you don't mind my asking, who did you hire for this transport?"

"I'm not supposed to tell you, but . . . Professor Wyborn."

Olivia couldn't believe this.

Of all the curse-breakers in this country, it had to be *him*. And his cockroach of an assistant. *Again*.

Now she understood why the Warden didn't have a proper transport containment plan in place. The professor was quite old and had long since retired to a more academic role, concentrating on teaching. He hadn't been out in the field in years. No, for a transport to another country he would send his assistant. And if Edmund Crowley was the man in charge of containing that wand . . . They were doomed.

"Is there something wrong with Professor Wyborn?"

There was something very wrong with his taste in assistants, that was for sure.

Olivia took a steadying breath. "You are severely underestimating the capabilities of this artifact, Mr Isaksson," she finally said, her tone grave. "This wand is capable of far more than you give it credit for."

She'd known four different Wardens since her career as a curse-breaker began, all of them transfers from other departments with limited experience dealing with cursed artifacts. None of them had lasted more than two years. She'd begun to wonder if this position wasn't some sort of departmental training exercise or something.

The first rule of battle was to know your enemy, and Isaksson was utterly clueless.

Olivia stood up abruptly. "I think you need a demonstration."

The Warden's startled gaze followed her as she rounded her desk. Turned out she was about to wake Jerry after all.

CHAPTER FOUR

OLIVIA CROSSED THE ROOM to reach her Wall of Doom. Since she couldn't surround the massive cabinets in containment wards because of the objects inside, she'd had to rely on good old silverstone chains for security. It was an absolute pain to open, was noisy as hell and made her entire office look like a medieval dungeon, but it kept the dangerous artifacts safe from wandering hands.

Reaching into the pocket of her tweed waistcoat, she pulled out a silver key, ridiculously tiny compared to the size of the hefty padlock it opened, which was almost as big as her head and weighed an absolute ton.

"What most people don't realise or want to accept," she gave Isaksson a pointed look, "is that after a cursing, your object has radically altered. With all this magic now flowing through it, it has become something very close to being alive."

Isaksson had put his elbows on the edge of her desk, propping up his chin, and followed her every move like a hawk.

Olivia opened the double doors of the central section, revealing deep shelves filled with a myriad of objects, all meticulously labelled. A music box that concealed a purplish glow, next to a leather spyglass and a cracked ornamental mask made entirely of the whitest porcelain, except for two black circles that represented the eyes and which, astonishingly, seemed to follow you as you moved. Countless other pieces adorned the shelves, each one giving off the same dark aura that warned you to stay very, *very* far away.

Olivia pulled on thick black gloves before reaching in to take one of the items from the top shelf.

It was an antique scroll holder, made from two rotating wooden cylinders, one on top of the other, that had been carved and polished. The thin and extremely long scroll was wound between them and could be read by slowly turning either of the cylinders.

The inconspicuous object looked innocent enough, if it weren't for the words pulsating and dancing atop the paper. And as soon as Olivia placed it on her desk, the nearby curse detector went haywire, emitting a high-pitched hiss as all five discs spun simultaneously to the highest measure of dark magic.

"This contains the Scroll of Eternal Life," she explained. "As the name suggests, it grants an immortal existence to anyone who touches it. However, what it really bestows isn't what most people would wish for." As she spoke, Olivia walked behind Isaksson to pick up something else, the glass dome he'd been examining earlier.

"There are many cursed objects I could tell you about, capable of terrible things that would make you shudder. But that's not what I'm trying to do here." She rounded her desk again. "I don't want to make you afraid of them, I want you to understand how intelligent they can be."

Isaksson hadn't reacted when she'd placed the cursed scroll holder in front of him, but as soon as she put the covered dome on the desk, he recoiled immediately.

"Mr Isaksson, meet Jerry." Olivia pulled the cloth away, and masked the scroll holder instead.

Beneath the clear glass was a plant with arrow-shaped leaves that shimmered in the dim light. Each one looked as if it had been cast in copper and then sustained a layer of verdigris rust. There were things sticking out of its densely packed roots. Golden and shiny, they were only visible when a stray ray of light reflected off their surface.

Isaksson regarded her like she'd grown another head. "Jerry. You named your weird-looking plant Jerry."

Olivia nodded.

"But why is it . . . rusty? It looks like an old statue."

"Ah, Mr Isaksson . . ." A small smile curved her lips. "That's because it is."

Olivia placed both hands on the glass dome. "All right, I'll take this out now. Don't say anything mean about him. He's quite sensitive."

Isaksson stared at her, eyes wide. "Wha . . . What?"

As soon as they were free, tendrils of the plant slithered towards Olivia to wrap around her hand. "Yes. Who's a handsome Persicaria?" she whispered softly.

She trailed the tip of her finger along a leaf, caressing it. The whole plant shivered in delight.

"Jerry isn't a real plant," she clarified. "This was originally a sculpture of a plant known as *Persicaria runcinata*, or knotweed. It once belonged to a Lord Remington who'd made his fortune through very questionable business dealings. He would often entertain potential clients at his home and proudly displayed Jerry on a large glass table in the library."

A few more tendrils slid silently across her desk, towards the gold letter opener she kept on the other side. They tried to hide from her by taking a detour behind a stack of books but, used to Jerry's antics, Olivia spotted them immediately.

"No, Jerry, I need that." She gently pushed the vines back. "Here." She pulled a silver button from a drawer and offered it instead. The nearest tendril accepted her offering and withdrew, vanishing a few seconds later inside Jerry's network of roots.

"Wait, you said . . ." Isaksson shook his head in disbelief. "This is a sculpture? Of a plant?" A small, contemptuous laugh escaped him. "I guess I'll never understand what passes for art to some people . . ."

Jerry froze.

All his leaves slowly pivoted towards Isaksson. With their peculiar shape and pattern, they looked like hundreds of eyes staring back at him. A slight tremor began to shake the whole plant, one that strongly reminded Olivia of a rattlesnake.

Isaksson immediately realised the error of his ways. "All right, my bad. Sorry, Jerry."

Olivia laughed softly to herself and stroked the leaves until the shaking subsided.

"After a series of unfortunate business dealings that cost him a good chunk of his fortune," she continued, "Lord Remington decided to turn to the dark arts. Jerry here is the result of an experiment gone wrong. All of his thirst for success, his drive for money and riches; all of it got imprinted on Jerry."

At that moment, Isaksson eyed another scouting tendril trying its luck. He grabbed the fountain pen before Jerry could snatch it.

"There are two things you should know about Jerry : what he desires and what he fears. I think you've already figured out the first one. Jerry covets all things gold and shiny. It's a direct result of the curse, as his master passed on his love of treasures. He's also quite possessive of them. He'll attack you if you try to steal them back."

When Olivia tried to grab something small poking out of its roots, Jerry immediately shifted them to swallow it back, and tendrils gently but firmly pushed her away.

"After being cursed, objects will only seek to fulfill the wishes their master has imprinted upon them. Jerry searches for gold and other jewels. He doesn't need food, warmth or water. Riches are his reason of existence, they are the purpose for which he was created. They should be the only things he craves, yes?" Her finger made another caress to the glossy leaves. "And yet, even though his master has been dead for decades and Jerry is just a cursed sculpture . . . He has developed a personality of his own."

"A personality? What do you mean?"

"For starters, he's quite proud, as you saw earlier. He's also very possessive of me and doesn't like people standing too close to me. That's actually the reason I keep him covered, he once tried to attack a client when we shook hands."

Isaksson looked warily at the squirming tendrils wrapped around her hand, all the way to her wrist. "And what is the second? What does he fear?"

"Now, that one's kind of ironic. Jerry is absolutely terrified of other cursed artifacts."

Olivia pulled up a corner of the black cloth, revealing a glimpse of the cursed scroll-reader. Jerry reacted immediately. All his vines came back to him, coiling tightly. His leaves folded in on themselves, as if to close his many eyes.

"You see how we've already gone beyond what most people think cursed artifacts behave like?" Olivia told Isaksson. "They are more than just vessels of a conjurer's will."

She removed her black gloves. "Direct contact with the scroll would send me into a vivid dream from which I would never wake. Not exactly the 'eternal life' that was promised, is it?" she said with a dry laugh. As she spoke, Olivia approached the scroll with her bare fingers. "Now, watch what Jerry does when I get close—"

She started violently when two things happened almost simultaneously.

First, Isaksson's hand shot out and wrapped around her wrist, stopping her in mid-air. In turn, every one of Jerry's leaves unfolded and swung towards him, hissing.

For a few moments, no one moved. Except Jerry, who shook so hard that his pot clattered against the desk.

Olivia stared at Isaksson with wide eyes. His whole body radiated tension, yet the big hand around her much smaller one didn't hurt at all, but instead felt strangely warm and reassuring...

"Ah. It's... all right, Mr Isaksson. I know what I'm doing. Trust me."

The Warden's gaze swung between her and the cursed scroll, not saying anything. Finally, he let go of her wrist, one finger at a time.

Jerry visibly relaxed.

Olivia's hand approached the cursed object once again, Isaksson following her movement with rapt attention. She didn't make contact, but hovered above it, her finger a breath away from the paper and the dancing words.

Immediately, Jerry trembled, distressed.

He began to move his roots around frenetically, expelling all the golden treasures he'd hidden inside until they formed a small mountain next to him. A few tendrils unfolded to push the shiny pile towards Olivia.

Meanwhile, Isaksson stared at the plant, mouth agape. "He's trying to stop you," he whispered.

"Yes." Beginning to feel guilty about this whole experiment, Olivia promised herself she would make it up to Jerry as soon as it was over. "He's afraid *for* me. He's trying to convince me to stop and is willing to give me the one thing he craves above all else to do it."

Deciding to end this, she pulled her fingers away from the scroll and covered it with the cloth again.

"I'm sorry, Jerry. Here, take them. Good boy." Olivia pushed the shiny coins, gold cufflinks, pen caps and other dazzling knick-knacks back towards him. His roots swallowed them all up, putting them back where they belonged.

When that was done, Isaksson still looked more than a little stunned. But he reached into his coat for his wallet, pulled out a gold coin and handed it to her without a word.

This Viking just kept surprising her.

She handed the coin to Jerry, who made it vanish in the blink of an eye. Then the plant let out what could only be described as a huge sigh of relief.

Olivia spoke again after a few moments. "One thing you learn quickly when dealing with old artifacts, is that this magic, this *energy* that gave them a semblance of life, has lingered for some time. Long enough for the object to have grown out of the constraints of the curse and become its own entity. You saw with Jerry how they can actually develop *feelings*. Have *desires*. They can act in much more complex ways than we think.

"You are not dealing with a simple dark magic wand that has a tendency to mess with people's heads, Mr Isaksson. In truth, this is a wild creature. And I don't know if we can build a cage strong enough to contain it."

The Warden regarded her gravely. He seemed to have finally heeded her warning. She sincerely hoped so anyway, for Olivia feared what might happen otherwise.

"If no cage can contain it . . ." he said. "What do you suggest we do?"

What indeed?

What did you do when faced with a predator you knew was more cunning, more powerful than you?

Olivia calmly stroked Jerry's leaves, her hand covered in writhing vines. "We throw in a tasty snack to distract it, of course."

CHAPTER FIVE

"I can't believe you let a client help you stuff a cursed artifact into a cage, Godwyn! What were you thinking?"

Olivia closed the office door and turned to scowl at him, hands on her hips. Godwyn immediately straightened from his sprawled position lounging in his office chair, two feet propped up on the desk.

A feminine, French accented voice drifted out from the other side of the room as Adeline sauntered in, carrying an armful of folders. "I think the problem might be that he *wasn't* thinking, actually."

Godwyn turned to glare at her. "I did not let him *do* anything, he simply jumped right in! I didn't even see him come into the office before he was yelling at me to grab the other side. Maybe if *mademoiselle* had deigned to lend a hand, we wouldn't have needed his help in the first place."

"A powerful arcanist like you?" Adeline huffed. She started pulling out drawers from the filing cabinets. "I thought you had the situation perfectly under control?"

Olivia raised her hand to stop Godwyn just as he was about to deliver a scathing reply. "Enough, you two. It's done now."

She covered a yawn with her forearm before collapsing into a chair. It had been a damn long day. All she wanted to do was get home and dive into that wand case report with a nice whisky.

"So tell us, boss," Cornelius drawled. Tiredness always made his smooth Louisiana accent thicker. By contrast, Godwyn's articulate, proper British voice grew increasingly rougher as the day wore on. "What did Isaksson want? Do we have a case?"

Forgetting her fatigue, Olivia leaned forward, a slow smile curving her lips. "Well, not exactly. *Yet* . . . But let me tell you, it's a good one."

Cornelius's eyes lit up. "How good?"

"Black magic wand with mind-based abilities. Extremely powerful. 14th to 15th century. And it has been driving the guards insane."

Godwyn frowned. "You mean it's been giving them trouble?"

"Oh no, no. They've heard voices, seen things. Some of them have experienced memory lapses or come back to their senses as they were opening cell doors. I mean, it's made them go *mad*. One even became convinced he was a medieval knight. Thankfully, he's all right now."

Olivia shook her head, still in utter disbelief at this artifact. "And that's not even the most impressive part. This wand is somehow able to control its residual magic. For weeks, it's been fully sucking its aura in, going completely dormant, so it could pretend it wasn't the one acting up."

Cornelius stared at her in astonishment. "*Ga lee* . . ."

His eyes were glowing with interest and he couldn't lean any further forward on his desk else he leaped over it.

Meanwhile, Godwyn had a grimace on his handsome face that was at risk of becoming permanent. "What?" he grumbled. "That's impossible."

"Yes. Isaksson actually thought it was another one. And right after he figured it out, the wand stopped trying to disguise itself."

"Incredible . . . Do you have an elemental analysis?" Cornelius asked. Olivia could almost see the wheels turning in his head. "What's the core made out of?"

"That, I don't know. It's all been redacted." Without leaving her seat, Olivia stretched out her arm and reached across the desk to hand him Isaksson's report.

"Redacted?" Cornelius produced a pair of thin round glasses which he perched on his nose before flipping through the pages.

With his dandyish looks, sensual charm and the honeyed cadence of his voice he inherited from his native New Orleans, he didn't resemble the typical scholar one bit. But Cornelius had a memory like a steel trap, read Old Arcane Tongue like it was nothing, and could spout morbid anecdotes about cursed artifacts all day long.

"I reckon they don't want to admit that the wand is made of illegal components," he said. "Especially since it looks like it's bursting at the seams."

"The Ministry doesn't always require a reason, but in this case I think you might be right. With what that wand has been capable of, it's certainly made of some highly restricted materials. And with that amount of power at such a large range . . ." Olivia's voice grew excited. "I think the core might even be a class seven."

Cornelius' amber eyes widened, but then he snapped his fingers. "You know, someone told me about this case in Italy, where they found a primary relic under an abandoned temple. What if it's not a gemstone inside the wand, but crystallised remnants of power? Maybe we should start looking for powerful mental mages of the period . . ."

Olivia tilted her head, thinking. "That's a good idea. I've got a few names that come to mind, we'll have to check. Honestly, it could also be a class four or five that's gone rogue. That used to happen quite often in Western Europe because of the ley lines."

"What do you figure the toxicity is?"

"I'd say no less than five hundred shaders."

Cornelius let out an impressed whistle. "That's some proper magic right there. Especially for a mental wand. Are you sure?"

Olivia nodded enthusiastically. "Oh yes."

She hurried around the desk to stand behind him. "Look at this report." She pointed to a particular section. "It would make sense, wouldn't it? I'm thinking something between a Bonelight and that White Veil plant that grows in burial grounds. You know? From the Bonaventure incident of 1905."

"I, for one, will remain eternally grateful that I haven't got the faintest idea what the two of you are going on about," a distinguished voice interrupted. Godwyn had been silent during their back and forth, but now shook his head. "It fills me with a sense of peace and serenity."

Cornelius and Olivia both looked up with expressions of pure, unadulterated innocence on their faces.

Adeline paused her file organizing. She had the twin of Godwyn's deeply disapproving frown marring her brow. "You're both *way* too excited about this."

Olivia laughed. "You sound like Isaksson."

"Don't tell me you don't find this fascinating!" Cornelius exclaimed.

"A mad wand that can give you psychosis?" Godwyn replied with sarcasm. "Thank you, but I'll pass."

Olivia shrugged. "I've never seen an artifact display so much agency before. I would be scared if I didn't find it so incredible."

To which Godwyn mumbled, "How did I know you were going to say that?"

"Well *I* can't wait to study it up close!" Cornelius said. "When do we go?"

Olivia winced. "That's the problem, we can't. Isaksson won't let anyone in to examine the wand, and he can't bring it out of the Cellars."

"You're kidding."

She just threw up her hands. "Mr Mysterious barely told me anything about it. All I have is this." She pointed to the Ministry folder, then reached inside her waistcoat pocket for the photographs and waved them in the air. "And these instant pictures. Besides, he only agreed to tell me that much because I already knew he was the new Cellars Warden. Which, by the way . . ." She pivoted towards her assistant, who'd gone back to stowing away files at the back of the room, "was incredible work there, Addie."

Cornelius applauded as Adeline winked and blew them all a kiss. The Baron just rolled his eyes.

"He wants to take the wand back to Romania, but hasn't hired us for the transport," Olivia continued. "He just needs a replica to put inside the cell. Something about the Ministry not wanting to admit they couldn't contain it, I don't know."

"What?" Cornelius scowled. "There's no transport? What does he think we do in here? Exactly how new *is* he?"

"Don't ask me that," Olivia replied with an exasperated sigh. "The Ministry is grossly underestimating their artifact, of course. I asked Isaksson what kind of containment system he would be using for the transfer, and he said they were planning on making a three or five-point null field. That, and I quote *"throw it in a crate lined with silverstone."*

Cornelius sighed. "Amateurs."

Leaning sideways, Godwyn snatched a few pages of the report from Cornelius' desk. "How much time do you have for the replica?"

Just as Isaksson was shrugging on his coat and preparing to leave her office, he'd left her with one last parting remark.

"By the way, I forgot to tell you, I'm on a very tight schedule here."

"How tight?" Olivia had growled at him, sensing trouble.

"I'll be back in two days to pick up the replica," he'd tossed over his shoulder. "Have a good evening, Ms Knight!"

And he'd left with a wink.

His chuckle still echoing in her mind, Olivia let out a resigned sigh. "He wants his replica done by Wednesday."

"Nice of him to give us ample time to work," Godwyn remarked sarcastically.

"Right, Cornelius, tomorrow I'd like you to see what you can find out about this wand," Olivia instructed him. "Anything you can tell me, no matter how small."

"What about me?" Godwyn asked her.

"If you like, you can come with me to Wardlaw Wands in the morning. The wand looks like it's made of ebony, but I'm not sure. I want to ask Ada for her opinion. But then I'll have to start on the replica, so you'll need to take care of the Baumer case. Should be standard procedure. Just be careful with the tombstone, I'm told it's feisty. And don't be late. Baumer will be expecting you to pick it up no later than mid-afternoon, and believe me, you don't want to keep him waiting." She smiled at his discomfit expression. "Or would you rather be the one to work on the wand?"

Cornelius had been furiously scribbling notes on a piece of paper, but at that, his head jerked up.

Immediately, Godwyn winced as if he'd swallowed something terribly sour. "I'm perfectly content to leave the insane wand to you two."

Adeline slammed her last drawer shut with her hip, all her files finally put away. Her heels clicked on the floor as she came over to lean against the edge of her desk. In the three years they had known each other, Olivia had never seen the other woman wear anything else. Through freezing rain or winter snow, she could be found prowling the city streets, as graceful as a panther in the deep forest.

"And what would you like me to do?" her assistant asked.

Olivia nodded at Godwyn. "You need to go with him. I'm pretty sure when he sees how Baumer's been containing his tombstone, he'll blow a casket. Pun intended. So I need you there to make sure he doesn't get arrested."

Adeline's smirk contained more than a hint of calculation. "That shall be my pleasure."

Indignation filled Godwyn's face. "Now, wait a minute. I am perfectly capable of dealing with clients on my own! Even when they behave like complete and utter imbeciles."

Olivia raised an eyebrow. He was not really proving his point.

"I think the Baron may have forgotten about the Bates incident," Adeline pointed out.

Godwyn sputtered, but Cornelius cut in, "Or the Yates case."

"What happened at Fawley Manor," Olivia added.

"And, oh!" Adeline went on, counting on her fingers. "Let's not forget that time at Hockcliffe Estate."

By now, Godwyn was throwing daggers at them all. "Are you quite done?"

Olivia held back a laugh. With his title, aristocratic upbringing, refined manners and elegant suits, one would think he would be the best choice for dealing with clients. One would be very wrong.

"Godwyn, I can promise you that when you'll come back tomorrow, you'll thank me," she told him. Then her voice turned excited. "By the way! I finished my new batch of curse repellent today! Do you want to take a vial and give it a try?"

Adeline's eyes widened. "Ah . . ." She cast a worried glance at the others.

"You know, why don't we leave it for an easier case?" Godwyn suggested diplomatically. "If Baumer is such a challenging client, perhaps it would be best to keep things as toned down and solemn as possible, avoid anything flashy."

Olivia hid a smile. He was simply adorable.

Instead, she let out a disappointed sigh. "Oh, well . . . I guess you're right. Maybe next time."

Out of the corner of her eye she caught Adeline turning to him and mouthing a discreet "thank you."

"At least we got a new case, so . . . There's that." Cornelius leaned back in his chair, twirling his pen between two fingers.

Godwyn grunted in agreement. "Indeed. Does anyone have any idea why things have been so dreadfully slow lately?"

Olivia didn't respond and went to lean against a window, her eyes fixed on the distant street below.

"We lost Ravenscroft?" Cornelius asked.

"He decided not to hire anyone after all," Adeline told him. "With the case closed yesterday, that leaves only two pending jobs, including this one." Her elegant fingers drummed on the desk. "You know, I haven't heard anything about other firms having such trouble getting new cases . . ."

There was a loud yawn, followed by two thumps as Godwyn put his feet back on a corner of his desk. He loosened the crimson tie around his neck and unbuttoned the top of his shirt before leaning all the way back in his chair, expertly balancing on two legs. "As if you would know, even if they did."

When he crossed his hands behind his neck, a wince escaped him.

Adeline rose gracefully to stand behind him. She slapped his hands away to massage his neck. "But *au contraire*, my dear Lord Mowbray. I would because I have a large network of informants. I know things. People talk to me."

Godwyn snorted, his eyes closed.

"Will you relax?" She rolled her eyes in exasperation and poked at his tense shoulders. "You're as stiff as a board."

"Perhaps he's afraid you'll wring his neck, *cher*," Cornelius quipped. "Or strangle him with his tie."

Godwyn opened one eye to point a warning finger at him. "Don't you give her ideas."

Adeline ignored them both, her voice thoughtful. "I hear Crowley is starting to make himself quite the circle of friends. He was invited to the museum gala last week, and he's often seen at the Fates Club . . . Could he have something to do with it?"

Olivia groaned as she took off her glasses, pinching the bridge of her nose. She didn't want to think about Crowley's wretched shenanigans.

Cornelius looked up with a frown. "Who's that?"

As their newest employee, he'd only been with them for a couple of months and obviously hadn't yet heard of the scourge of the curse-breaking world.

After working her magic on Godwyn's shoulders, Adeline hopped up to sit on a corner of his desk and crossed her mile-long legs. "Edmund Crowley is a witless cockroach who wouldn't know an higher-level curse from a haunting if it fell out of the sky to smack him right in the face."

"He's more of an opportunistic snake," Godwyn corrected her. "Always scheming in the shadows. Slimy and impossible to get rid of."

Adeline's red lips twisted into a grimace. "No, he's a condescending vermin whose arrogance is matched only by the amount of hair pomade he uses every morning. I swear he becomes a fire hazard every time he passes by a burning candle."

Cornelius's head snapped back and forth between them.

Then Godwyn snapped his fingers in triumph. "I've got it! A snobbish, stuck-up toad with delusions of utter mediocrity."

Conceding victory, Adeline leaned forward to shake his hand.

What Crowley really was, Olivia thought, was her worst enemy. Well, at least she was his.

"Crowley and I share a long history of despising one another," she explained, "ever since we were at University together. He loathes me and this agency, and well . . . As you could tell by these two, the feeling is quite mutual. He's Professor Wyborn's assistant."

Then Olivia's sour expression vanished and she rubbed her hands together. "But enough about that ugly troll. Even if it really was him, I don't care because I've just come up with the most brilliant plan. One that should provide us with an endless supply of new cases."

Well, a *plan* might be too strong a word for what she had in mind. A *crazy gambit* would be more like it.

"That's all?" Godwyn snorted, his tone clearly sceptical. He crossed his arms. "And what, pray tell, is that miraculous idea of yours?"

A satisfied grin bloomed on Olivia's lips. "My good Lord Mowbray, my idea is no miracle at all. What we have to do is actually quite simple. We're going to win this year's curse-breaking competition."

A stunned silence fell over the office.

"But . . . How can we win the competition without any cases?" Cornelius asked.

"Wait, earlier you said we didn't have a case *yet*," Godwyn said. Seeing Olivia's smug smile widen even further, he groaned. "You have *got* to be joking."

He obviously knew her best.

"How? I'm simply going to show Mr Isaksson the error of his ways and that it would be in his best interest to choose us instead for the transport of his wand."

"Do you know who he's already hired?" Cornelius asked.

"What you mean is who could ever be so daft to attempt such a challenging case without proposing an adequate containment plan . . ." Godwyn's voice trailed off.

"Ah!" Adeline barked out a laugh, her silver eyes sparkling. "You're going to steal Crowley's case? I love this plan!"

CHAPTER SIX

OLIVIA MUNCHED ON SOME sugar pumpkins she pulled out of a paper bag as she made her way through the serpentine streets of York, Godwyn at her side.

The sun had decided to grace them with its presence that morning, so she wasn't wearing a coat but a thin rust-coloured jumper tucked in a skirt that came to below her knees. Her favourite pair of walking boots and the leather messenger bag that held her equipment and never left her side completed the ensemble. It was the perfect attire for a day spent working on cases.

She glanced at Godwyn beside her and held a grin. They made quite the odd couple.

Lord Mowbray looked ready for a business meeting of the highest importance. He was wearing another of his daily suits, this one chocolate coloured, with a rich maroon shirt and not a wrinkle in sight. There was even a square of silk peeking out of his breast pocket. His jaw was clean-shaven, showing off pale skin and sharp cheekbones, full lips and an aquiline nose. His slightly curly hair was artfully slicked back and the green of his eyes thrown in sharp focus by the choice of suit colour. He also stood taller than most people and walked with a confidence in his gait that said he was used to getting his way.

In short, he looked every inch the noble heir he was.

Olivia offered him a sugar pumpkin, looking forward to not telling him when he would inevitably get a little powdered sugar stuck to his lip.

But he waved his hand dismissively, a far too serious expression on his face for so early in the morning. "Are you sure about this plan, Liv?"

Having bitten into another sugary treat, Olivia simply gave him a questioning look.

"We were only hired for the replica," he told her. "I cannot fathom why you insist on getting such a risky job."

Olivia didn't reply right away. She dusted the sugar off her fingers and reached into her bag to pull out her very crumpled copy of the latest *Cursed Herald*, curse-breakers' favourite publication. "I told you all last night. Winning this competition would mean not having to constantly worry about cases. But in order to do that, we need the most challenging, most impressive job. And this wand is definitely that. I'm surprised we don't have to fight every agency in town for it, to be honest. Whoever completes this transfer wins the contest."

Godwyn's voice turned sarcastic. "*If* that whoever manages to complete the job and not turn raging mad in the process, you mean."

Well, there was that.

As the magazine of choice for anyone in the field, the *Cursed Herald* reported every interesting piece of curse-breaking information. New techniques, fancy equipment, social events ... But the most interesting part was reading about other agencies' work.

Cases with notorious clients, peculiar artifacts, unconventional resolutions or just plain weird, the best ones always found their way into the magazine.

Olivia herself had had two jobs featured over the course of her career, something she was still immensely proud of. It certainly hadn't been easy, as the curse-breaking community could turn very competitive. Some might even say a tad bloodthirsty when it came to who would get the most exciting cases. All in fair game, of course.

Case in point, every year, the *Cursed Herald* held a competition to crown the most outstanding job. And every curse-breaking agency in the country fought tooth and nail to get to the podium. No one would sabotage another team's work, at least not openly, but short of that, curse-breakers were a ruthless lot.

Winning this competition would be the perfect answer to all their problems. It would officially propel them among the top agencies, guaranteeing them a steady stream of cases. And last but certainly not least, it would knock the socks off her colleagues.

Olivia wasn't above admitting she was particularly looking forward to knocking the socks off *one* colleague, in particular.

Having tried and failed to smooth out the magazine with her hand, she waved it in Godwyn's face.

"Have you seen it? Have you seen the despicable weasel they put on this month's cover?" She shoved the magazine at his chest. "Look at him. Look at his smile. He thinks he's already won. It's like he's sending me a personal declaration of war."

Godwyn pointed to the imaginative depiction of what Crowley would look like as a woodland creature she'd done on the cover. "Really?"

Olivia shrugged. "I took offence at his smug face."

That made Godwyn shake his head.

"I really don't understand why Isaksson chose him for the job," she continued. "Or why the magazine put him on the cover, for that matter. His case was nothing to write home to mother about. I mean . . . A cursed armoire that spits out nails?" She scoffed. "Flashy."

Godwyn laughed at her rant, but then his expression turned serious again. "You know, maybe the other agencies are staying away because they realise how dangerous that wand is, unlike Crowley. That artifact is unstable, unpredictable. Is it really wise to get involved? Besides, what do you know about that Isaksson, really? Can we trust him?"

Olivia snorted. "You're simply full of optimism this morning."

"I just don't want you taking crazy risks simply because you think we *have* to win the competition. I'm sure we can manage without it, we're not that far gone."

His solemn face made her sigh deeply. "I wouldn't be so sure. I received a letter from our bank a few days ago. They've somehow found out about our struggle and want to call in the loan in full."

"What?" Godwyn's green eyes sparked with indignation. "They cannot do that!"

"I'm afraid they can. We've been a little behind in our payments lately. I let it happen because they assured me they were willing to give us some leeway." Her voice hardened. "Obviously, they changed their mind. They're giving me three months to pay it all back or they're seizing the office."

Godwyn pressed his lips together. "Do you think Adeline's right? That it is all Crowley's doing?"

"I certainly wouldn't put it past him. The thing is, even if I somehow found the money to pay off the loan, we still need more cases. We won't survive for long without them. This competition, it's the best option we have."

"I realise that, but—"

Olivia cut him off. "I know this wand is very impressive, Godwyn, but at the end of the day it's just a cursed artifact and we're curse-breakers. This is nothing more than another case, another transfer. All we need is a tight containment, a strong bait and *voilà*."

Olivia knew she had what it took to make this wand comply. She was familiar with every curse-breaking technique there was, and she knew how to adapt them if necessary. This wand was tricky, no doubt, but so was she.

"Besides, you've got it all wrong," she added, something sombre creeping into her tone. "That wand has been so destructive because the Ministry doesn't have a clue how to properly contain its artifacts. It's people who are unstable and unpredictable. Curses . . . Curses, I can do."

Godwyn studied her for a long moment, not bothering to add what he thought of her arrogance. Finally, he said, "You know very well there's something not right with that wand."

Sly Baron.

Olivia avoided his gaze. "Fine, yes. Maybe I do know that," she grudgingly admitted. "But I'm not getting involved. The job is to grab the wand, escort it to Romania and get out. Nothing more."

She knew Godwyn was not wrong to be worried. The wand *was* behaving very differently than it should, and she really didn't trust Isaksson, as it was clear he was keeping important things from her.

But as she'd told him, she wasn't going to get involved or take any more risks than what was expected of her as the curse-breaking expert. Whatever else was going on was not her responsibility.

They walked in silence for a while before Godwyn added, "That's not all there is, is it?"

Olivia shot him a narrowed sideways glance. "You know me *too* well."

She considered her words carefully. "I've always believed that cursed artifacts were capable of more. Of gaining some semblance of life. But no one ever put much faith in my theories. They've always looked down their noses at me. This case may prove that I was right, that our techniques do need to evolve, to be updated. We have to start thinking of these artifacts as . . . as more than inanimate objects. They have needs and desires. Containments should be tailored to them, not just a bunch of centuries-old techniques thrown at them, hoping one will stick."

Olivia greatly enjoyed her work and took great pride in doing it well. She loved the satisfaction of closing a case, of taking unsafe, hazardous artifacts, treating them with the respect their age demanded, and finding them a new home.

To her, cursed objects weren't crazy things that howled or bit or shook uncontrollably. They were pieces of the past, relics of a time long gone. They carried history. They had once meant everything to their owners, who'd poured not only their magic into them, but their aspirations, their rage, their wounds. These artifacts deserved to be treated with care and compassion.

The Knight Curse-Breaking Agency was more than a job to her, it was her passion. Everyone on her team, each in their own way, was dedicated to it. They'd all worked tirelessly for years to make it into what it was now.

Olivia was tired of being brushed aside solely because she didn't have the right connections, or because she didn't play golf with York's elite every Sunday. It was time to show everyone what they were capable of.

"I'll convince Isaksson to give me this case. We'll escort this wand all the way to Transylvania, using cutting edge techniques and without a single hitch. Everyone will be impressed, Crowley will have to disappear back into the dark hole he crawled out of, and our work will finally get the recognition it deserves."

Godwyn saw the steely determination on her face. He sighed. "Well, I suppose that answers my question. If you're sure, then we've got your back. All of us. You know that."

Olivia smiled. She offered him a sugar pumpkin again, and this time he took it.

Godwyn hated sentient artifacts and mental magic more than anything, and yet he still supported her. When she'd taken a chance three years ago and hired an aristocratic heir who seemed to be running away from his family, knew next to nothing about curses and grimaced the first time he set foot in the office, she'd made the right decision.

Perhaps she might tell him about the powdered sugar on his lips after all.

The copper bell rang as Godwyn pushed open the door to the quiet shop. A voice immediately called from the back, "Just a minute, I'll be right with you!"

He held the door open for Olivia, who immediately unwrapped the scarf around her neck, thankful to be out of the biting autumn wind that had just risen.

Two large worktables occupied either side of the room, each made from a thick slab of reclaimed wood. One was immaculate and neat, while the other had clearly been used recently to work with clients. That one was covered with various instruments, from a brass set of scales to an array of measuring tools, on top of drawings scribbled on miscellaneous pieces of paper. A typewriter lay haphazardly to one side, one foot keeping another pile of documents from being blown away by a sudden gust of wind.

In the middle of the table stood a black storage chest, a crest reading *Wardlaw Wands* embossed in gold letters. Two doors normally kept it closed, but here were open, revealing a myriad of samples, including small wooden cylinders in mostly brown tones, punctuated by the odd bright purple or shimmering green. Drawers filled with various substances in tiny glass jars spilled out of the chest.

Beyond the worktables, the walls of the room were lined with heavy shelves holding books and old rolled up scrolls, and large display cabinets made up of the thinnest possible drawers, no wider than two fingers, containing hundreds of records of old wand designs.

Finally, a figure emerged from the back of the shop, but it wasn't who they were expecting.

The young woman was nearly as tall as Godwyn, with long legs and slender arms. She had the body of an acrobat, or a dancer. Her long, red hair was arranged in dozens of braids that fell to her waist, some of them adorned with tiny brass beads. The features of her face were delicate, almost elfin. She had pale skin dotted with freckles and some of the most captivating eyes Olivia had ever seen. They were a tawny colour in the morning light, already an unusual shade. But Olivia knew that once she used her magic, they would become a true, shimmering copper and seem to glow from within.

As Maeve's gaze settled on Godwyn, Olivia felt her magic brush against his for a second. His mouth opened slightly and his breath caught, before he schooled his expression back into a neutral mask. Olivia knew immediately that he'd recognised her particular ability.

"Maeve!" She grinned. "I thought you were in Winterdale assisting Professor Halford. What are you doing here?"

"He's taken the students on a field trip to Brocéliande Forest. My thesis is due in a few months, so I decided not to join them and came here instead. I was hoping for some peace and quiet while I wrote, but alas!" She sighed dramatically. "There's an international seminar of wandmakers happening in London this week. So when Ada heard I was coming, she immediately packed her bags and took Uncle Malachi with her, leaving me to look after the shop."

Olivia laughed. "That does sound like Ada."

She gestured to Godwyn. "Maeve, let me introduce you. This is my partner, Godwyn de Mowbray."

The two shook hands. To Godwyn, Olivia added. "Maeve and I have known each other since we were children. My father used to come here a lot, as he would always need a special material or other. He'd bring me along and stash me in the back room with Maeve while he and Ada talked business. I remember spending hours looking at all the strange jars stored in the back, wondering what they contained and where it came from."

Maeve laughed. "While *I* remember the time we saw Uncle Malachi's enclosure of glasswing butterflies. An enclosure he'd finally finished after months of wandering the woods gathering special plants for them to eat. Olivia convinced me that the butterflies needed more space to stretch their wings, so we opened the case and they all flew out the window. I don't need to tell you how happy my uncle was with us, considering these butterflies are extremely rare and only found in South America."

Godwyn glanced at Olivia, his expression amused. "So, if I understand correctly, she was the troublemaker between the two of you. Can't say I'm surprised."

Olivia rolled her eyes and elbowed him in the stomach for his impertinence.

"But you didn't come all this way to reminisce about our childhood exploits," Maeve said with a laugh. "What can I do for you?"

"We're trying to identify the type of wood used to create a dark artifact," Olivia explained. "A wand. I thought it was ebony at first glance, but I have my doubts."

Maeve's tawny eyes sparkled. "Ah. A wand of unknown conception, how mysterious! Let me see."

Godwyn winced. "That's why we're so unsure . . . We don't have the wand with us. Just pictures."

Olivia reached into her bag and handed Maeve the photographs. "I can see a strange reflection on the wood, especially in the handle. It could just be an effect of the light, but . . . What do you think?"

Maeve studied them carefully, a frown creasing her delicate face. "Hmm. No, I think there's definitely something there . . ." She brought the pictures closer to her face, squinting. "What kind of magic is it?"

"Mental. Very strong."

"Ah. Eastern European, right?"

"Romania. Around the 15th century."

Maeve hummed again. "Right, I don't recognise this type of wood off the top of my head. However . . ." She tapped her forefinger against her lips. "I can't shake this feeling that I've seen this before. There's something strangely familiar about it. Give me a minute, I need to check something." She turned on her heels and quickly disappeared through the back of the shop.

Meanwhile, Olivia dug around in her bag for the well-worn leather-bound notebook she carried everywhere with her. There was already an absurd amount of scribbled notes about this case, though most of them were unanswered questions.

Godwyn spun towards her with a gasp, "She's a Sensitive!"

Olivia nodded.

Godwyn had been working hard these last few months to become more perceptive to magic so that he could better handle cursed objects, so she wasn't surprised he'd picked up on Maeve's particular abilities. Still, she made a mental note to remind her friend to be more careful.

Sensitives were extremely rare arcanists who possessed the gift of sensing and manipulating magic itself. For them, arcane energy was a clearly visible and palpable force whose intensity and flow they could control. After her aura had brushed against Godwyn's for the briefest of moments, Maeve had been able to tell his level of power, his own abilities, whether he was cursed or bound by a Pact . . . Anything that had to do with his magic.

Of course, there were *other* aspects of a Sensitive's magic that were not so easily shown, and even less discussed in public . . .

Maeve hurried back, carrying a wooden crate that looked heavier than she was. The very second Godwyn noticed, he leapt forward to take it from her.

What a gentleman.

Behind Godwyn's back, Maeve made big eyes and pretended to fan her face. Olivia had to bite her lip to hold back a laugh.

The crate made a very distinct *thud* as Godwyn set it down on the table. It was filled with bulky kraft envelopes standing upright in a neat row, covered with handwritten notes.

"In her infinite grace and generosity," Maeve joked, "Ada left me a whole bunch of chores to do while she was away. One of which was clearing out the archive boxes in the back, which have been gathering dust since before I was born." She began shuffling through the envelopes. "I'm almost certain I saw a wood sample that looked exactly like yours. I remember because it was inky black with a beautiful sheen, and it reminded me of the wings of a magpie. I'm pretty sure it was called 'serpent something', or 'serpentine' maybe... Ahah!" She pulled out an envelope triumphantly. "There it is."

Unwrapping the tie at the back, Maeve emptied the contents onto the table. A few papers fell out, beside a long and rectangular piece of wood that would be just big enough to carve the replica. As she'd told them, it was indeed black, but with an emerald lustre that appeared every time the light fell on it in a particular way.

Olivia pulled her glasses up to the top of her head and swapped them for her reading ones, which dangled from her chest at the end of a thin gold chain. "It does look extremely similar..." She turned the wooden block this way and that, holding it close to her face and trying to catch the rays of sunlight coming through the front window. "What is it called?" she asked as she passed it to Godwyn.

Maeve reached for one of the papers spread out on the table. Frayed and yellow with age, it was badly crumpled, but the words were still perfectly clear.

"According to this importation application here, that's 'Serpent Wood.'" Maeve quickly read the form. "Apparently, this wood was ordered for a custom restoration project to repair a damaged artifact. It was agreed on the 15th of May 1912 and arrived five days later. Wow, that was crazy fast. Especially twenty years ago. It was done at the request of a certain G.H., but there's no name... What do you know! There's one signature at the bottom: a Mr Malcolm Knight."

"Your father?" Godwyn turned to Olivia, startled.

What a peculiar coincidence... Her father had been the one to repair the very artifact they were now working on. However, that wasn't what made Olivia frown. Her father had been an antique restorer, but he'd stayed away from cursed items. His speciality was complex mechanisms like clocks or hidden locks. What had he been doing with that wand?

"Can you tell us anything else about this serpent wood?" Godwyn asked Maeve.

She shook her head. "No, I'm sorry. There's nothing more here. But let me check the Catalogue."

She walked to the counter behind her and retrieved a huge leather-bound grimoire, thicker than Olivia's hand. The dark blue cover on the front had been engraved with the Wardlaw Wands insignia in silvery lines.

Maeve placed her open palm in the centre. A ripple of power went out and the brass claps on the side fell open with a *click*.

"Every wandmaker has one of these," she explained to them, "passed down through generations, and they consider it the apple of their eye. That's why it's warded, only a member of the family can unlock it." Maeve lifted the cover and turned the pages carefully, almost reverently. "This is a repertoire of all the family's knowledge and research. Like an ancestral Book of Shadows, but for wandmaking. So every time they learn something new, or discover a new substance or technique, they put it in here. Let's see what it has to say about your mysterious wood."

After a few minutes of searching, Maeve stopped on a page covered with precise handwriting in sepia ink, along with an intricate diagram and several annotations. She began to read aloud :

Extremely rare, I have only found a few suppliers who carry it in incredibly limited quantities. Unknown abilities. The emerald green sheen seems to run throughout the wood. It is likely a result of the sap of the tree permeating it. I ran the usual testing procedures. Very conductive of mental related magic, but attempts with other types have yielded very poor results. Extremely charged and volatile material, it hasn't agreed to work with any wand core I have tried.

Maeve looked up at them. "I think it's safe to say we found your mysterious wood."

It is my opinion that the sap of the tree, if magically potent, would make a most excellent core, as it seems to be the only substance the wood will accept. It remains to be seen whether the combination of the two forms a bond strong enough to channel magic.

Godwyn glanced at Olivia, who was furiously writing everything down. "And I think we've found the core," he added.

Maeve squinted at the page. "There's something written in the margin, there. It's a bit smudged, but I think I can make out what it says."

*I found a record of a legendary tree in Romania that seems to match the serpent wood. Folklore would attribute to it many incidents related to mental magic, including lost travellers, memory loss, trance episodes and catatonic states.
Legend has it that the tree*

Maeve stopped reading. "I can't decipher the end, sorry. The writing is completely rubbed off. But there's one last phrase. *The locals call it the . . . the Whi . . .*"

"The Whispering Tree," Olivia murmured.

Maeve and Godwyn both stared at her in amazement.

"How did you know?" Maeve asked her.

Olivia shook her head, as incredulous as they were. "I have no idea, it just came out."

"Perhaps you heard your father mention it . . ." Godwyn suggested.

"Yes, that must be it."

Only she couldn't shake the feeling that it wasn't.

It hadn't been her father's voice she'd heard in her head just now, calling it the Whispering Tree . . . It had been her own.

CHAPTER SEVEN

"*Sir Walter Thomas of Godolphin created the first official classification of artifact-bound curses in 1853. No, wait... in 1854. His theories have since been updated as the science evolved, but are still recognised to this day as the best system for dividing malevolent curses based on their effect on living creatures.*"

A sliver of black rained down, easily passing through the containment wards to join the small pile already accumulating on the towel below.

"*Type One curses are only capable of interacting with their environment at the most basic level. They can exert a physical force limited to rudimentary movement, and harness the energy around them to a radius of only a dozen feet...*"

Olivia's hand was steady, her focus razor sharp, and her lips moved almost soundlessly as she carefully carved the runes into the piece of serpent wood.

"*Type Two curses possess the ability to conjure up apparitions representing fragments of their past. They rarely attempt to interact with their surroundings, but are more intent on recreating scenes from their history through visions, sounds or smells.*"

Olivia's eyes left her replica, still floating peacefully in front of her, to dart sideways. No mist and no trees. So far, so good.

"*Type Three curses are recognised by their desire to communicate with those around them. They seek to direct visions into people's minds, share feelings and basic thoughts. As such, those objects fall under the Dangerous Substances Class Four category, and require a certification to be handled.*"

The specialised curse-breaking wand between Olivia's fingers crackled, a sign that magic was coursing heavily through it. Its touch grew hot.

Not yet. Hold on . . . Her heart sped up but she kept whispering under her breath, using the wand to cut off more shards of wood.

"Type Four curses are the rarest of all, possessing the uncanny ability to embody living creatures, making them the most dangerous variety. However, they . . ."

Crack!

A small cry escaped her as the wand in her hand snapped in half, its core cracked. The echo travelled the length of her arm to rattle her teeth.

Olivia put down the now useless wand and swore long and hard, massaging her sore wrist. She'd spent the whole afternoon working on that bloody replica, and so far had sacrificed two wands, four ash candles and her entire supply of Persian blue salt.

But the damned wood was as hard as adamantine and so arcane-charged, it had kept destroying her supplies one after the other. Even though she'd stuck it inside not one, but *two* different wards, trying to weaken it. There was one drawn on her desk using silverstone shavings that glowed bright silver, but when the replica had broken her first wand, she'd decided to pull out the big guns and construct a Lethe box.

It should have been enough, it should have been entirely *too much* for an inert piece of wood. And yet, as soon as Olivia had begun to carve into it, she'd started to see trees at the edges of her vision, felt wisps of gossamer touch her skin . . .

Just like the one that encircled her left wrist.

Olivia jerked her hand away. *For the love of . . .* She was definitely adding hazard pay to the Viking's bill.

"*The physical compulsion is achieved by direct contact,*" she muttered, "*whereas the mental one is a result of a breach of shields. Therefore, it is possible to break the compulsion with a strong enough push on either the physical or mental plane . . .*"

The phantom touch vanished.

This seemingly normal piece of wood was behaving exactly like a powerful curse, sending her visions and trying to entice her. And just like with those curses, the best trick was to distract the mind, to focus it on something else. Which was why Olivia had started to recite large passages from the *Compendium of Curse-Breaking Techniques.*

Still uttering under her breath, she picked up her last wand. This one was almost new, the metal cool and hard between her fingers.

Magic zinged through her hand and black dust rained down again as soon as she went back to work on the replica.

Unfortunately, the Lethe Box she'd had to conjure made her work ten times harder. A floating sphere completely surrounded the black wood, enclosing it behind walls of pure energy that looked like purplish glass, shot through by tiny lightening strikes. Those illuminated the black and glossy surface of the wood with an iridescent glow, almost like the surface of a pearl.

It made small details almost impossible to see, but she had to admit that she'd forgotten how beautiful it looked, especially with all this mist swirling around that resembled fluffy clouds . . .

"Ah . . . Boss?"

Olivia jerked her head up.

Cornelius was standing near the entrance to her office, staring at her. His fist was raised as if he'd just knocked on her door, yet she hadn't heard a thing. "Why are there tree branches dangling from the ceiling?"

"For Gods' sakes!"

Olivia jumped to her feet and in one smooth motion, threw a piece of silverstone netting onto the floating wand, over the Lethe Box. The hallucinations dissolved instantly, blocked by the metal.

That done, she slumped back in her chair and banged her head against the surface of her desk a few times.

"Was that . . . a Type Three?" Cornelius murmured.

Olivia shook her head. Without a word, she pointed a finger at the cloaked demonic *thing* hovering above her desk, which now resembled a cute little ghost knight, draped in chain mail. She still gave it a death glare.

"That was the *replica*?" Cornelius gasped. "But what . . . How . . . What *is* it?"

Olivia tucked a loose wisp of raven hair behind her ear. "It's annoying, that's what it is."

And to think she'd complained that this case was nothing more than a carpentry job.

"Please tell me you found something," she begged Cornelius. "I need some good news."

Her employee flashed her a grin, his honey brown eyes sparkling, and sauntered over.

In his mid-twenties, he was the youngest member of their team. With rich brown skin inherited from his grandmother, mischievous eyes and a sensual mouth, Olivia knew him to be quite the charmer. She'd been told that the ladies found his smooth New Orleans accent utterly irresistible, and that he'd once flirted with an entire female Feathurling team.

But Cornelius was much more than a ladies' man. In addition to his intelligence and incredible memory, he had the uncanny ability to make friends with just about anyone. He could walk into a room full of strangers and, within minutes, be sharing jokes and life stories. Olivia had lost count of how many people greeted him warmly as the Creole Devil, from the highest levels of Ministry administration, to the shadiest corners of the York underground.

After dropping a thick stack of papers on a corner of her desk not occupied by the wards, Cornelius grabbed a chair and turned it around to straddle it, resting his arms on the backrest. "Took me all bloody day, and I was ready to give up when I finally found it. But it sure explains why the wand's been acting the way it has."

Indeed, he'd rolled up the sleeves of his white shirt to his elbows but Olivia still spied a few specks of ink, and the purple tie around his neck had been loosened so many times that it was barely hanging on now. He was also wearing his thin, gold-rimmed glasses, something he rarely did, claiming they got in the way of his *"natural charm."*

Cornelius shuffled papers around and pulled out a few particular ones, decorated with intricate woodcut illustrations.

"This is from a book that records the history of Romania from the 11th to the late 15th century. There's an account of a general called Pál Torbai, who wielded a terrible weapon on the battlefields. One that could . . ." he flipped through a few pages, "*unleash visions of hellish landscapes and nightmarish creatures upon approaching armies.*"

"That sounds like our delightful wand," Olivia remarked dryly.

"And that's just the start, believe me. That general was something of a legend. He served the King of Hungary, Matthias Corvinus, and even ended up leading his Black Army. He was considered a military hero. It was said that he could win any battle, regardless of the odds. He had a fiercely strategic mind and would use any means at his disposal to gain an advantage. But that was until the last years of his life. Then he began to lose battles, even those where they had a clear superiority in numbers. All because he became obsessed with threats of conspiracy from within his own ranks. He didn't trust anyone. Imprisoned his seconds because he was sure they were plotting against him, banished and killed his servants thinking they were trying to poison him. I even found some texts that said he would roam the corridors at night, screaming that ghosts were haunting him."

Olivia understood immediately.

"Renuntiare Dominus," she breathed.

Cornelius' expression was both grim and ecstatic in equal measure. He nodded.

Latin for "to renounce one's master", Renuntiare Dominus was an extremely ancient concept in wandcraft, describing wands that turned against the arcanists who wielded them. Considered by many to be more myth than actual theory, it was based on the idea that over time, if wands were imbued with too much magic, they could become their own entity and choose to leave their masters.

It was a similar concept to Olivia's theory that the act of cursing could grant an object a semblance of life and decision-making power, but she'd never before heard of a credible example, and many scholars, including herself, considered it to be no more than legend. She had to admit, though, that this tale of the Hungarian general was making her reconsider.

"This is incredible . . . You're right, it explains why the wand has been acting the way it has." It was already showing a level of intelligence and autonomy rarely seen some five centuries ago, before it was even cursed. "What happened to him after that?"

Cornelius grimaced. "The general deserted and joined Vlad Tepes, the Walachian warlord. He was later initiated into the Order and became a Dragon Knight."

Olivia stared at him. "So you're telling me the wand made this military hero, leader of the Black Brotherhood, betray his king and join his sworn enemy?"

"Yes." Cornelius regarded Olivia intently, his voice turning sombre all of a sudden. "You'll have to keep a very close eye on it. If that wand could turn on its own master, it won't have any problem attacking *you*."

His solemn words hung between them, but Olivia forcibly put those dark thoughts to rest.

Her fingers drummed on the wood of her desk as she mused, "You know, there is something that's been bothering me. Why now? Isaksson told me that they've been having problems with the wand for years. So what's changed? Just like that piece of serpent wood. It's been lying around the Wardlaw Wands shop for years, not bothering anyone, yet as soon as I get my hands on it, it's giving me hallucinations, even through a Lethe Box."

Cornelius hummed in agreement. "It's odd, *non*? Almost as if . . ."

"As if it had been hibernating and was only now coming out of its slumber," Olivia finished.

"Exactly." Cornelius took off his glasses and leaned forward, resting his chin on his folded arms. "Perhaps Isaksson could give us the record of the wand's initial transfer to the Cellars? I reckon I could trace its origins that way."

"I already asked him. He told me he'd searched the archives of the Cellars from top to bottom, but the file no longer exists."

Cornelius sighed. "I guess it's one of those again . . ."

The Cellars were the result of countless years their Ministry had spent amassing powerful objects and other dangerous artifacts. Most of them accompanied by records that held varying degrees of accuracy and an even patchier knowledge of their capabilities.

Despite Olivia's excitement at all the incredible treasures they were rumoured to possess, she recognised the Cellars for what they really were: the biggest can of worms imaginable. She certainly didn't envy the Warden his job.

Cornelius was right, this wand was obviously the latest in a long line of artefacts their Ministry had preferred to entomb in the underground labyrinth, never to see the light of day again . . .

In fact, she was even convinced that more than a few relics were in a state of active cursing still, and so were realistically exerting that curse on something, or *someone*, somewhere in the world to this day.

A can of worms, indeed.

Cursed worms, to be precise.

Olivia shuffled through the rest of Cornelius' research. There were copies of pages from old history books, a few letters with the ink almost completely erased, maps bearing the insignia of the Order of the Dragon . . . And Cornelius' neat handwriting covering pages upon pages of notes. She could only dream that her own penmanship was this pretty.

"Have you found out anything about the properties of the wand? How it was made, the materials . . . Anything that might tell us what to use as bait?" she asked.

"*Non*. Nothing specific about the wand. But I might have a theory."

Olivia gave him a quizzical look.

"What if the wand is not really from the 15th century," Cornelius suggested, "but much, *much* older? After I found this Torbai general, I tried to go back in time, before it belonged to him. I looked everywhere, but there was nothing. How unusual is that? A wand that powerful and difficult to control, I should have found tons of records, right?"

Yes, that was one of the things Olivia found most incomprehensible about this wand. An unstable artifact that relished in driving people completely insane? There should have been an endless number of incidents over the years, not to mention plenty of crimes. That wand should have bounced from police custody, to government, to private institutions for years as no one could figure out how to properly contain it. Before the

Cellars had been created some decades ago, that had been the fate of many of its residents.

"Anyway," Cornelius continued, "since I'm not getting anywhere looking for the history of the wand, I'm going to track down the wandmaker who created it. I've contacted *mon bon ami* Andrei, who lives in Romania. Asked him to send me some records on famous wandmakers of the time. Hopefully it'll tell us what you can use as bait."

Cornelius leaned forward, brown eyes gleaming. "But if I'm right and the wand is much older than we think . . . There's only one place to look for answers."

Olivia finished for him, her voice almost reverent, "The Legendarium."

They shared a smile.

The precious tomes of the Legendarium were housed in a restricted library that, to Olivia and many other scholars, was almost considered a holy sanctuary. She could easily spend entire days examining the beautifully detailed illustrations and cryptic legends contained within the ancient leather-bound volumes.

She would have to take Isaksson to the Vaults the very next day. He, on the other hand, might not like the stifling atmosphere so much. Olivia found it peaceful and quiet, but she knew many others who described it as being locked inside a crypt. It didn't help that the Head Librarian, protector of the precious volumes and resident ghoul, was so tall, bony and gaunt as to resemble a living skeleton.

Olivia hadn't missed Cornelius' wistful look.

Ever since a rather disastrous incident a few weeks ago — involving a curse that had sneakily imprinted and then hid on Cornelius, before torching one *very* valuable scroll — he'd been banned from the Vaults by the Librarian.

Nicknamed the Dragon for the fierce way he ruled over his hoard of ancient books, the Head Librarian wasn't known for his mercy or forgiveness. Olivia hoped that with enough time, and the donation of rare scrolls she planned to make, Cornelius might be able to get back in his good graces.

"What bothers me," he said after a while, "is how the wand seems to simply appear out of thin air and then vanish just as quickly."

"What do you mean?"

"This General Torbai was not a nobleman or from a rich family. He was a commoner. A miller's son, I think. Who rose through the ranks because of his intelligence and ferocity in battle. So it's doubtful that he inherited the wand, it's more likely that he simply picked it up during a raid. And after his death, there's no more mention of the wand anywhere. It just disappeared. Same with the Cellars, the wand is just *there*. No record of how it got in, who had it before, nothing."

"What about the Order?" Olivia asked. "Didn't you say the general became a Dragon Knight? They must have taken the wand for themselves after he died."

"If they did, they chose not to use it for some reason. There's no record of it ever being used on a battlefield again after Torbai. My guess is that the wand was heavily cursed by then and no one could control it."

Olivia furrowed her brow. That seemed unlikely.

Not much was known about the legendary Order of the Dragon, other than how ruthless its members had been.

"It doesn't sound like the Order to have such a powerful weapon at their disposal and not use it," she said. "Not even if it drives the wand's master mad."

Before Cornelius had a chance to reply though, angry voices rose from outside. Olivia stood and moved quickly to the door, Cornelius close behind. They halted as Godwyn and Adeline barged inside the main office, their arguing growing steadily louder.

"Must you always be so annoying?" Adeline raged. "Can't you just say thank you for once?"

"What you did was incredibly reckless! What if he'd seen you? You could have—"

"I was perfectly safe! Besides, I was trying to protect *you*!"

Godwyn scoffed. "Please, I didn't need any help."

That earned him an exasperated snort as Adeline threw her hands up in the air. "Next time, I'll be sure to leave you down there, then! Do you know what you are? An arrogant, insecure man-child who feels threatened because I—"

"Oh, really? You want to talk about arrogance?" Godwyn marched up to her until he stood only inches away.

Refusing to back down, Adeline folded her arms across her chest, her eyes narrowing to slits.

"You only used your powers to show—" Godwyn stopped abruptly when he finally noticed Cornelius and Olivia standing at the door.

They, in turn, were staring shock-still at the angry newcomers, covered from head to toe in a faintly glowing, greyish goo.

Godwyn was the worst off, with the disgusting substance slicking back his hair, as well as covering his entire body, clothed in what had previously been his very expensive suit. He'd only managed to wipe it off his face, but there were still traces of the stuff caught in his eyebrows, giving them a strange phosphorescent glow, similar to uranium, which Olivia noticed still managed to bring out the colour of his eyes.

Adeline's once pristine heels were definitely ruined as they dragged the muck across the office floor. Underneath her tailored skirt, her long legs were glistening and her blouse had lost its lilac hue but, incredibly, there was not a trace of the nasty sludge in her elegant, pinned up hair. How she managed that, Olivia had no idea.

"Ah." Godwyn tried to hide behind a mask of cool nonchalance. "I see you're both back."

Olivia had to pick her jaw up from the floor to answer. "Yesssss . . . and obviously, so are you." Then she winced. "Wait, did my curse repellent do that? Oh my . . . Adeline, I'm so sorry."

"No, no, this isn't one of your creations," Adeline replied as she wiped some of the viscous goo off her arm.

Olivia waited for her to elaborate, but her assistant didn't add anything else, lips pressed into a tight line.

An uncomfortable silence poured between them.

"Well, that's . . . a relief, I guess." Olivia shared a bemused look with Cornelius, who'd leaned against the door frame, his hands in his pockets.

"Do we want to know what happened?" he asked, arching a brow.

"No!" Godwyn and Adeline shouted in unison.

Olivia frowned. "Do we *need* to?"

"The important thing is that we closed the case, so . . ." Adeline threw Godwyn a sharp look as she headed for the kitchen area. "Whatever happened was worth it."

There was a definite twitch in his jaw at her words.

Olivia crossed her arms, her eyes twinkling with unmistakable mischief. "You know, you didn't have to dig up that gravestone yourselves."

"Ah ah, funny," Godwyn retorted. "Next time there's a cemetery involved, send Cornel— "

A towel flew through the air to land right on his face. It slid ever so slowly down his slime-covered skin, before Godwyn finally wrenched it off.

The noble Baron De Mowbray stared at Adeline with what could only be described as the Look of Death on his face.

Unimpressed, she looked down her nose at him. "What? You stink."

The glare he levelled at her promised all sorts of retribution before he stormed off to their small office bathroom.

"Tsk, tsk. That man is infuriating," Adeline said with a shake of her head. "That's Hippogriffs for you. All Earth signs are."

She used another towel to gently wipe the sludge from under her manicured nails. Never mind that it covered the rest of her body as if she'd bathed in it.

Priorities.

CHAPTER EIGHT

THE NEXT DAY, OLIVIA was enjoying some quiet time in her home workshop, humming to herself and swaying to the sound of jazz playing in the background, when a pounding at her door startled her so much she almost fell out of her chair and sent the magazine she was annotating flying through the air.

Looked like the Warden had just arrived. And a good two hours before he was supposed to, as well.

Olivia tried to dodge the many piles of boxes scattered about to get to the record player, but when the pounding grew steadily louder, she had to give up and run.

"Coming!" she called out.

Flying down the corridor, she tripped over the edge of the carpet and barely kept her balance before flinging open the front door, gasping for breath. "What. Is. Wrong with you!"

"Ms Knight, good afternoon!" a deep voice boomed in reply, Isaksson pretending he hadn't just tried to break down her door.

Without waiting for an invitation, he pushed past her and proceeded to shrug off his long, dark coat. He was so tall and broad-shouldered that he almost took up all the available space in her small foyer. With his tousled blond hair, intense blue eyes and the edges of his tattoo peeking out on his forearm, he really did look like a proper Viking.

"So you have my replica?" he tossed over one shoulder.

Olivia glared at his large back as she slammed the door. "You're early."

He was damn lucky she'd finished earlier than she'd thought, else she would have simply slammed the door in his face.

"Oh yes, sorry about that," he replied absent-mindedly, not sorry in the least. He was looking around with interest, inspecting her various knick-knacks and picture frames. "Ah!" He pointed to one of the pictures on her wall. "That's you on a dragon there!" Then he started to laugh. "You already look green and the dragon hasn't even left the ground yet."

Of course, she looked green. She was on top of a huge beast that held no regard for the tiny human on its back, whom it could send hurtling through the air at any time, or simply crush like a gnat under its massive paw.

Before Olivia had a chance to reply, Isaksson had already turned to the other photographs immortalising her youthful exploits. "Look at this one! That's you as a tiny forest fairy."

Olivia made an exasperated sound. "Can we please get to work? I thought you were on a tight schedule."

When Isaksson finally deigned to look back at her, his eyes grew very wide. He turned to face her fully, a grin blossoming on his face.

Olivia raised a tentative hand to her head, scowling. "What is it?"

"Don't you think that's one pair too many?"

Olivia's fingers felt for the frame of her glasses and she groaned.

Her *two* pairs of glasses.

"Fine. I like to wear my close up and everyday glasses at the same time," she muttered. "Big deal."

This was part of her patented work-from-home uniform: a brown, loose-fitting shirt with questionable stains, tucked into a skirt with suspenders, a leather apron that held her own weight in tools, two pairs of glasses one on top of the other, and her long dark hair pulled back in a messy braid.

She would have changed if that damned Warden hadn't shown up so early, as if he'd sensed that would annoy her.

"Got your replica. This way." Olivia stormed off without a backward glance, infuriating chuckles echoing behind her.

Rather than build an outdoor workshop in the garden, where it would have been damp and cold, her late father had decided to move the kitchen and dining space upstairs and use one of the rooms downstairs for his restorative work. One room had turned into two, then three, until he'd commandeered the entire ground floor of the house as his domain. After his death, it had become Olivia's kingdom.

The Warden dutifully followed her out of the entrance hall, but then came to an abrupt stop. "Wow..."

Leaving a slack-jawed Isaksson behind, Olivia continued on, dodging boxes and crates with practised ease until she reached the record player at the back and turned it off. Then she moved to a small alcove in a corner of the workshop that served as an improvised kitchen and placed the kettle back on the heat. She'd barely slept the night before, so she'd reluctantly had to swap her beloved Darjeeling tea for coffee strong enough to raise the dead.

Over the course of her career and many experiments, Olivia had learned the importance of being prepared for all eventualities. Therefore, there were things *everywhere*.

Boxes overflowing with various parts and materials occupied every corner, tabletop and most of the floor. Shelves lined the panelled walls, equipment was stored haphazardly in large chests or metal trunks, and a tall glass cabinet housed hundreds of potions and ingredients she was currently testing. Uneven piles of books and other research folders littered the rest of the room, some perfectly straight, others leaning dangerously to one side.

Isaksson had better watch where he put his ridiculously long feet.

But the most startling aspect of the room was the dozens of lamps scattered everywhere. On tables, on the floor, on shelves... There was an ornate chandelier in the centre of the ceiling, and countless dēnglóng, or traditional Chinese red paper lanterns, dangled from the exposed rafters, drowning the entire workshop in a warm glow.

Curses, much like delicate plants, were known to be highly sensitive to the light of the sun and moon. Olivia pushed the theory even further and had learned to lull them into complaisance using the gleam of certain substances. That was why special Norwegian luminescent lichen hid inside storm lanterns, rune-engraved candles adorned the candelabras, and the impressive chandelier would cast an eerie purple radiance that could make even the foulest Type Three curse settle.

After the way the serpent wood had toyed with her all afternoon, Olivia had not wanted to take any chances.

"Your replica has been giving me much grief, Warden."

His cheeks creased. "Ah, I see how it's going to be. I will be 'Mr Isaksson' when you're frustrated with me and 'Warden' when you're annoyed."

"In that case, *Warden*, I'm afraid that . . ." Olivia suddenly had to run to snatch her Mask of Hydriana from his hands. "Don't touch that. It's haunted." She hurried back to pull the whistling kettle out of the heat and added, "Actually, don't touch anything in this room. I don't want to spend the next two hours prying a curse off of you."

Ignoring her royally, Isaksson continued to wander around the room, gawking at anything and everything with wide eyes. "What did my replica ever do to make you so mad?"

Olivia looked over to where it was resting innocently on a corner of a table, green light draped over the wood below. It had stopped misbehaving for the moment, surely mesmerised by the dēnglóngs' lights, so she'd removed all her wards, but she still didn't trust it.

"I managed to hunt down the original material your wand is made of," she said. "It's called serpent wood. It has no special abilities other than being extremely rare and highly conductive of mental magic. However, 'conductive' is definitely not the right word, as I've spent the entire afternoon seeing and sensing things that weren't there."

Isaksson immediately grabbed the replica to turn it over in his hands, not at all concerned by what she'd just described. "You saw things? Like hallucinations?"

"Yes. Just like with your wand. Except this *isn't* your wand, this is a fake. Or supposed to be, at least." She heaved a deep sigh. "Your case is turning stranger and stranger."

"Hmm. It feels incredibly similar to the real wand. There's even a slight tug on my magic."

Olivia took a small sip of her coffee and winced. *Heavens*, that was strong. "That's from the dracaena resin inside," she explained, dropping some sugar into her cup. "You're lucky I still had some left. Ordinary dragon's blood incense is easy enough to find, but this one comes from a particular strain of the tree and is quite unique. I only know of two shops that sell it, and it's pretty expensive."

Isaksson made a sound of disgust and promptly dropped the wand back on the table as if it had burned him. "Of course she would use dracaena," he muttered to himself. "Why am I surprised?"

Outside of curse-breaking, dracaena resin was a substance that had one very special use: to treat the Warped, those arcanists who had succumbed to the lure of too powerful magic, until their natural power turned into an unrecognisable force and they were literally consumed by it, their features deformed and skeletal-like.

Olivia's use of the crystals was far more prosaic, however. As they possess the ability to absorb energy from their surroundings like little leeches, they were excellent at purging traces of dark magic from client's homes, and she used them in retrieval jobs where she'd had to remove a particularly nasty curse.

"Since I didn't have a trace appraisal of your wand, I had to get creative," she explained.

She walked over to Isaksson, and traded the distinctively luminescent femur clenched in his fist with a coffee mug. "When you'll place the replica in the wand's cell, those crystals will fill with its dark aura. After a few minutes, it'll feel just like the real wand, but without the madness-inducing side effects. Although, after what happened to me today . . . I'm not so sure any more."

The Warden hummed quietly. He drank his coffee and kept his other hand raised, ready to poke at anything of interest. Olivia noticed, not for the first time, that he was incapable of sitting still for long, and was always moving or touching things.

Restless Viking energy, she guessed.

"Ms Knight!" Isaksson exclaimed.

He'd turned to the only wall in the room that wasn't covered by large shelves, where she proudly displayed her most prized possessions, and now threw her a bewildered look over his shoulder. "You did *not* tell me you collected antique weaponry!"

A smug smile curled Olivia's lips. "*Cursed* weaponry, to be exact."

His eyes widened even further. He leaned in close to examine each blade, completely mesmerised.

"Ah . . ." Isaksson pointed to her all-time favourite piece: an ornate Indian dagger known as a *bichawa* or *scorpion sting*, which had taken her ages to find and some fierce haggling to acquire. "Should I be worried? There's still blood on there."

Indeed, what looked like fresh blood still ran along the dagger's unusual serpentine shape, the crimson drops gleaming against the metal. Two twisting yalis had been carved into the golden hilt, winged mythical creatures with the face of a lion and the body of a serpent, associated with courage and protection.

Olivia laughed. "You're fine, I promise I haven't killed anyone."

"Is that really blood then? I suppose it's from the curse."

Olivia nodded. She gazed at the dagger fondly, it truly was her favourite piece of them all. "The story goes that it belonged to a legendary warrior, sometime during the Wadiyar Dynasty in India. This warrior was part of a secret order charged with protecting the most sacred Hindu sites and relics. It is said that one day during his explorations he discovered the exact entrance to Shambhala, the mythical paradise."

Isaksson had turned away and was now examining an ancient Corinthian helmet, turning it in his hands to take in all the details etched onto the metal, but Olivia knew he was listening intently. Which might be why he hadn't noticed the growing light pouring out of the eyeholes, which held a distinctly menacing glare.

She snatched the helmet before the awakened Greek warrior's spirit could have a chance to attack the Viking's hands that were handling him so callously. "As soon as his discovery was known, a member of his order pressed him for the information. When he refused to answer, the traitor took one of the warrior's own daggers and stabbed him. Before he died, the warrior cursed him so that his blood would forever stain his hands."

Olivia carefully returned the cursed helmet to its resting place when the Warden's gaze was caught by the metallic reflection of a large war hammer nearby, still oblivious to the stare that followed his every move.

CHAPTER 8

"To the Hindus, Shambhala is known as Aryavartha, or The Land of the Worthy Ones," she continued. "And so he made sure that everyone would know that the man who betrayed him was not worthy to enter this kingdom of paradise. The curse eventually imprinted itself on the dagger and," she gestured to the glistening blood, "here we are."

"I know this place..." Isaksson said, tilting his head. "It's also called the Land of Wonders, no?"

Olivia stared at him. "I wouldn't have taken you for a connoisseur of mythology, Mr Isaksson."

"I am not as ignorant as you think," he replied with a mischievous wink, but then turned back to her glass cabinet, his attention riveted by the glittering potion vials.

Olivia decided it was high time to start convincing Isaksson to choose her for the transport of the wand. But she had to tread carefully. If she said outright that she found the person he had hired utterly incompetent and that they were heading straight for a disaster, Isaksson might take offence and dismiss her warnings out of hand.

That had certainly happened to her before.

Adeline's many words of wisdom rang in her ears. She should start by finding something to agree with Isaksson on, and then slowly lead him to the only reasonable solution to his problem. She had to make him believe that *he* was the one who thought about hiring her... Yes, that seemed like an excellent plan.

"Edmund Crowley does not have the faintest idea what he's doing with this case," was what she said. "He's treating this artifact like any other when it's behaving in ways I've never seen before. Your wand is going to escape its containment in the first few hours, mark my words. You need someone else for this job, Mr Isaksson. You need me."

Olivia closed her eyes.

Well... So much for her excellent plan.

Isaksson turned around, not as taken aback by her passionate tirade as she thought he'd be. "You're very blunt."

Olivia cleared her throat. "Yes, well. It's been known to get me into trouble, but... I'm afraid after twenty-nine years, I'm stuck with it."

The Warden's blue eyes danced. "You and me both, then."

Indeed, he didn't seem the kind of man to beat around the bush or pretend one thing to gauge someone's reaction. He seemed much more like herself: direct and honest. She wondered how well he got on with the other Ministry officials.

Isaksson studied her a moment before he said, "So tell me. I suppose you have a better plan?"

Olivia picked up the very expensive bottle of Unspoken Water he'd been admiring and put it back on its shelf, before racing to retrieve a stack of papers. They were the real reason she had to drink coffee thick enough to keep the teaspoon upright: complete plans for a bespoke containment system.

Isaksson's eyes followed her with rapt attention, but he hadn't moved an inch so she stole his coffee cup and placed it on a small table next to her own.

"This is my proposal," she said, spreading out the papers. "A hybrid version of the Behr-Walde manoeuvre, modified to strengthen it against the wand."

His eyebrows crept up at her words. She shot him a questioning look, but he motioned for her to continue as he folded his large frame to sit across from her.

Olivia fished her battered copy of *A Compendium of Curse-Breaking Techniques* out of her messenger bag. It had certainly seen better days. The cover was scratched and scuffed on all four corners from taking it with her on every case, there were countless little pieces of paper sticking out acting as impromptu bookmarks, and she'd scribbled notes on every available page.

She flipped through the chapters in record time, knowing the book cover to cover, and stopped at the section detailing the manoeuvre, which included an illustration of the complex enchantment.

"Behr-Walde is the highest level of containment we have," she began to explain. "The way it works is that it creates a series of loops around the artifact, completely surrounding it. This allows it to channel the item's own energy into this grid, and that is what powers the wards. So the more the artifact tries to escape, the stronger the chains become—Isaksson, are you listening to me?"

The Warden's gaze snapped back to her after staring at her open book in bewilderment. "I can't believe you wrote in it!"

He pick it up and flipped through the pages, looking at all the annotations she'd made in the margins.

"Why? Do you have something against writing in books?"

"No, I just never thought of *you* as the kind of person who would." He gestured at her with his hand. "I mean, you're so . . . so . . ."

"So what?" Olivia's voice held more than a hint of warning. The Viking was on some very thin ice here. She folded her arms across her chest. "Maybe you don't know me as well as you thought."

The Warden tilted his head to the side and Olivia tried her hardest not to fidget under the weight of his stare. A lazy grin appeared on his face the next instant. "The ink is not permanent, is it?"

Of course it wasn't, she wasn't a psychopath.

Leaning forward, Olivia snatched the book from his hands. "Can we get back to business, please?"

"By all means, do carry on."

Such a magnanimous Warden.

Olivia cleared her throat. "As I was saying, this manoeuvre is very difficult for curse-breakers to pull off, which is why it's not widely used and only reserved for the worst cases. I know many colleagues who won't even try it. But when done correctly, it is an incredibly effective system, capable of containing the most powerful artifacts."

The Behr-Walde manoeuvre required an extremely precise hold on one's magic. Even then, the slightest fluctuation in power could cause the entire structure to collapse. Each strand of magic had to be exactly the same as the others, knotted at the exact spot, so that when completed, the artifact's energy could flow effortlessly throughout.

"So with this technique, the object is actually the source of the power that keeps it prisoner," Isaksson summed up. "Clever."

"Quite. That's why it's the strongest technique we know, the cage is as powerful as the artifact inside it. However, it has one very big drawback.

The connecting system around the item is highly susceptible to power fluctuations. That's one of the reasons it is so difficult to create in the first place. The threads of magic that make up the loops don't like to be uneven. So every jolt, every strong burst of unstable magic weakens the structure.

"Normally, this wouldn't be a problem, since artifacts are incapable of controlling their own power, unless they are wielded by an arcanist. However, your wand proved that it could when you were searching the Cellars to find the culprit, and it drew its aura inwards. Which is why I spent all night tinkering with the system."

She pulled out the detailed blueprints of the containment cage she'd drawn, a group of three translucent pages that overlapped to form the entire design of the cage. "This is what the wand will be transported in: a cylinder, divided into three chambers, made of arcane treated glass with a runic enchantment etched all around."

Olivia pointed to the left side of the cylinder. "If the wand ever shut down completely, as it did in the Cellars, then the entire cage would deactivate."

"But wouldn't it reactivate as soon as the wand used its power again?" Isaksson asked.

"In theory, yes. But it takes a moment for the energy to flow through the lines and arm the defences. It's barely a second, but the wand could potentially use that window to escape. That's why I added an auxiliary power source to keep the wards active at all times. So this chamber, here, will act as the reserve battery."

Isaksson pointed to the second empty space, this time on the right side of the cage. "And this?"

"As I've told you before, the best way to tame a curse is to tempt it with something it craves. So this is where we will place the bait. I've really built this whole structure around these two parts: the wand and the bait. Like a latticework connecting them. As the wand will expand all its energy trying to reach it, it'll be channelled into the lines and will power the wards all around. And in doing so, will keep the wand contained."

Isaksson studied her plans carefully. "And what will you use as bait? Are you sure the wand will be interested?"

"That, I don't know yet. But I can tell you from experience, once you find the right motivation, no curse will ever ignore it."

Isaksson pulled another paper out of the pile. This one showed an intricate design of interconnected circles, lines woven through with glyphs and arcane runes. "What is this?"

"That's the design of the runic enchantment. As I explained, the main weakness of the manoeuvre is its susceptibility to power fluctuations. Something the wand will have no trouble using to its advantage. If it decides to keep sending out bursts of power, it could cause irreversible damage to the construct. I've strengthened the threads as much as I could, but I can't make them completely immune. So instead, I added a series of fail-safes."

Olivia placed the open book with the traditional design next to her own plan and pointed to the new connections. "Each section of the runic enchantment you see here will shut down in the event of damage, independently from the rest. Like sealing compartments on a ship."

"What kind of damage?"

"Since this is a transport system, it could be physical. Impacts might sever the enchantment lines and disrupt the flow of energy. Or it could also be the result of a power surge, courtesy of the artifact, overwhelming the runes. But with these fail-safes, the cage can remain active instead of shutting down all at once."

Isaksson hummed in agreement. "You added fuses, then."

"Something like that, I suppose."

"Could the wand still break out of this?"

"Yes. Even with the fail-safes and the other protections, this is still just a temporary solution. Over time, the lines will eventually lose their ability to channel energy. Besides, a strong enough burst of power could break all the fail-safes one by one and sink the construct entirely. I'd say we have a window of up to three days to make the transport."

Isaksson raised his coffee to his lips, seemingly deep in thoughts. "I was told that the Beer-Waln manoeuvre was a cumbersome and overly complicated technique," he said finally. "One that was apparently reserved for the devil himself, and that this wand did not need."

"*Behr-Walde*," Olivia corrected him. "I'm guessing it was Professor Wyborn who told you that?"

The Professor was known for his use of dramatic phrases, and she had heard him use that one enough times to know it was his all-time favourite.

"I'd say that would be true if it weren't for the way your wand is able to manipulate its magic. I considered other systems, but none seemed to stand a chance against it. It is simply too intelligent." Olivia chose her next words carefully. "Professor Wyborn is a pioneer. He's done a lot to advance our understanding of cursed artifacts and how to handle them. But his theories are rather old and outdated. He and most of my colleagues are set in their ways and don't want to deviate from the usual methods. However, when it comes to special cases such as this wand, you need a more open mind."

Isaksson scratched his beard, feigning seriousness. "Hmm. You see, I was told by the Department that the Professor was *the only one* who could carry out this transfer. That he was the resident *expert* on the subject."

The bloody Viking was doing it on purpose.

Olivia tried hard but couldn't stifle her snort. "Some forty years ago, maybe."

Wyborn might be considered the father of modern curse-breaking techniques, his contribution to the field unparalleled, but come on . . . *"The only one who could do it?"* That was really pushing it.

"I take it you don't share that opinion," Isaksson said, his blue eyes alight with amusement.

Yet Olivia didn't return his smile.

She might have found her own sullen expression comical in his place, but they were talking about containing a particularly hostile and volatile artifact. One that had already attacked people.

She still had nightmares about the last time she'd underestimated a curse . . . She would *not* make the same mistake again.

So she downed the last of her coffee, winced at the bitter taste and took a deep breath. "Mr Isaksson, I'd prefer to be direct here. I consider my agency to be one of the best. Not because we resolve the most dangerous cases, but because we take the utmost care with every one of our assignment.

"We look at every detail, we study every angle. We pride ourselves on not taking anything for granted, but on researching things extensively so that we can be sure we are using the best strategies to do our work correctly and safely. This is partly why we have one of the best completion rates of any agency."

Isaksson's amused expression had vanished, replaced by the watchful gaze of a Warden.

"Your wand is a very intelligent construct, unlike any I've ever come across," Olivia continued, her voice grim. "It's very likely that it will test your defences in ways no other artifact has ever done. You need an agency willing to adapt its approach to counter it. We are that agency. You cannot simply rely on standard curse-breaking techniques, they won't be enough. Not here, not for this wand.

"Not when the very artifact you are trying to contain can convince you to open the door."

CHAPTER NINE

A SHRILL NOISE FLOODED the office.

Olivia jumped out of her chair, knocking over the three neat piles of folders she'd been sleeping on, then whirled around frantically.

When the strident ringing persisted, coming from the telephone on her desk, she dove for the receiver.

It was too late in the day for this call to be from a prospective client, but you never knew. There could be some kind of emergency with a cursed artifact . . . Or maybe it was Isaksson calling to assign her yet another last-minute job.

"Knight Curse-Breaking Agency, Olivia Knight speaking."

A grimace filled her face the very next instant.

"A little birdie told me that a certain Warden has been spending an awful lot of time in your . . . *establishment*." Crowley uttered that last word as if he'd called it a dump.

Even his voice was despicable, and immediately began grating on Olivia's nerves through the phone, worsening her headache.

"And here I thought a man as respectable as yourself would be above engaging in gossip," she replied with a sigh.

She dug out her rolled copy of the *Cursed Herald* buried under a pile of paperwork. Since she'd already fixed his picture on the front page to match his true likeness, she instead began adding antennae to Crowley's portrait on the inside article. "I'm pretty disappointed, I won't lie," she continued. "All my beliefs . . . shattered."

"You're playing with things that are way out of your depth," Crowley spat. "If you keep meddling in matters that don't concern you, I can promise you won't like the consequences."

Olivia's eyebrows jerked up.

Crowley might despise everything about her, but he'd never openly threatened her before. And what did he mean by *"it didn't concern her?"* Was he personally involved in this case? If so, how?

But Olivia put those thoughts aside for now, and instead made her voice cold and hard. Crowley seemed to have forgotten who he was dealing with.

"As much as I enjoy our antagonistic relationship and vigorous exchanges, the next time you threaten me or my team, it is *you* who won't like the consequences."

"That wasn't a threat, just facts. You need to stay out of this. The Warden may have chosen you for your so-called artisan skills, but that's all there is to it. Leave the heavy lifting to the professionals. This isn't a case for amateurs."

So he knew that Isaksson was the new Warden. She wasn't really surprised. Crowley was a gossip-monger who enjoyed grovelling to the higher-ups. He had to have heard about it before the Viking set a single foot in Scotland.

Olivia snorted. "Funny you should say that. I read about your latest case in the *Cursed Herald* the other day and I must say I found it dreadfully subpar. The Wagner technique, really? Maybe I should send you my review notes by dragonling. You might learn a thing or two."

Silence on the line.

Ha! He hadn't expected that one now, had he?

"You can only dream that your pitiful excuse for an agency would be so renowned as to be featured in the *Cursed Herald*."

And with Crowley's mystifying threats over, they were now back on familiar ground.

She huffed at his pathetic retort. "Don't you have another photo shoot to get ready for? And try to go lighter with the hair pomade this time, will you? Otherwise you'll blind the picture camera."

"Stay in your lane, Knight. I won't tell you again," he hissed before hanging up.

Olivia slowly put down the receiver, frowning.

Arrogant wart he'd always been, but there had been something different about Crowley tonight. Why was he so opposed to her involvement in this case that he would call to threaten her?

What the *hells* was going on?

Sighing, she stood and rubbed a crick in her neck, looking down at the disaster she'd made of her desk. After her team had gone home, she'd stayed behind to catch up on paperwork, but had ended up falling asleep on it instead.

She examined the heights of the large piles before her with a critical eye. She didn't know how, but she was certain the reports and various accounts had somehow found a way to multiply during her sleep. And how it was possible to have so many forms to fill out with so few cases, she had no idea.

Worse still, those hellish safety reports were taking twice as long to file, ever since the Ministry decided to decrease the volume of records they kept. Not by reducing the amount of information, no, that would make entirely too much sense. Instead, they'd decided to shrink the physical size of the files. More specifically, the size of the font used.

As a result, Olivia had spent the entire evening cursing under her breath and threatening bodily harm to the genius who had suggested making the words twice as small.

Thud!

What in the . . .

Thud-thud-thud!

Someone was pounding on her door. Groaning, Olivia ran. She didn't need to ask who was bothering her at this ungodly hour.

"Stop banging, I'm coming!" she yelled at the maddening Viking when he didn't stop his racket.

Luckily, her agency was the only business in the building, the last one having left months ago. Otherwise they would have lobbied for her eviction. Between the desperate howling of uncooperative artifacts and the occasional after-hours commotion of a certain Warden, she wasn't a very peaceful neighbour.

"Would it kill you to simply knock? Must you *always* try to break down my door?" Olivia exclaimed as she swung it open to reveal Isaksson standing in the hallway, his blond hair plastered to his head and his long coat completely soaked with rain.

She might have felt sorry for the Warden dripping all over the floor, if it hadn't been for the grin on his face and the twinkle in his eyes she definitely didn't trust. He'd worn the exact same expression while levitating on the ceiling and wrestling with the cursed Grimoire. "And what are you doing here so late? Is there something wrong with the replica?"

As usual, he didn't wait to be invited in, but stormed past her, closing the heavy door behind him. He shook off his drenched coat, projecting little rain droplets everywhere, including on her, and let out a satisfied sigh. He was like a big dog, happy to be inside and out of the rain.

With a scowl, Olivia gestured pointedly to the perfectly shaped and functional coat hanger he seemed to have missed.

"No, no, the replica's fine," he told her. "I would have come sooner, but I've been very busy. You wouldn't believe how much paperwork it takes just to move something from one place to another. *Jösses* . . . There has to be a competition running in the Department to see who can make the longest report forms."

Then Olivia watched him slowly turn on himself. What was he looking for?

"Ha!" He crossed the room in three of his ridiculously long strides, making his way to the corner of the office that acted as a makeshift kitchen.

"Coffee, yes?" he asked while his huge paws rummaged through the neatly stacked items on the table. "Please tell me you have some more of what we drank at your place earlier. I need something strong tonight. None of that tea nonsense."

Not waiting for an answer, he began to open all the little jars one by one, sniffing everything. "You know, I've been here a few months now, and I still don't understand this worship around tea. It just tastes like leaf-flavoured water to me."

Convinced she was still passed out on top of her paperwork and having a delirious nightmare, Olivia groaned as she marched towards him. "Because coffee isn't flavoured water too?" She slapped his hands away. "And quit messing up my tea corner."

Isaksson let her take over and moved to lean against a wall, arms crossed over his chest.

"Should you even be drinking that?" Olivia asked him. "It's very late."

In response, a loud yawn cracked his jaw. "Trust me, I need it. I've been trying to fill out some security report for four days. On top of all the logistics of the wand transfer and all the mischief it's been causing. I swear, once we get on that train, it's going to feel like a holiday."

"What security report?"

Isaksson ran a hand through his hair, leaving the damp strands standing upright. He looked as if he'd just come into direct physical contact with a particularly energetic curse.

"I think it's called RAC . . . 75 . . . Or something like that."

"Ah, yes. The RACCCOON? That one's atrocious."

"*Raccoon*? What are you talking about?"

"That's the name of the form. Well, not the official one, but what those of us who have to endure it, call it. The Risk Assessment Chart for the Conservation of Classified Offensive Objects Number 78." Olivia shrugged. "Or Raccoon for short."

Yes, she knew all about it.

That dreadful report was hellishly long and almost unreadable, with endless redirects between sections that kept you juggling pages, not knowing where to start. And the final table at the end was pure and utter chaos.

"I sympathize with you," she told him. "I have to fill out the Raccoon as well, and it's nothing short of cruel and unusual punishment."

Isaksson's gaze sharpened with interest. "Do you know how to fill in section IV-H?"

Olivia narrowed her eyes, wariness heavy in her voice. "I might."

This was the very last section and contained the never-ending table that had taken her so many sleepless nights to figure out, so she saved her hard-won tips like a dragon hoarding gold.

Isaksson raised his massive shoulders. "I did save your entire office from a demonic flying Grimoire. I mean . . . Who knows what might have happened if I hadn't been there."

Olivia scowled at him. There was absolutely no doubt that they would've been able to subdue the Grimoire . . . Eventually.

"We had the situation perfectly under control, you know." She closed the coffee tin with a little more force than necessary.

Isaksson scoffed, muttering something under his breath and her eyes snapped to him.

The Warden held his hands up in a placating gesture, chuckling. "All right, I take that back. How about a deal, yes? You help me with the raccoon, and I'll make sure to mention your name for any Department case involving a cursed artifact."

"I'll think about it."

Soon, the aroma of freshly brewed coffee filled the office, waking her and dispersing the last dregs of sleep. As she began to prepare a tea for herself — or a delicious cup of *leaf-flavoured water* — Olivia realised that she still had no idea what the frustrating Warden even wanted. "You haven't told me what it is you're doing here."

"You got the job," Isaksson announced, looking mighty pleased with himself.

Olivia's arm froze and the Warden hurried to snatch the coffee from her hand before she lost her grip on it.

"Seriously?" she breathed.

He regarded her over the rim of his cup, blowing on it. When he nodded solemnly, Olivia let out a victory cry and pumped her fist in the air. "Yes!" The grin that split her face was more than a little smug. "I can't believe you fired Professor Wyborn!"

What Olivia didn't say was what she would have given to see the look on Crowley's face when he found out. *This isn't a case for amateurs.* Ah! How right he'd been.

"I didn't fire him."

Stunned, Olivia's smile slowly slipped off her face. "Wha... But you just said..."

"I need both of you," Isaksson replied matter-of-factly, ignoring her look of pure horror.

"What do you mean, *both of you*?"

Surely he couldn't mean that she would have to work alongside Crowley on this case. She'd rather dive head first into one of those murky, alligator-infested swamps Cornelius told her about, to hunt for haunting echoes.

Isaksson grinned at her, a devilish twinkle in his eye. "You'll see."

Olivia had to take a deep, calming breath. It had been an incredibly long day and she didn't have any more patience for cryptic Vikings.

"Mr Isaksson, —" she began.

"Ryder."

"Ryder. It's very late. You've just barged into my office and are making absolutely zero sense. I'm giving you thirty seconds to explain yourself or I'm throwing you to Jerry."

The infuriating giant simply took another sip of his coffee, and Olivia resisted the urge to chuck her own teacup at his head.

"It's simple," he said at last. "You're the only one who has really understood this wand and what it can do. Your plan is a hundred times better than a null field." Isaksson huffed. "When I suggested the Beer-Waln manoeuvre to the Professor, he told me it would be like crushing an ant with a sledgehammer."

"Behr-Walde," Olivia corrected him automatically.

She couldn't deny that his words pleased her. She'd worked hard on those containment plans and was very proud of them. Especially of how she'd managed to negate their weaknesses.

She was also very glad that Isaksson had really *listened* to her, had heeded her warnings. She was used to dealing with her colleagues' disdain for her views, which they called "ridiculous" or even "scaremongering" behind her back.

But Olivia cocked her head, something about what he'd just said bothering her. "What do you mean *you* suggested the manoeuvre to him . . . When was that?"

A flash of mischief lit up Isaksson's expression.

And that was when it all dawned on her. The strange look he'd given her when she'd first mentioned her containment plan, or the amused way he'd revealed that Wyborn didn't have a proper one prepared . . .

"This was all a test, wasn't it?" Olivia was pretty sure he'd actually intended to hire her from the very first day they'd met, or had at least thought about it.

The devious Warden laughed. "I may not be an expert on curses, but I knew they were not taking the threat seriously. That wand managed to convince my men to open other artifact cages. Why it did not try to open its own, I do not know. But what I *do* know is that it could have, and there would have been nothing I could have done to stop it. You are the only one who can help me contain this wand, Ms Knight. I need you."

Olivia thought back to their very first conversation, when she'd explained to him how this artifact was different from the others, how dangerous it really was . . . She wondered how much of that he'd already known.

Oh, this Warden was a lot more shrewd that she'd given him credit for.

"But . . . What about Wyborn?" she asked. "What will he do then?"

"I may have misled you a little. The replica won't stay behind in the Cellars. It will act as a decoy and be transported to the Institute with all the other light artifacts, under Professor Wyborn's supervision. You and you alone, Ms Knight, will transport the real wand."

"A *decoy*?"

And there it was.

She knew he'd been hiding something. This blasted case was all sorts of wrong. First the amount of redacted information in the reports, then Isaksson's reluctance to tell her anything about it, and now this?

If Olivia were smart, she would walk away. Beware of night-barging Wardens, indeed.

"So all we have left to do now is sign the contract," Isaksson continued, oblivious to her growing unease. "Which is ridiculously long and complicated. And the reason why we need the coffee."

"Wait a minute," Olivia protested. "Why do you need a decoy to transport the wand? What is really going on here?"

He was transporting an artifact to another country's equivalent of the Cellars, there should have been no need for such measures . . . What was he so afraid of?

Isaksson waved a hand in dismissal. "It's nothing. A precaution."

Except it didn't sound *at all* like a precaution.

"Mr Isaksson," she said, her tone hard. "If you're afraid something might happen in transit, I want to know about it."

He sighed. "I really cannot tell you anything before you sign the contract. But—" he held up a hand to stop her before she could interrupt, "—I can promise you that I will take care of it. You can trust me."

Olivia regarded him for a long moment, then turned abruptly, taking the teapot with her. "Come. We'll be more comfortable in my office."

You can trust me. Could she? He was, after all, a Ministry official, which in her books meant he wasn't trustworthy, especially when it came to cursed artifacts. And if he'd lied about that, or deliberately withheld the truth from her, what else had he lied about?

She'd assured Godwyn that she wouldn't get involved. That she would retrieve the wand from the Cellars, bring it to Romania and get out. No reckless risks, no unnecessary commitments. But if Olivia's suspicions about the need for a decoy were correct . . . she might have no choice *but* to get involved.

She also knew that she was the only one with a plan that had a decent chance of success. It wasn't arrogance, but the simple truth. Crowley hadn't bothered to understand this wand, its history. He didn't know what it desired and how far it would go to get it. If she let him be the one to transport this artifact, people would get hurt. Or worse.

"Those are interesting holiday spots you got there." Isaksson looked at her over his shoulder, his blue eyes clearly amused.

He'd followed her into the room without a word, and was now studying the large map hanging on one of the walls.

Made from the darkest of inks, with torn edges betraying its age, the ancient parchment displayed all the most haunted places in Europe — crypts, forests, castles, even a completely underground city.

Olivia came to stand beside him and gently traced one edge of the map with a finger. "You mock me, but some of these places are hundreds of years old and have never been properly mapped. Who knows what might be lurking in those dark corners . . ."

Isaksson stared at her in disbelief. "And to you, that's a good thing?"

Olivia's lips curled. Sometimes, when she allowed her thoughts to wander, she found herself longing for some grand adventure. Unravelling mysteries and hunting treasures as she visited all those places dotting the map. She wanted to know what it felt like to leave her mark on the world.

Her love for her agency and her job had never wavered, but she had to admit that reality wasn't living up to the wild fantasies of her university days. Instead of gratitude, she was often met with contempt from clients, with lies. Sometimes outright suspicion that she might walk away with a family heirloom or two in her pocket. And from her colleagues, she'd long since stopped waiting for the inspiring advances, to settle for arrogance and outdated views.

"People think of curse-breaking as this wild and exciting job," she said, her voice soft. "The truth is, it's mostly paperwork and trying to get clients to confess how they've really cared for their artifact."

"Ah. You crave adventure and yet you hesitate now," Isaksson mused, his head tilted to one side. "Did one of your cases end badly?"

Olivia's head snapped up. Thankfully, his attention was once again on the map pinned to the wall and not on her troubled face, this mysterious Warden with the cocky smile and daredevil attitude, that hid a surprisingly astute mind.

Snap out of it, Knight, she chastised herself.

She couldn't afford to let her foolish, romantic thoughts lead her astray. Adventures were treacherous. Dangerous. They were nothing more than risky gambles, full of pitfalls and unpredictable outcomes.

The very idea of blindly following this stubborn Warden into one of the most dangerous jobs she'd ever come across should have been ludicrous. Especially given the scandalous lack of information on this case. An artifact like this required months of work and careful preparation, at the very least.

And yet . . .

No. She wasn't a thrill seeker like him. She liked rules, safety. And this case was about as unsafe as they came.

Then why was it so hard to convince herself she had to walk away?

It doesn't matter why, she told herself sternly. Because she didn't really have a choice, she never had. If nothing changed, very soon, she would have to close the agency. And she wasn't about to let that happen. Not without a fight.

Olivia sat down at her desk. "All right. I'll do it." She shook a stern finger in his direction. "But know I'm only accepting because it's the right thing to do, not because I want to go on an adventure with you. Also, I want to set some terms."

"Terms?"

"Yes. I want this to be a true partnership. I have a feeling I'm not going to like the things you've kept from me. I need to know that I can trust you. So no hiding, no secrets. As soon as I sign this contract, I want you to explain everything."

He nodded slowly. "I'll agree if you do the same."

Olivia didn't wait to start questioning her decision. She stuck out her hand. "Deal."

Isaksson grinned. He reached into his coat for the contract before placing it in her open palm. It was surprisingly hefty, almost bulging out of the kraft envelope it was in.

Something occurred to her then. She'd last spoken to the Warden a few hours earlier, in her home workshop, where she'd passionately advocated for her agency. There was absolutely no way he could have persuaded the legal department to draw up an entire transport contract so quickly.

She narrowed her eyes at him. "You had this done before today, didn't you?"

Isaksson raised his cup in salute.

What a crafty, sneaky Viking.

Olivia turned in her seat so she could toss the contract into the air beside her, with a practised wrist snap that activated the enchantment. The paper flew for a second before freezing, bobbing gently at about eye level.

She realised immediately why it had been so heavy, as the contract unfolded of its own accord, and went on and on . . . and on.

When the bottom of it grazed the floor, she gave the Warden an exasperated look. "You've only been here a couple of months. How did you manage to upset the legal department so quickly?"

"What?"

"This is the longest, most complicated transport contract I've ever seen. What did you do?"

Isaksson's face took on such a sheepish expression that she knew she'd been right.

He lifted a hand to scratch the back of his neck, wincing. "I may have expressed my . . . *dissatisfaction* with the amount of paperwork it takes to import anything into the Cellars. Really, it's ridiculous. I can't sit at my desk for five hours every time I need a new set of silverstone locks."

Olivia raised her eyes to the ceiling. "Please tell me you only sent a strongly worded letter."

"I went there in person."

"And?"

"And . . . They called security to escort me out and banned me from ever entering their premises again."

Olivia sighed deeply as Isaksson continued, unrepentant. "So I'm glad you said yes. You can be the one to deliver the post-mission reports once we're back from Romania."

Still shaking her head, Olivia switched her glasses and began to read the parchment. It was unnecessarily long and convoluted, but still relatively classic, as far as transport contracts went.

Without even taking her eyes off the floating paper, Olivia warned, her voice stern, "No touching." She felt more than she saw Isaksson put back what he'd snatched from her desk.

Finally, after a long while, she looked up again. "All right, everything seems to be in order. Let me get my contract quill."

She rummaged through the miscellaneous items on her desk, pushing invoicing envelopes and looking under piles of forms. "Do you see it anywhere? I just hope Jerry hasn't snatched—Ah, there it is."

Perpetual pens were an old invention, yet still used to sign all sorts of arcane documents. No ink was needed, as the signer simply imbued the tip with their magic. The resulting signature was therefore indelible, permanent and impervious to forgery or other alteration.

Or so the theory went. Because, as with all things in life, someone, somewhere, always managed to find a loophole.

And so, each year, virtually every business and agency in the country, in every field, upgraded their perpetual pens to the latest models, enchanted to withstand the new counterfeiting techniques.

Despite their name, contract quills were no longer made from feathers, but special woods, glass or sometimes even semi-precious stones. Olivia's favourite model, the 4th Edition Swift Quill, was spun from arcane treated glass and featured elegant swirls of shifting purples and golds.

She held the glass pen delicately between two fingers and called upon her magic. Slowly, the previously empty inner chamber filled itself with a shimmering "ink" that travelled along the twisting mechanism until it coated the glass tip with a coppery glow.

Olivia raised her hand to the floating contract and signed her name into the air, watching as it simultaneously appeared on the parchment as if written in liquid amber.

As soon as it was done, the contract folded back, tucking all its many sections inward until she could pick it up and hand it back to Isaksson.

"Now." Olivia wasted no time. "Why do you need a decoy to transport this artifact?"

In response, Isaksson stood up and began pacing the length of her office. His expression, usually either carefree and nonchalant or recklessly amused, had grown hard. "We've had three break-ins in the last few months. The last one in particular, came very close to success."

"How close?"

The Warden gritted his teeth. His eyes flashed with icy fire. "Too close."

CHAPTER TEN

Olivia's eyes widened. Sure, she'd had an inkling that this might be the reason, but... she'd convinced herself she had to be mistaken.

The Cellars were renowned for being impenetrable.

There was only one way in — an elevator located on a tiny island in the middle of rough seas — which took you straight down into a gigantic maze of underground tunnels. If, by some miracle, you somehow found your way into the tunnels, all the guards would have to do would be to simply lock the island and seal you in.

"I thought breaching the Cellars was impossible. How did they manage this?"

Isaksson's eyes had taken on a calculating glint. "I suspect the last attempt came so close because someone was helping from the inside."

Ah... Now the decoy made sense.

"I've gone over the incident reports a hundred times," he continued. "The thieves knew every single security protocol, every procedure. They got in unnoticed by any patrol and managed to find the right cell, which shouldn't have been possible either. The only reason they did not take the wand was because another artifact exploded. The first guard to come running saw them and sounded the alarm, but they vanished. We spent the rest of the night searching the tunnels from top to bottom. Nothing."

Olivia could feel Isaksson's angry magic dancing atop his skin. A very faint glimmer had appeared over his blue eyes, turning them almost silver in the dim light. She wouldn't want to be one of those thieves when the vengeful Viking finally caught up with them.

"The other thing that confuses me," he said — *'confuses'* looking more like *'enrages me to no end'* — "is how they were able to erase their arrival and departure from the Register. No one is supposed to pass through the entrance without being recorded."

Isaksson continued his angry pacing, large strides slowly digging a hole in her carpet, while heavy doubts and regrets crept into Olivia's mind. Taking off her glasses, she pinched the bridge of her nose.

Thieves . . . Good gods.

In her entire career, she'd never had to deal with smugglers or black market hunters. Her cases usually involved highly protected Ministry property, private heirlooms housed in wealthy mansions, or inherited artifacts that weren't that precious. What was she going to do when, and not if, the thieves tried to get their hands on the wand again? Her job was to contain curses, to protect people *from* them, not to safeguard them against attacks coming from the outside.

Olivia felt the strong urge to bang her head against the desk a few times, but instead she took a deep breath, put her glasses back on and straightened her shoulders.

Regrets would get her nowhere. She was already knee-deep in this case, and it might be turning into one spectacular mess right in front of her eyes, but she would be damned if she let it get the better of her. Besides, all this drama would only sweeten her victory when she would win the curse-breaking competition.

Her eyes fell on the abandoned cup resting on a corner of her desk. She might be determined to carry on, but she still needed something stronger than tea to get her through this evening.

"So, I gather that the plan is to leave behind a decoy to mask our presence," she said as she stood up and walked to a small display cabinet. "But they could still be monitoring the entrance to the Cellars. How are we going to get that wand out of there without being noticed? And I understand that you suspect people in the Department, but surely you don't think the police are involved. We could ask for help. I'm sure they'd be willing to provide a team to assist, or even simply an escort. Because you may look like you could crush someone's skull with your bare fist, but I'm afraid I am simply a curse-breaker. Duels are not on the agency's list of services, believe it or not."

The Warden chuckled at her tart words, as if she'd told a joke.

It hadn't been a joke.

"Not to worry, Ms Knight. This isn't the first time I've had to guard an artifact, I know what I'm doing. But if we want the plan to succeed, we can't trust anyone, not even the police. One mistake and it could all go to hell."

Olivia's lips thinned at his answer. Frustration hammered at her, along with uncertainty. She was putting a lot of trust in this man, whom she'd only just met. She also felt that he'd strong-armed her into this, and she didn't like it.

She thrust a glass of amber liquid in his direction, not bothering to hide her irritation. "And what *is* the plan then, may I ask?"

"To start, we'll have to use a more . . . *discreet* entrance. If they see you and realise you're a curse-breaker, they'll likely try to race us to the wand. I also have options in place for leaving the Cellars. There will be a ferry waiting to take us to Amsterdam. And then a train all the way to Romania." He gestured to the glass in his hand after taking a sip. "That's really good."

Olivia grumbled, "You're being awfully sparse with the details, Warden."

He paid her hard stare no mind as he carried on, "The less you know, the better. Ah, that reminds me, we're clear that you and I are the only ones who know about the decoy, yes?" Isaksson ran a hand over his stubbled jaw. "Perhaps I should have mentioned this before . . ."

"I'm sorry?" Olivia blinked, her eyes still following his back and forth strides, confused as to where he was going with this. Obviously the whole point of using a decoy was to keep their plan secret, so why on earth would he tell anyone else?

"Skelton, the head of the Dark Artifacts Department. He knows nothing about the decoy. He thinks Professor Wyborn will be taking the wand to Romania." Isaksson paused in front of her bookshelves and picked up one of the many books there, a slim tome containing ancient maps that supposedly showed the way to mythical cities. "So just to warn you, no one will be waiting for our arrival to escort us through the Cellars because what we're about to do is not strictly speaking *legal*." He leafed through the pages as he walked around her office some more. "You could even argue that we're kind of stealing the wand ourselves, but only if you want to get really technical about it. How trustworthy do you think this map to Atlantis is?"

The whisky caught in Olivia's throat and refused to go down. She was too stunned to speak for a long moment, eyes wide and voice breathless. "Wait, what? But that . . . That's a crime!"

"Hmm hmm. Stealing usually is," Isaksson said, before waving a dismissive hand. "Don't worry about it."

Her mouth dropped open. Actually dropped open.

Forcing it shut before it could freeze in that position, she managed to grit out, "*Don't worry about it?*"

Then she attempted to take a deep, calming breath, but her voice kept rising with each word. "Do you know the penalty for stealing Ministry property? That's ten years in prison and substantial fines! Not to mention stealing an object of this magnitude! We'll be lucky if they classify this wand as a historical artifact and not a dangerous weapon. But the prosecution will try to make it a level five Offensive Object, if not six! They could send us straight to . . . Oh, but that's not all! Since I'm not the curse-breaker assigned to this case, my going into the Cellars will be considered trespassing on Ministry restricted premises! That's another two to five years, in case you didn't know!"

Isaksson didn't interrupt her, an amused smile playing on his lips.

"And would you *please* stop your pacing, you're giving me a crick in the neck!"

The infuriating Viking closed her map book with a snap and sat back down again, calmly sipping his whisky. "Are you done?"

"Oh, Warden. I'm just getting started."

"Look, this is only for the duration of the transfer. As soon as the High Commissioner gets the wand, everything will be out in the open. Besides, I didn't *lie* to Skelton. It was just *assumed* that the Professor would be the curse-breaking expert on this case, and I did not correct him. But I got the contract and everything in your name, so it's all legal." He grimaced. "More or less."

Olivia looked toward the ceiling, praying for the strength and patience to deal with this man. "Your devil-may-care attitude may have worked for you in Sweden, Mr Isaksson. But here we have rules. Regulations."

"Ah, yes." Isaksson nodded, his lips twitching. "The English and their rules . . ."

Not at all amused, Olivia fixed him with a stare. "Any more surprises you might want to share with me?"

The grin he threw at her then, assured her that she'd just made one *very* big mistake.

"Well, there is one more thing we should discuss."

Oh no, what now? Olivia braced herself.

"We need to fly under the radar on this mission. Try to attract as little attention as possible."

Right. As if one of them wasn't a giant Viking.

"What exactly are you saying?"

"Your team cannot come with us to Romania. We have to be invisible. Ghosts." His expression was serious for once. "Impossible with five people."

Olivia immediately thought of Cornelius. He'd spent so many hours trying to learn as much as he could about this wand. And it had fascinated him so much. He was going to be absolutely gutted.

But she couldn't deny that she also felt a huge wave of relief. This case was turning out to be even worse than she'd feared. She didn't want to put any member of her team at risk, especially for a case that she alone had pushed for.

"Will that be a problem?"

No. But it meant spending a whole lot of time alone with him, and not chucking the cage at his impressively hard head.

"Not at all," Olivia replied. "Right, if we're putting everything on the table, you've yet to tell me when this transfer is actually supposed to happen. As you know, there's still a lot we need to work out." Her mind was already busy making lists of supplies and planning their next steps. "So when do we leave? Next week, after the fake wand is gone?"

Isaksson didn't answer for a long moment. A gleam of doubt had appeared in his eyes.

Oh oh . . . If even *he* was worried, it had to be something terrible.

"You do know the auction is in three days, right?" he asked carefully.

"Well, yes. But what does that matter? The decoy is the one that will accompany the cargo to the auction. Isn't that the whole point? To make everyone think the wand is on its way to Romania, when it is in fact still in its cell?"

He winced. "Not exactly. The real wand is too unstable, it can't stay in the Cellars indefinitely . . ." When her frown still didn't lift, he added, "We can't wait for the decoy to leave, it has to go now."

Olivia narrowed her eyes. "And when exactly is *now*?"

"I've arranged transport for tomorrow night. We should be in Romania the next day."

She gaped at him. "Tomorrow *night!* Are you mad? We still haven't decided what to use as bait! And I have to finish the containment cage!"

Isaksson crossed his massive arms over his chest and shrugged, not at all bothered. "You still have a whole day. Plenty of time."

Olivia had a sudden vision of herself jumping out of her chair, leaping across the desk and wrapping her hands around his neck. The force of their momentum would propel them both back to where Jerry was resting on a chest of drawers. He would enfold his tendrils around Isaksson's throat and they would both teach the Viking the true meaning of *plenty of time*.

She put her glass back on the desk with too much force. "You need to reschedule," she ordered him sternly.

"No."

"Yes!"

He shook his head. "No."

Argh! "It's too soon! We're not ready!"

"You'll get there," he replied.

"Your faith in my abilities flatters me, but I'm afraid I must disappoint."

Isaksson grinned and reached down to wave her freshly signed contract in the air. "Not possible. You already signed it."

This man was an absolute demon.

Olivia firmly told herself that killing him would mean an even longer prison sentence. So no killing the Warden, that was forbidden.

Instead, she raised both hands to massage her temples. "So let me make sure I understand correctly. This whole case was already a very dangerous, but theoretically feasible, transport of an object of power back to Romania. However, you're now telling me," she began to count on her fingers, "that thieves are after it, that no one knows what we're really doing and so the police could arrest us on sight, that we'll have no backup whatsoever from either the Ministry or my own team, and that we have to leave tomorrow night even though we're missing the cage and any way of forcing the wand to behave. Am I missing anything?"

"I don't think so."

"Great. Glad we cleared that up." She downed the rest of her glass in one go. "I take back our agreement. Don't ever mention my name for future Department cases."

Isaksson laughed. "You don't mean it. This is just the nerves talking."

By now Olivia was sure steam had to be coming out of her ears. She didn't know how or when, but she was going to get him back for this. "I should have known you were trouble the very moment I saw you flying through the air to tackle a Grimoire."

"Ah yes, that was *fun*! I hope you'll get more like it."

Olivia only sighed, the beginnings of a headache pulsing behind her temples. She'd agreed to take on this crazy case less than an hour ago and she was already cursing her decision.

"Why do I feel like I've just made a deal with the devil?" she muttered in a tired voice.

"Too late now, *Älva*."

Her eyes snapped open to stare him down. "What did you just call me?"

Blue eyes laughed at her. "It means 'pixie' in Swedish. Appropriate, no?"

CHAPTER 10

Olivia gritted her teeth.
Too late now, indeed.

CHAPTER ELEVEN

"No. You're both lying to me. Beetles cannot possibly eat an entire person in twenty-four hours." Godwyn's tone of voice broke no argument.

"I'm telling you, those ones can!" Cornelius insisted.

"You know, it's not that unusual," Olivia added. "I heard about a team of curse-breakers who stumbled upon a bear skeleton hidden in a hunting lodge once. Apparently, the owner was an Egyptology buff and tried to mummify the bear, but then got impatient and used scavenger beetles to clean the bones. They worked out that it must have taken them a week to do it."

"Where on earth do you even have to *go* to stumble upon a mummified bear?" Godwyn exclaimed, astonished.

Olivia shrugged. "Kent."

"Fun fact," Cornelius cut in, "there's a passage in the Egyptian Book of the Dead that talks about a mythical carnivorous beetle called Apshait, that feasts on the souls of the deceased as they travel through the underworld."

Godwyn stared at him as he held open the door to the building. "That fact is many things, Cornelius. However it is not *fun*." He waited for them to pass, but frowned. "Hold on. You said a team of curse-breakers found it . . . You're not suggesting the *bear* was cursed, are you?"

Olivia laughed. She adjusted the strap of the messenger bag slung over her shoulder while they started up the stairs that would lead them to their floor. "No. Of course not."

In front of her, Cornelius chuckled to himself. "Can you imagine?"

Olivia glanced behind her and saw Godwyn's face soften with relief.

"It was the beetles," she said.

She followed Cornelius down the corridor as they neared a peaceful and silent office for once. No vengeful portraits, no demonic Grimoires and no angry clients to placate. And most importantly, no infuriating Warden in sight.

As they came in and hung up their coats, Adeline emerged from the back of the room, a cup of tea in her hand. She smiled at them in greeting, then pointed to a still pale-faced Godwyn, standing frozen on the landing. "Which one of you broke him?"

Godwyn shook his head, no doubt trying to erase the images Olivia's story had conjured up in his mind. He also shrugged off his heavy wool coat, revealing a pale grey suit underneath, with an emerald scrap of silk peeking from the breast pocket. "It's too early for curses, Liv," he groaned. "Much too early."

Olivia tsked disapprovingly. "It's never too early for curses, Godwyn."

"Has the mail arrived yet?" Cornelius had taken off his hat and walked over to the tall windows, his eyes scanning the skies for a glimpse of a dragonling carrying his documents.

Shaking her head, Adeline resumed her bustle around the office, but as she did so, carefully avoided Godwyn's gaze or doing anything that would bring her anywhere near his desk. Olivia wondered for the millionth time what on earth had happened between them the day before, on the Baumer case.

She was about to make herself a cup of tea, but thought of more things to take with her to Romania, so she instead pulled out her notebook, before she could forget.

"I'm going to send Isaksson a telegram," she told Adeline distractedly as she scribbled everything down. *Let's see* . . . She would need her emergency repair kit, of course. Some of her silverstone netting, you never knew. Definitely any moonstone she could get her hands on. Maybe she should take a look at her concoctions, she thought. Ah, and what about her curse repellent? Might be experimental, but it was better than nothing . . . "To ask him if he wants to accompany me to the Vaults."

"There's no need for that. He's sleeping in your office."

"Hmm?" Olivia looked up with a confused frown. "Who's sleeping where?"

Her assistant grinned.

She came to sit on her usual perch, a corner of her desk, and tossed her long hair back, a mischievous look in her grey eyes. She held out a hand to inspect perfectly manicured nails and replied in a nonchalant voice, "Tall, blond hair, blue eyes, arms big enough to lift tree trunks . . . Ring any bells?"

Olivia froze. She closed her notebook with a snap. "What."

Any thoughts of working peacefully for a few hours vanished in a puff of smoke. It was as if the damn Viking took great pleasure in messing up her plans just to spite her.

Without another word, she strode into her private office.

Not surprisingly, the first thing she saw when she entered was Isaksson's booted feet hanging off her sofa. He was far too tall to be comfortable there, with his legs almost halfway out and his shoulders squished, but was sound asleep nonetheless.

One hand rested on his chest, while the other trailed off to the floor, and his mouth was slightly ajar. He'd tied his hair back today, but a blond strand had fallen across his forehead. Olivia's hand actually tingled with the urge to brush it back.

He looked so peaceful.

He'd been such a whirlwind ever since they'd met — all mischievous eyes, cockiness and bold grin — that Olivia found it strange to see him lying there so quiet. Her annoyance vanished, replaced by a strange wave of fondness that astonished her.

The Viking lived to annoy her. And yet, bantering with him had started to become . . . *enjoyable*. Not that she would ever admit it out loud.

Olivia shook her head to clear her ridiculous thoughts. She was sleep-deprived, that was all. Still, she made her way to her desk lightly, reluctant to wake the blissfully sleeping giant.

Only a few steps in, however, and she heard him stir. A loud yawn sounded, then his voice, even deeper and more rumbling than usual, "Your couch might be small enough to fit in my pocket, but it is surprisingly comfortable."

And just like that, her annoyance was back.

"You know, if my sofa displeases you so much, you could always try sleeping on your own instead."

Isaksson sat up, winced, stretched his arms. "Ah, but then I would miss that adorable scowl."

After another, *even* deeper scowl, Olivia dropped her messenger bag onto her desk with an unapologetic *thump*. Her eyes landed on a dozing Jerry as she did so, resting on a nearby cabinet. The cursed plant twitched every few seconds, causing all the leaves to rustle, as if taking in big breaths.

She frowned. She could have sworn she'd left him in his usual spot the night before. By the fireplace, where it was warm . . .

"I didn't want to cover him up, but he kept trying to steal my ring," a gruff voice said behind her. "So I put him over there. There was a nice ray of sunshine he seemed to like."

Another loud yawn cracked his jaw.

Olivia stared at him strangely. She really didn't understand this man. One second he was the most annoying Swede to ever walk this earth, and the next . . .

"What?" he asked, running a hand through his beard.

Olivia ignored him and returned Jerry to his usual place, careful not to wake him. The cursed plant was still rustling away when she walked back to her desk, after one last caress on a rusty leaf. "And may I ask what granted me the pleasure of your lovely snores so early in the morning?"

Isaksson stretched his torso, arms extended to his sides. The hem of his shirt rose and Olivia glimpsed hard muscles rolling beneath tan skin. She immediately averted her eyes, trying with all her might to suppress the hint of blush that was warming her cheeks. Instead, she busied her hands tidying up the stacks of folders on her desk.

"Got a telegram in the middle of the night saying I had to run down to the Cellars because the wand was raising hell with the other artifacts. Took us hours to quarantine everything. And that was on top of my guards seeing ghosts and shadows everywhere." He heaved a deep sigh, scratching at the light beard on his jaw. "If I don't get that wand out of there and soon, I'm going to have a mutiny on my hands."

Olivia patted the bag on her desk. "Good thing I finished the containment cage, then."

She hadn't slept more than a few hours either, having spent most of the night slaving over the construct. Luckily, she'd already had a rough skeleton of the cage she'd built a few months ago as a research experiment, so she'd only needed to make a few alterations and carve the runic enchantment. That last part was what had taken her so long, as each thread of power had to be carefully manipulated and placed. She might have let out more than a few colourful words and devoured her entire stash of fire whisky truffles, but she'd done it.

"Let me see." Isaksson demanded.

"Sorry, no time. We have to get to London."

"London?"

She'd planned to get some work done before heading to the Library Vaults, but since the Warden was already here, they might as well get started. So she ignored his confused expression as she slung her bag back over her shoulder and headed for the door. "It's actually a good thing that you came in so early, we'll be able to catch the first Portals. After nine, it's usually a nightmare. Come on, Cornelius must have received his books from his Romanian contact. With any hope, we'll have some answers."

But as soon as he saw them, Cornelius shook his head, a frustrated scowl on his face. "There's nothing. No trace of a wandmaker who crafted a wand with mental abilities like this one. And the records are very detailed. Sorry, it's another dead end."

Olivia sighed but Cornelius continued, excitement coming back to his voice. "So either we're wrong about the design and the wand comes from somewhere else, or . . . It already existed prior to the 15th century and was just altered during that time. That would certainly explain why it's so difficult to find any information about it."

Olivia drummed her fingers on the edge of the desk she was leaning against, thinking. "How old do you think it might be?"

"*Old*, really old."

Cornelius could be right. Many items of great power travelled through the centuries being remade, recast, added to other things . . . And to find no evidence of the creation of such a mighty wand was baffling.

Isaksson crossed his arms. "How exactly does this help us?"

"Generally, what cursed artifacts desire most in this world is either to fulfil the intent of the curse placed upon them by the conjurer, or more power," Cornelius explained. "Now, your wand has the unfortunate tendency of wanting to drive people insane, but if we could find what the core of it is, the source of its magic . . ."

Olivia continued, "Then it would stop at nothing to get it. And if it's busy reaching for it, then it's not trying to escape or using its power against us." She royally ignored the Baron sarcastically clearing his throat somewhere to her right. "From what Maeve told us, we think the core may come from the sap of this Whispering Tree. But that's just a theory, and I have no idea where we could find more of it. We need to learn more about how this wand was made. And if it really is as old as we think, then we already know where to look."

"But what happens if you still can't find what the core is?" Adeline asked. "Or if it really is the sap of this tree, but you can't get any more of it?"

"In that case, we'll just have to use some amplifier crystals and hope for the best. We don't have enough time to come up with another plan." Olivia shot Isaksson an annoyed look, but the Warden didn't even notice. He had a distant expression on his face and seemed to be deep in thought.

Olivia mistook it for concern so she quickly added, "But even if we don't find anything to use as bait, the containment plan will still work. This is just another precaution. We'd probably want to speed up the transfer, though. And we'd have to watch the wand even more closely."

Isaksson looked up at her. "Of course, yes. I'm sure you'll find something."

"Then what's bothering you?"

"Nothing. Just tired. Hopefully, we'll be able to relax once we're on the ferry." A slight smile curled his lips. "Although I have my doubts."

"Hmm."

"I'll head to Wardlaw Wands," Cornelius announced. "Perhaps Maeve will have some ideas, or she'll know of places where I could look for answers."

"And I'll see what we have in stock for amplifier crystals," Godwyn said. "Just in case."

But Adeline shook her head. "We're all out. We used the last of them on the Dunne job."

Olivia stifled a sigh of annoyance. Amplifier crystals were expensive, and unfortunately, if she was going to use them on this wand, it would require quite a lot. Looked like she was going to have to dip into next month's equipment budget, *again*.

"Godwyn, could you go up to Edinburgh to see Michael?" she instructed him. "Ask for the good stuff." They would need the strongest crystals he had if they wanted to get the wand interested. "And don't forget the family discount, will you?"

Godwyn huffed. "As if."

"Take Adeline with you," Olivia added. "They like her."

Michael had been happily married to his husband for close to ten years, but Olivia knew Adeline had the ability to charm a pile of rocks, so it was worth a try.

Her assistant's lips curled into a smug smile as Godwyn scowled. "For the record . . . They like me too."

Adeline lifted a hand to pat his cheek.

"All right, Mr Isaksson," Olivia said as she straightened. "We're off."

"Ryder," he corrected her immediately. "Also, are you ever going to tell me why we have to go to London?"

In response, Olivia marched to the front door and grabbed hers and Isaksson's coat, which she shoved at him. Then she leaned in close to whisper, "Brace yourself, Warden."

Ignoring his startled expression, she turned to the rest of the office. "By the way! I forgot to mention that Mr Isaksson swung by the office last night to make me sign the transport contract. So we've got the case! Hurray! However, he had a few surprises for me. None of you will be allowed to accompany us to Romania, as it is very important that we keep a low profile because thieves have been trying to steal the wand for months. Also, the Department doesn't know that we're the agency that's going to make this transfer. Again, so we can keep a low profile. Oh, and we're leaving tonight."

She barely paused to take a much-needed breath and clapped her hands. "So! I suggest you direct any and all remarks to the Warden, and I'm sure it would be his pleasure to explain his strategies in more detail. In the meantime, we're off to the Museum, so wish us luck!"

Her hasty explanation was met with a stunned silence, and then a chorus of exclamations and protests erupted.

Next to her, Isaksson muttered something in Swedish. He gave her a dark look. "You'll pay for this."

Olivia just grinned.

Grabbing his sleeve, she pushed him out of the office and shouted over her shoulder, "Can't talk now! Got to go!"

Amid the cries of outrage and demands for further explanation, she heard Adeline yell back. "Have fun, you two! And don't forget the offering!"

"An *offering*?" Isaksson asked as they stepped out into the cool autumn breeze.

A fine mist had settled in the air, and Olivia grumbled as droplets began to cover her glasses.

"The Arcane History Museum, or rather the Arcane Library," she explained, "has this very old, very precious series of manuscripts on legends. If Cornelius is right and the wand is much older than we thought, we should find some mention of it there. Once we finally know for sure what the core is, we'll just have to find more of it."

"And the offering?" Isaksson asked again. He held her back when a car passed a little too close.

"That would be for Pyke," Olivia answered. "He's the Head Librarian of the Special Collections Department." She chose her next words carefully. "He's . . . a little eccentric."

"From your tone, he doesn't sound just a *little* eccentric."

"Let's just say he's very passionate about his responsibilities." She dropped her voice conspiratorially and whispered, "He likes to talk to the books."

Isaksson stopped dead in his tracks and stared at her, *hard*. "Please don't tell me they talk back."

She shouldn't. She really shouldn't . . .

"Well," Olivia winced. "You know, some of these volumes are easily five centuries old, I mean . . . At least half of them must be haunted by now."

A car slammed on its brakes to avoid colliding with the Viking standing frozen in the middle of the road. Olivia had to run back amid the furious yells and push him out of the way.

"Think about it," she continued once they were safely on the pavement. "Haven't you ever walked into a library and felt a light touch of cold air on the back of your neck? Or left for a break and when you came back the book you were reading wasn't open on the same page you left it?"

Isaksson's eyebrows had reached his hairline now, and he kept opening his mouth to speak, then thinking better of it and closing it.

Ah, torturing him was simply delicious.

Olivia glanced at him with a solemn look. "York is an old place, you know. Full of . . ." She paused for dramatic effect. "*History*."

She tried very hard to hold on to her straight face, but her lip began to twitch uncontrollably and soon she was doubled over laughing.

Understanding dawned on Isaksson and he glared at her, muttering in Swedish.

"I can't believe you thought the books would talk *back* to him!" She had to wipe the tears from her eyes. "You should have seen the look on your face, it was priceless."

Isaksson pointedly ignored her as he started again. They'd crossed the busy city centre and seemed to have stepped back in time as they entered

York's famous Shambles, a maze of narrow shopping streets and winding alleyways, lined with timber-framed buildings.

And Olivia almost had to run now to keep up with the long strides he made no effort to shorten.

"I promise I won't tell anyone," she quipped.

"You better not." Isaksson pointed a finger at her. "And I'll have you know, you started this. With your talk of cursed things being alive and Odin only knows what else."

"Hmm hmm. If you say so."

The worn cobblestones beneath their feet stopped, and an elaborate arched roof, made of timber, wrought iron and glass, replaced their view of the sky. They'd arrived at the Portal Market, a particular place in York that could only be described as a small city within the city.

Decorated columns stood between colourful shop fronts, blending York's distinctive style of thick wooden beams with crimson brick walls and copper accents. Many people hurried through the market, visiting shops or stopping at vendors' carts for roasted chestnuts and hot chocolate.

"You never told me why we needed a gift," Isaksson groused beside her.

"The Head Librarian is very protective of the manuscripts in his care. He's been known to deny you access to a particular document if he feels you don't have a great enough need for it. He doesn't want to disturb them unnecessarily, you see."

"Right."

"But what a lot of people don't know is that he has a very sweet tooth. Which means that if we want to be left in peace today, it's in our very best interest to make a stop . . . right here."

Olivia stopped in front of one of the shop windows, the delicious smells wafting from the door making her mouth water.

The Ye Olde Sweets shop.

Turning back to Isaksson, Olivia found him gone.

Unimpressed by the candies, he'd wandered a few paces away and was standing by the nearby Dragonling Post platform, a sturdy metal pole with ledges on which dragonlings of all colours and sizes perched, waiting to be picked up to fly a parcel or resting after a successful flight.

The Warden was scratching under the chin of a small, icy white beast which let out tiny puffs of smoke and shuddered out of sheer delight. Olivia smiled as she spied the other dragonlings slowly edge closer.

Only one resisted his charms. A sleek, black dragonling was perched on the top edge of the resting post, enjoying staring at the humans going about their day. His head was held proudly in the air, away from Isaksson and his horde of admirers, but Olivia noticed him giving the blond giant looks out of the corner of his amber eyes.

Leaving Isaksson to his own devices, she quickly stepped into the shop to purchase her gift and emerged moments later with a colourful triangular paper box, decorated with little spikes along the edges and tufts of shiny copper paper at the top that looked like very realistic flames.

"You look very comfortable with them," she said to Isaksson, who was now petting not one but two dragonlings at once, and the puffs of smoke had upgraded to include small embers that flew into the air. The little creatures were in danger of spontaneously combusting from too enjoyable, under-chin scratches.

Isaksson smirked. "Former semi-professional dragon racer over here."

Why was she not surprised? Could the Viking have chosen a more dangerous sport than racing through infernal obstacle courses on the back of a seven-foot flying beast?

Isaksson gestured to the small white dragonling he'd stroked first, which was now pushing the other, much larger ones away with a warning growl to get all the attention. "Come closer, this one's a sweetheart."

Right.

As if the little beast had understood him, and was afraid of being denied the heavenly scratches, it gave Olivia a look that screamed *yes, do come closer and see.*

"Ah . . . Maybe some other time. My hands are full," she said, holding up the box of sweets she'd just bought.

Isaksson peered at it. "What are these?"

Olivia shot him an incredulous look. "You've never had a dragon egg before?"

"No."

She shook her head in astonishment. "That, is nothing short of a tragedy. Remind me to make you try one the next time we pass a sweet shop."

"That's not necessary, it's not that—" he started to say, and then took one look at her expression. "All right."

"Perfect." Olivia smiled. "I've got the gift. Let's go catch our portal."

After one final chin scratch, Isaksson followed her.

The imposing Portal arch stood in the very centre of the cobbled square, atop a raised circular platform. Made of thick stones, blackened by the passage of time, it held a delicate network of thin golden veins running through the massive structure, like metallic vines that glistened in the light.

Those metallic veins were a natural result of transportation magic and appeared on every portal gate as time went on. At first glance, they resembled inert threads of precious metal encased in the stone — gold, copper, silverstone or even adamantine, depending on the portals. But looking more closely, you could actually see them *moving*. The metal inside was kept in a constant liquid state, allowing it to conduct magic all throughout the massive stones. Just like the roots of a plant transporting nutrients.

Olivia retrieved two bright purple tickets from the bottom of her bag and offered one to Isaksson as they waited for their allotted time to cross.

"Is something wrong?"

Olivia looked away from a group of three gentlemen in elegant suits who disappeared through the Portal and glanced up at Isaksson's penetrating gaze. "Me? Nothing. Just thinking about the case..."

"You're sad."

How on earth did he always know what she was thinking? Was her face just *that* expressive?

When she asked him, he simply laughed. "To me, it is."

Olivia sighed. "Well, it's just that... You must have so many wonderfully dark artifacts tucked away in your Cellars! I really wish we had more time so I could have a look around." Her voice dropped to a low whisper, filled with awe. "I even heard you might have one of the Robes of Fate..."

An elderly gentleman with a walking stick and one snazzy top hat stepped onto the platform and disappeared, his gait as smooth and bouncy as a young man's, even though his hair had been a pure white cloud.

Next to her, Isaksson's expression had become inscrutable.

"Rumour has it, it's the golden one..."

A raised voice announced the last call for Sheffield over a loudspeaker, and a couple came barrelling down from one of the shopping streets. The man was juggling countless bags, his arm outstretched as if to grab onto the edge of the Portal itself. Meanwhile, the woman hurried behind, carrying a small, grinning girl whose eyes were bright from all the excitement.

"It is said to be woven out of pure sunlight and edged with gold..." Olivia continued. "So bright that it glows even in total darkness. It's embroidered with tiny yellow diamonds all along the edge... You're not going to tell me anything, are you?"

The Warden smiled.

Killjoy.

After the couple had gone through, a very stern looking employee came over, his severe frown so at odds with the cheerful Portal Network cap on his head that Olivia had to stifle a laugh. He led them to the platform and instructed them to stand in the centre of the intricate arcane circle etched into the stone.

Against one of the thick pillars of the portal arch was a podium that served as a command console, filled with various levers, dials and buttons. The Portal operator deftly pushed, turned and pressed, his pale hands flying over the controls in a complicated series of actions. He barely looked at what he was doing, staring blankly into space instead.

As he manipulated the controls, he took a deep breath, filling his lungs to the brim, and then intoned in a monotonous voice that came straight from the grave, "Good morning, ladies and gentlemen, and welcome to the Portal Network, the number one transportation system for the busy arcanist. My name is Alford and I will be your conductor for this crossing. We are now preparing your portal to reach Leadenhall Market. The journey will be instantaneous. Please make sure you have a valid ticket for your destination and keep it with you at all times. We would advise passengers not to keep it inside their clothing or bags, as it will self-destruct after use and surrounding items are at risk of spontaneously combusting. May I remind passengers to keep all their belongings close during the crossing. Any items left unattended will be removed and destroyed by security services."

Olivia noted with no small amount of awe that Alford still hadn't taken a single breath since he'd started.

"Passengers are reminded that oversized magical creatures and objects of power are not permitted to pass through our portals. A full list of prohibited items can be found at your nearest ticket counter. For your safety and comfort, please remain inside the circle while the portal is charging and do not attempt to leave. Thank you for choosing the Portal Network and we hope to see you again soon."

Alford finally paused to take a desperate, ragged breath, one that lasted a few seconds and shook his entire chest, as if he'd just broken the surface after nearly drowning at sea. Then he squeezed out one last dreary exhale, "The world awaits, let's catch Portals."

Olivia had no idea what the company had done to suck the joy out of him, but if they did nothing, he was going to turn into a ghoul.

Cold eyes glanced in their direction, before the austere employee pulled one last heavy lever on the far right of his console, this one huge and bright red.

The arcane circle beneath their feet ignited in an iridescent hue, growing in intensity with each passing second, as the previously empty space beneath the arch filled with energy. Moving swirls of every colour, resembling water that twisted and rippled, gathered until it turned opaque and obscured the view to the other side. Small particles of magic drifted into the air, like colourful embers from a fire.

Olivia shifted on her feet. She didn't particularly enjoy this next part.

A low hum began. A subtle pulse of energy in the air that grew and grew until she could feel her skin vibrating in unison. It reminded her too much of some of the nastier curses she'd encountered, bringing back not so pleasant memories.

Fortunately, the hum only lasted a short moment, reaching its peak before fading away. As it did so, the moving energy inside the arch twisted again and dissipated until it now showed a view of their destination, the Leadenhall Portal Market in London.

A light flashed green on Alford's counter. He dipped his chin an infinitesimal fraction, his own version of a go signal.

The Warden gestured for Olivia to go first, so she crossed the few steps to the arch, and stepped through to the other side.

CHAPTER TWELVE

After a few twists and turns through the streets of London, Isaksson and Olivia came upon the magnificent building of the Museum of Arcane History. Twin columns of imposing terracotta stones rose on either side of the grand entrance, where heavy oak doors stood half open, welcoming scholars and curious visitors alike.

Stepping inside, they were greeted by a cavernous room filled with worn stairs and corridors leading to every part of the massive building. Everywhere they turned, intricate carvings and detailed mosaics depicting scenes from the natural world awaited them. Not one corner of the Museum wasn't embellished with some captivating detail, not even the polished marble tiles they stepped on. Mythical creatures, ancient runes and legendary mages, all woven together into a tapestry of arcane knowledge. And above their heads, a towering archway supported the skeleton of a majestic dragon in flight.

Olivia led the way as they navigated to the western part of the building, the Arcane Library, and more specifically, the underground Vaults where their most precious scrolls and manuscripts were kept. She barely looked where she was going, the map of the gigantic museum as clear in her mind as the different ways to classify curses.

A large golden quote in Old Arcane Tongue, carved into the stone above an arch, heralded the entrance to the Archival Department. They arrived inside a massive circular room filled with desks arranged in concentric circles. Light poured in from all sides, thanks to tall stained glass windows depicting famous historical figures.

About a dozen people came and went, their arms filled with heavy volumes or pushing ancient manuscripts on wheeled carts. Others sat at their desks, bent over priceless parchments. A studious silence reigned, broken only by the sound of shuffling feet or the scratch of pen on paper.

And marching in the middle of it all, with a sneer on his face and an air of superiority as if he owned the place, was Crowley.

Olivia briefly hoped that he wouldn't notice them, but shark-like eyes zeroed in at once on their position.

In his thirties, Crowley was of average height, with a slender built that still made him look masculine. He was immaculately groomed, as always, with well-defined and patrician features. He wore a sleek dark suit, polished shoes that reflected everything in his path and matched his equally polished hair, and an expensive looking tie knotted at his neck in a complicated pattern.

He reeked of old money and prestige. And, of course, of boundless arrogance and so much narcissism he had to choke on it sometimes.

"Warden. What a surprise it is to see you here." His smile turned into a pompous smirk, tinged with contempt. No doubt that the surprise was good. "Especially considering the fact that you were ordered, just a few days ago, to stay well away from this case. I seem to remember the Head of Department being very clear on this matter. You are not to involve yourself in anything to do with this artifact. In fact, you are to remain in your Cellars where you belong. I know you haven't been a Warden for very long, but I trust you understand what this means?"

Olivia was so mad at Crowley's condescending tone that his words barely registered. But the sense of betrayal steadily growing in the pit of her stomach told her that she was about to have a few words with the Warden.

Black eyes turned to her, this time brimming with malice, and she stiffened.

"As for you, I must admit that I find your insistence particularly distasteful and unprofessional. Skelton put *me* in charge of this case. Surely you haven't sunk so low as to try and wrestle cases from your betters."

Olivia had been expecting it, and had been steeling herself ever since she'd spied his ugly, toad-like face across the room, yet she still saw red. Her fingers actually shook with the urge to throw something at his head.

"Is he always like this?"

Isaksson's even, calm voice helped her cling to her composure.

"Give him some time to warm up first, he's still feeling a little shy," she replied.

Crowley's scowl took on a lovely purple hue, but he recovered fairly quickly. "Knight, I knew you were foolish, insubordinate and defiant. But I at least thought you valued your career. Especially after coming so close to losing it once. We wouldn't want a repeat of your unfortunate last case with the Ministry, would we? You know how Lord Hadley feels about the Department. Or about you . . ."

"Murderer!"

Olivia felt herself pale.

"You did this! You killed her!"

The irate voice rang in her ears, an echo from that terrible day.

Isaksson must have sensed her distress because he took half a step, coming to stand slightly in front of her. Gone was his earlier cold indifference, he now looked ready to go to war.

"Listen, we are not here for the wand," he ground out. "Ms Knight is an expert I hired for an entirely different case."

Crowley let out an audible huff at *expert*.

Olivia was sure Isaksson could snap him like a twig with just his ring and pinky fingers. She would pay good money to see that.

"So feel free to report to Skelton that I'm following his orders to the letter," Isaksson continued in a cold, sharp tone, taking another half step forward.

He was now towering over Crowley, who had to crane his neck to meet his eyes.

"And now that you've had your little hour of fame, I suggest you leave before I decide to arrest you for obstruction of governmental administration."

"You cannot do that," Crowley huffed. "You don't have the authority."

"No?" Isaksson's voice dropped low and he spoke each word very carefully. "And yet I'll have still put you on the ground before the police shows up."

Crowley visibly flinched.

His gaze began to dart sideways, taking in the curious onlookers staring in their direction. His lips thinned.

If there was one thing he valued more than praise, it was his reputation. And clearly, the esteemed curse-breaker Edmund Crowley getting his comeuppance from an angry Viking god would haunt him to the end of his days.

His eyes flashing fire, Crowley took a step back. "You better watch yourself. Both of you," he spat and then marched off.

Olivia waited until he was out of sight before turning to Isaksson. "You warned me this wouldn't be all that legal," she growled, "but you sure failed to mention that they'd taken the case from you."

The Warden shrugged.

"Skelton forbid you from hiring me, didn't he?" she added.

"What happened on your last case with the Ministry?" Isaksson asked instead.

The biggest mistake of her life, that's what happened.

Olivia's hand slashed the air. "Nothing." She fought to keep her voice down. "I can't believe you were ordered to stay away! Do you have any idea how much trouble you've got me into? I could lose my licence, Isaksson! I could lose my agency!" When she'd only agreed to take this case so she could save it.

"You would never have accepted if I'd told you the truth."

"Of course not!"

Isaksson speared her with a look that was heated and slightly angry. He looked as if he wanted to grab her by the shoulders and shake her to her senses.

She was supposed to be the furious one here, damn it.

"There's no reward without risk, Olivia! Do you really think I could have worked with Crowley? Do you believe he has the slightest idea how to contain this wand?"

Olivia held on to her temper by the skin of her teeth. The arrogant oaf had no idea what he was talking about.

To him, risks were worth it. Of course they were, because he was clever and resourceful, and he knew beyond a shadow of a doubt that he would always manage to get back on his feet. That no matter if he broke the rules, disobeyed the hierarchy, outright lied to his boss, he would somehow charm his way out and land something else, a new job, maybe one even more exciting.

Whereas she would lose everything.

All those years studying, all those hours into the night preparing for cases that would get pulled from her first thing the following morning with yet another ridiculous excuse. All those conferences where she had to look at old men parading on a podium, congratulating themselves on having successfully contained a curse they didn't even know the first thing about.

And more importantly, she would have to live with herself if anything happened to her team.

Olivia took a step towards Isaksson, absent-mindedly rubbing her left forearm. "You took away my choice. You had no right to do that. Especially when we agreed there would be no secrets between us. I told you I needed to trust you. You've just destroyed that trust."

"I know, and I am sorry. But I can't regret what I did. Not when I knew it was the only way to get you on board."

Olivia took a deep breath, her hands fists at her sides. Then she marched away, throwing over her shoulder, "Let's go. We still have a legend to find."

The Warden followed her as she headed for a corner of the room, where a great cast-iron staircase loomed, encased in shadows, ready to spiral down into the Vaults — or the Dragon's Lair, as it was commonly known.

The sound of their footsteps sent echoes scurrying up the high walls. The staircase was so long and sombre, with only a few lamps here and there, that the whole descent was like journeying to the underworld.

If the Arcane Library they had just left housed the collection of rare documents the Museum was honoured to care for, then the Vaults were reserved for those it did not want you to know about. Dark magic grimoires and Book of Shadows, journals of black mages, spellbooks and much, *much* more . . .

Gaining access to this place as a researcher was a notoriously long and difficult process, requiring a thorough background check by the police. Normally Olivia wouldn't be allowed to take anyone down there with her. But she'd asked Isaksson to bring his Warden credentials and hoped that, coupled with her taking responsibility for his visit, he might be permitted temporary access.

As they descended, the air changed. It became heavy, oppressive. Because of all the precious manuscripts down there to protect, the entire space had been so heavily warded, one could almost touch it. Olivia felt their weight bearing down on her shoulders, pressing against her skin.

"*Vid Odens skägg* . . . Where are you taking us?" Isaksson muttered beside her, his low whisper echoing down. "This place is . . . I don't like it."

Well, too bad.

After a long descent, they finally reached the end of the stairs and entered another imposing circular room. This space was the exact twin of the one above. With the same arched doors lining the curved wall and the same circles of desks. But where the room they'd just left had been calm and studious, filled with light and hushed whispers, this one was dark and gloomy.

There were no windows anywhere, the only light coming from rows of lanterns hanging from the walls that cast an uneasy yellow-greenish glow throughout the room.

A few scholars worked at their desks, throwing worried glances at the man sitting behind the counter in the middle of it all. Olivia and Isaksson passed two people hurrying out of the room, their mouths pressed together in a tight line. The Dragon was in a foul mood today.

This would *not* go well.

But before Olivia could approach him, Isaksson caught her wrist.

"Look. I'm sorry I lied to you," he whispered. "Really. And I know you think I don't understand much, but I do know one thing: I have no hope of making this transfer without you."

His eyes did seem sincere. And yet he'd deliberately misled her, gone behind her back.

Even Godwyn had warned her, Isaksson wasn't to be trusted. Olivia knew it, and yet she'd followed him because some insane part of her had admired his recklessness. It had reminded her of herself, once upon a time.

"Skelton will do all he can to fire you, you know that."

"He'll certainly try. But when this is all over and we've successfully delivered the wand to the High Commissioner, he won't have much to complain about, will he?"

Olivia snorted. "Believe me, he'll find some."

Isaksson's eyes didn't leave her. "So? Are you still with me?"

What choice did she have? She was still fuming over his deception, but the truth was, she didn't want to stop. She didn't want to give up on her agency, didn't want to abandon the wand to its fate, didn't want to yield to Crowley . . .

Olivia exhaled a deep sigh. "Don't do that again, Isaksson. I'm warning you."

His blue eyes darkened. "You have my word."

The Head Librarian of the Special Collections Department, Mr Pyke, otherwise referred to as the Dragon, was a tall and lean man. He wore thin glasses over a gaunt face with cheekbones so sharp they cast deep shadows onto his cheeks. His dark hair was slicked back, showing off a distinctive widow's peak. His suit was all sharp lines and shades of black, with a high collar and tie. The only colour on him came from a gold signet ring on one of his bony fingers.

Olivia approached his desk, forcing warmth and friendliness into her voice. "Ah, Mr Pyke! It's a pleasure to see you again."

A long, dark eyebrow rose from behind his steel-rimmed spectacles. Pyke slowly lifted his gaze from the paper he was writing on to ponder her. His eyes were two chips of ice that attempted to shrivel up anyone who would dare to interrupt him.

"And how is your research going?" Olivia continued. "Have you managed to decipher the location of your mysterious Codex?"

"It's gone." Pike's voice was so flat and toneless, it might have belonged to a reanimated corpse.

"Pardon me?"

"An earthquake hit the dig site two weeks ago and swallowed everything up."

Oh, for the love of . . .

Next to her, Isaksson's chest trembled slightly, as if he was suppressing laughter. Olivia tried to surreptitiously kick him in the shin, but she miscalculated the distance and only managed to thump the leg of a chair.

"Ah, I'm sorry to hear that. That's some . . . unfortunate news. Well, we were passing through the Shambles on our way here, and I remembered how much you love dragon eggs," she said, reaching into her messenger bag and praying that she hadn't accidentally squashed the sweets.

The moment Pyke caught sight of the box, his fingers shot out to snatch it from her hands. There was even the slightest upward tilt to his mouth.

Success.

"I chose the diviner's pack," Olivia told him. "I remembered you telling me they were your favourite."

He'd certainly never told her such a thing, she'd just spied a small mountain of purple wrappers in his drawer once.

Her voice seemed to break the spell he was under, and the Dragon focused his attention on her once more. His face remained as impassive and austere as ever, but at least now, she didn't get the feeling that he was contemplating crushing her like a bug.

"Anyway, my companion here is Ryder Isaksson, the new Warden of the Cellars in Edinburgh. We're working on a very important job at the request of the Dark Artifacts Department, and we need to consult the Legendarium. I was hoping you might grant him temporary access."

"Hmm."

Olivia elbowed Isaksson, who reached into his pocket for his Warden credentials.

"You'll see here that he works directly for the Head of the Department, Mr Skelton, who personally selected us for this case," she added, the irony of the lie she'd told not lost on her.

Pyke stared at both of them in turn, while Olivia flashed him the most innocent and sincere smile she could muster.

A long moment passed before he unfolded from his chair, making all sorts of cracking noises, and made his way to one of the arched doorways that lined the wall.

With his long, thin limbs and the way he had of looking at you like a worm, he strongly reminded Olivia of a glasses-wearing praying mantis. And the possessive grip he still had on the box of sweets, clutching it in his clawed hand, certainly didn't help.

Pyke made a sweeping gesture with his arm and one of the heavy wooden doors pivoted on its hinges, making as much noise as the entrance to a castle's dungeon.

Through it, they entered a long, narrow corridor, no more than a couple feet wide, that led to a series of study rooms. Pyke escorted them to the very last door. He shot one last wary look in their direction, before pivoting on his heels and walking away without a word.

Isaksson watched him disappear through the arched door and close it behind him. The sound it made, accompanied by the feeling of the wards rearming, made Olivia think of a tomb closing in on them.

Lovely.

"We're stuck here, aren't we?" the Warden asked in a cautious tone.

Olivia laughed softly. She'd certainly wondered that once or twice. "No, the wards only keep people from going in, not the other way around. Don't worry, we're safe." Then she couldn't resist adding, "Well, except for the talking books, of course."

Isaksson shot her a dark look before following her into the study room.

A smile immediately blossomed on Olivia's lips. How she adored this place.

The faint light from the hanging lanterns on the ceiling reflected off the shiny surfaces of the desks. The room smelled of old paper and wood resin, and there was a particular aura in the air. A sense of such *history*. The weight of the past.

"What does that mean, Legendarium?" Isaksson asked as he looked around.

On one side, six tables were arranged for studying. Behind them lay the precious Legendarium volumes, stored on several rows of antique mahogany bookshelves. Some appeared to be in excellent condition despite their age, the leather bindings showing only slight blemishes and the gold letters still perfectly readable. Others, however, were hanging on by mere threads, their covers cracked and the gild worn away.

The other side of the room was completely empty. The far wall was just one giant wooden cabinet with countless tiny square drawers, each labelled with a string of runes.

"The Legendarium is a book of legends," Olivia explained. "Well, it's a collection of books, to be exact."

She dropped her heavy bag on the nearest table and clicked on the light. "In the 16th century, monks from the Mont-Saint-Michel Abbey in France decided to start recording arcane legends and myths. This mission eventually turned them into a full-fledged brotherhood, tasked with travelling the world to record every mythical tale in existence and compile them into a compendium. Any powerful and truly ancient artifact you can think of has most likely been mentioned in a legend at one time or another."

She walked to the far wall and drummed her fingers against the wooden drawers. Each one was roughly the size of her hand and decorated with a tiny brass pull, with hundreds of them stacked here. "However, the trick is to find the right legend. You see, the volumes were written in chronological order after each exploration campaign led by the brotherhood. So if you're looking for something specific — say, a particular tale, or anything related to a precise time or place — you'll have to find it using these."

Olivia opened the nearest drawer. Which went on . . . and on . . . and on.

It seemed like it would never stop, but the drawer finally came to a stop in the middle of the room. The whole length of it was longer than she was tall. That was why this half of the room had been left empty, without any tables or shelves.

Isaksson's eyebrows had risen higher and higher the further away the drawer went. Stunned, he looked at the near-endless, neat row of index cards that had now been revealed.

"*Va fan!* How did that even fit inside the wall?"

Olivia smiled and continued her explanation. "The entire collection of legends has been indexed according to various filters: region, date, type of magic, prominent items . . . So now all we have to do is find our wand."

Isaksson came over and gently tugged the drawer back and forth, watching as it was swallowed by the wall.

"And you're sure it's in there somewhere?" he asked her, but kept his eyes resolutely fixed on the moving drawer.

"I'm sure it is." Olivia replied. "Nothing that powerful can be kept completely hidden for centuries. I'm quite certain it's in even more than one legend."

Looking for the "Objects of Power" section, she moved to the right and cracked open a few drawers. That took a while.

"As I said, the challenge is to find it. Even though the indexing system is pretty good, there are thousands of legends written across hundreds of volumes. Some of which are even missing pages or chapters."

Olivia expertly shuffled her fingers through the index cards until she reached the desired section on Weaponry.

Looking up, she gave Isaksson a smug smile. "Lucky for you, I've been compared to a Legendarium whisperer."

The Warden rolled his eyes.

CHAPTER THIRTEEN

They were on their thirteenth try when Olivia suddenly gasped.

"Aha!" she exclaimed, waving a card in the air. "Got you."

Isaksson's head snapped up. "Are you sure?"

"*Category 3 Objects of Power, Section H Weaponry, Sub-section Æ Wands,*" she read out loud, "*Mental abilities. Core ingredient harnessed from mystical tree in dark forest. Origin story. Themes of corruption of the mind.* That's definitely the one."

Olivia turned the card over to read the reference on the back. "*Collection XXVIII, Volume 12, Book 8.* Let's go."

Behind her, Isaksson put both hands flat on the table and attempted to extricate his towering frame from the tiny desk where he'd been hunched over for the last hour.

"Pyke chose these chairs on purpose because they are torture devices," he grumbled. "I swear I sat on tree stumps more comfortable."

Olivia had to suppress a laugh as she headed for the shelves. He looked like a giant in a kindergarten classroom, with both legs sticking out from under the table.

Her eyes scanned the rows of books, a finger gliding along the wooden edge as she searched for the right section. "I don't know. You've seen how slender and bony he is, he might actually find these the epitome of comfort." She glanced at Isaksson over her shoulder. "I'm more worried about what would happen if I stuck him on the sofas in my office. He'd probably get swallowed up by the cushions."

Olivia turned her attention back to the bookshelves and the smile slipped from her lips.

The book was right in front of her face. Exactly where her finger had stopped.

And not at all where it was *supposed* to be.

She lifted the index card in her other hand and read the volume number again, her eyes flicking from the piece of paper to the innocent-looking red tome in front of her. Ancient and worn, the leather-bound volume was nothing remarkable. Traces of gilt still shone along its edges, half erased by time.

She'd handled dozens of Legendarium volumes just like this one. And yet she couldn't help the shiver that ran down her spine.

"What is it?" Isaksson asked her.

Olivia looked up with a guarded expression. "I found it."

He cocked an eyebrow when she didn't elaborate. "And . . . ?"

"And this is the right book, except it's not where it's supposed to be . . . Volumes 12 are over there." She gestured to her left. "And those are Volumes 4, Books 10 through 15."

The Warden simply shrugged. "Someone made a mistake."

Olivia didn't contradict him. Of course, someone could have been in a hurry and not put the book back where it belonged, but still . . . She couldn't help the sudden unease that washed over her. Her finger had stopped at the *exact* right spot.

Damn Pyke and his creepy attitude that always put her on edge, this was nothing more than a strange coincidence, Olivia told herself firmly. She dealt with curses for a living, she wasn't about to be frightened by an old book, for gods' sakes. Especially not after teasing Isaksson so mercilessly.

So she carefully slid the precious tome from the shelf and deposited it on the desk, while absolutely ignoring the way her skin crawled the whole time. She stepped away to grab a pair of protective gloves, trying very hard to keep her expression blank.

But the damn Viking was a true mind-reader, and he saw right through her.

"Why are you making that face?"

"What face?" She blinked up at him, her expression no more innocent than if she'd borrowed it from an angel.

He kept on staring at her. "You're spooked."

Olivia let out a dismissive huff. "I am not *spooked*. This is just a book. Just a very old . . . very precious . . . book."

And she definitely wasn't trying to convince herself of that.

"Right." Isaksson snorted. "And it has nothing to do, of course, with the fact that the hairs on your arm are standing straight up, or that you haven't opened it yet. Or that you aren't even touching it any more."

Olivia quickly looked down. She'd pulled up the sleeves of her shirt to put on the gloves, and her hair *was* standing up, damn it.

"You're imagining things. I'm just cold."

"Hmm."

Gloves on, she came back to the Legendarium tome lying so innocently on the desk. Isaksson also edged closer, his arms crossed. He looked as if he was waiting for a poisonous snake to jump out of the pages and attack them. Frankly, so was she.

Before she could lose her nerve and with one quick movement, Olivia grabbed the sides of the book and held her breath.

Nothing happened.

No snakes, no shivers, nothing.

"See?" She let out a sigh of relief. "It's fine, it's just a book." Still, she opened it carefully, mindful of its age and fragile leather binding.

A ripple split the air.

Like a wave travelling across a pond, it flooded the room, then slowly faded. They waited, Olivia's breath caught in her throat, but nothing more happened. Yet a strange echo lingered in the air.

After a long moment, she finally peered up at the Warden.

Bright blue eyes were fixed on the parchment pages, his entire frame tense enough to snap. One of his hands encircled her wrist, ready to pull her back at the slightest hint of trouble.

He eventually met her gaze, his expression daring her to try and deny what had just happened.

Instead, she pointed a warning finger at him with her other hand. Which wasn't trembling at all. "Don't say it," she ordered him, her voice strained. "You hear me? Not one word."

When Isaksson finally released her, Olivia didn't waste any more time, turning the pages as precautionary and quickly as she could. The sooner they found what they were looking for and got out of here, the better.

She didn't have to wait long before a striking illustration of a tree jumped out at her, announcing she'd found the right legend: The Fall of Erdőelve.

Written in sepia ink, the parchment page looked innocent enough. The sinuous branches of the tree wound around the written words, its deep brown trunk shot through with bright green veins. The leaves had been painted in shades of green, some dark, some light. A few even appeared shining bronze. The colours were luminous, vibrant, and made the tree seem almost alive.

Which was why it took Olivia a few seconds to realise that it was *indeed* moving.

The leaves swayed gently on the page, as if caught in an invisible breeze. The twisting branches of the tree moved as well, tightening their hold on the paragraphs ever so slightly.

"I'm not even going to comment," Isaksson growled from behind her shoulder.

Right.

The text spoke of a mythical tree, hidden deep inside a dark forest, rumoured to possess magic the likes of which had never been seen before. Every hundred years, the veins of the tree would bleed, creating green crystals that shimmered like the purest of jewels and illuminated the night. Lured by the tree's incredible power, many would venture into the dark woods in the hopes of harvesting it. But the forest was filled with many dangers, and not a soul was ever seen again.

As Olivia turned the page, she saw that the parchment was slightly darker. This time the illustration was of a mighty king, sitting on his throne. He wore heavy brocade robes, the burgundy colour so deep and rich that Olivia wondered if it would feel like velvet instead of parchment if she ran her naked finger over the page. The gold of his crown glistened, as if illuminated by candlelight. Advisors stood beside him, open books in their hands.

The text told how the ruler of Erdőelve, King Emeric, who was wise and noble, ordered that the crystals be retrieved and sealed in his most secure vaults. He sent his finest knights on this mission, and they returned triumphant. But the king feared for his crystals. An empath, he sensed the greed sweeping through his court at the sight of the mesmerising, glowing gems. So instead, he had them forged into a wand, and swore that the members of his bloodline would become its protectors.

In the right-hand corner of the page was an illustration of a kneeling man. And in his outstretched hands, laid the wand.

"We were right," Olivia said quietly, her eyes sweeping over the stunning illustrations. "The core is made from the sap of the Whispering Tree..."

She turned to the next page carefully, as if handling the most delicate of leaves.

The parchment was even darker still, this time the colour of burnt umber. At the top of the page, the king was brandishing the wand toward the sky, sat astride his powerful black horse. His armour shone as if it had been painted with pure gold. His knights framed him, their raised banners swaying in the wind.

Olivia read the text aloud:

King Emeric, in his wisdom, spurned the use of the Dark Wand, wary of its influence. Yet, dark shadows gathered around Erdőelve as neighbouring realms cast covetous glances upon its riches.

The dread of war loomed nigh, and Emeric, faced with impending conflict, chose the most perilous path of all.

Gathering leaders from afar, the King sought the wand's aid in forging a path to peace. A silent whisperer, it slithered into their minds, sowing seeds of accord, and the kingdom, saved from the ravages of war, sighed with relief.

Emboldened by his success and succumbing to the insidious voices of the Dark Wand, King Emeric wielded its power with abandon. He, who had once been revered by his people, blessed with the magic of a true Empath, fell into madness.

The downfall of Erdőelve's mighty kings was sealed as the noble kingdom became mere shade of its former self. Upon the death of King Emeric, the Dark Wand, bearer of doom, vanished into the shadows from whence it came.

Olivia's gaze fell to the bottom of the page, where wisps of darkness crept up, trying to reach the King.

"Did you hear that?" Isaksson's voice sounded uneasy.

She looked up. At first she didn't hear anything peculiar, but then she caught it. A faint whisper in the air.

She thought it might be coming from her right, but the sound was so soft that it would disappear if she concentrated too much on it. Yet as the seconds passed, it grew. Became stronger. Until it began to resemble something very familiar . . .

Olivia gasped. "Are the books . . . *talking?*"

A few paces behind her, Isaksson made a strangled sound. "I told you!" he hissed.

For it was unmistakably voices they could hear. Coming from the rows of shelves behind them.

Olivia caught something out of the corner of her eye and turned back to the book. She froze.

It wasn't open on the same page as before.

This one seemed to be the last of the legend. And this time, the parchment was completely black. A black so deep and true that it didn't reflect light any more, but seemed to absorb it. There was a text, written in grey ink. It seemed to float atop this pool of the darkest shadows.

An illustration of the wand adorned the page. Haunting. Captivating. Olivia found herself unable to look away from the faint iridescent shimmer emanating from it.

She knew Isaksson was still facing the talking books because there hadn't been any thunderous Swedish curses, so she reached behind her with a blind hand and felt for his shirt. Grabbing a handful of it, she yanked him to her side.

"Tell me you're the one who turned the page," he ground out.

Olivia shook her head.

"*Jeg er så ferdig med at ting blir levende!*" The Warden's voice was a ragged growl.

Olivia had to swallow a few times before she managed to whisper, her voice taunt with strain:

Carved from forgotten groves, the wand bore the shape of a serpent's coil, an emerald luminescence at its heart.

Once an instrument of great peace, it now mirrored the shadows it had absorbed. The darkness it spread no longer distinguished between friend and foe, but embraced them all within its sinister grasp.

"That explains what happened to the king," Isaksson pointed out.

"What do you mean?"

"He only wanted peace for his people. Sure, he manipulated the minds of the other leaders, but his intentions were good. So why would the wand turn evil after he used it?"

Olivia nodded as she continued his train of thought. "Because it not only feeds on its master's intentions, but also on those of its victims. So when the king used it on the other leaders, their desire for violence must have impregnated it. And that evil later spread to the hand that wielded it... If the wand was really able to turn an empath into a monster, no wonder it drove the Hungarian general insane after he used it on the battlefields."

"Or that it's trying to do the same thing to us now," Isaksson added.

The tiny hairs on the back of Olivia's neck rose in warning at the same moment as faint traces of handwriting appeared on the black paper.

"What is that?" Isaksson murmured.

The newly revealed words danced across the bottom of the page. Olivia squinted, but they were too fast for her to read. She saw enough, though, to realise that these weren't ordinary letters.

"It's Old Arcane Tongue," she told Isaksson. "But I don't recognise all the symbols . . . We'll need Cornelius. He's a linguistic genius, he'll be able to translate this."

"But why did they appear? Did we break a spell on the book?"

Olivia drew on her magic, about to wrap it around the pages to detect the remnants of a seal, but was startled to feel a tendril of it already going to the book before her, linking them.

"I think it's me," she replied with a frown. "I don't know how this happened, but my magic is what's calling the hidden inscription. As if it were a curse I was coaxing out of an artifact."

"So it's a curse, then?"

"I honestly have no idea," she breathed. "It might also be a . . ."

Her voice trailed off, eyes glued to the illustration of the wand. Something was happening . . .

The previous glimmer turned into a pulsating light, radiating from the core and eclipsing the black wood. The voices from the rows of books behind them also grew stronger, their whispers echoing all around the room.

Take me . . .

Olivia couldn't look away from the hypnotic glow. It danced on the page, calling to her.

Take me . . . the whispery voice commanded.

Olivia opened her mouth, but nothing came out. She tried again, but it was as if her mind couldn't form a single sentence any more.

Not even when she saw mist swirling around their feet. White waves that doubled in an instant until they reached their calves. Nor when she began to smell dampness in the air, or heard the unmistakable rustling of leaves.

Her hand rose of its own accord, moving towards the hypnotizing green light.

It wasn't until Ryder shot out and stopped her, gripping her fingers in an unshakable hold, that she realised . . . The wand was no longer just an illustration.

What appeared to be the real wand now rested atop the Legendarium page.

And it was not happy that Ryder had interrupted.

The voices that had been whispering softly in their ears howled in anger. A wind came out of nowhere, whipping Olivia's hair against her face. The hundreds of books behind them shook and rattled against the confines of the narrow shelves.

"What do we do now?" Olivia had to shout to make herself heard above the cries and the wails resonating around them.

Unbelievably, the wind was now so strong that she was struggling to stay upright. Tables and chairs were blown back and knocked over, a lamp fell to the floor and shattered.

"Hold on to me!" Ryder yelled back.

Olivia wrapped both arms around his torso, her hair blowing wildly around them.

The Warden flashed the book what could only be described as a wolfish grin, showing him all his teeth. He seized each side of the large volume and tried to close it. His biceps bulged with the effort and a growl escaped him, as if he were trying to lift hundreds of pounds. But the stubborn wand was no match for the Viking's strength and the book finally slammed shut.

Everything stopped. The wind, the mist, the howling... The sudden silence was so jarring that it made Olivia dizzy.

They didn't dare move for a long moment, their minds processing the abrupt disappearance of the raging storm. Only their matching, laboured breathing could be heard in the now peaceful study room.

Eventually, Olivia pulled away from Ryder. His blond hair was more dishevelled than she'd ever seen it, his eyes still a little wild. She didn't want to imagine what her own hair and face looked like.

That was when her gaze landed on his hands and her mouth dropped open in true horror. "You ripped them off?" Her voice was so strangled, she almost didn't recognise it.

Isaksson looked down at the pages between his fingers with an expression of disbelief. "No! I just closed it and... I have no idea how they got here!"

This couldn't be happening . . .

No matter that a miniature tornado had been unleashed in one of the most precious rooms of the Vaults, if the Dragon found out she'd torn off pages, he would kill her.

"Put them back!"

"What? How?"

"I don't care how, just put them back!"

But Isaksson shook his head. "I have a feeling it's more dangerous to leave them in there than to take them with us."

Olivia forgot how to breathe. "You want to take pages *out of the Library?*"

"They're already out, it's too late. Come on, let's go," he said and grabbed her hand to pull her towards the exit.

Olivia was still in such a state of shock that she didn't even struggle.

Thoughts swirled around in her head without pause. How had the wand managed to affect the books from all the way down in the Cellars? Were the wards there containing it *at all?* Had the real wand really emerged from the illustration, or was it a hallucination? What would have happened if she'd picked it up?

But most importantly, how was she going to keep the Dragon from murdering them both?

She didn't even notice that they'd already crossed the corridor and reached the central room where Pyke resided. Only he wasn't there, the whole room deserted.

That made Olivia pause. She'd never seen the Vaults empty before. Pyke considered them his personal kingdom and very rarely stayed away. She thanked her lucky stars, though. Maybe they'd be able to sneak out of the Library altogether.

Isaksson pulled her towards the spiral staircase, still holding her hand. They hurried up to the Archives Department on the ground floor and all of Olivia's hopes came crushing down.

Everyone was gone — all the researchers and scholars, the desks cleared — but Pyke remained. He sat behind the central counter, the box of dragon eggs opened before him. He must have eaten one already, for faint traces of smoke hovered around his mouth.

He really does look like a dragon, Olivia thought. Especially as he soared towards them, like a great winged beast swooping down on its prey.

She immediately raised her hands in a placating gesture. "My sincerest apologies, Mr Pyke, we had no idea we'd spent so many hours in the Legendarium rooms, we were—"

"What in the . . . What were you doing in there again?" he hissed. "And how did you get back in?"

"Time just ran away from us, we were so . . ." Olivia's voice trailed off, and she cocked her head to the side in confusion.

"Back?" she said, at the same time as Isaksson asked, "What do you mean *again?*"

The Dragon's dark brows knitted together in a thunderous expression. "No one can pass through the Vaults' protections without the key. What game are you playing here, missy?"

It was Olivia's turn to frown. "I have no idea what you're talking about. We came to you, remember? You unlocked the protections yourself."

"That was this morning!" Pyke exclaimed. "After that, you left!"

Olivia blinked. What was he on about? Had the solitude and oppressive air down in the Vaults finally got to him?

"We didn't leave, I assure you. We've been down there this whole time."

"What nonsense is this?" Pyke's voice grew shrill. "I saw you two leave!"

He was so agitated and upset that he looked more alive than she'd ever seen him. Which, Olivia realised now, was even more frightening than his usual cold and menacing demeanour.

"I don't understand how you managed to break the protections, but this is not right. I won't let this go easily, Ms Knight."

Olivia tried again to calm him down. "Mr Pyke, I assure you, this is all a misunderstanding. We haven't left the Legendarium rooms. You must have mistaken us for someone else."

"Olivia . . ." She heard Isaksson murmur from behind her, but ignored him.

The Dragon raised a bony finger in her direction. "I may not be your age, Ms Knight, but I still have two perfectly good eyes! I saw you leave this place with the blond giant!"

"That's not poss—"

"Olivia!" Isaksson shouted louder.

She whirled around. "What!"

He was staring at the tall stained glass windows, his back to her. Finally, he turned, a look of utter disbelief on his face.

"It's night outside."

"I can't believe the whole day is gone! We don't have the bait and we're supposed to get the wand in a few hours!" Olivia rushed down the steps of the Museum's entrance, Isaksson at her heels.

"What was that?" he exclaimed. "What happened in there?"

"Cornelius is a language genius," Olivia muttered to herself. "He'll be able to translate the inscription, I'm sure. But who would hide something in the Legendarium? And why behind a curse, of all things?"

"It was morning when we went in, it's pitch dark now! I'm pretty sure we just spent more than ten hours staring at that book!"

"We absolutely need a bait," she continued under her breath. "Even Michael's most potent amplifier crystals won't cut it, this thing is far too intelligent to fall for it. We need what's at the core. But where are we supposed to find the sap of a mythical Romanian tree?"

Not bothering to wait for him, Olivia quickly walked down the side of the Museum building and made her way back to the Portal Market.

"Olivia!" Isaksson called from behind her. "Pyke said he *saw* us leave! How is that possible?"

"Michael would know. If not, then maybe one of Cornelius' shady friends he likes to play poker with. Oh gods... And what am I supposed to do with the torn pages? When Pyke finds out, he's going to kill me!" She gasped. "Or worse, he'll *ban* me from the Library!"

"Olivia." Isaksson's hand latched onto her elbow and spun her around.

His blue eyes bored into hers, his voice deadly serious. "Tell me what just happened. Please."

Olivia took a deep breath, trying to slow down her madly pounding heart. "That wand is much more powerful than we thought. I've never seen anything like it. It figured out that we were here, in the Museum, and somehow connected to the Legendarium and all the other volumes. I mean . . ." She shook her head in disbelief. "It even sent Pyke the vision of us leaving so he wouldn't disturb us!"

She gripped the hand on her elbow tightly. "I think it has been lying about its true power all these years. Everything you've told me it did to your men . . . It's nothing compared to what it just accomplished tonight.

"It shouldn't have been able to find us there, in the Vaults. Shouldn't have been able to connect to the other volumes or get into Pyke's head. And not only did it do all that, but from all the way inside its cell!"

Olivia closed her eyes. "Ryder . . ." She struggled to find the right words to make him understand what had chilled her to the bone. "I don't think that wand has *ever* been contained in the Cellars, not really. If it had, this never would have happened."

Her voice dropped low. "I think it *chose* to stay there."

Isaksson didn't answer for a long moment, a muscle twitching in his jaw. Finally, he asked, "When the illustration of the wand detached from the page . . . What would have happened if we'd picked it up?"

Olivia's voice was barely more than a whisper. "That, I don't want to know."

CHAPTER FOURTEEN

"You... you *ripped* pages out of the Legendarium?" Godwyn had been leaning back in his chair, but now slowly brought it back down on four legs. "Are you mad?"

"You found a secret inscription hidden in the pages of the Legendarium in Old Arcane Tongue?" Cornelius interrupted him, his eyes practically bulging out of his head.

"You're lucky you got out of there alive," Adeline chimed in with a serious tone.

Isaksson snorted. "Believe me, I know..."

As soon as Olivia had explained what had happened at the Museum, the room had immediately erupted in chaos, questions and comments flying out of everyone's mouths.

"So the wand," Godwyn began, "took control of Pyke's mind and made him believe you'd already left." He paused, shook his head. "No. Just no. This is too much." His face had gone pale.

Cornelius exclaimed, "This may be the most exciting discovery since Sir Hatherall uncovered the missing pages of—"

"Please, as if you hadn't seen worse," Adeline cut in, turning to Godwyn. "You once had the text of an ancient prophecy literally appear on your chest..."

"What?" Cornelius shifted to stare at him too, his mouth open. "When did *that* happen?"

"It was nothing, she exaggerates."

"Do I? Lord Bewick's grandmother thought you were possessed by spirits and practically chased you out of the house with a fire poker..."

"It was a misunderstanding," Godwyn snapped.

"The police nearly arrested you . . ."

"Enough!" Olivia held her hands up, effectively silencing everyone. "Listen, we have to get the wand out of the Cellars. Tonight." She turned to him, "Cornelius, there were some very strange symbols mixed in with the Old Arcane Tongue, so you'll need the Codexes. They're in my bookcase, second shelf."

"Got it, boss," he replied, dashing into her office.

Olivia deposited her bag on Adeline's desk and flopped down into a chair.

Her assistant immediately dove in to retrieve the Legendarium pages, a cautious look on her face as she took great care to open the bag using only the tips of her fingers. Godwyn hovered behind her, breathing down her neck. When he lectured her to be careful for the third time, Adeline cut him a sharp look.

"What?"

Her voice was quiet and precise as she intoned with the sweetest smile, "If you tell me to be careful one more time, I will slice all your ties into ribbons and use them to knit Jerry a tiny pot jumper."

Isaksson came over to crouch beside Olivia's chair, looking mighty proud of himself. A chocolate bar was slid into her palm.

"Did you just steal this from Adeline's desk?" she whispered to him.

His expression was full of his usual mischief, but there was also concern in his voice when he asked her if she was all right.

Olivia tore into the candy as discreetly as she could, Ryder helping by angling his body to shield her from the other's view. "I'm fine," she said quietly. "Just tired and worried. You know she would have given it to me if I'd asked, don't you?"

"Ah. But doesn't it taste sweeter that way?" Ryder replied, the wickedness back in his voice.

The corners of Olivia's mouth twitched.

Cornelius returned to settle down at an empty desk. The table jumped when he dropped the heavy Codexes onto it. In the end, Adeline had decided to pinch the corner of each Legendarium page with two pens and was currently arranging them in front of him.

"Look at them . . ." Cornelius breathed, awe clear on his face.

As if sensing his admiring gaze, the previously hidden words danced and undulated merrily on the parchment like a group of will-o'-the-wisps.

Having wisely decided to give them some space, Godwyn brought a chair next to Olivia and sat, resting his elbows on his knees. "Far be it from me to spoil Cornelius' fun, but I really don't see what the point is. Aren't you supposed to leave tonight? You don't have time to go hunting for some mythical Romanian tree."

Olivia blew out a breath. "I know. I only asked him to translate the inscription because we still have a few hours. I'm not hoping for anything."

"Do you intend to use amplifier crystals then? We got the strongest ones Michael had in his collection." His eyes crinkled at the corners. "I have to admit, Adeline bargained beautifully for them. I thought he was going to throw her out at one point."

"I don't doubt it. But I won't use them. The wand is too intelligent, it won't fall for it."

Godwyn's lips pinched in disapproval. "Liv . . . Perhaps it would be wise to consider alternative options."

His cautious tone made Isaksson lift his head. "Alternative options?"

"If you simply waited another day to—"

"No," Olivia and Isaksson said in unison.

The Baron stared them down like they were aggravating children. "I am merely suggesting that you take the time to study the situation before—"

Olivia interrupted him. "Godwyn, I wish we could do that, I really do. But every curse-breaking instinct I have is telling me that if we don't get that wand out of there tonight, it's going to turn into an even bigger nightmare than it already is."

Godwyn pressed his lips together, but not before muttering, "What's common sense when you've got *instinct*?"

"*Oui!*" The triumphant cry rang through the quiet office.

Cornelius was waving a piece of paper in the air, his thin glasses slightly askew before he tore them from his face. "I did it!"

Adeline had to put a hand on his shoulder to keep him seated. He was even more excited than usual, almost vibrating in his chair.

"I had trouble translating this one symbol in particular because it wasn't written in the usual way. This was a different version of the script that's only mentioned in passing in the Codexes. So there's a chance that we've just stumbled upon a completely new subsection of the Old Tongue! How thrilling is that?" He spoke so quickly that it took them all a few seconds to catch up.

Olivia hid her smile at the flurry of groans and eye rolls that finally ensued.

"*Thrilling*?" Godwyn snorted. "We're talking about a language that's been dead for thousands of years, mate."

Adeline tapped him on the shoulder. "Come on, Cornelius, you're killing us with your weird symbols! What does the inscription say?"

"It's a small poem, or a prophecy, perhaps," he said, then recited:

*Beware the poison that seeps through
Unseen, unheard, it slithers.
Until the Gate, once broken, can be born anew.*

A confused silence followed his words before Isaksson scowled. "What's this *Gate*, now?"

"*The poison that seeps through,*" Olivia repeated. "Is it talking about the crystals? How they got into the king's mind?" Whatever she'd thought this hidden inscription meant, this wasn't it.

"I thought it was going to say where the tree is," Adeline mused. "Or at least give us some clues, like a treasure hunt . . ."

"Whatever this riddle means, I don't see how it helps us," Godwyn remarked dryly.

Olivia agreed. She stood and walked to the large windows, pinching the bridge of her nose.

"I wonder why the wand made the pages come out of the book," Cornelius asked behind her. "Is it trying to tell us something? Maybe it wants to go back to that . . . *Gate*. Maybe that's what it considers its home."

Isaksson muttered into his beard, "If the wand really wants to go back to Romania, maybe it should consider stopping being such a pain."

"Who would have added that inscription in the first place?" Adeline interjected. "And why? I mean, why hide it behind a spell? There's nothing concrete, it's all just vague words."

"I suppose it could be the Brotherhood itself when the Legendarium was written," Cornelius replied. "But I don't see why they would have hidden it, the whole point of the Brotherhood was to compile and study legends . . ."

Olivia stared down at the dark and empty street below. The light drizzle that had permeated the air for the past hour had turned heavier and promised to become a full-blown storm during the night.

Three words kept circling in her head without pause. And had done so ever since they'd returned from Wardlaw Wands.

The Whispering Tree . . .

How had she known what it was called? Had her father really told her about it?

If he had, then perhaps he'd told her something else, some small detail that might help them now . . . She couldn't shake this feeling that she'd forgotten something important, a clue. It kept nagging at her, but try as she might, she couldn't remember.

"I swear I got goose bumps when you read the prophecy," Adeline said quietly. "Up my arms and all. *Slithers*, ugh. That's such a nasty word."

Cornelius nodded. "Me too, *cher*. I got the *frissons*."

A flash of lightning lit up the sky.

And that's when it finally hit Olivia. What she'd been trying to remember for the past two days. The memory that kept slipping through her fingers. She remembered.

It had been late at night, one heavy with rain and thunder. She'd been alone in her room, deep under the covers.

An hour earlier, a man had banged on their door. She'd been sitting on her father's lap as he read her her favourite story. The man had had a scary look on his face, but her father had told her not to be afraid. They'd talked in his study for a long time, too low for her to hear even though she'd strained her ears. All she'd managed to catch had been the word "serpent."

And then the strange man had left. He'd given her father something wrapped in a black cloth. She hadn't liked the sight of it, it had felt . . . strange.

Her father had tucked her into bed right after, promising to read her two stories the next day to make up for it. She'd agreed.

After the first flashes of lightning had lit up the sky, she'd got out of bed and padded downstairs in silence. Everything had been dark, but the dying flames in the fireplace had helped her see. The door to her father's workshop had been pushed, but not closed. She'd been able to hear soft voices whispering inside, though she hadn't recognised her father's deep tone.

A green light had poured out from the gap under the door.

She'd come closer and pressed her eye into the keyhole. Everything had been green.

Intrigued, she'd slowly pushed the door open. The green light had grown stronger and stronger. The voices, too.

That was when a large shadow had fallen over her. "Olivia!"

Her father had scooped her up and stormed back into the office, shutting the door to his workshop firmly behind him.

He'd plopped her down on the sofa, his big hands engulfing her shoulders. He'd been angry.

"I told you not to go into the workshop without me, Olivia! What were you thinking?"

"I heard voices. Who were you talking to?"

Her father's entire body had frozen at her words. "You heard voices?"

His expression had frightened her then. She'd managed a tiny nod.

"What did they say?"

He'd shaken her when she hadn't answered. "Olivia, tell me! What did the voices say?"

Olivia's lip had begun to quiver. "I don't know, I couldn't hear very well . . ."

He'd heaved a big sigh then, hands gentling on her shoulders. "It's all right. Don't be scared. Just . . . Don't ever do that again, alright? Promise?"

At her nod, he'd hugged her tight. "Come on, let's get something hot to drink before bed."

The memory faded and Olivia became aware of someone saying her name repeatedly. Adeline was standing beside her, gently shaking her arm.

"I remember," Olivia breathed. "I remember the night my father worked on the wand. I remember everything . . ."

She quickly recounted her memory of that night.

"The Whispering Tree . . . That's why I've been thinking about it ever since we came back from seeing Maeve. I heard whispers that night—" Olivia gasped, her eyes going wide. "I know what they are! They're Serpenthyst!"

Then she shook her head. "I should have realised this before. The mental abilities of that wand are simply too great. It couldn't have possibly been anything else."

When Olivia finally noticed that no one was speaking, the others exchanging bemused looks between them, she added, "Serpenthyst crystals, otherwise known by their more modern term . . . Ophite stones."

Adeline whistled.

Isaksson crossed his arms and began to pace, while Cornelius winced.

Only Godwyn's confused expression remained. "What's wrong? Why are you reacting like this?"

Adeline was the one to explain. "These crystals are very dark magic. Extremely powerful, extremely dangerous. They can open the mind to suggestion and manipulation, and have been used for all sorts of terrible things in the past: altering people's memories, messing with their heads to hunt for secrets, forcing them to do things against their will . . ."

Godwyn ran a hand over his slicked back hair. "Marvellous."

Olivia continued, stifling a sigh, "And now for the other bad news. They've been banned for at least fifty years. You can't buy them anywhere. So we're back to square one." *Gods damn it.* Every time she thought they were making progress, another surprise knocked them back.

"What?" Isaksson turned to stare at her, disbelief in his voice. "Don't tell me none of you know someone who sells a little contraband."

Olivia opened her mouth, but nothing came out.

"Aren't you supposed to be working for the Ministry?" Godwyn asked incredulously.

Cornelius just laughed. "I like you, Isaksson."

Olivia finally remembered how to speak. "But . . . I . . . They've been *banned*." She'd sunk extra gravitas onto the last word, just in case he'd failed to understand its full significance.

Lips twitching, Adeline was clearly fighting back a grin as she said, "My dear Warden, you will soon learn that Liv does not take kindly to a little rule breaking."

"If it can land you in prison, I don't find it very *little*," Olivia muttered.

The Warden in question winked at her. "If you get arrested, I'll tell the Ministry it was for the good of the mission and get you out. I promise."

Arrogant Viking. If they were caught with Serpenthyst crystals, they would *both* end up in prison.

"But this is more than just contraband," Cornelius told him. "Ophite stones were already incredibly rare back when they were allowed, so now . . ."

Isaksson simply shrugged. "Then I guess we don't have a choice. We have to go down."

Down?

Olivia's brow furrowed, but then her mouth fell open. He couldn't possibly mean *Down-Below* . . . "You can't be serious."

Godwyn blinked. "He certainly *looks* like he's serious."

Isaksson grinned, wild blue eyes gleaming. "Oh, believe me. I am."

"What if we managed to find this mysterious G.H on Maeve's old papers?" Cornelius suggested. He'd taken off his thin glasses and was leaning back in his seat, expertly twirling a pen between deft fingers as if it were a poker chip. "The one who commissioned the importation of the serpent wood. It has to be the stranger from your memory, right? And if he gave your father the wand all those years ago, he might have some Ophite stones."

Godwyn snapped his fingers. "That's actually a really good idea, we could—"

"I know very well who it is," Olivia interrupted them.

They all turned to stare at her.

"You do?"

"Hmm mm. It was Griffin."

Each member of her team nodded then, not surprised. "Ah, that makes sense," Adeline even said.

"She means Griffin Holmes," Cornelius explained to Isaksson.

"Who's tha—" the Warden started to say, then went completely still. "*Griffin Holmes?* Of Holmes and Hastings?"

"He's a family friend," Olivia added.

The Warden gaped at her before repeating slowly, "The Purveyor is a family friend."

"He invited us all to dinner not long ago," Godwyn told him. "We were given a tour of the back room of their shop. Quite impressive, I must say."

Cornelius continued, "They'd just returned from an expedition to South America. Showed us a jade ceremonial mask they'd dug up from a ruined Mayan temple, it was incredible."

"Michael made us a traditional Ghanaian dish," Adeline finished. "It was a lovely dinner."

Isaksson stared at each of them in turn, his jaw slack, and Olivia couldn't fight her twitching lips.

A tapping sound broke the silence.

Olivia looked around in confusion when the tapping came again.

Adeline rose and approached one of the windows in the corner of the office. She arched an elegant brow. "It's a dragonling."

"At this hour?" Godwyn asked.

Adeline grabbed their dedicated fireproof glove and opened the window. Sure enough, there was a black dragonling waiting not-so-patiently on the ledge. It immediately climbed onto her covered hand, showing the envelope dangling from one of its front paws.

"I think that's for me."

Olivia turned to Isaksson. Eyes narrowing, she crossed her arms. "Something *is* going on with you today."

"Then perhaps you could come and take this off yourself?" Adeline called out. "Because this dragonling is giving me the evil eye."

She was right, the creature's amber eyes were fixed on her, and they did *not* seem pleased.

The dragonling flew back into the night after Isaksson came to collect his missive, ready to transport another important package.

Olivia approached as the Warden quickly scanned the message, his face growing darker and darker. She placed a hand on his forearm. "What's wrong?"

Isaksson looked up, his eyes two blocks of ice. He handed her the message without a word and emptied the rest of the envelope, pulling out a thin folder marked confidential.

As Olivia read, she felt her face turn equally dark.

"Liv?" asked Adeline. "What's going on?"

Isaksson looked at Olivia for a second before letting out a big sigh between clenched teeth that sounded more like a hiss. "I recently found out that this isn't the first time people have tried to transfer this wand out of the Cellars. I don't know why I wasn't told before, but there had been a previous attempt. And it went terribly wrong."

"What happened?"

Olivia answered, "It says here that a team of four curse-breakers was assembled. All experienced. The *incident*, as they're calling it, happened before they even had a chance to cross the border."

Adeline's hand went to her throat. "Did they die?"

Isaksson had quickly shuffled through the thin folder and now shook his head, passing it to Olivia. "They fell into a catatonic state. All of them were committed to a psychiatric facility." His voice came out hard and cold. "That was six years ago. They're still there."

Silence fell between them before Adeline asked, her face drained of colour, "I've never heard of this before . . . You?"

Cornelius shook his head as Olivia joined in, her voice grim. "Me neither. The Ministry must have covered it up."

"And you didn't know?" Godwyn stood to glare at Isaksson. "How is it possible that you didn't know?" He crossed his arms over his chest. "Exactly what kind of Warden are you?"

A muscle played in Isaksson's jaw. "I don't know why. And believe me, I am *not* pleased."

"You're asking her to risk her life for a lost cause!"

The Warden levelled a warning look at him. "It isn't a lost cause, we have a plan. It will work."

Godwyn bit back, "Maybe you should tell that to the last curse-breakers who tried."

Isaksson straightened to his full, impressive height and stepped forward, angry energy rolling off him in waves. "I suggest you watch your tone, Baron."

Godwyn only raised his chin. Lesser men might have fled for their lives, but he was clearly made of sturdier stuff. Either that, or his expensive suit doubled as armour. "Or what?"

Olivia shot them both an exasperated look. "Gentlemen, this is hardly helpful."

"What is the matter with you, Godwyn?" Adeline cut in. "Olivia knows what she's doing. What do you think will happen if Crowley gets his hands on that wand?"

Armageddon, no doubt.

"She's right," Cornelius added. "Crowley doesn't have a clue what to do with it."

Godwyn scoffed. "Trust me, I am well aware. But we didn't create this mess in the first place, why should we be the ones taking all the risks?"

"If not us, then who?" Adeline retorted, her voice rising. "No one else can do this transfer! You've seen what happened to the other team that tried."

"Exactly how is this any concern of ours? Why doesn't the Ministry step in then?"

Adeline gestured pointedly at Isaksson. "Well, isn't *he* from the Ministry?"

Godwyn rolled his eyes and growled, "You know perfectly well what I meant."

Adeline whirled to Olivia, throwing up her hands. "Please don't tell me you agree with him!"

Olivia knew she shouldn't. That she should feel the noble ardour gripping Adeline, not the cynicism that Godwyn displayed. That, as a curse-breaker, it was her responsibility to protect the population from this wand, even if it was extremely dangerous.

And yet, she *did* agree with him. She hadn't created this mess, so why should she be the one to risk going into a catatonic state to fix it? Besides, there had been a time when she'd tried everything to protect, to save. And all it had done was blow up in her face.

"And what if I do?" she retorted. "I'm tired of having to take care of Ministry's blunders." Her gaze whipped to the Warden. "Unfortunately, we don't have a choice any more."

Isaksson's eyes narrowed to slits. "Now, hold on a minute..."

"Because *someone* here decided he knew better than everyone else and lied to his superiors, sending them to pick up a fake after they explicitly forbade him from hiring us! Which, of course, I only found out after signing the bloody contract!"

"You knew very well there was going to be a decoy before you signed it!" replied the Warden, his face turning into a thunderstorm. "And don't pretend it would have mattered either way, you've been dying to get this case since the very beginning!"

"That was before I knew about any of this!"

Adeline's voice rang cold and precise, and could have frozen the air in the office when she declared, "Anyone who would rather trust Skelton and Crowley with this transfer, is either a coward or a fool."

Godwyn stepped forward. "Have a care who you call a coward."

Adeline hissed, her silver eyes flashing, "It's not my fault if the truth hurts, Baron—"

A shrill whistle pierced the air.

Everyone turned to Cornelius. "It's the wand!" he shouted. "Look!"

Olivia sucked in a breath when she saw the green tendrils of mist covering the entire floor of the office, all coming from the forgotten Legendarium pages.

There was a flurry of curses behind her, but Olivia barely heard them. She'd had *enough*.

"Cornelius, get me the *De Arcana Opuscula*. Everyone, stand back." Her magic whipped around her, an angry bronze current.

She used it to roll up the carpet, and Adeline barely had time to snatch up her typewriter before her desk joined the others in a disorderly heap across the room.

Cornelius rushed back, a book in each hand.

"Left one," Olivia replied to his questioning look.

That made him gasp. "You want to do a Sidus Vortex."

"What's that?" Isaksson asked.

"I've had it with this wand!" Olivia snapped, ignoring his question. "I'm going to remind it who's the curse-breaker here."

That got everyone moving.

Godwyn hurried to the supply room and returned a few seconds later, his arms full of an assortment of chalks, vials of ash and pouches of precious crystals. Next to him, Adeline juggled a marble pestle and mortar with some potion bottles. They dumped everything on the floor.

"Which ones?" Godwyn asked Olivia simply.

She pointed to the leather pouches. "Malachite. And aspen ash."

At some point during all this, Isaksson had stationed himself out of the way, leaning against a wall. He'd crossed his arms and ankles and watched the flurry of activity unfolding around him with an intent stare.

When Godwyn had finished mixing the ashes with some clove oil, he brought the small clay pot to where Olivia knelt on the hardwood floor. Without her having to say a word, she simply looked up at Adeline and immediately, a small paintbrush flew through the air, passing over Godwyn's bent head.

Armed with the greyish mixture, Olivia began to paint the circle, while Godwyn added the appropriate script next to it with the crushed up malachite Adeline had just ground up.

Then Olivia used her powers to levitate the Legendarium pages and place them inside the finished circle.

When everyone had taken a few cautious steps back, she placed the palm of her right hand in direct contact with the ash line. Her power punched through the circle like a gong being struck, releasing a vibration that rippled through the air.

Light burst from her hands and ran down the chalk lines, igniting them as it passed, like fire travelling along an oiled up cord. It also reached the runes and characters wound through the pattern. The green symbols sparked, rising from the ground until they floated above it, glowing with power.

Olivia lifted her arms and concentrated. The circle began to spin, sending puffs of chalk into the air. Magic popped like a firecracker, the lines spiralling faster and faster until they rose to form a solid, spinning arch around the pages.

A dull ache began between her temples, but Olivia ignored it.

She fed more power into the circle and the green characters shot higher. They speckled the spinning dome, changing from an emerald shade to liquid silver.

Slowly, the crackling faded, replaced by a low, steady hum. A solid wall of magic now enveloped the Legendarium pages, resembling a view of the galaxy, the twinkling runes like stars.

There would be no more green vines or messing with their heads, that was for sure.

Getting up took some effort, but Olivia dusted her palms, a determined look on her face as she squared her shoulders. "Warden, lead the way to the Cellars. We're getting that wand out, right now. Cornelius, when that's done, we'll meet you to go *Down Below*."

Godwyn protested, stepping into her path to grab her shoulders, "Liv, wait. This is a terrible idea. Even Cornelius thinks so. And coming from him, that should mean something."

A paintbrush flew through the air to hit the Baron's back.

Adeline added, a dissatisfied twist to her red lips. "It hurts me to admit this, but Godwyn may be right. You won't have any bait. How will you get the wand into the containment cage?"

"This *is* a terrible idea," Olivia conceded, her voice tense. "The only problem is, it's the only one we've got."

She straightened to her full height. "Listen, that wand has been toying with us for far too long. I'm tired of letting a curse get the best of me. If it wants to play, I'll throw a hex at it so fast, it won't even have time to release the mist. I've got a lot of pent-up frustration I need to let out. As for the bait . . . I'll think of something. I'm going to that prison and I am *not* leaving without that wand."

Godwyn shook his head as he scowled at Isaksson. "I knew he was going to be a bad influence."

Olivia started for the door but paused suddenly. "Cornelius, where is it exactly? The entrance to the black market?"

"It used to be under a yew tree near Craigmillar Castle, but now . . ." He pulled a shiny copper coin from the pocket of his jacket. Olivia had noticed he liked to play it between his fingers, when he was deep in thought.

He now examined it, tilting his head before finally looking up. "Greyfriars Kirkyard."

Godwyn threw up his arms. "See? Nothing good can come from a market held beneath tombstones."

Olivia ignored him, grabbing her coat as she stormed out of the office. "We're curse-breakers, Godwyn. Ghosts and tombstones are our business."

CHAPTER FIFTEEN

"Not so bloody tight, *Älva*. You're strangling me."

"I still can't believe I let you talk me into this!" Olivia hissed, but still loosened the death grip she had on his neck.

As she'd discovered a few moments ago, the Warden so-called "discreet entrance", meant putting her under a cloaking spell and tricking the Cellars wards by disguising her magic with his own. It had sounded like a reasonable enough plan, right until she'd spotted the crazy glint in his eyes. The next thing she knew, he was uncermoniously lifting her onto his back and telling her to keep quiet.

"*Talk you into this?*" Isaksson repeated with a snort. "You kept slapping me away, I had to lift you up there myself."

"You're damn lucky it's not Professor Wyborn you have to haul around on your back!"

Olivia's hushed words were sharp with outrage at being carried around like a child, but Isaksson's answering chuckle was deep and slightly heated. "Oh, believe me, I *know*."

A rush of heat came over her cheeks, and it was then Olivia realised just how tightly she'd wrapped herself around him in an effort not to fall. Her legs were locked around his waist and her arms crossed over his broad chest. And she was *absolutely* oblivious to the feel of his muscles shifting and rolling on his frame, or how strong they felt under her fingertips.

She thanked her lucky stars that the Warden couldn't see her flaming face.

She was distracted by another wave that tipped the boat sideways and sent her stomach roil with it. She sacrificed an arm to grab the swinging oil lantern beside them before it had a chance to smack Isaksson right in the face.

They were racing towards the island at breakneck speed, thanks to their crazy captain, and were being pummelled by strong winds that had started the moment they took to sea. The rickety wooden boat made all sorts of cracking noises as it broke against the waves.

Olivia squeezed her eyes shut and pressed her cheek against the firm curve of Ryder's shoulder. Between the heavy rocking of the boat, the icy howling winds whipping the ends of her scarf around, and the salty mist from the waves stinging her eyes, she concentrated on holding on to him and nothing else. Ryder, being the Viking that he was, had no problem keeping his balance and was grinning with excitement.

"Almost there!" their captain shouted.

Olivia risked opening her eyes mere slits. Slivers of the moon peeked through the angry clouds, enough for her to see that he was right.

Beyond the waves was a small, ugly building, like a dark block of stone thrusting up from the sea. Only one story high, it stood on an island not much larger than it was, the distance between the black water and the walls a mere thirty feet at most.

The boat docked at a tiny wharf that appeared even more rundown than it was. Isaksson thanked the captain and stepped out, still carrying her. His strides were as assured and quick as ever. He didn't seem to care that a full grown woman was wrapped around his back like an octopus.

Olivia tried to shield her face from the biting wind as best she could and nestled it in the crook of his neck. When the tip of her nose touched his warm skin, they both jerked.

Olivia quickly pulled away. She couldn't *wait* to get inside and be on her own two feet again. After that, she would have no choice but to threaten Isaksson not to breathe a word of this to another soul, under pain of death. Especially not to Adeline. If she found out, her assistant would never let her live this down.

"All right, we're coming up to the wards. Don't move," the Warden instructed her quietly.

He released his power and wrapped it around both of their forms. Olivia could see a faint blue sheen appear at the edges of her vision.

She felt the exact moment they entered the wards. There was pressure against her skin, the sense of magic enveloping them. Thankfully, their trick seemed to work and they emerged on the other side, unscathed.

After a few more quick strides, Isaksson cracked open a heavy steel door and stepped inside the building.

The room they entered wasn't very large, with only a desk and a few chairs lining the walls, and two doors at the back, marked as staff quarters. The majority of the space was taken up by a massive hole in the centre, where a tiny elevator lay suspended at the end of a steel cable.

Olivia audibly gulped.

A guard was on duty behind the desk, looking as if he was struggling to keep his eyes open. Next to him, a massive open book rested on a wooden pedestal.

This had to be the register that recorded every arrival and departure from the Cellars that Isaksson had told her about. He'd warned her that he had no idea how the would-be thieves had managed to avoid it, and so the book would record their own passage, cloaking spell or not. But he'd assured her that the guard on duty wouldn't bother to look at the register, not with the Warden on the premises. A security flaw they would use to their advantage, and one he would remedy as soon as they returned from Romania.

Isaksson greeted the guard and asked him how his artifacts had behaved.

"We caught a situation, but everybody's calm now." He shrugged. "Turns out 'twas a false alarm."

Famous last words, Olivia thought with a wince.

Isaksson seemed to think the same because he groaned, "Never say that, man. Don't you know it's bad luck? Has there been a shift yet?"

At the guard's negative reply, Isaksson continued, "Right, I'm going down. If you spot Amesbury, tell him to find me straight away."

Olivia tried very hard not to choke Isaksson as he approached the never-ending pit and manually slid the grille of the elevator open.

Well, an elevator was a fancy name for what it really was. It looked more like a cage made up of crossed iron bars, that dangled above the void at the end of a thick cable and a system of pulleys.

And as Isaksson stepped inside, gods help her, it *swayed*.

Olivia's whole body clenched in terror and she gripped the lapels of his coat with white knuckles. She could feel Isaksson's chest quiver as he repressed a laugh.

She decided she didn't care any more if her grip suffocated him.

Isaksson pressed one of the brass buttons on the control panel. There were a few seconds when nothing happened and they lay there, suspended in the cage.

And then they fell.

Olivia gasped, her shriek stuck in her throat.

Alright, they weren't exactly *falling* per se, but they were hurtling down a whole lot faster than normal elevator regulations would allow.

The criss-crossing iron bars that made up the sides of the elevator cage allowed her to see everything as they spiralled down into the Underworld.

The Cellars were simply a massive cylindrical hole dug into the ground. A series of suspended metal walkways and bridges connected the levels, with stairs also lining the rock walls in a descending spiral.

They were falling too fast for her to make out the individual cells carved into the walls. Instead, they blurred together like black splotches dotting the grey stone.

Unconcerned about being trapped in a sinking cage, Isaksson patted her ankle reassuringly. "Relax, Olivia. Everything is fine, I promise."

"Everything is *not* fine, Mr Isaksson," she managed to say past her gritted teeth. "It is very far from fine! We are falling to our deaths!"

He laughed. "I do this every day, you know. And I'm still here."

"You have to do this every day?" Olivia croaked. She could scarcely believe it, her stomach was ready to jump out of her throat.

"Oh yes. Gets the blood pumpin'," the crazy Viking replied.

Olivia hissed a strangled sigh in response, and just held on.

Down they went, until it seemed they must be halfway to Hells by now, but the cage finally came to a stop after one last abrupt jolt.

When Olivia remained perfectly still and made no move to get off his back, Isaksson cleared his throat. "*Älva?* Did you notice we stopped?"

She said nothing, so he tried again, "The coast is clear, and the cloaking spell is still active. You can come down. No one will see you."

Olivia unclenched her jaw enough to hiss, "I don't think I can move."

That made him laugh, *again*.

"Allow me," he said and gently but firmly, dislodged her legs from around his waist.

The Warden pushed open the gate to the elevator cage and sauntered out as if he'd just enjoyed an invigorating evening stroll. He made a flourishing gesture with his hand. "Ms Knight, welcome to the Wheel."

Olivia glared at his broad back as she followed at a much slower pace. She had to grit her teeth and her legs shook uncontrollably, but at least her blood was *"pumpin'."*

She didn't ask him why this place was called the Wheel. Thanks to her unobstructed view as they'd plummeted down, she could guess it was because of all the suspended walkways radiating out from the elevator shaft, like the spokes of a wheel.

They weren't even at the lowest level, having stopped about halfway down this never-ending pit, and were now walking on clanking metal that didn't fill her with the utmost confidence.

Around the suspended platforms, a multitude of torches had been placed against the rough surface of the walls. The air was stuffy and damp, as you'd expect in underground tunnels, but strangely not as unpleasant as she would have thought. Her mind must have been playing tricks on her, but she swore she could even feel a semblance of a refreshing salty breeze on her face, as if they were in a cave near the ocean rather than hundreds of feet underground.

It was mostly quiet, save for the clatter of the elevator going up and down and the sounds of guards walking the pathways, with the occasional muffled conversation or whistled tune. Beneath it all, Olivia could detect a faint hum in the air, a slight vibration she was very familiar with and only came from the proximity with powerful artifacts.

Each cell was nothing more than a crude hole dug into the stone walls, the edges of the entrance rough and uneven. There were two rows of cells for each level, the upper one accessed by the most unregulated-looking system of ladders Olivia had ever seen.

The barriers guarding the cells were much more elaborate. Twisting diaphanous bars locked in a complicated pattern shifted and swayed, as if made of pure smoke. Olivia had expected sturdy silverstone and was fascinated by this unknown substance.

But before she had a chance to brush her fingers against one of the smoke bars, a young man in a guard's uniform suddenly appeared in their path.

He looked to be in his twenties, with a mop of tousled brown curls that he'd unsuccessfully tried to tame with some pomade. It was even worse than Isaksson's hair when he ran his hand through it in frustration. The young man's crazy curls contrasted with his very serious expression and his tightly pressed uniform. Only his eyes brought some warmth to his face, sparkling with intelligence and wit.

"Amesbury," the Warden greeted him. "Who's in charge of the dark sectors tonight?"

"I am, sir."

Isaksson sighed. "Amesbury, I may not have been here long, but believe me, I know what's going on. This is the third time."

The young guard grimaced. "It was supposed to be Glover's shift, but he asked me to cover it."

Olivia heard Isaksson's voice harden. "What you mean is that he didn't show up for his shift because he got scared and you had to cover him so there wouldn't be a hole in the patrolling grid. I'll talk to him, but later. Right now, I need you to come with us."

Amesbury fell into step beside him with a frown, but didn't ask any questions.

They all entered Isaksson's office, where a simple desk took up most of the space, leather chairs on either side. A tall bookcase stood against one wall, much like the one Olivia had in her own office, with large filing drawers at the bottom. On the other side of the room, the wall had been completely covered in wood panelling and filled with hundreds of tiny doors. Rows of protective runes had been carved down the sides.

"I'm going to lift the cloaking spell, Olivia," was the only warning Isaksson gave before she felt his magic release her.

Amesbury jumped when she suddenly materialised a few feet away from him.

They'd agreed that Isaksson would be the one to provide the cloaking spell so that he would still be able to see her. Besides, this kind of magic wasn't Olivia's forte. She hadn't wanted a random arm to pop up into existence if her concentration slipped.

She held out her hand to Amesbury with a smile, greatly enjoying his look of astonishment. "Evening. It's nice to meet you. I'm Olivia Knight."

The young guard stared at her outstretched hand. "I . . . You're . . . Edward Amesbury."

Meanwhile, Isaksson had unfolded a map on his desk, placing a bottle of whisky and three glasses on each corner to hold it in place. Olivia peered at the label: Bowmore 12 Years Old. Not bad, the Viking had good taste.

"Amesbury," he said. "You'll be relieved to know that tonight is the night that wretched wand is leaving us. Ms Knight is a curse-breaker, she'll help me transport it out of the Cellars."

The young guard frowned. "But what about . . ." he started to say, then understanding blossomed on his face. "Ah, so that's what you've been doing."

The Warden grinned, mighty pleased with himself. "I hid a fake wand in the cell. When Crowley—"

Olivia's head snapped up. "What about Crowley?"

"He'll be here tomorrow to pick up the fake. They're supposed to catch a Portal—"

"A *Portal*? Crowley is taking what he thinks is the real wand through a Portal?"

"It's not just any Portal," Isaksson explained. "There's a specialised Ministry one in—"

"It doesn't matter if it's a specialised one, the wand would have broken it going through! Not to mention, I don't think the Portal itself would have let it come near. What the hells is he thinking?"

Isaksson sighed and shared a look with Amesbury. The young guard kept a straight face, but couldn't hide his twitching lips.

"Olivia, please don't forget we're the ones with the real wand, yes?" the Warden said in an aggravated voice. "Now, can I please explain what the plan is without you interrupting me every five seconds?"

"Fine," she muttered. "But for the record, you're damn lucky to have me as the curse-breaker on this job." She said it without any excessive pride, she just couldn't believe the recklessness with which Crowley was handling this case.

"Believe me, I am well aware," Isaksson replied. "Right, we only have—"

An urgent knock on the door cut him off.

The Warden had to close his eyes for a moment.

He finally went to crack open the door to his office, and returned with a telegram. His slight frown turned into a full-blown scowl as soon as he'd finished reading it. "We're about to have company."

"What do you mean?" Olivia asked him.

"Skelton and Crowley are on their way." He flashed them an impish grin. "Guess they're afraid I'll do something foolish."

What an irrational notion, Olivia thought sarcastically. "How much time do we have?"

"Not long."

"Let's get to it, then." She immediately reached inside her leather bag and unwrapped the containment cage from an old hand-knitted scarf, Amesbury and Isaksson leaning in close.

All around the thin glass cylinder, where the wand would later be suspended, she'd etched an intricate design of interconnected circles and runes, each line turned to molten starlight by the combination of her threads of power and crushed moonstone crystals.

"I'm no specialist, but looking at it, this containment feels definitely powerful. I think it might just work," the Warden said.

Olivia's eyebrows rose. It *felt* powerful and *might* just work? "I sure appreciate the confidence, O Mighty Warden."

Of course, Isaksson immediately tapped his finger on the glass. Just like a child trying to make the fish in an aquarium react.

"These lines are incredibly precise," the young guard told Olivia as he examined her work attentively. "You used moonstone powder, didn't you? For its ability to channel energy."

Finally, someone who knew what they were talking about.

"Yes, exactly," Olivia replied. "Besides, moonstone crystals have the added benefit of being extremely stable. With this type of construct, you need very steady materials."

"Ah, I see. Why not something more powerful, though? Like feyroot?"

"Amesbury, stop flirting with my curse-breaker," a gruff voice interrupted.

The young guard smiled, revealing two adorable dimples in his cheeks, while Olivia sputtered, "Excuse me! I am not *your* anything."

But Isaksson ignored her as he marched over to the wood-panelled wall, his eyes sweeping over the multitude of doors, each marked with a series of runes. Opening one revealed a bright silver, very odd-looking key, hanging from a hook by a leather string.

It resembled a thin metal rod with no teeth, engraved with symbols along its length. At the top was a sphere that could roll in every direction as it was encased in concentric circles, like a miniature globe.

"Is that really where you keep the keys to the artifacts?" Olivia remarked. "That doesn't look very . . . secure." She'd expected a vault or a large chest, with booby traps and hidden mechanisms that shot fireballs.

Isaksson chuckled at her cautious tone. "Believe me, these are no ordinary keys."

"Is that a tiny compass at the top?" Olivia craned her neck as she tried to get a good look at the *key* he held possessively in his hand. Without thinking, she tried to grab it from him, but he easily evaded her.

"Sorry, *Älva*. Can't let you touch it. Secret Warden business."

She was so curious that she didn't even reply when he used her ridiculous nickname once again. Her gaze shifted from his clenched fist to the unrolled map on his desk. "Why would you need a compass to find the cells, you've got a map. Unless . . ." She gaped at him then, her eyes widening with the realisation. "The cells are *moving*."

Isaksson didn't answer, but he had a smug smirk on his face that was as much confirmation as a resounding yes.

"Wow," she breathed.

So that must have been what he'd meant when he'd asked the guard if the "shift" had happened. He'd wanted to know if the cells had moved yet.

She leaned in close to study the crinkled map. Lines of brown ink marked the structure of the Cellars, made up of a nightmare of interlinked levels, all arranged around the central elevator shaft. Unnamed blocks marked the individual cells, which had been carved out absolutely wherever they would fit.

"How are we going to find the right cell if they keep moving?" Olivia asked them.

"I really shouldn't be discussing this with you . . ." Isaksson mumbled, then resigned himself to explain: "We get a shift every day. But in theory, they could happen at any time, especially if the Cellars get spooked." On the map, his finger tapped the jumble of paths and detours that was the Wheel. "There hasn't been one yet, but I can guarantee it's going to happen, especially after we start messing with the wand."

"What do you suggest?" Amesbury asked. "Should we wait for the shift? What if it's late?"

Isaksson grinned. "Then we make it happen sooner."

The young guard made a sound of understanding. "You're going to provoke a shift."

"Exactly. I want you to go on your security round, locate the O'Brien Widow's music box and release it."

Olivia's head snapped up. "*O'Brien?*"

She knew all about the O'Brien mansion, and the countless ghosts of family ancestors that had been crammed into a little music box by the Lord's widow. She'd left it behind as a parting gift after her cruel brother-in-law had ordered her to leave her home.

"It should make enough of a wave to wake the Cellars, but isn't too dangerous." Isaksson turned to Olivia. "You agree?"

She nodded, excitement shining in her eyes. "Yes. And you know, if he's going to handle a cursed artifact, maybe I should go with him. You know . . . as backup."

Both men stared at her with knowing looks.

"Nice try, *Älva*. But I need you with me when we search for the wand's cell. You know, for the transfer we're trying to make?"

Olivia sighed. "Fine."

"Right. We'll wait for Amesbury to provoke the shift. Then we'll use the key to locate the right cell, we'll extract the wand, replace it with the decoy and get out of here. Any questions?"

Olivia and the young guard both shook their heads.

"Let's do it then." Isaksson opened the door to his office, but put a hand on Amesbury's arm before he could walk out. "Be careful," he told him.

"Looks like the wand is behaving itself for now," Olivia declared when Isaksson came back in.

The Warden groaned and threw up his hands. "Great! Now you've jinxed it."

He marched to a corner of his office and threw open the doors to a small armoire.

Olivia huffed out an exasperated breath. "I didn't *jinx* anything. It was a simple observation. The wand hasn't reacted since we entered the Cellars with the—"

The sudden shriek of the alarm made her jump.

Oops.

Isaksson turned to her, his eyes accusing. "See? I told you, you jinxed it!"

Olivia's eyes widened when she saw the short sword in his hand. "Ah . . . Is that really necessary?"

Amesbury burst into the office then, out of breath and his eyes wild. "Warden!"

"What's going on out there! What happened?" he exclaimed.

CHAPTER 15

"It's . . . the shift!" the young guard managed to get out between panted breaths. He looked as if he'd just run down the entirety of the Cellars like the flames of hells were after him.

Isaksson grabbed his shoulder. "Amesbury, breathe! What do you mean, it's the shift? Did you free the O'Brien? Did it work?"

"No, I didn't have time!" Amesbury paused to take in some much-needed air. His words came in quick, breathless bursts. "All the cells keep shifting, they won't stop! The artifacts are going crazy!"

CHAPTER SIXTEEN

They stormed out of Isaksson's office and crashed into pure pandemonium.

Guards were running every which way, up and down the stairs, clanking along the metal pathways, bumping into each other. Shouted warnings and cries for help echoed from every direction. The air was thick with smoke and iron.

All three of them ran to the elevator shaft and looked down. Olivia grabbed Isaksson's shirt as he went right to the very edge, unconcerned about the free fall that awaited him if he lost his footing.

On the lower levels, the cells lining the walls appeared and disappeared in a mad rhythm. They were being swallowed and spat out by the stones, blasts erupting from the artifacts within. And above it all, the shriek of the alarm continued to echo, drowning out thoughts and battering against their ears.

The wand was awakening all the artifacts in the Cellars, one by one, like a terrible wave.

Amesbury pointed down. "Looks like it's stopping at level eight!"

But the wand wouldn't just *stop*, and the wave kept growing. It swallowed that level, prompting an eerie, high-pitched scream and a roll of thunder, accompanied by flashes of white as the artifacts came into range.

Isaksson's eyes widened. He swore. "*Jävla!* That was the Mirror!"

Amesbury shared an alarmed look with him. "Which means its neighbour is next!"

CHAPTER 16

Olivia's hands turned into claws around Isaksson's shoulders as he leaned even further into the void. "You're going to fall down!" she screamed.

But the Warden ignored her, instead barking a series of orders to the guards running below. "Bring me all the silverstone, we need to seal off the levels! Chains, net, whatever we have! Amesbury, grab the obsidian mirrors and bring them down here!"

"What's going on?" Olivia asked as the young guard ran off. "What's its neighbour?"

"A cup that absorbs energy. The Cup of . . . ah . . . " Isaksson frowned. "It's silver. There are ugly little faces all around it."

"The Lunar Chalice?" Olivia shrieked, her jaw dropping in shock. "The Chalice that can consume everything within a thirty foot radius? Including the wards locking all your cells? *That* Chalice?"

"That's the one! But don't worry about the wards, it's one of the most stable artifacts we have," Isaksson replied as he met her gaze.

As one, they rushed towards the spiralling staircase.

"If you have the Lunar Chalice, then you must have the Sun one, too!" Olivia panted as they all but flew down the stairs. "Please tell me you didn't put them together!"

She'd pressed a steadying hand against the wall and felt the rough stones grow progressively icier.

"Does a ceiling count?" Isaksson yelled over his shoulder.

"What?"

"They're like twins! Why wouldn't you put them together?"

"Because they feed off each other! Do you even *know* how they work?"

A running guard, his face blotchy and red from the exertion, passed Isaksson who promptly picked up the heavy silverstone netting in his arms and slung it over his own shoulder with barely a grunt. He didn't even stop running.

"I'm warning you, when this is all over," Olivia managed to get out between ragged breaths. "You'd better hire me for an expert audit!"

Isaksson slowed as they neared the Lunar Chalice.

The bars on the cell were gone. Thin, silver veins had spread from it and up the walls, bringing rivulets of magic towards the Chalice, sucking the power from the walls, the wards, the nearby artifacts... anything they could reach.

Inside the cell, the faces of the saints carved into the blue-hued metal, glowed as the artifact absorbed all this power surrounding it. The small platform on which it rested was encased in a thick layer of ice, and sharp icicles hung from the ceiling.

But what stole Olivia's breath was what she could just make out in the cell above.

The Sun Chalice was floating upside down, its golden metal blinding. Small grains of sand wafted through the air like dust. It was an almost perfect replica of the one below, but where the Lunar Chalice took energy, this one *radiated* it.

Crackling golden vines flared from the cup, spreading as quickly as the icy ones from its twin. Before Olivia's very eyes, the rivulets grew and grew, until the streams became rivers of molten metal, suffused with magic. The glow from the two metals intensified, the cups vibrated.

As the Lunar Chalice swallowed it all, bloating itself with energy, the Solar one expelled it.

Finally, the Chalices could take no more, and two violent jets of power erupted, gushing out like water from a geyser. A golden stream surged out, shot through with amber flakes, so bright it hurt to look at. It sank right down to the stone floor, and reappeared in the cell of the Lunar Chalice below, this time silver-blue, sparkling with lightning and holding shards of ice.

"Olivia!" Isaksson cried, but she could only stare transfixed at the powerful display of the Chalices' magic.

The suspended walkways shook beneath their feet. The air grew thinner, as if they'd scaled the top of a mountain.

The Warden had to shake her arm to get her attention. "Any expert advice would be appreciated!"

"Ah..."

CHAPTER 16

A yell rang out. To their right, guards dropped to the floor in the nick of time as a beam of pure energy shot out of a cell, a colourful ray sizzling with power that crashed into a wall, leaving a blackened and smoking crater.

Then jets of what looked like ruby shards erupted from another cell, and only Isaksson's lightning-fast reflexes prevented them from stabbing Amesbury right in the chest. The young guard had returned with his arms full of shiny, black, palm-sized obsidian mirrors, which he was handing out to the others. Olivia understood that they were preparing to use them to generate a level-wide null field.

Isaksson pulled off the heavy piece of silverstone netting draped over his shoulder, ready to rush in and throw it over the Chalice, but she grabbed him. "That won't do anything, once the Chalices have bonded, there's no stopping them!" She ducked to avoid another stream of ruby shards. "The only thing to do is to get the wand out of there, it's the reason they're behaving like this!"

Isaksson whirled around and bellowed a volley of orders at the frantic guards, trying to make himself heard over the still shrieking alarm and the thundering artifacts. "Everyone, evacuate the dark levels! Protocol W̄-9! Burgess, Coleman, as soon as we're down, activate the mirrors and seal off the levels on either side of these Chalices. I want no less than eight men on those fields, understood? Everybody else, gather all the silverstone you can find!"

Before Olivia could ask him questions, Isaksson had grabbed her hand and was pulling her into a run. Amesbury followed as they dashed along the metallic pathways and then down the spiralling stairs.

While they descended the levels, dodging beams of energy or shots of dragonfire that scorched the air, the atmosphere changed. It became heavy, oppressive, as if a storm was about to break. It was also so cold that Olivia could see each one of her ragged breaths.

At least the sounds were muffled. The shrill of the alarm faded to the point where it seemed to be coming from another building entirely.

The Warden pulled out his strange-looking key and waved it around, trying to locate the wand among the shifting cells. "This way!"

They followed him as he took a hard left through a tunnel dug into the wall. And then they sprinted down a dark corridor, up a small flight of stairs, to the left again, then down. Olivia quickly lost track and just focused on watching where she was going as the torches became fewer and fewer.

But that didn't stop her from gasping suddenly and crashing to a halt, her eyes wide.

Turning back around, she ran a few paces until she reached the sight that had stopped her dead in her tracks. Her hands gripped the shadowy bars of the cell. "The Robes of Fate!" she breathed in utter awe.

Strong arms grabbed her around the waist and she was unceremoniously lifted into the air. She had no choice but to let go of the icy bars as Isaksson carried her forward, still running.

Whenever they passed guards, the Warden would direct them to the Wheel to help seal off the affected levels. They careened down yet *another* flight of stairs then came to an abrupt halt.

Olivia narrowly avoided crashing into Isaksson's back. Panting hard, she put her hands on her knees, her laboured breaths wheezing out of her. "What is it?" she managed between gasps. "What's wrong?"

No one answered. Straightening up, she noticed that Isaksson and Amesbury were staring straight ahead, transfixed.

She tried to crane her neck, but couldn't see anything from her position, hidden behind the Warden's broad back. With no other choice, she ducked under his arm to get to the front. The sight that greeted her made all the hairs on her arms stand up.

Ghostly figures stood at the end of the corridor. Made of bright green mist and slowly gaining shape, they lay there motionless. More wisps of smoke slithered out of the walls to join them, slowly turning into shadows of men. Swords hung from their sides. Some wore what could be a helmet.

Olivia opened her mouth to speak, but then the sounds began.

They were faint at first, just a whisper, a vibration in the air. But they grew.

Boots.

Boots stomping on the floor and the clinking of metal against metal. The whole corridor echoed with it. The rustle of fabric, the sound of swords leaving their sheaths. And then voices joined in.

Suddenly they were all around them. Echoing from every direction, seemingly coming from the stones of the Cellars themselves. The voices turned angry. Someone cried out in a language Olivia vaguely recognised, begging for mercy. An anguished scream pierced the air, a cry of despair. It brought tears to her eyes.

Swords clashed, blows fell. Olivia smelled tar, smoke and the overwhelming stench of blood.

She felt the chill lingering in the air wrap around her, smothering her. It grew stronger, tangible. The cold weight pressed against her chest, an irresistible torpor creeping through her entire body.

Olivia froze completely. She was so numb, cold. Afraid.

A part of her brain registered that this feeling was somewhat familiar, and she came back to her senses with a jolt. The apparitions had almost managed to Lock her In.

Unfortunately for the wand, she was a curse-breaker and knew all the tricks.

She wrestled savage breaths from her uncooperative body. Willed her heart rate to pick up, shook her head to clear her mind of the icy fog.

Forcing herself to turn her back on the apparitions, she saw that Isaksson and Amesbury were still rooted to the spot, staring at the ghoulish visions.

Olivia's fingers were frozen solid, but she forced them to grab Amesbury's sleeve and punch Isaksson in the arm. It took her a few tries to find her voice, but when she finally did, she shouted, "Don't look directly at them! Close your eyes if you can't turn your head!"

She pulled on Amesbury's uniform and dug her fingers into Isaksson's biceps, but they only stirred slightly. So she gritted her teeth, raised her arm high and slapped Isaksson across the cheek. *Hard.*

The Viking came to with a gasp and stared at her wide-eyed.

"You with me?" she asked briskly, before turning to Amesbury.

"Are you going to slap me again if I say no?" Isaksson winced, working his jaw. "You sure pack a punch for such a tiny hand, *Älva*."

They didn't have time for a more delicate approach, so Amesbury's cheek got the same treatment as his boss. The young guard stumbled back, let out a pained groan, then shook his head to clear it.

"What *are* those things? What happened?" Isaksson narrowed his eyes but avoided looking at the apparitions.

"That was Locked-In Syndrome, wasn't it?" Amesbury asked. "What Type Two curses can do."

Isaksson raised his compass-key and swore. "*Helvete*! We can't go that way!"

Clearly, the compass didn't care that their path was blocked by greenish silhouettes that were getting closer and closer.

"We need the map—"

Olivia shove it against his chest.

The Warden stared at her, looked down at the map, sputtered. "How-You . . . You stole the map from my desk?"

"I did not steal it, it's right there in your hands!"

Something shifted behind her in the shadows of the corridor. A twisted silhouette, then another, and another. The apparitions were trying to surround them.

"Hurry!" Isaksson shoved Olivia through an empty corridor to their left.

They sped through another dizzying criss-crossing of paths and flights of stairs, stopping only when the Warden had to find them a new path. The trampling of boots followed them, sounding as if an entire army was on their tail.

They were racing down a curved corridor when Amesbury suddenly called out, "Look out!" He leapt over something, barely keeping his balance.

Olivia was running far too fast, so she simply jumped where he'd jumped and yelled, "What was that?"

"Roots!" He threw over his shoulder.

She tried to look down as they zipped past more corridors, but could barely make out anything in the dim light. So she followed Amesbury's lead every time he veered or jumped, his keen eyes spotting a patch of sickly green sprouting from the stone floor.

They made a sharp turn and finally caught sight of the wand's cell, easily identifiable by the thick green mist pouring out of it. Isaksson made a sharp movement with his forearm, but before they could jump into the cell, the stone wall had swallowed it back.

Isaksson cursed and slammed his hand against the stones.

Something out of the corner of her eye made Olivia whirl, and she was running before she'd fully registered the wisps draped across the floor, licking at the walls.

She was about to slam head first into the bars, but they vanished just in time for her to fly into the cell. She gulped down air, a huge grin splitting her lips. "Made it!"

From outside, she heard Isaksson laugh. "You all right in there?"

"Fine!"

The wand's resting place was tiny, more of a hole in the wall than anything. She squeezed in front of the stone pedestal where the wand rested. "I'll start the transfer, you stay out there and keep watch. If you see the apparitions again, don't look them in the eye! And whatever you do, don't let them touch you!"

There was a second of charged silence before Isaksson's voice rang out, wary. "Olivia . . . What happens if they touch us?"

"Ah . . ." To be honest, she had no idea. Cornelius and her had argued long and hard about whether the curse was a Type Three or Four, but without a proper analysis, they couldn't be sure. All she knew was that avoiding the apparitions sounded like an excellent plan.

"Just keep your hands to yourself and you'll be fine!"

She heard the Warden mutter something to himself but didn't comment. Pulling her containment cage out of her bag, she narrowed her eyes.

The wand was emitting its familiar emerald glow, along with tendrils of smoke that wrapped around it and draped over the stand. It was being far too quiet, too complacent. Olivia's skin barely prickled.

She was sure it was taunting her. This was the same artifact that had followed them all the way to the Legendarium, tried to burst out of the pages. It was the reason her days were numbered now and Pyke would try to have her head. It was the artifact that had conjured up ghostly apparitions to roam the Cellars and prodded the Chalices into causing all sorts of mayhem.

Olivia didn't trust this.

She didn't trust this one bit.

Keeping a wary eye on the wand, she studied the protections in place. Unlike the other artifacts, the Warden had added heavy wards inside its cell. Blue lines floated in the air: two connected pentagrams, held within a spinning circle holding lines of glyphs. Olivia touched one of the lines with her fingertip and it flashed white.

The Shield of Trinity.

A standard level three binding ward, but not a bad choice for this artifact. They would need Isaksson to use his Warden magic to drop it, and as soon as that happened, Olivia knew for sure that the wand would try to break free. That was why it was being so docile right now.

Olivia needed to think of it as an extremely intelligent animal. A viper, lying in ambush. Right now, it was watching her every move, patiently waiting for the perfect opportunity.

"Ah . . . Ms Knight?"

"Just a second!"

She would have to erect her own wards to make sure it couldn't escape while she pushed it inside the cage. Olivia doubted the diaphanous bars at the entrance did anything. But which ones? She only had time for a strong level three, anything higher was out of the question.

The wand was also sneaky. Olivia needed a ward that was not only strong enough to withstand a direct hit, but also one that didn't have many weak points, otherwise the wand might find a way to slither in.

"Olivia?" the Warden called.

"I'm a little busy here, gentlemen!" she yelled back.

A Vector Equilibrium would have been perfect, but it was quite complicated and required a lot of precision. Perhaps a Valentijn Lock would do the trick. It wasn't as strong, but the weaknesses weren't obvious, so the wand wouldn't have time to find them before she stuffed it into her cage.

"Olivia!" Isaksson tried again. She could hear a hint of annoyance creeping into his voice. "Amesbury and I would very much appreciate it if you could come out and see this."

Groaning, she stepped back towards the entrance of the cell, making sure to keep one foot inside so the walls wouldn't swallow the cell up again.

As soon as her head emerged, though, she froze. "Ah."

Isaksson was standing in the middle of the corridor, his back to her. A glance over her shoulder revealed Amesbury on the other side, also facing away. And they were both staring at the guards who stood frozen in place, looking back at them with unseeing eyes.

"Huh, Cornelius was right," Olivia said with a tilt of her head. "That curse is definitely a Type Four."

"What?"

"Well, you see, Type Threes can impact some sort of desire onto you, but it's nowhere near as strong as Type Fours, which can almost—"

"Is *that* what happens if the ghosts touch us?"

Olivia didn't need to reply. An eerie acid-green sheen rolled over the guards' irises and they started towards them. Pistols clicked out of their holsters, batons left their belts. A few hands wrapped themselves in magic.

Amesbury took a few steps back, his hand wrapping over his own weapon.

"Both of you, get inside the cell!" Olivia exclaimed. "Isaksson, you can lock it, that should hold them off!"

A shield of bright, shimmering blue erupted around the Warden. He widened his stance, rolled his shoulders back, his magic gathering just beneath his skin. There was a wolfish grin on his face and his eyes all but glowed as he glanced back at her. "Take care of the wand with Amesbury, I'll hold them off!"

As if in response to his bravado, ghostly apparitions came out of the walls to stand among the compelled guards. That only made the Viking laugh.

He beckoned them with his hand. "Bring it! The more, the merrier!"

Olivia rolled her eyes as she ducked back into the cell, Amesbury right behind her. She muttered a prayer asking for patience, and furiously rifled through her bag. She was about to turn it upside down when she finally found the belt of black salt grenades she'd stolen from Cornelius, and thrust it at Amesbury. "Here, give that to your boss."

"What is it?"

"Trust me, he'll like it."

As the young guard dashed outside the cell, Olivia turned back to the wand.

Right. The ward would have to be done quickly and it would have to be precise. She rolled up the sleeves of her shirt, straightened her shoulders. A smile spread across her lips. *Here we go.*

With a fleeting thought, she realised that she had to look exactly like Isaksson right now.

She visualised the shape of the Lock in her mind, concentrating on the lines, the geometry.

"What can I do to help?" Amesbury asked her.

She reached into her waistcoat for her curse-breaking wand. Working in the Cellars, she guessed the young guard had to own a pretty powerful wand, but hers would be more effective against the curse. "Use that."

Amesbury's brows rose, but he took it without question.

There was a loud *bang* from outside their cell, followed by a delighted cry and a laugh. "Ha! I love those things!"

Olivia's hands rose as she called upon her magic. It bathed her fingers in copper light and she began to draw the first pentagram in the air.

Just as she'd predicted, a spectral arm pushed through the stones of the cell, reaching for her. Looked like the wand was done acting nice and wanted to play.

Amesbury didn't even hesitate. He raised her wand and blasted at the shadowy fingers.

Another *bang* sounded, then another and another. The air began to smell of burning salts.

As Olivia drew the second pentagram, grabbing tight onto her concentration, she saw three more translucent arms stretch out of the stone, long-fingered and bony. Amesbury fired at them in quick succession.

Around the wand, the tendrils of mist that had been lying still now flexed and undulated, writhing like snakes. The stomping of boots returned, making the ground shake. Olivia heard the sound of a sword leaving its sheath, followed by a Viking's roar.

Greenish roots sprouted from the cracks in the stone floor. A ghostly hand reached out behind her, straining to grasp her shoulder, but Amesbury was faster. He drew his own wand with his left hand and pulverised it. He moved to stand at her back, both wands raised.

A flash of light caught her eye. Isaksson had pulled back until he was standing near the entrance to the cell, swinging his sword at the greenish apparitions.

Roots were hanging down from the ceiling now, slithering along the walls. The spectral hands were coming from everywhere. Amesbury kept blasting them away, sweat dripping down his temples. He barely blinked.

"Almost there!" Olivia groaned as she drew the glyphs as fast as she could. "Isaksson! Get ready to pull the wards back!"

A green root wrapped around her ankle. She didn't allow her hands to falter a single second. Even as she felt it slither up her leg.

The second pentagram armed itself with an audible *clink*. It joined with the first, pulsing with power. The outer circle began to spin and the glyphs suspended in the air sparked bright copper.

The entire ward radiated light and a solid wall of magic, like a barrier of translucent metal, formed around the artifact.

"Now!" Olivia shouted, and the previous blue lines vanished.

Pure power erupted from the wand. Tendrils of mist burst out and collided with her new defences.

Olivia tried to pull them into the cage. They resisted.

So she called to her magic, leaving herself open, and dangled it in front of the wand.

She didn't stop to think about how reckless she was being, just focused on drawing the curse in and into the cage. She made her power shiny and bright, sparkling with life.

The wand didn't hesitate. It went after her power like a hungry raptor after its prey. It swooped down, writhing tendrils turning into razor-sharp claws, ready to sink into her magic, but Olivia slammed down the lid of the cage and caught it.

For a while she could only stand frozen in place, her arms still outstretched. Sweat drenched her hairline and her heart pounded furiously in her chest. That had been close.

Too close.

She swore she could feel phantom scratches where the curse had almost caught her.

The icy sensation around her leg disappeared. The green roots and shadowy hands that had invaded the cell vanished into smoke. The roar of battle faded.

"Well," a deep voice said into the sudden silence. "I'd say that worked."

CHAPTER SEVENTEEN

"Let me do the talking. Try to act natural, like you've been here before. But be on your guard. Don't touch anything. Don't look at anything. And whatever you do, don't draw attention to yourself. Or to anyone else." Cornelius rattled off rules one after the other, his voice crisp and stern, a far cry from his usual Louisiana drawl. "We want to get in and out as quickly as possible."

"*Cornelius,*" Olivia growled.

He'd been rambling on ever since they'd entered the nondescript alley, or snyckelwynd, tucked to the side of the Three Cranes Inn in York, to emerge all the way up north, in Edinburgh's Candlemaker Row.

"Liv, there's still time to go back," he insisted. "*Down Below* is a rather... unsavoury place, as Godwyn would say." His eyes flickered to the bag at her hip. "If they sense it, they won't hesitate to attack us."

"Which is why I've brought along some big muscles to protect us."

Isaksson visibly perked up at that. "Are we talking about me?"

"And what if it starts acting up again?" Cornelius insisted. "What if you can't control it? We should have left it at the office."

Olivia rolled her eyes. "You're beginning to sound like our dear Baron. You know as well as I do that the black market will be filled with counterfeits. I'm not sure I can tell the difference between fake ophite stones and the real deal. But the wand will."

When his eyes darted to her bag again, she hurried to ask. "Tell me more about it. How often does the market change location? And do the police really not know where it is?"

Cornelius sighed at her obvious attempt to deflect. "It doesn't move, only the entrance switches. There are many all throughout the city, but only one is ever in use at a time. You also need a token to get in." He gave her a warning look. "And don't ask me how you get one."

She wasn't going to.

"So the police never come?" Olivia eyed the silhouettes moving around the graves as they entered Greyfriars Kirkyard, clearly not resembling weeping mourners.

"Oh, they know. But a raid would be much more trouble than it's worth. People have got used to being constantly on the move. If a detective ever showed his face, you wouldn't find anything more dangerous down there than a class two amplifier."

Olivia noticed Isaksson shooting her a sideways glance. It was the fourth one since they left the office, and she knew it had nothing to do with their destination. "Come on, ask."

"I still can't believe Griffin Holmes is your family friend!" he exclaimed.

Olivia immediately shushed him. "Not so loud!"

At their surprised looks, she winced. "I don't think mentioning his name in here is such a great idea." Because a good portion of the *unsavoury* people inhabiting these parts were sure to have a history with the Purveyor of Favours.

"I also don't want him to ever find out we were here," she added. "He's like the boogeyman. Just saying his name might bring him out."

"Are you afraid of him?" Isaksson asked her. "I thought you said he was a friend."

That made her laugh. Of course, she was afraid of him, who wouldn't be?

"My father used to do a lot of work for him and his husband, restoring artifacts they brought back from their travels," she explained. "I remember seeing them a lot as a child. When my father died, they decided to watch over me. They're like . . . my two fairy godfathers."

After losing her father in a tragic accident eight years ago, and when they weren't off on some crazy adventure on the other side of the world, Michael and Griffin had become a constant presence in her life. Sometimes

Michael would drop by the agency for an evening chat with a bottle of aged whisky and some slightly psychedelic tea. Other times, each member of her team would receive an invitation — handwritten on thick paper, of course — to dinner at their home.

"Isaksson, if we're discovered, I should warn you. They can be a little . . . unusual. You must promise me you'll be on your best behaviour."

The Warden narrowed his eyes. "Unusual how?"

"Let's just say that everything you've ever heard about them, especially Griffin, is both completely fabricated and also very true."

Cornelius had been shaking his head at her. Now, he laughed. "I find it hilarious, *cher*, that you're more afraid of being found out by Holmes than you are of entering a den of cut-throat thieves and smugglers."

"That's because I've got my priorities straight."

They followed Cornelius as he weaved his way through the weathered and crumbling headstones, his eyes studying the statues and grave markers. From the pocket of his vest, he retrieved his strange, copper coin and paused before a statue of a weeping angel. Beneath it lay a tombstone, the engraved inscription faded with age.

"Here lies Sir Lancaster's grave," Cornelius said as he removed his hat and knelt before the statue.

Amidst the wet leaves and patches of moss, a small symbol had been hidden between two folds of the angel's wings. An arcane character, meaning "Key."

Cornelius placed his coin directly atop the etched symbol. "He was a constable in the 1840s and dedicated his long career to putting thieves and criminals behind bars."

"And now his grave is the gateway to the black market," Olivia commented. "They certainly have a sense of humour."

Cornelius closed his eyes and whispered something under his breath.

There was a rasping sound as the tombstone slid to one side, revealing not the decaying remains of Sir Lancaster, but a deep black hole.

Olivia couldn't help the shiver that ran down her spine. The entrance loomed ahead like the open maw of some great monster.

Cornelius threw a glance over his shoulder. "Are you sure about this?"

Steeling her spine, Olivia nodded.

"Lead the way," Isaksson said.

Cornelius hovered his foot into the dark hole. He swung his leg around until it collided with a step that materialised from the mist, dozens more appearing after it, ready to lead them down into the tomb.

As they went down into the bowels of Edinburgh, the air growing thick with the pungent scent of damp and unknown odours, Olivia tried very hard to suppress an intense sense of foreboding.

The underground tunnels unfolded before them like the roots of some gigantic tree. Each was like a real street, with stalls draped in shadowy cloths lining each side of the narrow passage. This was like a city beneath the city, but for the forbidden and the rare.

Everywhere she turned, Olivia saw vendors hawking items of questionable origin: potions that promised miraculous effects, artifacts that exuded powerful enchantments, creatures whose eyes glinted in the shadows. The atmosphere was an almost palpable pulse of excitement and trepidation as people manoeuvred between the various stalls, some eager, focused on their quest, others wary, looking for the best price.

To Olivia, this was the sort of place where fortunes could be made or fate embraced.

"Stay close to me," Isaksson whispered to her.

The hilt of his gladius was clearly visible behind his shoulder. He was following Cornelius' instructions to the letter: not looking at anything too closely, staying on his guard, but keeping his gait relaxed. Gathering her courage, Olivia tried her best to copy him.

A low chatter enveloped them, filled with muttered conversations, hushed tones, the clinking of coins and the occasional growl or rustle of feathers. To her left, a gleaming wave of . . . *something* foul and utterly wrong was leaking from a cast-iron cauldron. She gave it a wide berth and tried to ignore the scratching sounds that seemed to be coming from within it.

Olivia marvelled at Cornelius' ability to navigate as he turned left then right, winding his way through the tunnels.

He halted at a large stall where a stooped figure sat behind the counter, eyeing them with a mixture of curiosity and deep suspicion.

"Looking for something special, dears?" the vendor croaked.

As his face tilted, it caught a beam of light from the nearby torch and Olivia nearly recoiled. His skin was a mixture of greens and yellows, textured like some deep sea monster. It also looked wet or oily, as if he'd just stepped foot on dry land.

Cornelius nodded at the strange man, the edge of a playful smile on his lips. "Something special, indeed," he drawled, then stepped closer to converse quietly.

A few other figures were examining the wares displayed on the stall. Olivia scanned the row of goods, curious yet apprehensive of what she might find. There were glass jars of strange insects suspended in formol that she didn't dare look at too closely, rare potion ingredients thrown together in wicker baskets, glowing talismans . . . and an assortment of what were advertised as "First Grade Echoes", remnants of curses that were supposedly used to power all sorts of rituals.

Olivia couldn't help the sneer that escaped her. "That piece of rock is as much an echo as the laces on my boots."

Beside her, Isaksson's chest rumbled with suppressed laughter.

As the man to her right scratched his arm with jerky movements for the third time, Olivia ventured a glance. He was wearing a coat that swallowed him whole, the hood up. His hands were hidden inside dark gloves, the stitching worn and falling apart.

She was about to take a cautious step away when she caught a glimpse of the man's face and froze.

He was Warped.

His face was unmistakable. Gaunt, with sunken eyes and hollow cheeks. On his trembling hands, the fingers had turned inward, like claws. What she'd thought was the finger of a glove splitting apart at the seam and falling off, was in fact his real finger, bent at unnatural angles.

Warping came as a result of playing with too powerful magic. Either the caster would accumulate too much power and it would destroy his body from within, or he would use every last shred of his power to complete a spell, leaving him a powerless husk.

Dracaena resin could be useful in the very early stages, when the case wasn't too advanced, but its effectiveness was still relative, and unfortunately reversing a Warping was still a very rare occurrence.

Which was why despicable individuals had begun selling what they advertised as Warped medicine. Made from dried herbs and the crushed shells of some African beetle, this remedy did nothing except pray on people's despair.

And that was precisely what the man held possessively in his gnarled hand, the other fumbling with the strap of his wallet.

When Isaksson noticed Olivia shaking with anger, he leaned close, "What's wrong?"

"This is fake."

At her words, a hushed silence spread through the market like wildfire.

The vendor with the scaly skin slowly pivoted to stare at her. His eyes were as cold as two lumps of coal. "What did you say, dearie?"

Olivia watched as darkness rolled over Isaksson's features. His hand went to her arm in warning.

But Olivia drew up to her full height. For one thing, apologising now would be a sign of weakness, and while she was no expert on black markets, she understood this: showing any fear in a place like this was a bad idea.

For another, her blood was boiling and she was far too mad to back down. "I said this is fake. There is no such thing as Warped medicine. I thought you were selling quality goods. Obviously, I was wrong." She turned to Cornelius. "Come on, let's go."

Olivia spun around and started to walk away. She tried desperately to keep her spine straight, even though she could feel the vendor's eyes boring into her back and could almost feel the cold metal of a dagger plunging between her shoulder blades.

Her fingers began to tremble, but then Isaksson's breath kissed her temple as he bent down to whisper, "Keep walking, don't look back. I've got you."

A shaky breath escaped her lips. When Cornelius subtly took the lead of their group once more, she concentrated solely on following him and not drawing any more attention to herself.

They went deeper and deeper into those tunnels, and with each new step, Olivia felt a palpable shift in the atmosphere. And it wasn't because of the scene she had caused earlier. No, this was new...

Whispers echoed through the tunnels, coming from faraway. Bits and pieces. Like a thousand voices, speaking all at once.

What is it...

Where does it come from...

It feels familiar to us...

Olivia didn't dare allow a single false step as she glanced at Isaksson. The Warden was focused on everything around them, projecting at once confidence and laziness, as if this visit to the bowels of the city was as common to him as a stroll through the gardens of Princes Street.

And she knew... Olivia knew that the haunting voices were inside her head.

What is it...

After a few more minutes of wandering through the serpentine tunnels, Cornelius finally stopped them at a particular stall. This one seemed bigger and richer than the others, with a sturdy table covered in silk, not worn cloth. It also had fewer things on display, mostly dried plants and small bottles.

But the real goods were all neatly hung on the wall behind it.

Cages.

Olivia gritted her teeth, her hands balling into fists at her sides.

Ravens, owls, exotic birds with colourful feathers, tipped in gold. All with big, frightened eyes. They were strangely silent, shrinking away from the bars, not making a sound.

Olivia's jaw ached from how hard she was clenching it. She couldn't cause a scene. Not after what she'd done with the Warped medicine. Not if they wanted to get out of these tunnels alive.

They just had to get the ophite stones. Just get the stones.

Warmth brushed her knuckles.

Olivia didn't care if it betrayed her weakness, she gripped Ryder's rough-skinned hand tightly, intertwining their fingers.

"Cornelius! It's been a long time since I've seen you down here." A spindly man was watching over the stall. He wore a large, dark hat pierced by a crimson feather straight out of a buccaneer's tale. "And you brought your boss with you, how peculiar." He chuckled in a raspy voice that sounded more like a cackle. "Don't you know this place is illegal?"

Olivia swallowed past the lump in her throat. This was the first time she'd ever met this man . . .

She forced a tight smile, pretending not to be fazed by his knowledge of her, or by the ghostly voices growing steadily louder in her head. "I wanted to see where all his money went."

That earned her a delighted cackle before he turned to Isaksson and said, "You, however. I do not know." *Yet*, his look and tone implied.

Not missing a beat, the Warden inclined his head a fraction. "Indeed," his deep voice confirmed.

"We're looking for something in particular," Cornelius declared. "Serpenthyst."

"Ophite stones, eh?" the merchant rasped, tapping his knuckles on the counter. "Dangerous business, that. And expensive."

Cornelius managed an easy smile as he waved a hand. "Ah, how you wound me! You know I'm always good for the money."

As if summoned by their words, a figure emerged from the concealed passage behind the stall, draped in a tattered cloak that seemed to absorb the light. The hood obscured the man's face, leaving only the gleam of bright, *bright* eyes.

"I hear you're in the market for ophite stones," the mysterious figure said in a low, gravelly voice as he pondered them. "Be warned. Such desires do not come cheap."

"I don't believe I've ever done business with you, *mon ami*," Cornelius replied, his Louisiana accent thickening. "But rest assured, my coin is as good as any."

The vendor cackled softly, his great feather fluttering, and the man raised his hands to pull back his hood.

Next to her, Isaksson tensed. Even Cornelius had a small reaction as Olivia took a full step back.

The man had yellow eyes, as luminous as a burning flame, slit by a long, black pupil. He stood motionless, unblinking, his stare that of a viper.

Beneath his tattered cloak, elegance dripped from every seam of him. A finely cut, charcoal grey pinstriped suit hugged his frame. Under the heavy jacket, a crisp ivory dress shirt with French cuffs peeked out, secured by silver cufflinks that glinted in the dim light.

Cornelius began bartering with the merchant, the mysterious figure remaining silent at his side while Olivia's pulse raced. The haunting voices were sounding all around her now, as if coming from right behind her shoulder.

What is it, what is it, what is it . . .
We know it . . .
What is it, what is it, what is it . . .

Oh gods, coming here had been a mistake. A terrible mistake.

"You hear them, don't you?"

Olivia's head snapped up. The cloaked man's reptilian eyes were boring into hers. His lips hadn't moved an inch, yet she'd heard his grating voice clearly.

A cold shiver ran down her spine. Ryder's fingers tightened around hers.

Looking inside herself for the shields that protected her mind, Olivia expected to find them in tatters, her soul wide open. Yet the amber light was as strong as ever, encircling her entire mind. So how had he done that?

Cornelius' voice brought her back to the present. "We'll need to inspect the merchandise first, you understand."

"Of course, of course," the vendor cackled, rubbing his hands with a wolfish edge to his smile.

The silent man parted a thin curtain between the cages to reveal a dark passage leading into the stone wall. As he turned, the tattered ends of his cloak kissed the ground. It was then that Olivia realised they'd been swaying from the moment he'd appeared, even though there was no breeze to be found anywhere in these tunnels.

He beckoned them in with a twist of his hand.

She didn't want to go inside that passage.

He waved them over again.

Gods damn it. Steeling herself, Olivia followed Cornelius into a long corridor that reeked of a distinctive metallic smell.

Blood.

They were very probably walking into a trap, but they needed those stones. Otherwise, the job would be over before it could even begin.

Another set of curtains and they entered a large chamber filled with . . . *things.*

It was as if this one room contained an entire tunnel's worth of wares. Steel crates, wicker baskets, apothecary jugs and skinny glass vials. An assortment of dried herbs and potted plants. Horns, antlers, scales. And bones, so many bones: in bundles, packaged in clear sachets, in boxes to be scooped out with a ladle.

"You shouldn't have come here," said the voice that shouldn't be in her head. *"Don't you know you're being hunted?"*

"How can you talk to me like that?" Olivia dared to ask.

No reply.

"So, where are they?" Cornelius demanded, steel creeping into his voice.

The stranger made no move.

Olivia felt herself blanch. This was a trap.

Beside her, Isaksson's hand went to the hilt of his sword. "What have you done?" he growled.

Olivia was about to summon her magic when something made her pause. She went motionless as her nape prickled in warning.

Her eyes went to the right, where another shadowy passage disappeared into the thick stone. It was pitch black inside, even though two burning lanterns glowed on either side of the entrance. And as she watched, the shadows inched slowly forward, out of the passage and inside the chamber she was standing in.

She must have made some kind of noise, for Isaksson turned his head sharply. Metal whispered as he drew his sword.

Impossibly, the shadows grew even more, slithering along the walls and creeping across the floor. Dark power rumbled through the stones, rattling the collection of glass jars on the shelves.

Oh uh . . .

Olivia stifled a grimace as the mysterious man murmured, "Purveyor."

A pair of piercing gold eyes appeared in the darkness, almost sparkling against the shadows. A figure silently emerged and approached them, taking the form of a man.

Isaksson had pivoted to face him fully, his entire body coiled like a wolf about to pounce on its prey.

Jet black hair, stroke through by a dramatic strand of pure white, framed a face with angular cheekbones, a straight aquiline nose and a sharp jaw, sheathed by dark stubble. Through all this darkness, his tawny eyes shone like two polished gold coins.

Jagged lines marred his alabaster skin, one running down his cheek to his chin, the other scoring across his left eye and brow. It added a savage edge to his otherwise aristocratic profile, turning him even more menacing.

Something he absolutely didn't need, as he already regarded them with so much piercing intensity that sweat was drenching her hairline.

"Olivia . . ." he rumbled, his voice ice. "What exactly do you think you are doing?"

Where did it go . . .

We need it . . .

We want it . . .

Olivia took an unconscious step back, assaulted by the ghostly voices ringing inside her head. A small whimper escaped her.

"You need to leave. All of you."

It was the strange man who had spoken, turning to Holmes. Meanwhile, Isaksson reached for her shoulder, concern clouding his voice. "Olivia, what's wrong?"

"You can't stay here. She'll lead them right to it," the mysterious man stated. Then he moved, his long fingers fastening on her wrist. "What are they saying?"

Isaksson immediately pushed him back to stand in front of her. "Don't touch her," he snarled.

Cornelius also took a step forward, his eyes darting between the strange man and Holmes. "Who's *they*?"

"They want it," Olivia said, her voice trembling. "They're coming."

Some sort of silent conversation passed between Holmes and the strange-eyed man before the latter thrust his chin to the dark passage on their left, from which Holmes had come. "Go. Now."

He went to the centre of the chamber and stood still with his feet firmly planted on the floor, his cape twirling around him, arms outstretched to the side and palms up.

Olivia only had time to glance over her shoulder before Holmes pushed her out. What she saw almost caused her to stumble before Isaksson wrapped an arm around her waist to propel her forward.

A small dagger had appeared in the stranger's hand. He used it to cut deep into his arm, uttering harsh words under his breath. Old magic rose, so ancient and ice-cold that it took Olivia's breath away.

A miasma of crimson smoke burst into life above his head and surged out, spiralling around him like an erupting volcano. The ruby currents of power licked the walls of the room, swirled around the ceiling, spread across the dirty floor.

Blood magic . . . The mage had just used blood magic.

The most forbidden of all.

They followed Holmes' hurried instructions and arrived before a massive well. It was old, very old. With cracked stones along the rim and moss running down the side, along with a few withered vines.

Olivia looked around with confusion. "I don't see any Portal . . . We must have made a wrong turn. We should go back and find Holmes."

He'd left them at a crossroads, saying he needed to take care of things and would meet them back at his shop.

Olivia let out a startled yelp as Isaksson's hands cupped her waist and lifted her onto the lip of the well.

"Wh-What do you think you're doing?" she squealed, her voice high.

Her entire body had locked in place, knees bent and arms outstretched. She was pretty sure her heart had stopped as well. Anything to remain perfectly still and not fall into the never-ending abyss.

"This *is* the Portal," Isaksson said.

Olivia's eyes widened as she saw him, then Cornelius, jump on the edge of the well.

"What? Oh, no. No, no, no."

"It's all right, Liv," Cornelius tried to reassure her, but she was too busy not panicking to listen to his explanation. "You'll have to jump in."

"*Jump?*"

A glance down revealed that they might not be lying. The pit inside the well wasn't a black hole as she'd feared, but lit with the same opalescence as regular Portals.

She still wasn't jumping in.

"Go on, Cornelius," Isaksson told him. "We'll be right behind you."

Cornelius nodded and let himself fall before she could stop him.

Olivia wasn't proud of the shriek that escaped her.

Then Isaksson turned to her, but she shook her head vigorously. "No, no. I can't do this."

"It's all right. Close your eyes. That's it, keep them closed."

"Really, Isaksson. I can't—" Olivia yelped when big hands lifted her, and in the next heartbeat, they were falling.

Her stomach rose to her throat, her blood roared in her ears, but then after a few moments, Olivia had to admit it wasn't so bad.

Had to be a trick.

She became aware that the Warden was laughing softly when she felt small puffs of air against her face. His deep voice landed right next to her ear.

"Olivia?" he cajoled.

Her fingers tightened and she vehemently shook her head. Her body was pressed against him, hands clutching his neck for dear life.

They were going to fall, for real this time. Any minute now.

"Olivia?" Isaksson tried again. "We're here. You can open your eyes."

What?

"You're lying. I can't feel the ground!"

He laughed again. "That, *Älva*, is because you're hanging on to my neck and you're too small."

Olivia dared open her eyes mere slits.

Ah.

Brick walls surrounded them now, and a lamppost above their heads illuminated what looked to be the corner of a deserted street. She could even see Cornelius standing a few paces away, his lips pressed together to hold back a laugh.

Olivia cleared her throat, and released the tight grip she'd had on Isaksson's neck.

"Hmm. Thank you, Warden, for your ah . . . assistance."

Isaksson sketched a bow, eyes gleaming with mirth. "My pleasure."

CHAPTER EIGHTEEN

THE SHOP FRONT WAS too small.

Olivia knew full well that the interior was a real labyrinth. So the midnight blue façade in front of her, tucked between two larger establishments advertising the finest collection of exotic teas for one, and the services of Argent & Co, a prestigious art broker for the other, was entirely too small.

With elaborate corbels and mouldings, sweeping gold letters and two spiral columns on either side etched with tiny vines, the shop front screamed elegance and old aristocracy. A multitude of antique gilded lanterns hung from the top, softly illuminating the damp street in a warm, golden glow.

"No reckless Warden shenanigans," Olivia said, cutting him a sharp look. "You promised."

"I remember," was the growled reply.

Isaksson took a step toward the finely carved door, but Olivia grabbed his arm before he had the chance to raise his big Viking fist. "Don't you dare."

He rolled his eyes, but stepped aside so that Cornelius could be the one to *gently* tap the brass lion's head knocker against the wooden frame. But before he could move, the door swung open and Michael Hastings appeared.

In his fifties, he stood tall and muscular. His skin was a rich brown, a few shades darker than Olivia's, with strong, handsome features: black eyebrows, a prominent nose, full lips and a square jaw hidden behind a short beard that held more than a little silver. His dark hair was cut close to his head. His hazel eyes, usually alight with intelligence and a touch of mischief, were at this moment dark, stern and focused on them.

"Ah. There you are."

Ignoring his severe expression, Olivia crossed the threshold to hug him. "I believe you already know what happened."

Michael was still watching Isaksson like a hawk when he drew back. "Indeed. I know all about your recent escapade. Come in, all of you."

The door closed behind them with a snap that hadn't sounded at all like a normal lock.

Walking past hundreds of rare items displayed on several heavy shelves, Michael led them to a tapestry at the back of the shop, depicting two medieval knights engaged in a duel. Pulling it aside revealed a corridor, the walls made of old, thick stones that looked as if they belonged in some ancient castle. The air that came out of it was cold and heavy.

He stepped inside first, for Olivia knew there were nasty surprises awaiting any fool who tried to enter this place unescorted. She still vividly remembered the very first time Griffin had brought her here, shadows swirling around him as he walked. She'd felt as if Count Dracula himself was escorting her through his castle. The elegant baroque of the street front seemed very distant now.

The corridor was drenched in darkness, but as soon as Michael passed, the hundreds of runes and arcane lines carved into the walls came to life, igniting around them with an intense golden fire.

At the end of the passage stood a heavy wooden door, partially closed, decorated with swirls of forged iron in the shape of two open wings. They swung open of their own accord, unveiling something that shouldn't have been possible.

The four of them were standing on a small balcony overlooking a cavernous circular chamber, wider than two ballrooms put together.

Winding staircases flanked either side of the balcony and could take them down to the main floor or along the catwalk on the second floor. That level was entirely filled with bookcases and display cases, metal railings lining the walls with rolling ladders. The books up there were old, dusty, the covers torn or completely falling apart. Some rows were even chained.

Without even thinking about it, Olivia started edging towards the books — her fingers actually tingling with the urge to caress the ancient spines — but Michael descended the stairs and Cornelius shot her an amused look. She reluctantly followed suit, running her hand along the golden banister, carved to resemble the sinuous tail of some serpentine creature.

On the ground floor, the walls were a mixture of dark wood panelling, medieval tapestries and priceless works of art in large gilded frames. Bronze statuettes rested in wall niches among antique weapons and ornate shields. A few heraldic banners hung from cast iron poles.

Michael led them to a monumental fireplace, all carved iron inlaid with green marble, darkened by age and soot. It stretched the full height of the wall to the top of the very high ceilings, its roaring fire radiating a welcomed warmth.

And illuminated Godwyn and Adeline, who sat on the sofa before it, calmly sipping tea.

Olivia felt the skin at the base of her neck tingle. She turned to see Griffin leaning against one of the marble pillars on the side, his arms crossed over his chest.

After the events of the black market, she was relieved to see him in one piece, even if the anger currently wafting out of him was obvious. "Griffin, I'd like you to meet Ryder Isaksson, the—"

"I know very well who that is," Holmes interrupted her, his voice like a whip. "You were enlisted by the Swedish Ministry to hunt down their dark relics before becoming our new Warden of the Cellars. How long you will remain as such, however, is unsure, judging by your last conversation with your Head of Department. Did I miss anything?"

Well . . . She *had* warned him that there was no point in trying to hide anything from Holmes.

The Warden threw Griffin an impudent smile. "You forgot to mention my uncanny ability to charm everyone around me."

Olivia rolled her eyes. Isaksson had no sense of self-preservation.

"I'm afraid threatening looks have an unfortunate tendency to sour tea," Michael said, his tone amused. "Come join us, all of you."

Except Griffin and Isaksson didn't stop their staring contest, each one refusing to be the first to look away.

In the end, Olivia decided to grab the Warden's arm and push him towards the sofas before thrusting a cup of tea into his hands. Adeline was watching them in turn, riveted, as though enjoying the latest episode of her favourite soap opera.

"What I would like to know," Griffin said as he turned his disturbing eyes away from Isaksson to focus on her, "is what possessed you to go nosing around *Down-Below*." His gaze dropped to the satchel held protectively at her side. "And with *that*, no less."

But Olivia had some questions of her own. "The man with the yellow eyes asked me if I could hear them, the voices. What were they?"

"Who was that man?" Isaksson asked.

"And how did you know we were there?" Cornelius cut in. "Did he tell you?"

Adeline and Godwyn's heads followed the back and forth questions, brows arching in surprise.

"Was he really a . . ." Olivia's voice trailed off under the intensity of Holmes' warning glare.

In the tense silence that followed, Godwyn leaned forward. "What *happened* to you three down there?"

Griffin didn't reply for a long time. Finally, he said, "The tunnels under the city are old, Olivia. Very old. Older than the streets above. There is forgotten magic there. Forgotten and . . . locked away. Don't bother asking me any more questions, I won't tell you." His stare was stern, unyielding. "As for that man . . . All I can say is that if you ever see him again, do *not* trust him."

Adeline leaned forward to squeeze her hand. "Liv, you and I are going to have to talk."

"What were you doing down there anyway?" Michael asked them. "What did you want?"

Olivia cleared her throat and fidgeted with the rim of her cup. She was definitely about to sour the tea. "Ophite stones. Or rather, Serpenthyst crystals."

Holmes' head snapped to her, and her mouth went dry. He speared her with a look that froze her in place, his expression almost feral as he growled, "Do *not* tell me you are trying to do what I think you are."

"We have to," Olivia replied. "It's too dangerous to stay here."

"It's also too dangerous to be moved. Not to mention you're doing exactly what it wants."

Michael laid a calming hand on his husband's arm. "I feel like I might be missing something?"

Before Olivia could open her mouth, Isaksson beat her to it. "I'm afraid our case is highly confidential. We cannot divulge any information about it. But I can assure you that Ms Knight will not be in any danger. I will keep her safe."

All three of them scowled.

Griffin and Michael, because they either didn't believe him or didn't like the idea of her ever needing safeguarding, and Olivia, because she *definitely* didn't need the protection of an arrogant Warden who had no idea what he was talking about. If *she* wasn't there to protect *him* and keep the wand in check, it would only be a matter of hours before it made Isaksson howl at the moon.

"Warden. I think the time for secrets has passed." Griffin's voice was sardonic. "We all know, all of us in this room, what artifact you're talking about. And I also know it has caused you a great deal of grief these past few months."

Beside her, Isaksson's voice remained easy as he replied, "Which is why I've hired Ms Knight. As you know, she's an expert in her field."

Ah, flattery. It was a nice try.

Michael insisted, "So I take it you're not planning to use the crystals to strengthen the wards of its cell, are you?"

This time it was Griffin who explained, rumbling between clenched teeth, "They want to take the wand back to where it came from. Back to Romania. And they plan on using the crystals for it."

"What exactly do you need them to do?" Michael asked.

Olivia winced. "I'll use them as bait to make the wand behave during transport."

Griffin closed his eyes as a sigh that sounded more like a hiss escaped him. "You," he finally growled, "are playing with fire."

Michael picked up his cup again, calmly sipping his tea as if they weren't a hair's breadth away from a duel. "That is quite something, indeed," he said. "I can only imagine the gravity of the situation if you need such a dark substance to contain that wand." His voice turned concerned. "But you need to take care, Olivia. Serpenthyst crystals are not to be messed with."

"You know me. You know I'll be careful."

Lips pressed into a tight line, Griffin walked to a corner behind the sofas where a crystal decanter sat on a glass-topped table.

"Was it the Order?" Olivia couldn't stop herself from asking. "*Down Below*?"

Slowly, so slowly, Griffin pivoted to face her. "Now. Why ever would you ask me that?" His tone was silky with menace.

Olivia glanced at the others uneasily. "The man with the yellow eyes said we were being hunted."

"And what precisely would make you think an extinct secret society, hundred of years old, might be hunting you?"

A rough-skinned hand brushed her own and Isaksson growled, "Will you stop it with the threatening looks? Just answer the bloody question."

Michael laughed softly. He turned his head to share a pointed look with his husband. Some sort of unspoken conversation passed between them before Griffin waved a hand, some of the tension finally draining from his face. "Very well. What do you know of the Order?"

Cornelius cleared his throat. "Not much. I was able to find out that the wand belonged to a Hungarian war general who was a member in the late 15th century. After his death, it most likely ended up with them."

Holmes plucked the teacup from Olivia's hands and replaced it with a thick crystal glass before doing the same with the others.

She dipped her lips into the amber liquid with the ghost of a smile. Smoked, dark, with notes of sherry and spices. That was some expensive whisky. Holmes didn't share his fancy alcohols with just about anyone. This business with the wand had obviously rattled him.

Needing to stretch her legs, she stood and walked the few steps to the impressive fireplace, examining the crest resting above it : a griffin and a stag holding a shield engraved with two crossed keys. From her father's many lessons, she knew that this crest had been carved from something called Noir de Mazy marble, its deep black highlighted with streaks of gold. Shards of amber had been set for the griffin's eyes, and Olivia could swear they were following her every move.

"There's not a whole lot in the history books," she said. "I know they almost disappeared at one point, but the House of Draculesti brought them back to life. Especially its warlord, Vlad Tepes."

Adeline made a strangled noise. "That's an interesting choice of words, Liv."

"Wait a second. Vlad Tepes..." Isaksson's voice held warning. "You don't mean... Vlad *Dracula*, do you?"

Olivia grimaced.

The Warden heaved an aggravated sigh. "Of course she does," he muttered, and took a healthy swig from his glass.

"They were a very secretive group," Cornelius continued, crossing his ankle over his knee. "Even more so than other societies. They've been involved in many conflicts in their time, but never overtly, always in the shadows. Their pursuit of powerful weapons, however, was well known. They'd been hunted by the Black Brotherhood for years, and eventually, both groups faded out of existence sometime during the next century."

"You are not mistaken," Griffin rasped. There was something very peculiar about the way he pondered them, some faraway look Olivia couldn't place. "But I question whether any of you truly appreciate the scope of their schemes and intrigues. The Order of the Dragon had a hand in every territory, every circle. They took part in every major conflict and event that shaped history. Their reach seemed to know no bounds. As did their list of enemies."

He came to stand on the other side of the fireplace, twirling the liquid inside the tumbler between his hands. "It is also much older than you think. It has had many names, changed forms. Evolved. But you could say that a certain version of the Order has always existed. The only reason they were able to remain in the shadows for so long was because keeping their existence secret was at the core of their precepts. And hiding in plain sight is their specialty."

Olivia did not miss Holmes' use of the present tense.

"Their legacy goes far beyond what you've read in the history books," he said, his voice deadly quiet. "You would all do well to remember that."

"Speaking of hiding in plain sight," Adeline cut in. "We know you hired Olivia's father to restore the wand before it ended up in the Cellars, but how exactly did you come to have it in the first place?"

Holmes's head swivelled towards her, but she only met his sharp stare with a sweet smile as she sipped more of her tea.

"This wand has been in my family for many generations," Griffin admitted. "The records of how it came to us were lost long ago. Over the years I have tried to find out more, but no one I've spoken to could offer me any real answers."

What an utterly unconvincing lie. Olivia shared a knowing look with Adeline.

If there was a rare and dangerous artifact lying around in his family's vaults, Griffin would have moved heaven and earth to find out what it was doing there. The Purveyor wasn't a man who tolerated secrets.

It was precisely what she'd begun to suspect. She didn't know much about Holmes' family or history, but she had learned that he came from a very old, very powerful bloodline in Romania, and he seemed to know an awful lot about that wand . . .

"Are you warning us against people who might try to steal it?" Olivia asked, doing her best to keep her expression impassive.

"I am telling you that this artifact is no mere dark object," Holmes replied. His voice sent icy shivers down her spine. "There are those who would use it to further their plans. Plans that go beyond simply harnessing its power."

"If the wand is truly that dangerous or coveted," Isaksson asked him, "why would you ever surrender it to the Cellars?"

"For the same reason you are now trying to get rid of it. The wand grew restless and I couldn't contain it any more. I tried to reinforce the wards as much as I could, but they would inevitably wear down. I have many more artifacts in my collection. When it started affecting them, I knew it had to go." Griffin's voice gained an edge, his golden eyes sharp as he studied them in turn. "I doubt you realise how terrible that artifact really is. How insidious. This wand can creep into your mind and draw out your deepest fears, your most secret insecurities. It will use them against you in ways you could never have predicted. And as you've seen for yourself, its reach extends beyond any containment ward, no matter how strong. You will need to be on your guard at all times."

Olivia didn't answer, doubt settling heavily in the pit of her stomach. She was beginning to feel as though she might have made a terrible mistake in accepting this case.

Her gaze fell on the amber liquid in her glass, and she stared at it absent-mindedly. "We came across something really strange while researching the history of the wand," she said. "Does the word *'Gate'* mean anything to you?"

The shadows that were Holmes' power exploded out of him, drowning out the light. Olivia didn't even have time to take a step back.

In moments, they had slithered onto the floor, climbed the walls, covered the roaring fire until they were standing in a corner of utter darkness. Olivia's glass shattered on the floor.

Holmes' amber eyes brimmed with magic, all but glowing from within. Olivia couldn't look away. Her blood was rushing through her veins, her heart pounding too loud and too fast.

Her dangerous, self-proclaimed godfather had vanished. In his place stood an angry mage who had unleashed his magic.

She belatedly realised that Ryder was shouting her name, but it sounded as though it was coming from a million miles away. He was pounding his fists against the black tendrils, but they had grown as solid as adamantine. Olivia couldn't even feel the heat of the flames dancing right behind her.

Within their circle of darkness, Holmes took a step towards her. He didn't stride out, but rather glided across the floor without making a sound, like a mythical wraith coalescing from the shadows. He was focused only on her. Nothing else existed. She had the griffin's undivided attention.

"What do you know about it?"

Cold shot through her. Even his voice was different. It was gravelly and raspy, reminiscent of the very creature he was named after.

Olivia had to wet her lips several times before she could answer. "When we looked in the Legendarium, a hidden inscription appeared on the page. It was in Old Arcane Tongue. Cornelius translated it."

Another step. "And what did it say?" the griffin rumbled.

Its golden eyes beckoned her to respond. No, they *demanded* that she answer. She couldn't have lied or stayed silent, even if she'd wanted to.

"*Beware the poison that seeps through,*" she whispered. "*Unseen, unheard, it slithers. Until the Gate, once broken, can be born anew.*"

"Do you know more about it? Have you researched it?"

"No. We only translated it about an hour ago, right before we went to the black market. I have no idea what it means."

Holmes' voice dropped low and he spoke each word very distinctly. "Who knows of this? And do *not* lie."

His voice chilled her to the proverbial bone. Sweat ran down her back. "My team. Isaksson."

"Good."

At once, the shadows disappeared and the room was flooded with light again, so suddenly that it blinded her.

Olivia felt herself being thrown back against a wall. She squeezed her eyes shut, her heart pounding madly in her chest. She expected to feel pain, but strangely it never came.

"There's no need for that, Warden," she heard someone say.

After a few deep breaths, she dared to open her eyes.

It wasn't a wall she'd hit. It was Ryder.

He'd wrapped one arm around her waist and now clutched her to him, her back against his chest. His other arm was outstretched towards Holmes and he'd conjured a shield that warned him to stay back. It shone with a furious glow, the same intense blue as his eyes.

"What is wrong with you?" he barked.

Even Michael regarded his husband with a strange expression, as if he barely recognised him.

Godwyn walked around the corner of the sofa. Olivia realised it was to get closer to a shell-shocked Adeline, a pale hand encircling her throat. To grab her if Holmes summoned his shadows again.

"You've stumbled into something you shouldn't have," Griffin snapped at them, his voice harsh and commanding. "And if you value your lives, you won't do anything about it or breathe a word of it to anyone else."

If he wanted to defuse the situation, this was the entirely wrong thing to say. Then again, at least it was honest.

The arm clutching Olivia tightened protectively, feeling as solid as arcane steel. "Are you threatening us?" Ryder's voice had fallen to a dangerous calm.

Godwyn casually draped his hand over Adeline's hip and pushed her behind him. She didn't struggle, simply rose onto the tips of her high heels to peer over the Baron's shoulder.

"I am merely stating the facts, Warden."

Godwyn's face darkened and Ryder bristled against her. Olivia could feel the magic coiling around him, his power ready to lash out.

She patted his hand as if taming a wild beast. "We should all calm down," she said softly. "Why don't we sit back for a minute, yes?"

Michael immediately gestured towards the couches. "I think that's an excellent idea. Let's sit down."

It took Ryder a moment to agree. Reluctantly, he released his hold on her and they all sat, except for Griffin, who began pacing in front of the fireplace. Traces of his magic slipped out of him, trailing after his body.

Ever the perfect host, Michael took Olivia's teacup and poured her some more tea. When he handed it back to her, her hand trembled only slightly. She met Griffin's gaze at that precise moment and caught the regret that flashed across his face. But it was gone in a blink, his features snapping back into an impenetrable mask.

"You cannot tell anyone about this," he ordered, his raspy voice full of menace. "I mean it."

"And tell them what, exactly?" Ryder replied angrily. "What's this Gate?"

Griffin shook his head. He clasped his hands behind his back, pacing so furiously that his hair swayed with each rapid stride. "All I will say is that very few people know of this secret, and they would kill to keep it that way. Forget you ever heard that word," he told them. "Forget all of it."

Olivia was too stunned, and still a little afraid of him, to react. But she thought no less of his command.

"Where is the book now?" he demanded. "In the Library?"

"Ah." Adeline hesitated. "Actually, the . . . the pages detached themselves. From the book."

Griffin stared her down, gold swirling in his eyes. "What do you mean, they *detached* themselves?"

Olivia admitted, her own voice unsteady, "Well, I guess the wand somehow sensed that we were there and connected to the book. The illustrations came to life. There was mist, howling wind . . . And then, when Isaksson closed the book, the pages came off."

"And where are they now?"

"In the office."

And also copied in her notebook, along with the secret inscription, but Olivia kept that to herself.

"As soon as we're done here, I'll be coming with you to pick them up," Holmes declared. It didn't sound like a request.

Well, at least it was nice to know that they would be going able to leave this place. He'd had her wondering there, for a second.

"We still need to discuss the Serpenthyst crystals," Olivia said, keeping her voice low so as not to startle the raging beast.

Holmes stopped his pacing and turned.

Ah. Spoke too soon.

That cold, sharp gaze of his cut into her. Though this time, his look was calculating instead of murderous. That was an improvement.

After a long moment, he declared, "I will require some insurance."

Isaksson scowled, but Olivia inclined her head, not the least bit surprised. Holmes might act like her eccentric godfather, but he was still the Purveyor of Favours, so she'd expected no less from him.

Michael put down his teacup. "Griffin, perhaps we should . . ."

But his husband held up a hand. "No. She knows my price."

Olivia immediately felt Isaksson tense up beside her, so she stood before he had a chance to stop her. "I agree. What is it you want, Purveyor?"

A small, if not a little cunning smile stretched his lips, making the faint lines at the corners of his eyes stand out. "The same thing I ask of most people who want to deal with me . . ." he rasped in a soft, almost cajoling voice. "A favour."

"Then let's sign a Pact," Olivia said, coming to face Holmes in front of the gigantic fireplace.

Arcane Pacts were one of the oldest recorded uses of magic. Among arcanists, they acted as contracts in which two parties agreed on a set of terms and bound that agreement to their powers.

If one party renegaded on the agreement, the Pact would punish them severely, inflicting a wound on their magic. He would become an Oathbreaker, and until the deal was made right again and the Pact satisfied, would forever carry this scar. For many, having this gaping wound was unbearable and drove them to fulfil the oath, whatever the cost.

"Are you ready?" Griffin asked her solemnly.

Olivia nodded and gripped his forearm as he did the same. Magic rose, sending waves of shivers down her spine. A binding ribbon appeared — ethereal, twisting, as if made of pure smoke — and wound itself around their clasped arms.

"My oath today is to let you leave this place with the Serpenthyst crystals you have requested," Griffin declared.

At his words, the band encircling their arms grew brighter. No longer as fragile and colourless as before, it began to gain substance.

"My oath today," Olivia said, "is to return the crystals to you at the end of our journey." Struck by a sudden thought, she quickly added, "And to the best of my ability, in the same condition as they are now."

Her hasty addition made Griffin regard her, his face calculating, before he finally tilted his head.

The ribbon of moving mist turned completely opaque. Magic pulsed through it, like a river of molten silver.

"Let it be done," Griffin said.

Olivia repeated, "Let it be done."

As soon as the words left her lips, she felt a tug at her magic from deep within. The silvery glow around their arms intensified before the bond ignited, sending small particles of silver ash rising into the air.

Olivia rolled up the sleeve of her shirt, Griffin doing the same beside her.

Each Pact left a mark on the bodies of both parties, as a memento of their agreement. It would slowly fade into the skin and remain invisible unless one of the parties broke their oaths, in which case it would stand out in bright lines that were unmistakable, warning everyone that the person was an Oathbreaker.

Looking down, Olivia discovered a graceful design of swirling vines and flowers, forming the finest of lace, encircling her forearm. It resembled a traditional Mehndi and was a cheerful copper colour that stood out against her dark skin.

Each Pact trace was different and suited to the individual's magic. So when she glanced at Griffin's arm, she saw intricate and twisting lines of ebony that faded from the blackest shade to light grey and then finally disappeared into his alabaster skin. They looked exactly like the tendrils of shadows that were his magic.

Griffin turned to exchange a weighted look with his husband. Olivia held her breath.

At last, Michael inclined his head, though his mouth was thin. "Very well, if you're sure."

He crossed the huge room to a trio of imposing bookcases and raised both hands in the air. Soon, wood groaned against stone as one of them pivoted to reveal what lay behind.

An antique tapestry hung on the wall, depicting a great tree with veins of glowing green running through its trunk, and hundreds of leaves in shades of greenish-blue and bronze in its winding branches.

The Whispering Tree.

Just as it had done on the pages of the Legendarium, the tree moved its limbs, the branches twisting and swaying to an invisible breeze. At the bottom, an inscription had been woven in gold thread, written in what Olivia assumed was Old Romanian.

Michael placed the palm of his right hand on the tapestry, at the centre of the tree's trunk. When he lifted it a few seconds later, the wood buckled and twisted. Groaning, it expanded and seemed to rearrange itself until two tiny doors appeared.

Using the very tips of his fingers, Michael reached for the minuscule doorknobs and pulled a long, thin cardboard box out of the tapestry. Entirely black, the corners and edges worn down by time, it was covered with a piece of paper bearing the Ministry's insignia.

When he closed the doors, the tree rearranged itself, moving its bark around until it made them disappear once more.

Michael pivoted towards Olivia, the box resting on his outstretched palms.

As soon as her fingertip made contact, a ripple split the air.

Just like what had happened in the Museum's Vaults, it felt as if a wave of power poured out of the box. An old power. And once again, the smell of damp woods and the sound of rustling leaves filled the room.

Olivia's eyes widened and muffled curses floated from behind her. In more than one language.

Ignoring them, she moved to a small table and retrieved the containment cage from her bag. Prickles down her spine told her that Holmes was standing right behind her, even though she hadn't heard him move.

Long fingers took the cage from her.

While he inspected her work, Olivia's gaze landed on the scars marring his face, made even sharper by the flickering light of the fireplace.

She'd always imagined that he'd received those while battling some terrifying creature armed with claws and fangs in some desolate part of the world. Deep down, though, she suspected that another, *far* different kind of creature had inflicted the blows, judging by the haunted look she sometimes caught him with.

A dark brow arched and a startled gleam appeared in Griffin's eyes. Surprise and respect. It was only there for a fleeting second, but Olivia saw it and would savour it for the rest of her life.

She pushed aside the paper covering the black box, some sort of crime scene evidence form, to reveal a vial of Serpenthyst crystals resting on a bed of velvet. They glowed with a gentle radiance, nowhere near the piercing light of the wand.

"They look kind of dull," she mused under her breath. "Compared to the wand."

Her remark caused a muscle to twitch in Griffin's jaw. "Indeed. The ones inside the wand are much, much more powerful."

Taking a steadying breath, Olivia opened the small chamber on one side of the containment cage and dropped the ophite stones inside.

Everyone stood still, waiting.

Lured by the power, the wand immediately reached out, its dark magic slamming into the enchantment design, flooding the lines and causing the runes etched into the glass to burn. Wave after wave, the energy poured out as it tried to reach the crystals, but the defences showed no difficulty in channelling all this power and keeping it prisoner.

Just as Olivia had predicted.

After a few minutes, she finally raised her head. "It worked."

They were now in possession of the sturdiest cage she'd ever built, a solid containment strategy and Serpenthyst crystals that would hopefully keep the wand occupied.

Olivia just prayed it would be enough.

CHAPTER NINETEEN

"You know a storm is coming, yes?"

Olivia glanced over her shoulder with a frown. That seemed a bit . . . dramatic. "With the wand, you mean? Are you so sure they'll try to steal it again on our way to Transylvania?"

Isaksson came over to lean against the railing beside her, his hair tumbled by the salty wind. He gestured at the dark and angry clouds she could make out on the horizon. "I meant *those*."

"Ah. Right."

She could see him laughing softly out of the corner of her eye, so she raised a threatening finger in his direction. "Don't make me bring up the talking books incident."

Isaksson only muttered into his beard. Then he held out a steaming tin cup. "Here, got you this."

Smiling in thanks, Olivia took a sip. The tea was harsh and bitter, as one would expect from a group of gruff sailors, but she was grateful for the warmth that spread down her throat.

Isaksson was right, of course, a nasty storm seemed to be closing in on them, the wind beginning to whip her braid around. But for the moment, everything was rather calm, the sea tranquil, glimpses of the moon peeking out from behind silvery clouds. So she rested her forearms on the railing and just let her eyes wander over the waves.

After leaving Holmes' shop, they'd hurried to the district of Newhaven, careful to keep to the shadows. Olivia had had to fight the feeling of eyes on them the entire way to the harbour. Isaksson had chosen the small, inconspicuous-looking steamer all the way at the end of the pier, and immediately begun haggling over their passage.

They'd stashed their luggage in a corner between two crates of vegetables, Olivia had discreetly checked that the wand was still contained, and Isaksson had gone to explore the ship. That had been around an hour ago.

"I had a talk with the captain," he began. "He agreed to let us use the private cabin below deck. It's smaller than a broom closet, but at least you won't be serenaded by the crew snoring all night."

"Did you threaten him?"

"I made a strongly worded argument."

The corner of Olivia's lips twitched before she said, "I have to admit, when you said we were going to take a ferry, that's not what I was expecting."

Once upon a time, the ship's hull had been a lovely brick-red, but was now covered in rust, the rest of her paint a dirty grey. Her single funnel was chipped and dented, sending forth a thin spiral of black smoke that mingled with the leaden mist around her. Olivia hadn't checked the area below deck, but she'd be lying if she didn't admit she was relieved for Isaksson's presence beside her.

He had the good grace to wince. "Yes, sorry about that. But trust me, it's for the best."

Without warning, a smug expression bloomed on Olivia's face. "Can you believe that right now, Crowley is transporting my decoy, thinking it's the real thing. I can just imagine the look on his face when he arrives in Transylvania to deliver it, only to be told it was a fake all along." She shrugged. "It's the little things in life, you know."

"From what I've seen, he really doesn't like you."

"Ah! That's quite the understatement. He thinks he's so much better than us because he can afford to buy ultra special Namibian desert salt. I don't need fancy salt to close cases, you know." Olivia huffed with annoyance. "We've been struggling to get new cases for months now. Adeline is convinced it's because of him. That he somehow finds out who our potential clients are and keeps pushing them to other agencies."

Isaksson crossed his arms as he leaned against the railing. "So that's why you really wanted this mission. You wanted to take your revenge, is that it?"

It was then that Olivia realised he had no idea about the competition. And how could he? It was a curse-breaker thing. "Ah... Not quite."

All of a sudden, she was nervous. She recognized how, from an outsider's perspective, competing for the most dangerous and impressive job could sound a little... *crazy*. "You see, there's this thing we do... We, as in curse-breakers, I mean. Hmm. We have a specialised magazine called the *Cursed Herald*, and every year it lists all the cases of notice that have been accomplished. And, well, there's a sort of... winner. That is, the person who—"

"Wait a minute. You have a *tournament*? For curses?"

Olivia winced. To her horror, she felt pink blossom on her cheeks. "It's more like an award, really..."

But Isaksson shook his head and laughed, not listening to her. "Ah, I get it now! I can't believe you hold championships for your cases! Wait. Is there a trophy?"

Olivia groaned. "And now you're making fun of me."

"No, no. I'm being serious! And I would like to point out that if there is a trophy, I want one too. I mean, you wouldn't have got the case if it wasn't for me, so it seems only right."

"There's no trophy."

"No trophy? What kind of tournament doesn't have a trophy? Not even a plaque?"

Thunder rolled in the distance and a fat drop of rain landed on Olivia's shoulder. Looked like the storm had finally caught up with them. And not a moment too soon.

She downed the last of her tea, then turned on her heels and headed for the ladder that descended below deck. "Going to bed now, good night!" she threw over her shoulder.

But Isaksson followed her. "You know what? I already know where to put my plaque. In my office, right next to the keys to the cells, where I can see it every day while I drink my coffee and remember the fun little adventure we had together. Yes, I like that." He gasped. "You could even curse it! Yes, you could put a curse on it! Like Jerry, turn it alive."

"You leave Jerry out of this." The wind angrily whipped her hair around her face as Olivia hurried to the ladder. That one drop had turned to furious rain in a flash.

"I think I should add a shrine to my plaque. I'll make some..." Isaksson's voice stopped abruptly.

Startled, Olivia turned around.

He stood frozen in the rain, all trace of humour gone from his face. His head tilted to the side.

"What is it?" she asked him quietly.

She doubted he'd even heard her. He kept his head cocked, as if trying to decipher something beneath the crash of thunder and the rising howl of the wind. His eyes swept the deck of the ship, and then slowly lifted to the skies.

His right hand reached behind his back and he drew his gladius.

Oh, no. What now?

Olivia had to bite her tongue to stop herself from interrupting him. The cold sent shivers down her spine, but she forced herself to remain still.

The tranquil peace of a few moments ago was a distant memory. The rain was falling down hard now, and the ship rocked with every wave. She had to widen her stance to keep her balance.

Finally, when Olivia thought she couldn't keep her mouth shut any longer, he declared quietly, "I think I hear a dragon flying."

Olivia sucked in a breath.

If he could hear it above the thunder and rain, then the dragon was circling right above them, close but hidden in the clouds. And that could only mean one thing...

They were about to be attacked.

Isaksson's eyes dropped to the satchel across her body, where he knew she kept the wand. He reached inside his boot for one of his daggers and handed it to her. The metal felt cold and heavy in her hand. She gripped it tight, trying to keep her fingers from shaking.

"Go. Find the captain. Tell him we've got company and barricade yourself in his cabin," he ordered her.

His eyes had turned a lighter shade of blue, almost icy. He'd called forth his magic and it buzzed across the surface of his skin, ready to be released.

Olivia hesitated. She didn't want to leave him alone, not when they had no idea how many were coming, and especially not when a bloody *dragon* was about to board the ship. "What about you?"

Ryder reached for her shoulder. His eyes were clear and focused. "I'll be fine. Go."

Olivia turned her back and sprinted for the door leading below deck without looking back. She ran down the ladder and almost missed a step when she felt it. A vibration that shook the entire ship.

A dragon had just landed.

Olivia cursed. Her fingers clenched on the handrails, turning her knuckles white. Her eyes flicked to the door behind her. but then she gritted her teeth and continued down even faster.

If anyone could fight through a nasty storm in the middle of a dangerously rocking ship, it was her crazy Viking.

She passed a few bewildered crew members who stared as she raced down the corridor, then jerked open the door to the captain's cabin. Two men whirled towards her.

One was standing by a small desk littered with maps and nautical instruments, his hand caressing his bushy, ragged beard. The captain. The other had introduced himself as his first mate, a burly man with reddish hair and a pipe stuck to the corner of his mouth.

"Captain!" she exclaimed, out of breath. "We're under attack!"

She opened her mouth to explain, but something held her back.

She'd interrupted them in the middle of a quiet and intense conversation. Now, the two men exchanged a glance. There was obvious surprise on their faces, but a sixth sense whispered to her that it wasn't surprise at the attack, it was surprise that she was *here*.

Olivia's hand tightened on the strap of the messenger bag across her body. The captain's eyes flickered to it.

She didn't even think, she just acted.

She threw herself to the side, barely avoiding the chair which flew across the room, and crashed into a small armoire. The chair shattered against the wall, raining wood splinters down on her. The first mate had hurled it at her with a speed she'd never expected from a man his size.

Before he had the chance to send her something else, she scrambled to her feet and hightailed it out of the room, running up the ladder as fast as her legs would carry her.

The sight that awaited her on the main deck almost made her lose her balance. She desperately tried to stop, her arms flailing in the air, but her momentum propelled her forward.

She crashed right in the middle of a duel between Isaksson and four other men. Two wore long dark capes and hoods that covered their faces, the other two were part of the ship's crew.

"Olivia!"

Isaksson managed to halter the course of his ball of energy before it could hit her in the face. The icy blue orb, brimming with furious magic, disappeared into the water with a hiss.

Olivia slid on the wet floor and almost toppled over, but with an agility and grace she hadn't known she possessed, managed to regain her balance, dashed between the startled men and all but flew across the deck to the other side of the ship, the captain and first mate still hot on her heels.

"I'll be fine!" she shouted over her shoulder. "You carry on!"

A bark of laughter answered her.

She almost rolled her eyes. The Viking was having *fun*.

Olivia ran past the ship's single funnel to the back of the deck and turned around to face her attackers. She ran a hand over her wet face, pushing back the hair plastered to her skin. That's when she realised she'd lost Isaksson's dagger somewhere during her mad dash.

The captain and first mate slowly approached her, knowing they had her boxed in. They were joined by one of Isaksson's previous attackers, a deckhand with small, beady eyes who stared at her with a nasty smirk.

Olivia's gaze darted to the sides. There was nowhere to hide, everything around her was half-broken pallets of supplies and cages of food. And, of course, the vast blackness of the ocean. The dragon was nowhere to be seen, but there was a peculiar shadow in the sky, moving around the clouds.

The captain's snicker drew her attention back down, his hideous beard twitching as he laughed. "You're wrong here, little girl. You won't be fine. Not unless you give us what we're after."

Little girl?

Olivia snorted. She didn't bother to reply as she conjured up a shield, the golden glow illuminating the deck.

The captain didn't waste his breath on more useless threats. His face darkened as sparks ignited around his hands. They flared and grew until bright silver lightning danced on his fingertips. Olivia squared her shoulders.

The thunderous explosion crashed against her shield with the force of a miniature bomb. It lifted her off the ground and threw her back a few steps.

Bloody hells!

Olivia managed not to fall and kept her shield up, but the captain's blow had sent a jolt through her body that had rattled her teeth.

That's when she saw the big first mate's hands burst into flames and she cursed long and hard. She only had time to brace herself before a wave of fire crashed against her shield, along with more blasts of pure energy.

The heat bathed her face, her arms. The light blinded her.

Olivia clenched her jaw. It was so hot, so violent, that for a second, she didn't know if her shield still held or if she was on fire.

When it finally stopped, it took a while for her eyes to adjust back to the darkness.

From far away, a familiar bark of laughter rang out between rumbles of thunder. It made Olivia grin, even through the next onslaught of fire against her shield.

"Nice try, big guy!" she yelled. "That one tickled!"

Olivia had no idea where her bravado was coming from. All she knew was that it had been trouble after trouble for days now, and she just wanted a second of bloody *peace*!

The flames on the first mate's hands grew brighter. His face twisted into a furious grimace. "Give it up, or I'll make you regret it!"

Not if *she* made him regret it.

Lifting her eyes, she spotted the arm that was used to pick up cargo crates, conveniently hanging directly above their heads. *Ah ah!* And luckily for her, it was old, sea-worn and rusted, just like the rest of this ugly ship.

Sparing a flicker of her power, Olivia began to press on the thick bolts of the pulley that connected the arm to the mast. It was hard to concentrate while also keeping her shield up, and she groaned when her magic slipped.

The rain and wind blinded her, the heat from the fire scalded her face. But she gritted her teeth against the pain and *pushed*.

Finally, the last bolt went flying. Olivia watched as the wooden arm came crashing down on its unsuspecting targets. Only the captain caught sight of it at the last possible moment and jumped out of the way, taking his first mate with him.

Dammit.

Still, the deckhand with his ugly sneer took the crane right on his thick skull and fell to the ground in a satisfying heap.

"You're gonna pay for that, Missy," the captain growled as he struggled to get his big hunk of a first mate on his feet.

Little girl and now *Missy*?

Olivia was going to knock the moustache right off his ugly face.

Their relentless attack resumed, slowly pushing her towards the railing and the churning waters below. She tried her best to maintain her position, but felt herself slipping backwards on the flooded floor with each new blow. She needed to find a way out of there, and fast.

An enormous fireball raced straight towards her. It would have surely thrown her overboard if she hadn't dived to the side instead, and crashed into the wooden crates.

For a moment, spots danced in her vision. Her shield swayed and flickered, but she held on to it by the skin of her teeth.

Olivia allowed herself a few ragged breaths to clear her head. She was plastered against the mountain of cargo boxes and something was stabbing her in the kidneys. With a grimace, she tossed a bunch of carrots to the side.

Her legs buckled and she slid down until she was kneeling on the cold, wet floor, biting back a moan of pain. Her trembling arms were stretched out in front of her, still holding onto her shield. It wasn't as bright as it used to be, and alarm shot through her when she realised it was riddled with holes.

The two men took menacing steps towards her crumpled form. They knew she wouldn't last much longer.

Olivia risked a glance at the other side of the ship. She glimpsed Isaksson's sturdy frame, slashing and dancing with his sword... He was truly a sight to behold.

"Just give us the wand and you have my word we'll let you live!" the captain shouted.

Olivia's face hardened. They'd let them live, yes... live while they threw them overboard and waited for the sea to drown them, more like.

But before that, she had one last gift for Ugly Beard and his first mate.

"I don't know what they've told you about this wand," she called back. "But it'll turn your entire crew mad before you can get to port! You can't handle a curse like that!"

While she distracted them, Olivia shifted her shield to one arm, and fumbled in her coat pocket with her other hand.

"Ah, but *you* can, right girlie? Maybe we'll just take care of the giant and keep you here instead!"

Olivia snorted. "Good luck with that," she muttered.

Above the howling of the wind, the sound of rain and thunder, her own blood rushing to her ears, she could hear Swedish exclamations and battle cries along with the clash of swords. If they thought they could handle the giant, they should think again.

Her fingers finally found what she was looking for and she nearly recoiled. It was so cold and wrong that it made her hand tingle all the way up to her shoulder. *Perfect.*

A smug grin formed on her lips. She didn't need any fancy blast waves or jets of hellfire. She might not be a great duelist, but she was an *exceptional* curse-breaker.

Olivia pulled the item out of her pocket and threw it across the deck. It slipped on the wet floor and came to a stop right between the two men. The small gilded box, adorned with glittering stars and perfect little bows, looked as lovely as ever, even on the deck of this decrepit old ship.

The captain and his second had immediately lunged out of the way, protecting themselves from what they'd assumed was a bomb.

When they realised nothing was happening, they slowly rose from their crouch. The two men looked down at the small box on the floor that was shaped like a glittering night cloud. Their dumbfounded expressions slowly changed to condescending grins. The first mate burst out laughing.

"I think you may have made a mistake here, little miss," the captain boasted.

"And I think you spoke too soon, Captain Moustache," Olivia replied and used a flicker of her magic to open the lid.

A perfect, tiny carousel horse sprang up, with silver hooves and a mane of opals. It made a slow turn on itself, its minuscule saddle glittering like a falling star.

And then the curse erupted.

A terrible wailing exploded from the box as all the O'Brien ancestors were set free. Eerie, shrill, it immediately surrounded the entire ship, coming from every direction.

Then the mist came. Dense and black, it poured out of the box in huge waves. It swam along the bottom of the ship, climbed over barrels and cargo cages, disappeared over the railing and into the waves. In the blink of an eye, it was everywhere.

The captain and his first mate stumbled back. They tried to kick it away, but the tendrils of fog wrapped around their legs. Up and around they went, from ankle to knee to thigh, impervious to their furious attempts to shake it off.

As they watched in horror, the fog gained substance, transforming from an ephemeral cloud into a swarming dark sea. They both cried out at the sudden pressure around their limbs, their muscles cramping.

And at the sight of the hands that reached out from the smoke.

The captain screamed in earnest. He shook his legs madly, but the dark hands gripped him tight, clutching his trousers between black and long fingers. They rose and rose, climbing over his coat in an effort to reach his throat.

The first mate's hands erupted into flames again. He tried to stop the rising fingers with bursts of fire.

Bad idea.

Olivia watched as the big, burly man jumped and spun around as if caught in a crazed dance, cursing and shouting. He got too close to the cargo crates and one of his hands set the rope net on fire.

Soon, the entire exterior of the box was ablaze and the wind helped spread it to nearby ropes, even under the relentless rain.

Olivia's eyes widened. That had *not* been part of the plan.

That's when a large shadow appeared behind the two screaming men, gleaming sword in hand.

The Warden had arrived.

He'd been running full-tilt towards them, but at the sight of the black fog, the wraith-like hands coming out of it, the two screaming men and Olivia still on her knees, staring calmly at it all, he jerked to a halt.

Both of his eyebrows rose to his hairline.

Olivia wiped the rain from her face. "Yes, I admit. The fire is an unforeseen development." She had to shout to make herself heard.

That seemed to snap him out of his surprise. A quick blow with the hilt of his gladius send both men to the floor, unconscious.

Isaksson strode over to her, undisturbed by the edges of the mist that licked at his shins. He knew Olivia held total control over the curse and she wouldn't let it get a taste of tender, Viking flesh.

He grabbed her hand. "How did you do th . . ." He started to pull her upright, but then froze. "Wait. Is that one of mine?"

Olivia stood and used her foot to discreetly push the music box under a thicker patch of fog. Her magic splayed out around them, containing the wailing and the wraith hands, pushing them all back where they belonged. "Hmm? What do you mean?"

Isaksson gaped at her in astonishment. "You stole an artifact from the Cellars?"

Just then, Olivia caught a flash of white at the edge of her vision. Without thinking, she grabbed the labels of Isaksson's coat and threw them both to the side.

The blast of ice barely missed his thick Warden skull. Thankfully, they landed on a pile of what looked like folded wool, which cushioned their fall somewhat.

Looking down, she realised that she'd fallen right on top of him, both her hands on his chest.

Well.

"I can't believe you stole it!" Isaksson exclaimed, not making the slightest move to push her away. "When did you even . . . How . . . I have so many questions!"

"I didn't steal it!"

"No? Then explain to me why I just saw you put it in your pocket."

Olivia groaned. She used her grip on his coat to push him upright until they were crouched behind the relative cover of their pile of fabric.

"Now is really *not* the time!" she snapped.

A hail of bullets thudded around them. They sneaked a glance to the other side of the deck. Three crewmen who'd previously stayed out of the fray were marching towards them, and this time they were carrying firearms.

Isaksson let loose a string of curses. *"Jävla helvete!* How many people are on this bloody ship!"

He retaliated with a swing of one of his bristling balls of energy. It was wild, just like him, bucking and straining to be let loose, like a miniature thunderstorm in the palm of his hand. It hissed as it flew through the air to crash against their shields.

One of the deckhands tried to sneak in from the side. Olivia used her magic to send a nearby wooden barrel flying and he went down like a bowling pin. She smiled. Her eyes searched for another one to swing at them, her new favourite trick.

That was when she darted a look over her shoulder and blinked. "Ah . . . Isaksson?"

When he didn't answer, she tapped him on the arm, her gaze still fixed on the back of the deck.

Another bullet whizzed past but missed, hitting the metal funnel instead with a *tink*. Isaksson grinned a savage smile. His magic shot out, this time both hands erupting into sizzling orbs of power.

She tapped his arm again as he released the small supernovas. "Ryder!"

He growled.

This time, she grabbed his chin between her fingers and swung his head around. His jaw tightened when he realised that all the crates behind them were going up in flames.

"What do we do now? There's no way out of this ship!" Olivia yelled.

Ignoring the thunks of the hails of bullets still echoing around them, Isaksson frowned for a while, deep in thoughts, before slowly turning his head to face her. He grinned then, a devilish twinkle in his eyes. "There is still *one* way out of this ship."

Olivia's stomach dropped. *What was he up to* . . . She gasped. "No."

"Yes."

She shook her head categorically. Tried to crawl away from him, placating her hands in front of her. "Now, let's be reasonable about this . . ."

That made him laugh, the demon. "Oh, believe me. I am."

Isaksson lifted his head to the skies and let out a long, high-pitched whistle.

"Really. This is a terrible idea," Olivia said, her voice beginning to waver.

But he ignored her and grabbed her around the waist, forcing her to stand. He looked around them before staring at one of the wooden crates behind. The inscriptions on it revealed that it contained bottles of aged whisky, and the rope around it had just caught fire.

Olivia felt Isaksson's magic wrap around the massive crate. His arms flexed and bulged as if he was lifting it himself. The wooden crate lifted a few inches off the ground. A vein shook in his neck. It rose a few more inches, and then, with a pained groan, Isaksson sent it barrelling across the deck at top speed.

The crate crashed and exploded in the middle of the ship with a huge *boom,* spraying fiery liquor and splinters of wood everywhere, and creating a barrier between them and their attackers.

But Olivia's attention was quickly drawn to the large shadow in the sky, flying smaller and smaller concentric circles around the ship, looking for a place to land. Only Isaksson's firm hold on her waist prevented her from running away.

"I know you have this unnatural bond with dragons," she said, her voice getting progressively higher, "but really, why would he even listen to you? You're not his rider! I rather think he'll take the opportunity to swallow us whole. Besides, dragons don't like me. I mean, big or small, it seems to be a universal feeling among all species, I . . . I really would rather take my chances with the strange men shooting fireballs."

Isaksson whistled again to lure the dragon closer. "Trust me, I've got this."

I've got this, I've got this . . . What Olivia *got* was that she wasn't getting anywhere near that thing.

She decided to change tactics. "Do you know the statistics on dragon riding accidents? And the survival rates? They are low, Ryder. Really, *staggeringly* low."

The boat rocked as the black dragon finally landed in front of them, on the tiny part of deck that wasn't engulfed in flames. It held its wings slightly extended, as if ready to take off again, and its head swivelled between them and the still shooting figures. It seemed jumpy and afraid, unsure of whom to trust.

Isaksson finally let go of her waist. Walking very slowly, and before Olivia had a chance to stop him, he approached the skittish creature. His hand was extended in front of him in a fist, his eyes glued to the dragon's amber ones, and he kept whispering under his breath.

The dragon reared its head and a puff of smoke escaped its nostrils.

Olivia let out a trembling breath. "Ryder . . ."

But he didn't falter. He moved closer, one slow step at a time, until his knuckles were a breath away from the scales on the dragon's nose.

Her heart in her throat, Olivia watched as the large creature contemplated the foolish human before it, surely wondering if it would make a tasty snack.

She was rooted to the spot with fear, but strangely mesmerised. There seemed to be some sort of silent exchange taking place between them.

For a few endless seconds, nothing happened. But then the dragon inclined its head slightly and touched its nose to the Viking's fist.

Isaksson grinned, more Swedish whispers flowing out of his mouth, then turned to Olivia. "See? Told you."

Her lips parted, she could only stare as the flames reflected off the dragon's dark scales.

Isaksson strode to her and before she knew it, had lifted her into the air and onto the dragon's back.

Olivia felt the blood drain from her face and wrapped both arms around her messenger bag, clutching it with all her might.

There was a blur of movement. She thought she saw Isaksson haphazardly tying their bags to the back of the saddle, but she was in such a state of shock that she honestly wasn't sure. A few terrified heartbeats later, he was behind her.

"Don't worry!" he yelled. "Ex-professional dragon racer, remember?"

"Somehow, that doesn't make me feel any better!" she managed to get out over the panic stealing her breath.

And then her heart fell into her stomach as they took off.

CHAPTER TWENTY

Isaksson was the first to spot land. He squeezed Olivia's hip to get her attention. "We're almost there!"

Olivia didn't have it in her to utter one thing that wasn't a string of curses, so she simply nodded.

She was in pure and utter *hell*.

The wind and freezing rain hadn't relented *one minute* after their hasty departure from the boat, only turning to drizzle in the early hours of the morning. She was exhausted, shivering, both her thighs were on absolute fire and her left leg was completely numb.

Of course, Isaksson, with his brilliant ideas and complete disregard for her well-being, was having the time of his life and kept grinning like a maniac.

She was never working with him again. *Never*.

After what seemed like another eternity, she finally felt their dragon dip to their left and closed her eyes in relief. Thank the gods.

Their dragon flew towards a cobbled square and made a graceful landing that still managed to turn her stomach. The few people hurrying about gave them curious looks, but thankfully no one ran off to alert the police.

Olivia pushed her hair out of her face with trembling fingers as Isaksson dismounted behind her, then grabbed the bags he'd attached to the saddle.

"You all right?" he asked her. His damp, blond hair was sticking to his skin but his eyes shone, more blue than she'd ever seen them.

Managing a small nod, Olivia let him take her messenger bag, and its precious cargo, from the protective embrace in which she'd kept it during their flight. He then encircled her waist in his big hands to help her down.

As soon as her feet touched terra firma again, Olivia's knees immediately buckled. Her hand shot out to grab Isaksson's arm in a vice-like grip.

He chuckled, but wrapped his arm firmly around her waist. "Not a big fan of dragon flying, I see."

Meanwhile, their dragon waited patiently beside them, curious eyes looking all around. He didn't seem all that fazed to have been kidnapped by two strangers and brought to an unknown city.

"So I guess we have a dragon now," Olivia muttered. "What are we going to do with him? I mean, what do you even *do* with a dragon anyway? Should we find a refuge or something?"

When she could finally stand on her own two feet without fear of toppling over, she let go of Isaksson's arm.

"Don't worry about him," he replied as he walked over to affectionately pat the scaly neck of their new companion. "He knows where to go. Dragons always find their way back."

In their mad rush to escape the steamer ship, Olivia hadn't noticed that he wasn't actually black. The scales were a very dark green, with an iridescent sheen that reflected the light in a rainbow effect, like a smooth opal. The early morning light made the few drops of water on his scales twinkle.

Sensing her stare, the dragon turned his head towards her. His glowing eyes were a deep amber, and she could swear they were laughing at what state she was in.

Isaksson whispered something else to him as he scratched the scales on his chin. Then he took a few steps back and the dragon spread his wings to their full width in a graceful arc.

Olivia held her breath. He was magnificent.

One mighty jump, and he took to the sky.

They both watched him fly away in silence, before Isaksson turned to her. By now Olivia was ready to keel over from exhaustion, while the Viking was practically buzzing with adrenaline. "Come on, our train is waiting for us and we definitely don't want to miss it. Let's go, yes?"

"Gods, I'm freezing," Olivia said as she rubbed her hands vigorously, trying to bring some feeling back to her fingertips. "I don't think I'll ever feel warm again."

In response, Isaksson approached the small, cold stove in the corner of the compartment and the air around his fingers sparkled. A blue flame came to life inside his open palm and leapt to the kindling underneath the coal, igniting it.

"Show-off," Olivia couldn't help but mutter under her breath.

She thought she'd been quiet enough, but Isaksson spun around to stare at her, his eyes amused. "Don't tell me you're impressed by a little fire?"

Olivia took off her drenched coat and motioned for his as well, before shuffling until she sat as close to the stove as she dared without setting herself on fire. "Please," she scoffed. "Don't flatter yourself."

She was trying very hard not to notice the way his soaked shirt was now plastered to his skin, clinging to the hard, corded lines of his body. Instead, she examined what would be their living quarters for the next two days.

Due to the need for secrecy, and so that Olivia could tend to the containment cage in peace, Isaksson had managed to book them an entire suite on this train, consisting of two connected compartments and a sitting area. It wasn't large by any means, but Olivia had to admit that working for the Ministry had its moments.

Isaksson, however, didn't seem to think so as she heard him let out an impressive string of curses after banging his head on the chandelier for the third time.

Olivia snickered. "Turns out being short isn't such a hardship. Lucky for you, you have a hard head." She reclined in the plush seating banquette, the soft velvet under her hands and the warmth slowly enveloping her body a far cry from their earlier mad dash through the storm.

Isaksson shot her a narrow-eyed glance, vigorously rubbing his forehead, before grabbing the humongous bag he'd been lugging around all day and setting it down on the opposite bench. Olivia leaned forward, curious. She watched as he unfastened the leather belts that held it closed and unfolded it to reveal the perfect Viking away-from-home kit.

Straps held an assortment of knives of various shapes and sizes, including a set of small throwing daggers that looked to be made of arcane treated carbon steel. Olivia wasn't surprised that he had good taste in blades. To the right were two hand grenades, a length of rope and three sticks of dynamite. A couple of pockets here and there had to be hiding more sneaky surprises.

Out of the corner of her eye, she caught Isaksson reaching for the hem of his shirt and instantly froze.

He took it off in one swift move, used it to wipe the rain off his face and then draped it over their makeshift drying rack. "You don't mind, do you?" he said. "And you should get out of your clothes too, or you'll freeze."

With her mouth suddenly as dry as the desert, Olivia could only nod. She firmly ordered her eyes to look anywhere but at the faint goosebumps she could see appearing on his chest. For a Swede and someone who lived in Scotland, his skin was surprisingly tanned and covered in a thin layer of blond hair . . .

Olivia tore her eyes away. Grabbing her own bag, she dug around for the snacks she'd stuffed inside what seemed like a lifetime ago, eyes glued to the contents. She began to inventory their impromptu breakfast, placing everything in a neat row on the table in front of her.

Let's see . . .

Three packets of fizzly drops, different flavours, in stellar condition.

Two sugar pumpkins, crushed beyond recognition, but assuredly still delicious.

She threw a furtive glance at Isaksson, catching him as he twisted his bloody arm to inspect it.

A waterlogged chocolate bar. Damn it.

A couple of frosty bites that looked more like frosty *powder* with some chunks in it.

The tiniest packet of mystic moon biscuits, still intact, and a nuts bar, interestingly scorched down one side. Olivia tilted her head, wondering how that was possible when nothing else in her bag got roasted. In any case, the charring might actually give it more flavour . . . *Wait.*

She jumped to her feet. "You told me it was just a scratch!"

Isaksson looked up in surprise. "This? I've known worse, believe me. This is just a mosquito bite."

Olivia grabbed his hand with an eye roll. She pushed him down onto her bench and had to step around his ridiculously long legs.

A mosquito bite. *Please.*

She wondered if all Vikings were born with an innate sense of foolish recklessness, or if they had a sacred handbook they shared among themselves. Some sort of family heirloom, passed down from father to son, outlining all the ways in which a true Viking should put his pride before basic common sense.

She slapped Ryder's hand away and properly examined the bloody gashes that marred his arm. There were a few scraps all around, but the worst were three large lacerations that ran from his collarbone, all the way to his biceps.

He indulged her, staying perfectly still as she rotated his arm this way and that, trying to get a good look at his mosquito bite. He only hissed once, when her icy fingers brushed the sensible skin of his side.

"Stay there," she ordered, before quickly ducking inside her compartment.

Olivia went to the small vanity unit in the corner to wet some clean towels.

The mirror above revealed her tired eyes, the hollows beneath her cheekbones, the tightness around her lips. Strands of her hair were plastered to her temples. Her clothes were wet and rumpled. Her once neat braid was a windswept mess that could rival a cuckoo's nest, but above it all, there was a glint in her eyes that should not be there.

It was the exact same as Isaksson's. When he'd fought five men on the ship, when he'd jumped onto their dragon's back. When he'd taunted the apparitions in the Cellars to come and try to get a piece of him.

It was a silly thing to be excited by danger, she knew. To *welcome* it. Foolishness, indeed.

Then why, in the name of all hells, was there a small smile dancing on her lips?

Olivia jerked her gaze away from her inexplicable reflection and marched back to the main compartment, but the sight that greeted her stopped her in her tracks.

Ryder was leaning back in the seating banquette, his sculpted chest and flat stomach on full display. The soft morning light played with his skin, showing all sorts of dips and hollows.

Olivia swallowed the lump in her throat. She pushed him back until she could sit on the edge of the bench, their legs presser together. Ryder kept his blue eyes on her the whole time, a weight in his gaze she'd never seen before.

Ignoring it, she began to gently clean the blood on his chest.

The tips of her fingers actually tingled where they came into contact with his skin, and she could feel a blush rising up her neck. The way he had of staring at her like a starving winter wolf sure didn't help.

Olivia threw her concentration on the task at hand, commanding her eyes to *not* wander. Instead, they fell on his open bag and all its many tools. "That's some interesting gear for a Warden," she pointed out in a strained voice.

She'd known the previous three, and they'd all been more administrators than this rugged warrior. One of them had never even been out in the field before . . . Hang on.

She'd asked herself a hundred times why the Department would hire someone like Isaksson to be their new Cellars Warden. And Holmes had used the word "enlisted" when talking about his work for the Swedish Ministry. As if he hadn't had a choice in hunting their dark relics. Not to mention, why would a Department official know anything about the legend of Shambhala?

Because the Land of Wonders was believed to contain a temple made of pure, glittering gold, that was why.

"Dear gods, you're one of those, aren't you?" she breathed. "A treasure hunter."

Isaksson gave her a wicked look. He inclined his head, using his left hand to dip an invisible hat. "At your service."

A bemused smile curled Olivia's lips in spite of herself. "That explains so much . . ."

Treasure hunting wasn't explicitly forbidden, but it was well known that they engaged in various degrees of rule-bending while on a hunt. So this was ultimately the fate that awaited many notorious hunters. Their Ministry would have enough of their rogue expeditions and decide to conscript them into their service by threatening to press criminal charges.

Since hunting dark artifacts was an extremely dangerous business, not many people volunteered, so they'd had to turn to reckless, thrill-seeking hunters to do the job. On behalf of their Ministry instead of a bounty, this time.

It didn't surprise Olivia in the least that Isaksson had been one of them. What did surprise her, however, was how little a treasure hunter knew about dark magic. The Warden seemed to have as much understanding of curses as Godwyn had when he'd first arrived at the agency.

Her hands continued their task of cleaning his torso as she asked, "I'm curious. What exactly does a treasure hunter *do*?"

Isaksson's voice was dry when he replied, "Try to win duels, mostly. Avoid being bitten by a hydra or attacked by wild wolves. Freeze to death."

Olivia's surprise must have shown, because he chuckled. "Not what you were expecting? Treasure hunting is kind of a catch-all, we were sent to retrieve all sorts of things. Relics, treasures, artifacts, sure. But also people, creatures . . . You'd be surprised how many think it's a good idea to hide in the wild. That they'll be safe there because the conditions in Sweden are so harsh." He shrugged. "It was our job to prove them wrong."

"So you haven't dealt with many curses?"

"A few. But nothing as strong as this." Ryder tilted his head sideways as his eyes gleamed. "Perhaps we should form a team, you and I. With your extensive knowledge of artifacts, I bet we could make a fortune."

Olivia shook her head. "Now, explain to me how a semi-professional dragon racer becomes a treasure hunter, to then end up running a prison for artifacts?"

She'd meant her question as a tease, but when she noticed the shadow passing over his face, regretted it at once.

His eyes had taken on a distant glaze when they shifted to look at the trees beyond the window. "It's a long story."

Silence fell, heavy and tense.

Though deeply curious about his past, Olivia racked her brain for something to say that would ease the thick tension on his face. He would tell her more if and when he ever wanted to.

"I'm afraid that doesn't look pretty," she said in a light voice. "The arm might have to come off."

Ryder heaved a big, dramatic sigh and his eyes shifted back to her. "Maybe I should get a fake one."

"You could add all sorts of fancy gadgets to it. Like a big, heavy hammer that you'd swing at all your many enemies."

Ryder jerked his chin towards his bulky supply bag. "I've got a M-kit in there."

Olivia's hands stilled. Mendix kits were a controversial invention, used to heal and stabilise all manner of wounds, arcane-inflicted or otherwise, from gashes to creature's bites, burns and everything in between. These kits bonded with the user's magic and used it to power their regenerative properties.

As such, the drain on their arcane energy could be enormous, sometimes fatal. Repeated use could even lead to long-term consequences, such as weakened natural healing powers or an erratic hold on one's magic.

Olivia wasn't surprised that the Viking carried one of those kits in his pack. "Absolutely not. They're too dangerous."

"It'll be fine. You don't want to know how many I've used in my life."

"You're right, I don't want to know."

"You wouldn't want my arm to rot, though, would you?" Ryder insisted. "Or fall off . . . Not to mention sepsis."

Olivia rolled her eyes. "You're insufferable." Then she sighed. "Fine, if you insist. Where is it?"

At his nod, she reached for the small tin box sticking out of one of the pockets. "And what's that one over there?" She pointed to another, smaller box packed next to it.

Ryder's grimace was eloquent. "Venom kit."

"That doesn't sound fun."

"Believe me, it's not."

"Have you ever had to use it?" Olivia asked, opening up the M-kit.

Ryder nodded grimly.

"What for?"

He brought up his other arm, where three tiny circular scars encircled his wrist. Olivia took hold of his hand, angling it towards the light so she could better see the faint silvery marks.

"Poisonous Shadow Lake eels," he explained.

Olivia cringed and let go of him, as if the nasty creatures were still hanging off his wrist. "What were you doing in there in the first place? Taking a midnight dip?"

Ryder snorted. "I wish. People had warned us that the eels were big, but those things were bloody huge. It wasn't a fun night, I'll tell you that. Nasty *jävel*."

Olivia folded the towel to get a clean side and began to gently dab at the edges of the wound on his collarbone.

"How did you get that?"

Ryder's voice broke her concentration. She looked up in surprise. "What?"

He caught her hand and gestured to the curved line under her thumb. "How did you get that scar?"

"Ah . . . Now, that is quite the tale. With macabre details. Are you sure you can handle it?"

His eyes lit up at the challenge in her voice. "Tell me."

Olivia's mouth quirked up. She untied the knot securing the M-kit and unfolded it on the table. A bandage, smeared with a brownish ointment that smelled strongly of ginger, was held within a long and wide black strip. She held the bandage carefully by the edges before positioning it over Ryder's three worst lacerations.

"We're in this incredible, majestic, ancestral home," she began. "Centuries old, with antiques everywhere, and quite a few ghosts. It's the middle of the night. We'd been called in because one of the resident artifact in the attic was acting up and they didn't know what to do. Godwyn is nowhere to be seen. I don't remember what he was doing, but I'm alone. Cautiously making my way through the attic with only the light from a small candle . . ." Olivia laughed unexpectedly when she noticed his arm. "Are you getting goosebumps?"

"You're alone, at night, in an attic full of ghosts, of course I'm getting goosebumps," Ryder muttered.

"And that's just the beginning, I'm afraid. Right, so. Candle, pitch dark. And then suddenly, I see a flash of colour to my right. But before I can turn around, my candle is snuffed out. I light it again and it's snuffed out again. Third time, same result. And that's when I start to hear a piano playing. I don't have to tell you there were no pianos in that attic."

Ryder groaned. Her big, strong Warden might look uncomfortable with her story, but he was hanging on her every word.

"Lift your arm." Olivia wrapped the long black strip around his bicep, careful to leave enough length to loop it around his torso. "The piano continues to play, the music picks up. I'm still desperately trying to get any light into this room. And then the music reaches its climax and suddenly, everything lights up. Every candle, every lamp. Even the older than dirt chandelier above my head. And right in front of me, stands the ghost of a woman. Dancing.

"She's wearing a cocktail dress with jewelled sleeves. Pinned up hair with a tiara. There's no more music, but I can hear glasses clinking together, even hushed conversations. The woman slowly turns towards me and she says something . . ." Olivia's voice trailed off.

Ryder was transfixed, his mouth sightly open. "What? What does she say?"

Olivia took on a deeper voice. " *'My dear, your outfit needs some serious sparkle.'* And then Godwyn bursts through the door, the ghost of the woman vanishes into thin air and the artifact, which had been the diamond necklace she was wearing, catapults out of a chest and howls so loudly that it shattered the windows."

Ryder stared at her for a long moment. "But . . . What about your scar?"

Olivia pulled the band tightly around his chest before tying the two ends together. Her eyes were wicked. "Oh, that? I just tripped over a chair coming out of the attic and fell into a crystal fruit bowl."

Ryder chuckled, shaking his head at her. "That was quite the story."

"I aim to please."

With his wounds bandaged as neatly as she could get them, Olivia looked away from his half-naked form and slumped back into the banquette with a sigh.

"And this one?"

Olivia's eyes flew open.

The tip of Ryder's finger was hovering above her collarbone, above the old scar there, a thin line darker than the rich bronze of her skin.

All traces of humour were gone from his face. The timbre of his voice had also changed. It was deeper, more rumbling. Olivia's breath caught, her lips parted.

Ryder bent his head, his eyes so impossibly blue. They were fixed on her neck, on the pulse that matched the crazy beating of her heart.

Even sitting, he seemed to tower over her. Which should have made her uneasy, or even annoyed her, but all she felt was the warmth emanating from him that had chased the ice from her bones. A strand of blond hair had fallen to his forehead. Her hand hitched to comb it back.

"Ah . . . I don't know if I remember," Olivia managed to whisper.

"Hmm." So slowly, his finger came down and Ryder traced the delicate skin of her neck, light as a feather.

Olivia cleared her throat. Had it always been this hot in here? She swore it had been freezing just moments ago . . . "I—so—how's your shoulder? Not too tight?"

There was another long pause. Ryder's eyes still looked a little wild as he pulled away and rotated his shoulder slowly before shaking his head.

Olivia, on the other hand, frowned as she looked sceptically at her work. The modest M-kit was stretched tight around his muscles and looked far from secured. "Your arm is monstrously big for that tiny bandage."

That made him bark out a laugh. *"Monstrously?"*

Olivia reached for the silk scarf in her bag. She wrapped it around his arm to hold the kit in place. "Less mockery, more gratitude."

Ryder's chuckle faded, but she could still see his lips twitching furiously.

When she'd tied the last knot, he gripped the hand that cupped his bicep. "Thank you."

She nodded before jerking to her feet. Which was a mistake because black dots instantly appeared at the edges of her vision and she swayed.

Ryder grabbed her waist to steady her. "Easy now."

Olivia could feel his hands practically burning her skin, even through her clothes. She took a small step away from him. "I'm fine, just stood up too fast."

He eyed the small mountain of snacks on the table. "Maybe you should eat something." He started to reach for the nearest one, but a knock stopped his hand.

Olivia frowned. She headed towards the suite door and glided it open to reveal Godwyn standing in the narrow corridor.

He was wearing a crisp midnight blue suit tailored to his tall frame, and carried a well-worn leather satchel under one arm, a garment bag and folded newspaper under the other. He was also sporting an exasperated frown and was about to speak when Adeline and Cornelius appeared behind him, all carrying suitcases.

Olivia's brows rose in surprise. "What are you all doing here?"

That was when she heard movement behind her and Ryder emerged, still shirtless, bandaged, his hair a mess.

Adeline's mouth dropped open, Cornelius did a double take and Godwyn looked like he'd just been punched in the face.

Olivia's cheeks warmed. "Yes. So . . . We have a lot to tell you."

CHAPTER TWENTY-ONE

After a hurried explanation for their current state and one heated debate, Olivia had managed to convince her team to give them a few moments before pestering them with more questions. Adeline had obviously continued to stare at Isaksson's naked chest unabashedly, and Olivia thought that might have been the reason why Godwyn had finally agreed to wait for answers.

She'd barely had time to check on the containment cage, change into some dry clothes and attempt to tame her hair back into some semblance of a braid before her time was up and she'd had to hurry to the lounge car.

"So, what's going on?" Olivia asked as she approached the table where her team had gathered. "Why are you here?"

Cornelius replied in a sombre tone, "You were attacked only hours after leaving the city. You have no idea what might happen on the way to Transylvania. You need our help."

Ryder glanced at her in surprise.

Olivia smothered a sigh as she sat down. "Holmes," was all she said. Then, she insisted, "Still, you didn't *all* have to come. You could have just sent Godwyn."

Of course, she was glad to have her entire team by her side, but she hadn't wanted them to follow her on what was quickly turning out to have been a foolish decision ... And Isaksson was right, a group of five people was easy to spot.

Her assistant huffed and rolled her eyes. "Please! And leave him alone in a foreign country when he doesn't speak anything other than English? He wouldn't last two days."

Godwyn glared at her. "I have been on many trips abroad, I'll have you know. And I have always managed fine. I don't need to speak . . . ah . . ."

"Dutch?" Cornelius supplied.

"Exactly, yes — *Dutch* — to get around."

Adeline arched an eyebrow, unimpressed. She eyed the steaming cup he held in his hand and her crimson lips curled into a grin. "So I suppose you've had a sudden craving to replace your usual black tea with . . ." She leaned in to take a whiff. "Hot chocolate?"

Godwyn's eyes narrowed to slits. He defiantly took a very large gulp of his drink.

And immediately began choking and coughing furiously. Adeline only smirked.

Ryder leaned close to Olivia to whisper, "Are they always like this?"

"No. I think they're trying to be good because you're here."

He chuckled as Godwyn continued to cough and Cornelius gave him a few big pats on the back. Olivia smiled faintly at their antics, then raised a tired hand to massage her neck.

Something tapped her shoulder.

"Here," Ryder said as he nudged her with a chocolate bar. "You're exhausted. Eat."

Olivia tore the wrapper open with her teeth before taking a huge bite.

Ryder had straddled his chair backwards and was leaning over the back of it, his chin on his forearms. Brooding.

"What's bothering you?" she asked the big, sulking Viking at her side. "If you keep glaring at that waiter, I'm afraid he'll start to fear for his life."

Adeline passed them both a coffee and a steaming cup of tea, which they gratefully accepted. Olivia felt as if her extremities were only now beginning to thaw.

When she looked up, Ryder was still lost in thought, deep lines marring his brow. "So?" she pressed. "Come on, tell us."

"It's about the attack last night, on the boat. Something feels off."

"What do you mean?" Adeline asked him.

"The way they attacked didn't feel coordinated at all. Why board the ship as their first move? It makes no sense. The crew should have attacked first and then used the dragon riders as backup. But they waited for the dragon to land and only joined the fight when you ran to them for help. That's a terrible strategy."

Adeline frowned. "So? Maybe they're not trained in fighting tactics."

"But the raids on the Cellars were perfectly planned and executed. That doesn't fit."

Ryder was right. They'd had to be, to get that close to stealing an artifact under constant surveillance, in an underground tunnel system with only one way in or out.

"Could be that whoever is after the wand has hired multiple teams to steal it. We might be dealing with different groups," Cornelius risked.

That made Godwyn pinch his lips in aggravation.

"It did feel like two different groups, with no unified strategy," Olivia agreed. "And now that I think about it . . . I wonder if I didn't see one of them attack the captain."

"Are you sure?" Cornelius asked her. "Maybe it was just friendly fire. I mean, even if they're not on the same team, they're still on the same side. Attacking us while also fighting each other doesn't strike me as the brightest idea."

Godwyn grunted, his voice thick with sarcasm. "Honour among thieves?"

Ryder said nothing as he took a gulp of his coffee, grimacing slightly when he moved his shoulder.

"That's not all that's bothering you, is it?" Olivia insisted.

That earned her a bemused glance. "You're reading my mind now?"

Olivia pointed to the space between her eyebrows. "It's just that you have this big line, right there, that's getting deeper and deeper. If you're not careful, it'll turn permanent, you know."

"I'll keep that in mind . . ." Ryder pretended to take another sip of his coffee, hiding his lips, and mouthed *"Älva."*

Olivia decided that finding his most prized possession, and then chucking it out the window would be her first priority as soon as they were done here. Perhaps his set of throwing daggers . . . After all, they looked *suspiciously* well oiled.

Or she might just steal them and keep them as a souvenir of their fun little adventure. Yes, that sounded like a much better idea.

"But you're right, that's not all." He heaved a big sigh and rested his head on the wall behind him. "Everything about this mission feels wrong. I don't have a clue how they even found out we were on that ship. And now it looks like there might be not one, but two teams after us." He dragged a hand through his hair, the frustration evident in his voice. "I also keep thinking about Skelton. Why was he so against hiring you for the transport? And insisted on picking Wyborn, who is clearly the most predictable choice ever?"

Olivia certainly agreed. Not only was there no real reason to choose Professor Wyborn, who hadn't taken on a case in years, but they all knew there was a mole lurking somewhere, watching their every move. So why not act as unexpectedly as possible?

"Wait. He specifically rejected Olivia for this case?" Godwyn turned to her with a scowl. "Did you know about this?"

Olivia glanced at the Warden. "It has been brought to my attention, yes."

"To be honest, it doesn't surprise me," Adeline pointed out.

"Really?" Ryder asked her. "Why?"

Olivia winced. "Let's just say we have some history, the Head of Department and I."

"What did you do?"

Olivia sputtered. "Why are you automatically assuming that *I* did something—"

"She yelled at him," Adeline interrupted with a wicked grin. "On the phone. And in person. Several times."

Ryder gaped at her, while Olivia narrowed her eyes at her assistant. "I may have expressed my dissatisfaction with the way a certain situation was being handled . . . It was *one* time!"

Godwyn, Cornelius and Adeline all shook their heads at the blatant lie and Ryder burst out laughing. "I can't believe you scolded me after I complained to the Legal Department! You did exactly the same thing!"

Olivia scoffed. "I wasn't expelled by security though, was I? So it's not the same, sorry."

She took another bite of chocolate, her thoughts returning to their earlier topic. "How were you approached to take over as Warden?" she asked in a careful tone. "Did you know Skelton beforehand?"

Ryder crossed his arms. "Subtle, you are not. You can say it, it really looks like he might be our mole."

Well, if the cat was out of the bag . . .

"That would sure explain a few things," she declared. "How the would-be thieves managed to get so much information. How they erased their passage from the Cellars register. Possibly how they found us on that ship, too."

Even though she had no respect for Skelton, she had to admit she still found it hard to believe he could be involved in such illegal activities, even if it seemed the most plausible explanation.

It also meant there would be no help from home, should they need it. No support from the Ministry. They were truly on their own.

"If the Head of Department has been our mole all along," Adeline pointed out, her voice grim. "Makes you wonder who else might be involved . . ."

Olivia opened her mouth to argue, but then Ryder let out a grunt of agreement.

Skelton, she might understand, but . . . Adeline wasn't suggesting they might be dealing with a *conspiracy*?

"Pardon me. You cannot possibly be implying that Skelton, the head of the Dark Artifacts Department, might have been in cahoots with criminals?" Godwyn gave a dismissive snort and pointed at Adeline with his spoon. "I think you've been reading too many spy novels, darling."

Adeline's lips pressed in a tight line. "No, my lord. Of course, I'm not *implying* that. I'm *saying* that Skelton has likely hired multiple groups of professional thieves to get the wand and possibly sell it at a parallel, illegal auction." She narrowed her eyes at him. "And you leave my novels out of this."

Olivia shot her assistant an incredulous look.

Adeline simply took another sip of tea. "What? It makes the most sense."

"Think about it," Cornelius added. "If the Head of Department isn't behind this, then why would the thieves have waited so long before trying to take the wand? The timing is too suspicious."

Olivia stifled a groan. This was simply too crazy. She had *not* fallen headfirst into an international smuggling ring of cursed artifacts, had she?

But the memory of Holmes' behaviour flashed behind her eyes. His explosive reaction to her mention of the "Gate", his insinuation that they'd stumbled onto something much, *much* bigger than they thought . . .

And to think she had dragged her entire team into this mess, despite Godwyn's repeated attempts to warn her. It would teach her to chase spectacular cases and adventures. Boredom was underrated.

Oblivious to the tumultuous thoughts raging inside her mind, Ryder declared, "The High Commissioner has to be in on it too."

Olivia stared at him in astonishment. "Constantin Mitrea?"

They were saved from further arguing by the appearance of an attendant who politely asked Isaksson to follow him because a telegram was waiting for him at the Salzburg stop.

As the Warden disappeared through the compartment door, Godwyn and Adeline also excused themselves before marching off in opposite directions of the train, pretexting a need for fresh air for one and a sudden desire to read the Austrian newspaper for the other.

Olivia pressed her head against the plush high-backed seat, her mind reeling and her stomach in knots. In contrast, her eyes lost themselves in the peaceful scenery outside, the beautiful mountains and lush rolling hills mingling with the train's puffs of steam.

"Did any of them told you what happened on the Baumer case?"

Olivia turned to Cornelius in surprise. He'd fished out a familiar copper coin from his pocket, and was expertly bumping it around his knuckles. She wondered how many on this train would recognise it for what it truly was. "You mean the phosphorescent stuff that was all over them? I think it might have been some residue from the—"

"Nah," Cornelius cut her off. "I'm talking about what went down between them. I've tried asking, but they won't say nothing."

Ah. Olivia, too, had wondered, but Adeline had been tight-lipped about it.

"I guess they got into an argument. They're like cats and dogs, those two." She tilted her head to the side. "It's not like you to care about gossip."

Cornelius shook his head slightly. His eyes were surprisingly serious, not mischievous like they usually were. "That's because I don't think this is," he declared. "Before we left to join you, we got a call from Baumer. Adeline answered and I could tell she was nervous. As if she was expecting something bad to happen. Godwyn too. He kept fiddling with his cuff links."

"What did Baumer want?"

"From what I got, he kept apologising over and over, saying he never thought the ghost would be that strong. He said it was safely contained now, and the extraction team would take care of the swamp. Even offered us a bonus."

Olivia thought back to their argument that day. Godwyn had accused her of being reckless, that someone might have seen her . . .

Dread settled over her. Oh, no . . . She couldn't have been that careless, could she?

Olivia hid the sudden tightening of her lips behind her teacup. Instead, she shrugged non-committally.

If Adeline had really done what she suspected, they could all be in a lot more trouble than they were now. She would have to talk to her, and this time Adeline had better tell her exactly what had gone down.

"You're right, it's strange," she admitted, fiddling with the edge of her napkin. "I'll try to ask again, but you know how they are. I'm sure it was nothing, though. Just Godwyn being overprotective."

Cornelius didn't seem convinced, but his eyes drifted to the window and the grassy hills they were passing.

"I want to ask you something," Olivia said quickly, changing the subject.

CHAPTER 21

The corners of Cornelius' lips quirked upwards. "That sounds rather ominous. What is it, *cher*?"

"If I'm not mistaken, you've been known to have an inkling of what goes on in . . . perhaps *questionable* . . . circles, yes?"

His smile broadened into a grin. "I have friends in the city's underground, you mean."

"Yes. Well, have you ever heard anything about Skelton? Could Isaksson be right about him?"

"Ah . . ." Cornelius' voice trailed off as his long fingers tapped the edge of the window sill in time with the chugging of the train. "I can't say if he's right, but I wouldn't dismiss it. I've heard Skelton's name floating around in . . . *questionable circles*, as you said, and . . . It wasn't told in anger, but rather a sort of careful prodding. And coming from black market dealers . . . Interesting, no?"

Olivia hummed softly. She had every confidence in his opinion. Cornelius had an affinity for reading a room or taking the pulse of a city and was rarely wrong in these matters.

"What about the High Commissioner?" she asked him next. "What do you know about him?"

This time, Cornelius's warm brown eyes sparkled with unmistakable mischief. "Are you sure you want to know what I think of your idol?"

Olivia scoffed and fiddled with the edge of her braid. "He's not my *idol*."

She'd only spent countless hours, since her first days at Winterdale University, following every one of his legal battles and tribulations with bated breath, or read his speeches so many times she could recite entire paragraphs from memory.

"If you say so," Cornelius drawled, his honeyed voice clearly amused. "I'm afraid I don't have any juicy tidbits to scandalise you. There's a lot of gossip, sure, but most of it doesn't sound even remotely close to plausible. All I know is that he seems to have made quite a list of enemies, standing up to corrupt organisations like he has. He's been High Commissioner for what . . . seven years now?"

Eight.

"So he's lasted much longer than any of his predecessors," Cornelius continued. "Which could be either a good or bad sign."

"Hmm." Olivia took off her glasses and rubbed the bridge of her nose. "I'll be relieved once we're back in the office, and the only thing I have to worry about is getting the good greatwood bark at a reasonable price."

"You could do it too, you know."

"Do what?"

"What Mitrea does," Cornelius said. "Shake up the old institutions. Create more laws to protect the artifacts... You certainly know what you're talking about. I heard you recite the Dark Substances Act of 1889 by heart once, when you were cleaning Jerry's leaves. All twenty-eight sections of it."

Olivia felt heat warm the tips of her ears. Thank the gods Isaksson hadn't heard that, or he would have spent the rest of the journey teasing her mercilessly.

Once upon a time, she might have longed to do exactly what Cornelius had suggested. She'd wanted to march through the halls of the Ministry and shake some sense into them all. It infuriated her how all those old professors and so-called *experts* could turn a blind eye to what they knew was really being done with cursed artifacts.

But that had been before.

Before she'd learned the price to pay for playing with those old powers.

"I don't think I could, I don't have the patience," she replied with a soft laugh. "Besides, I'm not like Crowley to woo and make alliances and whatnot... I'm just a curse-breaker."

She was content to stay where she was. Curses might howl and bite and explode, but Olivia understood them. She could study them, learn their behaviour, predict their actions. They were familiar. Unlike the treacherous waters Crowley liked to swim in.

Guess you shouldn't expect a toad not to enjoy wading through swamps.

Cornelius studied her for a moment before interlacing his finger atop the table and leaning forward, a particular gleam in his eyes that only came from the discovery of an especially juicy curse-breaking story. "Have you heard about the Richmond case?"

"Isn't that the one with the abandoned mansion and the little cemetery on the grounds? The Lochlan team went in."

Cornelius nodded. "That's the one. The whole neighbourhood had been complaining for weeks about loud bangs at night and a strange purple mist coming from that graveyard. Well, the team narrowed it down to one particular grave and dug it up, thinking whoever was inside had been buried with a cursed heirloom . . . But do you know what they found instead?"

Olivia's eyes widened, her breath caught. "Do tell."

As Cornelius explained all about the near-empty coffin, the three hundred year old skull covered in purple handprints and the fangs of the unidentified creature in the sealed jar, Olivia smiled inwardly.

This was what she was meant to do. Swap gruesome curse-breaking stories with Cornelius or discuss the best types of salt to use on Type Twos, listen to Adeline and Godwyn bicker, work on her experiments . . . She'd leave the inflamed speeches, the political intrigues to the High Commissioner, and the bold, daring missions to Isaksson.

She was a curse-breaker. Nothing more, nothing less.

CHAPTER TWENTY-TWO

T HERE IT WAS.

Spread out on the floor of their suite when the table hadn't been enough, all in neat little piles: instant pictures on one side, the medical evaluation of the curse-breakers' condition from the asylum on the other, and the report of their failed mission in the middle. Olivia stared at it all, feeling the guilt slowly engulf her and burn away at her insides.

She'd done it. *Again.*

A shuddering breath escaped her lips. Studying those papers hadn't given her any insight, she hadn't been able to discern what the curse-breakers might have done wrong, nothing that could help them now. The only thing it had done was make her feel even more guilty.

Olivia rubbed her eyes. Maybe she should go look for the others, see what they were up to. She obviously wasn't going to be much help here, all by herself.

A faint cry dragged her back to the present. Olivia frowned as she strained her ears. She thought it might have been a child crying.

Strange . . . She couldn't remember seeing any small children on this train. Getting to her feet, she headed for the door and entered the narrow corridor. A few compartments down, another door slid open. A little girl with bouncy ringlets stepped out, her white dress swaying as she ran. At the sight of the crimson ribbon in her hair, Olivia nearly cried out. Something inside her twisted so violently that her knees buckled and she had to catch herself with one hand on the wall.

She had died in a terrible accident. Her body had been buried in a mahogany coffin, the corners decorated with silver lilies, under a pure white headstone that seemed to glimmer when it caught the sun's golden rays.

How could she be running down the corridor of this train, the hem of her dress flowing behind her and sobs echoing down?

Olivia pushed herself away from the wall and ran.

It couldn't be. And yet, it was her. Olivia had stared at the portrait beside her grave until she could recall every detail of her face in her sleep.

The little girl approached the door leading to the other car and disappeared before Olivia had a chance to reach her.

Her fingers were like ice as she clawed at the handle, trying to open the heavy steel door. She lost precious seconds but finally a blast of air hit her and she hurried into the dining car.

Olivia spun around, her gaze frantically searching every direction. Tears stung her eyes. Had she imagined it?

Something grabbed her forearm.

Olivia looked down and stifled a cry.

The previously angelic face that looked back at her was torn, hideous. Blood drenched one side of what was left of it, spilled down her entire body, soaking her white dress. It had stained the hair lying in clumps around her head, the same colour as the ribbon in tatters above it.

"Why have you done this to me?"

Olivia tried to wrench her arm away but the girl held on. Bloody, lifeless fingers clawed at her skin.

"Why did you kill me?"

Olivia's blood froze inside her veins. *Please, please, make it stop.*

"Why didn't you save me?"

A choked sob escaped her.

Bang!

Olivia screamed.

She whirled around to see a man wearing a dark uniform enter the car, an apologetic expression on his face. "My apologies, *Domnișoară*. I'm sorry if I startled you."

Olivia's frantic gaze searched around, but the girl was gone. Panting, she mumbled what she hoped was a vague apology before stumbling back to her own car.

As the door to the compartment latched behind her with an audible clang, Olivia slid to the floor and finally let the tears roll down her cheeks.

Olivia's hand reached blindly for the box of sweets beside her, her eyes never once leaving the thin vial she was twirling between her fingers.

"Why are you that strange colour . . ." she murmured to the pale, glimmering blue liquid. "It's almost as if the vanadium and the lagoon waters fused together to form a third substance that looks surprisingly stable. I wonder if that would make the . . ." She popped a fizzly drop into her mouth and chewed, wincing as the sharp, sour taste of the candy overwhelmed her taste buds. "Maybe I should try Fuhrmann's approach . . ."

She reached for another drop, still deep in thought. "Hmm, yes. I'll mix you up with some—"

"Do they ever talk back?"

The fizzly drop flew through the air to bounce against the window.

Ryder chuckled before dropping onto the bench opposite her. He was still laughing when she glared at him over the rim of her glasses, one hand pressed to her racing heart.

"Sorry. Did I scare you?"

Olivia's eyes narrowed. "The only thing that scares me, Warden, are your ideas."

Unrepentant, he stretched his limbs across the way, encroaching on her bench seat and scratched his beard. "What are you doing?"

"Working," she snapped. Then a smile curled her lips. "Did you win?"

Ryder groaned. "You know damn well I didn't."

The last time Olivia had seen them, before retiring to their suite for some much-needed peace and quiet, the Warden had been about to teach

Adeline some Swedish card game, an arrogant glint in his eye and a cocky smile.

"You could have surprised me."

Ryder only shook his head. "That French assistant of yours is a menace."

He tried to steal one of her fizzly drops and Olivia swatted his hand. "Have you seen the others?"

"I passed Godwyn, he was reading a book in the other lounge." His voice dropped to a low whisper. "He looked . . . unwell."

Olivia straightened immediately. "*Unwell*?"

"Hmm hmm. The window beside him was open and his face had gone grey. He even took off his tie. I don't think he likes trains that much."

Olivia couldn't help the snicker that escaped her. If Godwyn had lost his expensive tie, he indeed wasn't feeling well.

Having finally managed to steal one of her sweets, Ryder popped it into his mouth and watched with rapt attention as she dragged her curse-breaking kit closer, before pulling out instruments and substances one by one and placing them in a neat line in front of her.

"Where did you run to after lunch?" Olivia asked, peering at him from behind her glasses. "I didn't see you anywhere."

"On a security sweep." He picked up a small magnifying glass and turned it over, a puzzled frown on his face. Instead of a single glass lens, there was a small hinge mechanism on the side that allowed it to switch between four lenses, each one a different colour.

"Have you ever thought about getting a bigger one?" Ryder jerked his chin towards her kit but never took his eyes off the peculiar tool in his hands. "Yours is about to burst." He was switching the lenses on the magnifying glass and looking around, testing them all to see what different things they would reveal.

"I'll have you know this kit has been with me since my very first case. It's sentimental, all right? The weight of memories."

Ryder huffed. "It certainly looks sentimental. You're handling it like a baby bird." He was now trying to superimpose two lenses, one a mossy green and the other an opalescent sheen.

"Well, the things in there are experimental for a reason," Olivia replied. When all her tools were perfectly straight and evenly spaced, she unwrapped the containment cage, revealing the wand still blissfully floating inside. "They're not all that stable."

She pulled a leather rolled up kit closer and untied the knot, revealing a row of five test tubes. Each filled with a different substance, they were accompanied by small folded notes she'd slipped behind. Her precious supply of moonstone, the silvery-blue powder of the vanadium she'd just experimented with, the highly poisonous 'screaming fairy helmet' mushrooms and the wyrmscale she'd asked Cornelius to purchase for her on the black market... Hmm. Maybe unveiling those in front of the Warden hadn't been such a clever idea.

After surreptitiously pushing the kit a little to the side, Olivia picked up the vial of woodhorn and carefully extracted one of the dark cuttings with a pair of tweezers, careful not to damage the delicate horn. She then dropped it into her small bottle full of the shimmering blue liquid, before corking it up again and shaking it vigorously. She was careful to keep her thumb on the cork, just in case. Inside the vial, the mixture frothed and foamed before settling down, now a purplish powder.

Ryder eyed the substances spread out before her warily. "What exactly do you mean by *not stable*? And what are you doing with that?"

"This is one of my creations," Olivia explained as she sprinkled the newly created powder over the runes of the cage. "An energy enhancer. Made from vanadium powder and the waters of the Hacachina Lagoon in Peru."

The powder bubbled where it came into contact with the glowing runes, then settled after a few seconds. Now the runes were a little brighter and there seemed to be a pulsating effect to their glow, almost like the beating of a heart. Jackpot.

She corked the vial with a satisfied smile and shrugged. "And I mean that, *theoretically*, some substances might have the tendency to combust or explode if handled too aggressively... Not," she added hastily, "that this has ever happened, mind you."

Ryder let out a snort, utterly unconvinced.

He pointed at her vial as she tucked it safely back into its leather pouch. "Will it make the containment last longer? How much time do you think we have?"

"It's hard to say for sure, but I think the cage will hold for about a day. Give or take a couple of hours." Olivia glanced at him. "And put that back, it's fragile."

Ryder ignored her. "The train is due to arrive in Brașov tomorrow morning," he said. "So if all goes well, we'll have plenty of time."

He finally stopped fiddling with her magnifying glass and picked up her Wagner-Cozma meter instead, which was used to measure the levels of dark magic nearby. He held it in the palm of his hand and swung his arm back and forth, watching the needle lose it when it would detect the caged wand.

Olivia muttered, "It's the 'all goes well' part that's worrying me."

She leaned across the table and snatched the precious meter out of his hands, placing it back on the neat row of tools in front of her. "Will you leave my equipment alone? They're not toys."

"I didn't have such cool gadgets when I was a treasure hunter. It sure would have saved me a lot of time." He popped another fizzly drop into his mouth and grimaced. "And a few scars."

Fishing her notebook out of her bag, Olivia began jotting down notes on how her energy enhancer had performed.

"Look at you, writing in your tiny notebook with your tiny pen."

Olivia made an exasperated sound. Why hadn't she tossed the Viking out the window yet?

Taking advantage of that moment of distraction, Ryder yanked the pen from her hand and held it up to the light. "Look at the size of this," he said in amazement. "It's smaller than my finger."

And he was right. In his broad hand, her perfectly proportioned and normal pen looked as if it belonged to a child.

"Maybe if your fingers weren't so enormous, it wouldn't look so ridiculous."

"Do you have to buy them custom-made for your tiny pixie hands?" Ryder shot back.

Olivia scowled at him and retrieved her pen. "Don't you have another security sweep you could be doing instead of pestering me?"

Instead of answering, Ryder reached into his jacket and pulled out a folded piece of paper. He straightened it, handing her what appeared to be a new telegram.

Her brows shot up in surprise as she read the message.

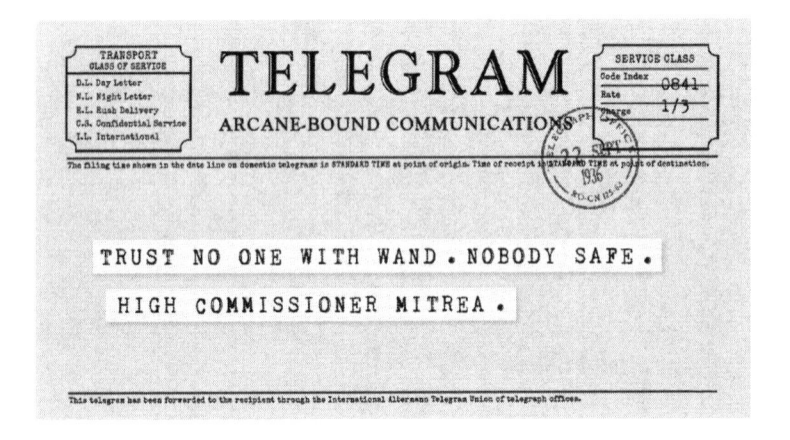

```
TELEGRAM
ARCANE-BOUND COMMUNICATIONS

TRUST NO ONE WITH WAND. NOBODY SAFE.
HIGH COMMISSIONER MITREA.
```

"That's an . . . interesting development."

Ryder didn't smile at her baffled tone. In fact, he looked uncharacteristically serious as he pushed a hand through his hair. "You don't think he's involved."

Olivia smothered a sigh.

"He was the one who arranged the transfer in the first place," Ryder continued. "He's got the right connections, the power, the resources . . . He's friends with Skelton. It all makes sense."

Olivia fiddled with the edge of her notebook.

Except that the man was a legend.

Constantin Mitrea had dedicated his life to preserving and protecting dark relics from governments and private collectors alike. Incorruptible, uncompromising, he'd gone up against rigid institutions and powerful men relentlessly. Olivia had followed his political battles for years, she couldn't imagine him trying to steal an artifact now.

It was much more likely that he knew about the whole thing, and was trying to stop it.

"Besides, he's the one running the auction, right?" Ryder added. "I thought you hated it."

"I do. But you're wrong about him. I've followed his career for years, Ryder. He's not corrupt like the rest of them, he really does everything in his power to protect the artifacts. He's been trying to abolish the auction since the very beginning of his mandate, but the Romanian government has always interfered. So he decided to be the one to organise it instead, so that he could keep an eye on the auction pieces. Make sure nothing too rare or dangerous made it onto the list."

"Hmm." Ryder ran a hand through his hair. "It doesn't matter anyway, we still can't give him the wand."

That made Olivia frown. "What?"

"Even if you're right, he could be targeted and the wand stolen. We can't risk it."

"I'm sorry, I don't follow. Who else would we give the wand to?"

Ryder stared her down. "Olivia, we were attacked in the middle of the ocean where no one should have been able to find us. Where can the wand go that'll be safe?"

"But . . . I . . . This exchange is part of an international agreement. We can't just *decide* to ignore it. That would be considered a crime. They would send the police after us, treat us as fugitives. If they caught us, we could go to prison. Listen . . . I understand what you're saying, but we can't keep the wand. That's simply not an option."

Ryder waved a hand dismissively. "The Ministry will understand why we did it once we have a chance to explain. We won't end up in prison."

Olivia refrained from voicing all the retorts that pressed behind her teeth. Instead, she ground out, "If you think the Ministry capable of being fair and just, you're being naive."

She might have shared his opinion at the very beginning of her career, but she'd certainly learned her lesson since then.

Ryder regarded her carefully, taken aback by her fierce reaction.

She tried to rein in her bitterness, to make him understand. "I've dealt with them before, Ryder. They don't care about suspicions, or about what's right. All they worry about is not losing face. Even if they have to throw you to the wolves for it."

No, under the veneer of science and research, the Artifacts Department was as politically motivated and cut-throat as the highest levels of Parliament.

"Even if it turned out that we were right not to trust the High Commissioner, they would still call what we did a terrible violation. I can't have my business or my employees associated with this. I'm supposed to get my team out of trouble, not deeper into it!"

Incredulity made Ryder's brows knit together. He looked as if he wanted to reach across the table, grab her by the shoulders and shake some sense into her. "That wand is a terrible weapon," he ground out. "Just think what they could do with it! We have a responsibility here."

Olivia couldn't help the snort that escaped her.

As if she didn't know what that wand could do. As if it wasn't *her* skills and knowledge alone that kept it from turning Isaksson's mulish brain inside out. "My *responsibility*, as you say, is to deliver the wand to the High Commissioner. That's what you hired me for. I'm neither a detective nor a spy."

"There are lives at stake here, Olivia! Real lives, that could be hurt. Don't you care about them?"

His own growing frustration only fuelled her ire. How dare he imply she didn't care, that she didn't want to help. Of course, she did! But getting involved in such games only ever blew up in your face.

"All right then," she snapped. "Let's hear it. Let's hear this plan."

Ryder crossed his arms while leaning back in the bench. "You're mad."

Mr. Detective, indeed.

"Am I? I'm simply waiting to be properly dazzled by this wondrous plan of yours that will ensure not only the safety of this wand, but that none of us ends up mad or in prison, and that will guarantee you the praise of the Ministry and the congratulatory handshake of the Head of Department."

CHAPTER 22

Ryder's stare turned stormy. "Is that all? Or is there something else you want to add? Like the part where you win your competition, maybe even get knighted for your troubles, until you're buried under so many cases that you have to hire Crowley as an intern."

"I'd rather turn down clients that let that snake anywhere near my agency."

"Open your eyes, Olivia," Ryder growled. "This is the real world, you can't guarantee how things will turn out. But it doesn't mean you have to give up and hide."

"I'm not hiding," she hissed. "I'm looking after my own, there's a difference. I care about my team, Isaksson. I'm responsible for what happens to them. They followed me here to help and you want me to risk their lives on a wild goose chase!"

She closed her eyes and took a deep breath, trying to regain her composure. "Even if we wanted to, we simply don't have the time. The containment will only last until tomorrow. After that, we have no way of keeping it secure."

"At any moment, that wand could decide to blow through the containment wards and make everyone on this train completely insane," she stated, her voice rough. "Not to mention, the two teams — that we know of — that are actively trying to steal it and could attack us at any given time. My team and I are already in incredible danger, Ryder. But you need our help to get the wand where it's supposed to go, so we'll help you. We'll do what you hired us to do. After that, it's not our problem any more. I won't risk the lives of my team to play a game of spy that we have no clue how to win."

"You're afraid," Ryder snapped, his tone hard. "And you have been from the very beginning. That's really why you didn't want your team to come."

Olivia flinched as if he'd slapped her. Sudden anger made her clench her fists tightly at her sides and the words escape her mouth with barely any thought. "And what's so wrong with that? They're my team, my friends! Do you really think less of me because I don't want to see them hurt? You don't understand because you're just one man. You go wherever you please, act however you want, and you only have yourself to worry about. You don't understand what it's like to have people depending on you. It's easy to be reckless when you don't care what happens to anyone else."

Olivia regretted what she'd said as soon as she said it. "Ryder, I . . ."

"I get it." He got up and headed for the door. "If you need me, I'll be on my security sweep."

CHAPTER TWENTY-THREE

THE PIANO WAS CURSED.

Not enough to bite players' fingers or cause a riot when it suddenly came to life in the middle of the night, but Olivia could feel the energy left inside by a previous owner. It wasn't a malevolent presence, simply the love an artist had had for his instrument, which had permeated the wood, even after his death.

She watched as an elegantly dressed woman approached amid soft applause and sat down on the small bench. Her satin gown rustled as she lifted her sleeves, and her graceful fingers began to dance over the black and white keys.

Olivia wondered if she could feel it. If the woman could tell that this piano wasn't like any other, that it impregnated whatever lovely note she played with something... *more*.

That was how Adeline found her, her chin resting in her hand as she swirled the wine in her glass, quiet conversation filling the saloon car.

"What happened?" Adeline asked as she perched on a leather stool beside her. She waved the waiter over for a glass of her own, then turned to Olivia with a raised brow. "And don't even bother pretending. What did Isaksson do?"

Olivia lifted her eyes to the ceiling. "He's an obstinate, self-righteous, arrogant knight in shining armour who won't listen to reason. That's what happened."

Adeline took a sip of her wine, humming in agreement. "And?"

"He thinks we shouldn't trust anyone with the wand. He wants us to keep it."

"That sounds wise."

Olivia's head snapped to her. "Have you forgotten that thing can drive us all mad?"

"That's precisely why we shouldn't give it to just anybody," Adeline replied pointedly.

"It's also too dangerous to *keep*. And this is not our fight. The Ministry should step in and take care of it." The words burned her throat coming out, but that didn't mean they weren't true. It was dangerous, might very well get them hurt, imprisoned or killed. And it wasn't their responsibility. Olivia knew how to contain curses, not unravel political intrigues and conspiracies.

Adeline said nothing. She swivelled on her stool to face the other passengers, her elbows resting on the table behind her. She crossed her long legs and surveyed the crowd, her sharp eyes no doubt analysing every move, every glance.

Olivia's fingers drummed on the rim of her glass. After a few minutes, she couldn't take it any more. "It's not like you to stay silent."

Her friend shrugged, her tone matter-of-fact. "You already know what I think."

"Then you're mistaken," Olivia ground out, fingers clenching on her glass.

"Am I?" Adeline turned to her. The light tone was gone from her voice. "You're afraid of making a mistake. But we made our own choice to come here. All of us. We knew it would be dangerous, and we came to help you anyway because we care about you."

Olivia raised her glass, a sarcastic smile on her face. "Then I shall repay you by turning you into criminals and putting you all in terrible danger."

Adeline sighed in exasperation. "You're missing the point."

Her next words were soft, spoken with care. But they cut nonetheless. "We're not children, Olivia. This is nothing like the last time."

Olivia drew back immediately. "You don't know what you're talking about."

Adeline didn't let her tone deter her. "No, I don't. Because even though we've been friends for years, you've never talked to me about it."

She hadn't talked to *anyone* about it. And probably never would. "That's because there's nothing to say. It's in the past."

"It's clearly not in the past if it makes you this upset."

Olivia held on to her temper by the skin of her teeth. Her friend was simply trying to help. And she might be right, too. Olivia knew she had changed after the incident, she was not the same person as before.

She straightened her shoulders, hiding her emotions, even as she felt her hand under the table clench into a tight fist. "What's wrong with wanting to keep you all safe? And why should we risk our lives trying to right other people's wrongs? I don't even know if we *can* do it. There's simply not enough time to untangle all this . . . mess. We're curse-breakers, Adeline. This is police work."

And it was her who had insisted on taking this case. All so she wouldn't have to shut down a business she loved, one they'd spent so much time and energy building.

Her friend's steel grey eyes were fierce as they held her own. "We're not helpless, Liv. We're a team, strong and capable. I'm not worried about us. I'm worried about everyone else. You say what if one of us gets hurt should we get involved, but . . . what if hundreds of people get hurt should we don't?"

Olivia didn't reply for a long moment. Her gaze drifted to the music player, her long and delicate fingers dancing on the piano, as tenderly as a lover's touch. How many people had caressed those keys like this? All of them leaving a piece of themselves behind: sometimes in anger, sometimes in the hopes of catching an admirer's eye, to seduce or to forget. They probably hadn't even known they were doing it. Yet Olivia knew very well that every life left behind an echo.

She didn't want to pry into Adeline's private life, but if what she suspected was true, she couldn't keep quiet any longer. They might all be in danger on this case, but in a way, Adeline was even more at risk. "What happened with Baumer?"

Her lips pressed together. "It was an accident."

"I don't mean that. I mean how did you convince the ghost to move?"

Adeline didn't pretend to misunderstand. "No one saw me."

"Addie..." Olivia closed her eyes on a frustrated breath. "Someone could have. You know how dangerous it is to use your power. All it takes is just one person talking, that's it."

"I am well aware," was Adeline's tart reply. She lowered her voice. "I didn't do it on purpose. It just came out. Godwyn was about to drown and... He's quite angry with me, even though I saved his ungrateful ass."

"And he's right. You should have been more careful."

Adeline straightened, her eyes spitting fire. "And exactly what choice did I have? I wasn't going to let him get killed..."

"You need to take more care!" Olivia hissed. "Need I remind you that Isaksson works for the Ministry? If he catches you using these powers, you know very well what will happen... You should never have come here. At the next station, I want you to get off this train and take the first one back."

Adeline threw her napkin on the table and rose from her seat. "If you think the threat of my power will stop me from doing what I must to save any one of you, then you don't know me at all," she said, her voice cold and her lips set in a flat line.

And with that, she turned on her heels and stormed off.

Before Olivia had a chance to call after her, Godwyn appeared, a severe expression on his handsome features.

"What's wrong?" Olivia asked him. She couldn't resist patting the bag at her hip in reassurance, making sure the wand was still inside and safe.

"We have a problem. You need to come back. Right now," was his brisk reply.

They followed him at once, Adeline asking as soon as they entered their private compartment, "What's happened? Is someone unwell?"

Cornelius and Ryder rushed in and Godwyn shut the door firmly behind them. "No. The replica is here, on this train," he said. "With Crowley and an entire delegation from the Ministry."

"What do you mean *Crowley's here?*" Ryder demanded. "He's supposed to be already in Romania."

Godwyn shook his head. "He's on this train. With some Ministry officials, a couple of security guards and the Head of Department. They're all crammed into carriage eight."

CHAPTER 23

"You have got to be kidding me!" Ryder began to pace the small length of their sitting area, his brows knitted together and his jaw as hard as a block of granite.

"Apparently, the Portal took one look at their artifacts and shut down," Cornelius explained. "Godwyn and I overheard two of the Ministry officials talking. They weren't being discreet."

Olivia sank into the bench and pinched the bridge of her nose. She knew the Portal wouldn't agree to transport the replica, even if it was a fake. Imbued with as much dark magic as it was, there was no way in hells. Damn that incompetent cockroach, he couldn't do anything right!

"We need to get off at the next stop, we can't stay here," Ryder ground out.

"What?" Cornelius frowned. "Crowley didn't see us. I just figured we'd have to be more careful."

"That's not the problem," Olivia explained. "Crowley and the other Ministry officials could have led the men trying to steal the wand right to us. As you said, they're not very discreet."

"If they're here for the wand, they'll attack them," Adeline said. "As much as it pains me to say it, we need to warn Skelton. Even if it's just to prevent innocent bystanders from getting hurt."

"I agree, but I'm not sure that's such a good idea." Olivia winced. "Crowley's already threatened me to get me to drop the case. If he sees any one of us, he'll cause a scene." She turned to Ryder. "Perhaps you could have a word with the Ministry officials instead."

The Warden continued his angry pacing. "And say what? If I tell them the truth, that they're transporting a fake, and word gets out, the whole plan goes to hell. Not to mention how Skelton will take it."

"Could we leave an anonymous note?" Adeline suggested. "Warn them to be on their guard?"

Right at this moment, Godwyn returned from his compartment, his jacket in one hand and a piece of paper in the other. "We don't have to worry about Crowley," he said, a grim look in his eyes. "They already know we have the real wand."

An hour later, Olivia followed Ryder into the dining area, the sound of hushed conversations and clinking cutlery surrounding them.

The message had been simple and to the point. "Meet us in the dining car. 8 o'clock. " Godwyn had found it on his pillow.

Why bother with an invitation to dinner when they could have simply tried to take the wand by force, no one knew.

They'd debated the best course of action for a while, before deciding that Olivia and Ryder would go to this cryptic rendezvous, leaving the wand under the others' supervision. They would wait in the next car, close enough to hear if mayhem ensued and flee with the wand. Ryder had taught them several escape routes and had set a time and place to meet, in the event that everything went to hell.

The mysterious senders of the message were easy enough to spot. Two men sat at the table furthest from the entrance, in a corner. They seemed to be making small talk, sitting relaxed, but their eyes took everything in.

One was older, perhaps in his mid-forties, with black skin and hair, a slightly crooked nose and keen eyes. He appeared to be of medium height and build, wearing a smart but unremarkable suit. He was smoking, with an easy expression on his features. He could just as easily be a wealthy businessman on a European holiday, an academic professor on a research trip, or a foreign diplomat.

The other man looked nothing like him. As soon as he spotted them, he tried to feign nonchalance, but Olivia had picked up a few tips from Adeline's astute observational skills over the years, so she noticed the slight twitch in his fingers and the way he'd shifted in his chair, as if to give him as much room to move as possible. He was almost as tall as Isaksson, with beefy arms and broad shoulders, and there was no disguising the intensity in his aura. He was nursing a drink, strong fingers wrapped around the glass. Olivia could just as well picture them encircling someone's neck.

The two men stood as they approached. The older one smiled, nothing but warm courtesy and respect in his expression. "Ms Knight, Mr Isaksson. Thank you for agreeing to meet, please have a seat."

CHAPTER 23

He sounded American, Olivia noted, but without any accent she could make out.

She shared a cautious look with Ryder before settling into the chair he'd pulled out for her. As she sat down, she could swear the older man narrowed his eyes at her covered right arm, where the mark of her Pact with Holmes was. But whatever sharp expression he had was gone in an instant, replaced by his friendly demeanour.

"I think some introductions are in order, no?" he said. "My name is Sean Walker and this is my colleague, Logan Pierce."

A waiter materialised beside their table to take their drink orders and disappeared just as quickly.

"Now, what would you say if we jumped right in, hmm? We are part of a very old institution that has been protecting the public from the most dangerous threats for generations. A rather pompous job description, I know." He raised his glass to his lips with a chuckle and a slight shake of his head. "What we *actually* do is step in when government agencies are not equipped to deal with a particular threat. When they don't have the knowledge or the resources to contain it. Unnatural magic, corrupt mages . . . You name it, we've done it all."

He looked at his stone-faced colleague. The other man hadn't said anything, but he was still watching Isaksson as if he might sprout fangs and claws at any moment.

"We pride ourselves on having something of a proactive approach," Walker continued. "We like to take care of things before they even have a chance to become a problem. However, one such problem is currently travelling among your luggage, so we find ourselves in a bit of a pickle."

A *pickle*. He really did say that.

Olivia also hadn't missed his use of "unnatural magic" either, and it had immediately put her on edge. She would have to be extremely careful to keep Adeline well away from these men.

"What institution are we talking about, exactly?" Ryder asked.

"I'm afraid that is classified information. But even if I told you, it wouldn't mean much to you. The existence of our group is a very well-kept secret—"

"You're Black Knights."

Olivia's words floated in the stunned silence that followed.

Ryder smiled at the two men with a particularly cocky grin, and she barely avoided rolling her eyes at his display of smugness.

It really hadn't been that hard to guess. The Guard was the only institution with the authority to operate across country lines, but if those two had belonged there, they wouldn't have bothered to keep it a secret. Or to negotiate, for that matter. Guardians weren't known to bargain for what they could *take* instead.

With her growing suspicion that the Order of the Dragon was indeed alive and kicking, it wasn't much of a stretch to imagine that its historical counterforce might have survived the centuries as well . . . And had been *hunting* it still.

Walker waited for the waiter to serve their drinks before leaning back in his chair and studying her intently. With slow movements, he pulled out another cigarette from a silver case inside his jacket and lit it. "I have to be honest. I greatly underestimated you."

"Indeed you have. In more ways than one," Olivia said. "Mr Walker, let me make myself perfectly clear in return. You can spare us the lecture on how dangerous that wand is, or how much damage it could do if it ever fell into the wrong hands. Believe me, the Warden and I are well aware. Unfortunately, both you and your colleague currently fall into that category."

"Now, Ms Knight, there's—Olivia. Can I call you Olivia?"

"No."

The look he gave her then was the one you bestowed upon petulant children. "Ms Knight, there's really no need for this hostility. We all want the same thing, to keep the wand safe. To keep *innocents* safe. So far, you've done a terrific job of protecting it, but frankly, this artifact is much, much more powerful than you realise. For some, it would be the key to unleashing terrible evil upon this world. It is far more valuable than you can imagine. I mean no disrespect, but you are not equipped to handle its protection. The risks are simply too great. It's time for us to take over."

Unleash terrible evil... The memory of Holmes' outburst of dark power flashed behind her eyes again. Was Walker talking about the Gate the wand seemed to be connected to? Was the Order trying to extract something from wherever it led?

For the millionth time, Olivia wondered what she'd got herself into.

"And I suppose you are," Ryder scoffed.

"As I said, we have decades of experience dealing with the darkest of magic." Walker smiled again, creating small crinkles at the corner of his eyes. He took a deep drag from his cigarette and waved his hand. "We are all reasonable people. There is no reason why we cannot resolve all this in a peaceful manner."

A muscle shifted in Ryder's jaw. The atmosphere around the table suggested that the manner in question would be anything but peaceful.

"Exactly how reasonable were you when you appeared on dragon's back in the middle of the night to attack us?" Olivia couldn't help but snap.

Walker simply laughed, undeterred by her tone. "What gave us away?"

"Apart from the way you've both been staring at Isaksson like he was about to jump over the table," she began, before gesturing to his timepiece. "You're wearing your wristwatch on your left, which means you're probably right-handed, and yet you're picking up your drink and smoking with your other hand. And your companion is trying his best not to bother his ribs." Her lips curved upwards. "Courtesy of the Warden's magic, I gather?"

The other man's eyes snapped to her.

By contrast, the look Walker gave her was sheepish, almost contrite. "Not our wisest course of action, I grant you."

Olivia had to grit her teeth to smother her retort. These men had attacked them on that ship and they certainly hadn't softened their blows. Ryder had been hurt, they both could have been killed. And now here they were, behaving like perfectly respectable gentlemen. Heroes. Guardians of the people and the peace.

Please. The note ordering them here had been left on Godwyn's pillow. A less subtle threat, she'd never seen.

His Pierce colleague still hadn't said a word. He simply stared, watchful, calculating. It unnerved her.

But beneath her anger, Olivia was starting to feel like a deer in the woods, knowing that a predator was circling around her. Looking for her weaknesses, waiting for his chance to pounce. She hated the cold sweat that dampened her shirt.

A broad hand closed over hers under the table, squeezed.

She didn't dare glance at him, didn't let any reaction show on her face when Pierce was still following her every move, but Ryder's warmth slowly seeped into her cold fingers. She wasn't alone. He was with her and he would protect her. No matter what.

Because she knew perfectly well where this conversation was going. She would not give them the wand, and they were not going to yield.

Olivia raised her chin. Her eyes were clear and sharp. "And how do you expect us to believe you?" she declared. "For all we know, you could be one of the people you're warning us about. We are under government contract, part of an official repatriation programme. We are acting under the orders of High Commissioner Mitrea. Even if we believed you, we cannot simply *give* you the wand."

Walker's reaction to the mention of the High Commissioner didn't escape Olivia. His lips pressed into a thin line, his eyes darkened. It was gone a moment later, but she saw it. It had been anger, but with a hint of disgust.

"If you're really concerned about the safety of the wand," she continued, "you'll have to take it up with the Romanian Ministry."

Walker hummed softly. "It seems we might be at an impasse here."

The new smile he flashed her was all teeth and had more in common with a shark's grin than with his previous attempt at harmlessness. "Believe me, Ms Knight, I understand that we're responsible for your lack of trust in us, and rightly so. However, we do not have the luxury of waiting for you to believe us. This is a courtesy meeting. We will take that wand and keep it safe from anyone who might try to use it."

Ah, threats. Finally.

Olivia had grown tired of their strange dance. Beside her, Ryder was still but ready. His magic coiled around him like a wolf ready to pounce.

"I don't need to remind you what happened the last time you attempted to take the wand from us," she said.

She felt more than she saw, the pride flashing in Ryder's eyes. He smirked as Pierce's hands clenched into fists.

"Besides, are you really going to attack us in the middle of a crowded train? For an institution that likes to keep its identity a secret, that doesn't seem like such a bright idea. There is an entire delegation from the Ministry, all piled up in car eight."

"Ah, Ms Knight. Now it is your turn to underestimate us." Walker crushed his cigarette butt on the crystal ashtray in front of him. The nonchalance on his face sent tiny shivers down Olivia's spine. "You're correct, we would never attack you in the middle of a crowded train. Which is why you'll bring the wand to us."

Ryder tensed all over, ready to leap over the table and tackle him. The air around him shimmered with faint traces of icy blue.

But Walker held his easy, relaxed pose. He knew where the threat was coming from. All six feet of it currently vibrating in his chair with restrained fury. One wrong move and the Viking would be upon him before his creepy companion had the chance to blink.

So he barely moved, all he did was clench his left hand into a fist. But it was enough.

Olivia's lips parted in a startled exhale.

Immediately, Ryder's head snapped to her. His eyes roamed around her frozen form, trying to discern where the threat was coming from. "Olivia?"

She didn't answer. Couldn't move a single muscle, couldn't turn her head. She knew her face had to be white as death.

Invisible arcane lines burned around her. She was inside a circle, one of the most volatile and aggressive she'd ever felt.

Anger rolled off Ryder in waves. "What did you do to her?" he growled.

"Ms Knight is currently in the middle of a hidden circle, set to detonate if she tries to leave." Walker leaned forward. None of his easy, laid-back American persona remained. He simply wasn't the same man as before.

Now he was focused, cold, deadly. He looked predatory and slightly vicious. His flat voice raised all the hairs on Olivia's arms.

"In one hour you will come, alone, to the baggage car and hand over the wand. Do that, and we will spare your lives. If you try anything, or alert the Ministry delegation, the circle will blow the lovely Ms Knight to bits. Are we clear?"

Olivia could feel it, the edges of the circle vibrating with leashed violence. She didn't dare probe too much for fear that the slightest touch would set it off.

These weren't empty threats.

Out of the corner of her eye, she saw Ryder's face contort with dark rage. She thought she'd seen him angry before, but this . . .

He pinned Walker with a deadly stare. "If anything happens to her before then, you'll regret it."

He stood. His magic brushed past Olivia, as wild and raging as a thunderstorm. His eyes met hers. What she saw in their depths made her heart settle inside her chest. It was steel, strong and unwavering.

The Viking was coming back for her.

A shaky breath left her lips before she set her jaw and nodded.

Ryder turned on his heels and walked away.

CHAPTER TWENTY-FOUR

OLIVIA'S FINGERS SHOOK.

She was clenching her hands tightly to hide it, not wanting to give them the satisfaction. Or the wrong idea, for that matter.

Her mind might be a whirlwind of emotions: fear, frustration, regret. But above all else, she was incredibly, *monumentally* angry.

So angry, in fact, that it was all she could do to keep her mouth shut and not let loose the torrent of words that pressed behind her gritted teeth. It would not help her situation one bit, even if it would make her feel a whole lot better to express to her captors exactly what she thought of them.

She was also becoming increasingly unnerved by the feeling of the circle trapping her. It was invisible, yet it chafed and scraped her, like prickly vines wrapped around her body. It also felt distinctly like Walker, which was the most revolting part. Tasted like a lying, deceitful, sanctimonious, two-headed snake and she could hardly bear it.

She'd spent the last hour thinking furiously, trying to come up with anything that wouldn't end with her turning into curse-breaker confetti, but hadn't had any luck. She would have to trust her team and the Viking to get her out of this.

And did that not fill her with the utmost confidence . . . She had faith in her team, in their hearts and their abilities. But she also knew that they could be as reckless and foolish as Isaksson. She couldn't help but be wary of whatever plan they'd concocted, and hope they wouldn't land in even more trouble than they were in now . . .

Speaking of the Viking, he materialised from behind a pile of suitcases at the other end of the car, and marched towards them.

As soon as Pierce spotted him, he smirked. It was an evil kind of grin that made Olivia shudder. He was glad to fight the Viking. He acted as if he'd been looking forward to it.

She just hoped that Ryder would get the chance to even out his ribs with another one of his powerful blows.

Walker, who'd been lounging against a huge wooden crate, arms crossed over his chest, straightened from his position. "Ah, Warden. Right on time."

But Ryder barely looked at him, his eyes fixed on her. "You all right?"

Olivia nodded. She got to her feet and pushed the trunk she'd been sitting on to the side, out of the way.

"Now, I'm sure the lovely Ms Knight is anxious to get out of the circle," Walker said. "So hand over the wand and we can all enjoy the rest of this delightful journey through the Carpathians."

Olivia slanted a dark glance at him. She swore if he called her lovely one more time . . .

"I don't have it," Ryder replied.

Walker sighed in exasperation. He pinched the bridge of his nose as if he were dealing with a frustrating employee. "Mr Isaksson, I thought I'd made myself perfectly clear. Hand over the wand or I will detonate the circle around Ms Knight with her inside. You obviously don't want any harm to befall her, that much is evident. Why are you making this so difficult?"

"You misunderstand me. I do not *have* the wand," Ryder ground out. "When I got to our compartment, it was gone."

Olivia's breath caught. Was he serious? Or was this some part of his plan? She couldn't tell . . .

"Do you really expect me to believe that?" Walker huffed.

"You're welcome to search our compartment, search us, do whatever you want, but the wand is not there. If you're as familiar with dark artifacts as you claim to be, then you know that this one's special. It's devious, it has a mind of its own." Ryder shrugged his massive shoulders. "And obviously, it's not too interested in coming with you."

Pierce took a menacing step forward. "He's lying," he hissed.

Ah, so the rabid guard dog *could* talk after all.

Meanwhile, Walker was considering Ryder in silence. His face had lost all its false polite veneer. Only cold menace remained, sharpened by intelligence and resolve. This man was more dangerous than the hunk of muscle that flanked him.

"You see, Mr Isaksson," he declared. "I don't think I believe you either. I think you are bluffing."

Pierce moved, brutal and blindingly fast.

Ryder's back hit the steel wall of the train with a sickening crunch. The next instant, Pierce's meaty fist had hammered a punch to his jaw, followed by one to his gut.

Ryder doubled over, but before the other man could pin him down, he'd managed to scramble away.

Olivia's face paled. The force with which Ryder had slammed into the wall had shaken the entire car and she hadn't even *seen* Pierce move.

His left hand erupted into dark flames. Ryder didn't hesitate and rammed straight into him. He blocked his left arm and jabbed the heel of his other hand into the man's nose. Pierce grunted but didn't back away.

Olivia started to move forward, but Walker suddenly focused his gaze on her. "I wouldn't," he said coldly.

She halted, fists clenching at her sides.

Pierce's dark flames reappeared. He sent them hurtling towards Ryder.

He'd obviously expected the Warden to duck and twist to avoid them, his fist waiting. But instead, Ryder summoned an icy blue shield in the nick of time that absorbed the dark blow.

Pierce's fist whistled uselessly past his face while Ryder used the opportunity to snap a vicious kick, his foot smashing into Pierce's already injured side.

This time, Pierce let out a harsh yell and clutched his midsection, staggering back a few steps.

Clever Viking.

Ryder grabbed a heavy railway lamp lying nearby and swung it at Pierce's face, *hard*. Not giving him any time to recover, Ryder punched him again, turning his body into it. Pierce went down on a knee, his mouth bloody.

"That's enough."

Walker hadn't raised his voice, so both men ignored him and stood ready to go again, knees bent and fists clenched, but Olivia's anguished cry stopped Ryder in mid-strike.

Walker had restricted the circle around her, prickly chains tightening mercilessly.

His hand encircled her wrist, his fingers digging into her flesh. "Isaksson, don't think for one second that I'll hesitate. The life of one curse-breaker compared to thousands if the wand fell into the wrong hands. That's not a bad trade."

Ryder's eyes blazed with anger. He slowly raised his hands in the air and backed away from Pierce.

"I'm glad we can be reasonable about this. Now, about that wand—"

At that moment, the door to the car swung open with a bang. Godwyn emerged, his face and shirt bloodied, pushed forward by a merciless grip on the back of his head.

He staggered closer and the man restraining him came into view. Olive-skinned with short, dark hair, he had the same featureless suit as Walker and the same cold, ruthless eyes. "Got it," he said.

No . . .

For clutched against the stranger's chest was the containment cage and within it, the cursed wand.

Olivia saw Walker's satisfied smirk. "Well done. Right on time, too."

The man holding Godwyn gave him a final shove that sent him stumbling. Ryder grabbed his shoulder, steadying him.

"You got what you wanted," the Warden snarled. "You have the wand. Now, release her."

"I should refuse on principle, since your lie renegaded on our deal," Walker said, "but I am a gentleman, so I'll keep my word." That last part sounded as much a promise as a threat.

The invisible chains binding Olivia tightened even more and she let out a pained whimper, but then they unravelled, as if sliding down her body before landing in a heap at her feet.

Walker pushed her away, and only Godwyn and Ryder's quick reflexes prevented her from falling face first to the floor. She clung to Godwyn's arm as Ryder stepped in front of them.

Pierce had risen to his feet, his stare murderous. He seemed to want nothing more than to get back to his fight, but a nod from Walker had him grit his bloody teeth and turn to a particular section of the car. The muscles in his arm bunched. With a sharp tug, he actioned the large sliding doors, letting in a blast of night air that ruffled their clothes.

"In exactly two minutes, this train will cross a bridge over the Danube river," Walker explained. He'd raised his voice to be heard over the wind.

Olivia's pulse sped up. They couldn't be planning to push them overboard, could they? The fall might kill them instantly, or they could drown, break every bone in their bodies . . . She glanced at the opening. The night was so dark, lit only by the occasional sliver of moonlight, that it would be like plunging into an infinite black hole.

"Don't worry, Ms Knight," he added, having read her mind. "This is our way out, not yours. A boat awaits us below."

"You have what you came here for." Ryder's voice held an edge. "You can let us go."

"I have," Walker agreed. "There is just one hiccup."

Oh no . . . They really were going to throw them overboard.

Olivia's eyes settled on what appeared to be a heavy toolbox. As soon as the others made their move, she was going to hurl it at Walker's face, knocking him off balance. Ryder would take care of Pierce, finishing him off once and for all, and Godwyn would occupy the third one. They might even have a chance to wrestle the wand back . . . All they needed was the element of surprise.

"No one can know we were here." Walkers's words fell like heavy bricks, his intent clear. "We're supposed to be a secret group, after all."

"But . . . you said you would spare us!" Olivia exclaimed.

A dangerous light flared in his soulless eyes. "Indeed, I did. And I will keep that promise. However, I said nothing about what condition you would be left in."

His words didn't make sense to her until he extended his hand towards the third man.

She sucked the air into her lungs with a sharp gasp. "No!"

"Hand me the wand," Walker ordered. "We'll make sure they remember nothing of our presence here tonight. Only that their mission failed and the artifact they were trying to contain turned on them."

"You can't do this!" Godwyn cried out.

Olivia's world shrank to the cage in Walker's grip. Her eyes fixed on the shimmering lines, glowing softly in the dim light. The floating wand was barely visible beneath the glass, surrounded by green wisps. It looked so peaceful, so serene, and yet it contained the worst magic Olivia had ever handled.

"Walker, listen to me," she urged. "You told us that you've dedicated your life to protecting innocents from dangerous artifacts. You cannot let that wand out of its cage, it will turn on you. All it wants is freedom. If you take it out, you'll never be able to put it back in." An invisible fist had clamped her throat and was squeezing it, making it painful to speak.

"Please, listen to us!" Godwyn yelled over the howling wind. "This is suicide, the wand will drive you all mad! There's no controlling it once it's out!"

Walker lifted the sleeve of his suit to check his timepiece. When he looked up again, his eyes were ice-cold. "It's almost time."

Fear chocked Olivia. *No, no, no.* It couldn't end, not like this. Suddenly, there wasn't enough air on this bloody train.

"Please, don't do this," she begged.

But Walker ignored her again. He simply gestured to the other men, his expression merciless and unyielding.

He was going to doom them all. The wand would take complete control of their minds, they wouldn't be able to fight it. And then it would drive everyone on this train mad, locking them in their worst nightmares . . .

A burst of magic erupted from the third man, the one who'd brought Godwyn. It whistled past Olivia's head and catapulted Pierce through the opening and straight out into the night.

Ryder lunged. His arm whipped out.

He wrestled the cage from Walker before sinking a mighty fist into his gut that knocked him off the train too.

Godwyn hurried to the sliding door and groaned as he slammed it shut. The roar of the wind died abruptly.

Olivia blinked.

Someone ran inside their car. Adeline. "Are you all right? Did it work?"

Olivia had to force her jaw to unclench. "What."

The unknown third man looked pointedly at Adeline, and the next moment, Cornelius' face was staring back at them.

Olivia's mouth fell open. She couldn't believe this . . . Adeline had used her illusion magic. In public. Right in front of Black Knights.

"Tell me I'm hallucinating," she breathed. "Tell me you haven't done that."

"It worked great, no?" Ryder grinned, hands on his hips. He looked very proud of himself.

"Believe me," came a resigned voice from behind her. "I tried."

Godwyn was pressing a handkerchief to his face, wincing. Looked like the blood hadn't been part of the deception.

"What were you thinking?" Olivia hissed. "Those were Black Knights! They'll realise what you've done, they're no fools!" She spun around to face Ryder. "And you! Aren't you the expert in impossible situations? How could you let this happen?"

Ryder didn't snap back. Instead, his voice was calm, reasonable, and that only enraged her further. "We had no choice, we had to save you. And if that doesn't convince you, maybe this will: we had to save the wand."

"You should have found another way!"

Olivia did her best to keep the angry words from flying out of her mouth, especially after the fight she'd already had with them, but she couldn't believe this. Adeline hadn't just let her powers slip, she'd *deliberately* used them against members of a secret mercenary group that had flat out admitted they hunted all unnatural magic.

As soon as they understood what had really happened in those final moments of the fight, they would hunt her down. They would reveal her identity to the police, who would arrest her and throw her in jail for breaking the Forbidden Laws. And then, she would end up in—

"I don't regret it."

Olivia pivoted on her heels.

Adeline stood with her back ramrod straight, her mouth a thin line and her silvery eyes clear. "I did it to save you and to protect the wand. I would do it again in a heartbeat if I had to."

Olivia brought a hand to her brow. Of course, she would. Because Adeline was a strong and brave woman, loyal to a fault, who would never hesitate to risk her own life to save those she loved.

Olivia should never have brought her here. They should all have stayed behind in York, safe. Whatever happened now, was entirely her fault.

"Don't do that." Adeline's voice was scathing.

"What?"

"You're blaming yourself. This wasn't your decision to make, it was mine. What I do with my powers, with my life, is only up to me. You don't have a say in it, no matter how much you might wish otherwise."

It was all crumbling down.

All her careful planning, all her talk of safety, rules and being smart, and Olivia had led her team into the most dangerous case there ever was.

Yet, their plan had worked. It might not have been a good or safe plan, but it had worked. If it hadn't been for them, the wand would be with the Black Knights now. And if it had been for *her*, the wand would be lost.

"Maybe if you took greater care with your life, I wouldn't have to worry so much," Olivia said. Then she turned and left.

CHAPTER TWENTY-FIVE

*T*HE COURTROOM WAS SUFFOCATING. *Or maybe it was her, she couldn't tell. Lord Marston had just finished his closing argument, gesticulating and raising his voice as if he were on stage. One edge of his wig had lifted from the intensity of his fervour, before he'd put it back in place.*

It was such a ridiculous look, she'd thought. She couldn't pretend to be half as intimidated by him as she should be.

"Order!"

There were shouts, people were standing. The judge called for order, policemen rushed in. Olivia blinked. What had happened?

Something grabbed her, wrenching her out of her seat.

Bang!

Her chair clattered to the floor.

Lord Hadley's face came into focus. He was shaking her, yelling. His hand encircled her arm, digging into her skin like vicious claws. She jerked back, but it held.

"Murderer!"

His eyes were bloodshot, his face contorted with rage. His skin was so pale, made whiter still by his grief and his shock.

Breath caught in her throat.

It looked as if a wraith was clutching her, demanding that she be dragged into the depths of hell for what she'd done.

"You killed her!"

Olivia gasped awake, her heart pounding inside her chest. She rubbed her left arm, which felt as if it was on fire.

There was the softest knock on her compartment door, then a deep voice whispered from behind, "Olivia? Are you all right?"

She recognised Ryder immediately. Without thinking, she jumped out of bed and slid the door open, careful not to wake Adeline, who was sleeping in the top bunk.

She opened her mouth to say something, but her throat suddenly closed, trapping the words inside.

Ryder's worried gaze swept over her. When she still hadn't spoken, he simply asked, "Do you want to go back to sleep?"

When she shook her head, he held out a hand.

Knowing there would be no more rest for her tonight, and with her blood still rushing through her veins, pounding in her ears, she put her hand in his much larger one and let him lead her to the sitting area of their suite.

She sat down on one of the benches, tucking her legs underneath her. Perhaps Ryder could teach her how to play his Swedish card game and she would forget all about the painful consequences of past mistakes. Or maybe he'd let her have a taste of the flask of whisky she knew he always kept in his pocket.

His supply bag lay rolled out on the table. It looked like he'd been cleaning his weapons, as she spotted various rags and an open bottle that was probably oil.

He hadn't lit the main ceiling lamp, instead the only light came from a small hidden sconce above the window. It cast a warm glow over the interior of the compartment, reflecting off the dark wood panelling and crimson drapes.

"Looks like I wasn't the only one having trouble sleeping," Olivia said, a shiver running down her body. She was dressed in her nightclothes and a brightly patterned robe, the slumbering coal stove the only other thing to combat the train's chilly drafts.

"Can't say I'm not glad for the company," Ryder replied as he retook his seat opposite her, stretching his long legs on the banquette. "I was getting bored."

"What shall we do then?"

In response, he reached inside his coat for his small silver flask and handed it to her.

Predictable Warden.

Olivia took a sip of the smoky liquid, welcoming the burn down her throat. Ryder had turned his head away, parting the velvet curtains at the window to peer outside. His gaze lost itself in the distance and Olivia used the opportunity to study him.

Even in the dim light, with half his face hidden in shadow, there was no mistaking the impact of the day on him: fatigue overlaid his features, wariness tugged at the corners of his mouth and a grim determination set his jaw. He looked worn, even rougher than usual, as if he hadn't rested in days. He was still sharp, still ready, but it was the dangerous edge of a warrior in the lull between battles.

Olivia wondered how anyone could ever mistake him for a simple Ministry official.

She trailed a finger along the edge of the table, instead of reaching out and running it across his brow, like she wanted to. She longed to see him soften, if only for a moment.

He'd changed into a dark linen shirt that stretched over the solid strength of his chest. The sleeves were rolled up, revealing the tattoo on his forearm, the scars dotting his skin. He must have bathed recently because his shoulder-length hair looked darker than usual, slightly curling at the tips. It should have made him look young, boyish. All it did was draw Olivia closer, this hint of a soft side he never showed anyone.

And she had been so unfair to him.

She handed him his flask and when their fingers brushed, Ryder frowned. "You're cold." He reached for the coat he'd bundled into a makeshift pillow and handed it to her.

Olivia wrapped herself in the thick black wool and sighed in contentment.

It felt so deliciously warm that she couldn't help but burrow deeper into it. Ryder laughed softly, but she decided she didn't care, even though she knew she looked like a baby owl, with her dishevelled hair, glasses hanging low on her nose and the coat that practically swallowed her whole.

Olivia shifted, trying to make herself comfortable, but something pointy was lodged in her side.

Ryder winced. "Careful, *Älva*. Don't wiggle like that."

"There's something... poking me in... the hip," she managed as she tried to arrange and shift the heavy coat over her shoulders. "What the hells have you got in there? More knives?"

"You don't want to know."

Olivia's brows rose. Oh, she wanted to know. She *very much* wanted to know.

Ryder reached across the table to put a hand on her shoulder. "Really, Olivia. Stop fidgeting."

She huffed out a frustrated breath but stopped moving, instead patting the area to smooth it. "Fine... Seriously, what is it? You're acting like there's a bomb in there."

The slow smile that spread across his lips trapped the breath right in Olivia's throat.

She immediately withdrew her hand. "A bomb?" she croaked.

Ryder reached into the coat himself, eyes twinkling with mischief. His fingers returned with a small and oddly shaped box, all black with pale blue lettering and the drawing of clouds.

"I'll have you know this isn't just *any* bomb," he said, sounding very pleased with himself. "This baby carries one hundred and four grams of Tenebris stones and is capable of creating a black cloud fifteen feet wide. No wick to light, all you have to do is throw it."

Olivia gaped at him in disbelief. "I've got snacks in my pocket, Isaksson! Snacks! While you've been carrying a bomb around all day! That's a disaster waiting to happen!"

The Warden shrugged.

He deftly opened the box and dropped a small transparent sphere into the palm of his hand. Despite her better judgement, Olivia moved closer to examine it. The orb was tiny and filled to the brim with what looked like dark beads.

"The mist that comes out of this is so dense and opaque, it's like ink," he explained. "Perfect as a distraction to get out of a tight spot. There's no need to act so shocked, Ms Knight. Isn't Cornelius' luggage full to the brim with some sort of grenade?"

She grimaced. "Well, he's always been more of a . . . field agent. Whereas I like to stick to the research and technical side of curse-breaking. The *sensible* part," she added with emphasis.

Ryder couldn't hide his amusement. "What a terrible lie." He folded his arms across his chest. "I've seen the things you hide in that bottomless bag of yours. They're anything but sensible."

"It's not the same."

"You're right. Your . . . *experiments* also explode, but the difference is mine are supposed to. Yours, not so much."

Olivia's lips twitched. When she shook her head in disbelief, the smugness on Ryder's face dissipated and, to her profound delight, a slight pinkish hue appeared atop his cheekbones.

"What?"

"I just thought you'd use, I don't know . . . military grade."

Ryder shrugged and looked away, scratching the back of his head. "It's not my fault Fiery Fancy has the best stuff," he muttered.

Olivia took another swig of whisky when he handed her the flask. At some point during their bickering, her heart had settled in her chest. The guilt was still there though, like a heavy cloak she couldn't shake.

"You've gone pretty quiet over there."

Olivia mimicked his position, arms crossed and legs along the bench. Her face turned away, she kept her attention riveted on the knots in the mahogany table. "It's just . . . Nightmares. That's why I couldn't sleep."

Except it wasn't really nightmares that plagued her. Nightmares didn't exist.

This one was the truth.

Ryder simply hummed. She was grateful he didn't push.

"I heard you earlier," he declared, his voice soft. "You said you were sorry."

Ah. Spoke too soon.

Olivia tried to shove aside the memory of Lord Hadley's desperate cries, the way he'd squeezed her arm, tight enough to leave bruises. Damn Viking had the ears of a bat. "That was because of something that happened a long time ago. It's just the stress of this job." She clenched her fingers around the cold metal of his flask so he wouldn't see them tremble. "And what about you? Why couldn't *you* sleep?"

Her voice had held somewhat of a bite, convinced he wouldn't answer her and that would be it, the conversation would be over.

Only he replied, "Same as you. This mission is bringing back unpleasant memories."

Olivia blinked at the sincerity in his tone. The look he gave her was unguarded, full of emotion.

"Do they have anything to do with why you came to Scotland?" she couldn't help asking. "Holmes said something about a mission gone wrong."

Surprising her still, he didn't hesitate and nodded.

He pulled the window curtains further apart, revealing snow-capped mountains gilded by moonlight. In stark contrast to the beauty outside, his eyes held a distant and unpleasant look. "My last mission ... didn't go as planned. You've already guessed that I didn't choose to work for my Ministry. And since we were potential convicts, they didn't exactly treat us like respectable members of society. They gave us the worst jobs, the most impossible ones. You know me, they were actually my favourites," he said with a twist of his lips.

Olivia snorted at that.

But his expression turned sombre again. "This one had been gruesome. Things went from bad to worse very quickly. We tried to save it by doing what we did best, which was to take even more risks. That didn't work."

Those simple words told Olivia everything she needed to know. Ryder had lost men on that mission. And he blamed himself.

She could see it in the shadows swirling among the blue of his eyes, the cautious edge to his jaw. The way his fingers had edged closer to the knives laid out on the table between them.

Shame coated her tongue. She'd accused him earlier of not caring about anyone's life but his own. She'd immediately regretted saying it, but only now did she understand how wrong she'd been.

"You see, it wasn't any one man's fault," he went on. "It was everybody's fault, really. Some rash decisions, some bad thinking. A lot of things to prove. That made it harder later, not having anyone to blame. Or everyone, you might say."

His voice trailed off. Silence fell between them, broken only by the soft rattle of the train.

He may not have said many words, but Olivia knew they had meant a great deal to him. He'd let her peek at his guilt, his wounds.

She'd certainly never talked about her own nightmares, Adeline alone knew about the incident. But only the bare facts, not the heavy weight she carried over it still. A part of her had always held back, not even to confide in a dear friend of many years.

But in the quiet, the stillness, with only the rumble of the train to be heard, Olivia found that perhaps she could crack open that particular door. It felt safe to do so. Right here and right now, like a moment suspended in time. With a Viking warrior who would never judge or pity her.

For there was a kinship between them. The kind that came from similar ghosts haunting you. Yet, where she'd used hers to harden herself, to make better choices and smarter decisions, Ryder had remained the same person he'd always been. Reckless, rash, infuriating, yes. But . . . alive.

And she realised with a start that some dormant part of her longed to do just that.

"I worked for the Department before I started the agency." Her voice sounded hoarse and grating. She didn't stop. "I loved it there at first. But I quickly learned that politics played a huge part in how we were supposed to look after the artifacts. I caused quite a lot of trouble before I had to quit."

Before *they* made her quit.

"I was assigned this case of a family with a cursed mirror in the attic. A father and two little girls. They'd just inherited the house after the death of the grand-parents. I'd prepared the containment plans beforehand, so all I had to do was get into the house and build it around the artifact. Routine stuff."

Olivia took a breath to steady herself. Ryder wasn't watching her. He'd picked up one of his throwing daggers and his oil rag, and was slowly wiping it over the blade.

"But what I found in that mansion . . . It was a ticking time bomb. That artifact was stuffed with so much dark magic that I couldn't even get close. It was beyond unstable, I expected it to explode at any moment. Absolutely nothing even remotely close to what we'd discussed. I got out of the house, I was fuming. I didn't care about causing a scene, I shouted for the owner and confronted him in front of everyone. His staff, his business partner, some of his family who had stayed there after the funeral. As you can imagine, he didn't take it too well. Told me to get the hell out. But I refused to leave until he had evacuated everyone. I was preparing to call the police on him.

"Suddenly, I saw Skelton's car screeching down the driveway. He grabbed me and proceeded to explain what he thought of my lack of tact with influential clients. I was ordered to set up the protections like I had planned, or I would be fired. I was about to tell him where he could shove his orders, it was on the tip of my tongue. But then I stopped."

Her voice turned rough. If only she could go back to that moment.

"I thought about how proud my father had been when I got the job at the Ministry before he passed. I realised I didn't want to be fired. Yes, I hated the politics and I'd get into a lot of arguments with my boss, but I'd worked so hard to get there. And if I was fired, my reputation would be ruined, no one would hire me again. So I swallowed my pride and did as I was told."

Olivia clenched her jaw. The words didn't want to come out. They gathered in her throat, choking her. "That very night, one of the little girls went up to the attic and the artifact exploded. She was killed instantly. The other girl was badly injured, as were three members of staff sleeping in the next wing. Their injuries were so severe that they spent seven months in hospital. The little girl has a permanent limp and her face is covered in scars. She wanted to be a ballerina."

Ryder didn't say anything. He didn't look at her either, and she couldn't begin to explain how relieved that made her. It had taken everything she had to utter this story. And she still didn't really understand why she'd done so.

"It made the news. An investigation was launched. After a few weeks, the police cleared me of any wrongdoing, but the Ministry forced me to resign. They were under pressure from the higher-ups, who wanted someone to be responsible. It wasn't a question of the dangerousness of the artifact or anything else I'd tried to tell them. In the end, my containment failed and it was my fault. So I left. And that was the end of it."

"But it wasn't." Ryder placed the dagger back in his bag, put the oil and the rag away too, before meeting her gaze.

Olivia stared at him, the soft orange glow of the gas lamp turning his eyes from ocean blue to a midnight shade, and for once, she didn't try to hide.

"You carry this with you still," he continued. "That's what your nightmare was about. It wasn't the end for you."

"I can't let it go." Her admission felt like ripping out a piece of herself.

"You tried to make them listen."

A bitter laugh escaped Olivia. "I didn't try hard enough. In the end, I chose my career over their lives."

Ryder surprised her again when he nodded silently. He didn't offer her any platitudes, didn't say how sorry he was. And most of all, he didn't tell her that it wasn't her fault and that she shouldn't carry that guilt.

Because it was, and she did.

Olivia brushed the back of her knuckles across her cheeks, trying to swallow back the heartache stealing her breath. "Ryder . . . I want to apologise for what I said earlier today. I didn't mean it. I know you care about what happens to us, I've never doubted it."

At that, a shadow passed over his face and she wished once gain she could take back her words.

"There's no need," he replied. "I understand why you said it. Even more so now."

She took another sip from his flask, the liquor stinging her throat as it went down. She hoped it could just as easily burn the aching twist in her stomach. It seemed she hadn't been able to do anything right today.

"Adeline's mad at me too," she said, her fingers playing with one of the buttons on his coat.

"You should be careful. She's dangerous, that one."

The ghost of a smile flickered across her lips. "And she's right. But it's . . . not easy."

Ryder took the flask back, downed some whisky.

Not easy to trust, not easy to risk what you love most. Or to shoulder the burden of responsibility. The knowledge that if she failed, and the wand went on to do terrible things, it would be no one's fault but hers. *Again.*

Yet, that was exactly what Ryder was doing. Had done from the beginning. He hadn't permitted his past to drown him, not the way she had.

She'd been so angry. Angry at Adeline for being reckless, angry at Ryder for allowing it. But mostly angry at herself for putting those she loved in danger. She'd spent so much time and energy being angry, she was exhausted.

Adeline's earlier words came back to her. *This is nothing like last time.* She wasn't alone this time. And maybe now, if the worst happened, the guilt and the weight would be easier to carry if it was split between them all.

"I think you're right," Olivia declared. "This case is too big now."

Blue eyes bored into her. "What are you saying?"

"I'll help you. *We'll* help you. To investigate this whole thing, to carry out this mission. Protect the wand. Hide it, if we have to."

Ryder watched her. There was unmistakable pride in his gaze, as well as relief.

Olivia felt some of the tension ease from her shoulders. She'd made a decision, marched on from where she'd been stuck at a crossroads. Only time would tell if she'd got it right this time.

"How about a toast, then?" he asked her. "To seal our new partnership."

She gestured to the flask in his hand, but Ryder shook his head. "No, no."

He dug around in a corner of his pack for a moment. His eyes were twinkling.

Olivia watched as he produced a box of dragon eggs, the sides a deep crimson with tufts of golden paper spilling from the top.

"I noticed it in the service wagon." He looked down, frowning. "I hope I got the right one, I'm not even sure what flavour this is supposed to be."

Ryder smiled as Olivia snatched the colourful box from his hands before delicately opening it, as if she was handling the rarest of artifacts.

From the dozen or so eggs rolling inside, she selected two bright amber ones and placed them on the palm of her hand. "Come on, try one."

Ryder leaned closer. He didn't reach for the eggs, but picked up one of the daggers from his pack and used the tip to roll them around.

Only about one inch tall, they looked just like what they were called, two shiny little dragon eggs. That would soon end up tiny piles of crumbs.

Olivia pulled her hand back. "Stop it. No smashing my toast."

Ryder discarded his dagger. "They look harmless enough."

"Don't tell me a big, bad Viking such as yourself is afraid to try a candy," she teased him.

He shot her a dark scowl, but decided to pick up one of the eggs and bring it to his nose for a sniff.

Satisfied with the smell, and after another suspicious glance in her direction, he popped the whole thing inside his mouth. A few seconds later, his frown relaxed as he murmured in relief, "It's not bad."

But just as quickly, his entire body froze and he watched, wide-eyed, as a faint orange smoke began to emerge from his mouth. His eyebrows shot up when the smoke started coming out of his nose as well.

Olivia laughed, savouring the look on his face.

"I told you," she said, and swallowed hers whole.

CHAPTER TWENTY-SIX

OLIVIA WATCHED HER STEPS as she juggled the tray with one arm, compensating for the small movements of the train with her body. Her other arm was tucked behind her back, out of sight. She could hear Cornelius snicker behind her, but made no comment.

She used her foot and some clever knee manoeuvres to slide the compartment door open. "Feel free to help anytime!" she threw over her shoulder.

"Oh, you seem to have the situation well in *hand*, boss," was his cheeky reply.

They entered the lounge car where Godwyn, Adeline and Ryder were sitting, chatting quietly. It wasn't too early, but the train had lost most of its passengers at the last few stops, so they were the only people here this morning. Cornelius slid into one of the empty seats and no one wasted any time digging into the delicious breakfast.

Isaksson looked at everything laid out on the table with a sad little frown. Olivia hid her smile. What a fearsome Viking he was.

When he glanced at her, she winked and brought her hand out from behind her back. His eyes properly lit up as she placed the steaming cup of coffee in front of him.

"Right, then," Godwyn began. "What happens once we reach Romania?"

"We disappear," Ryder replied simply.

Olivia's teacup froze halfway to her mouth. After their conversation last night, she knew what was coming but . . . to hear it so plainly was still jarring.

"We *disappear*," Godwyn repeated.

"I think we're about to break around eleven laws right now," Olivia muttered. "Just off the top of my head."

Cornelius grinned as he twirled a spoon around his fingers. "Only eleven? That's not as many as I expected, I'm kind of disappointed."

Olivia shot him a dark look over the rim of her teacup. "No Yule bonus for you."

"I sent a telegram this morning," Ryder continued. "To my police contact, an inspector I trust completely. I asked him to gather as much information as he could and then come join us here."

"The same detective who gave you the file on the other team of curse-breakers," Olivia guessed.

Ryder nodded. "He's a good man, he'll help us. We can trust him. But in the meantime, we need to find a way to extend the containment of the wand."

"While avoiding the Romanian authorities who will surely be looking for us," Godwyn finished in a harsh voice. "You're turning us into fugitives from the *law*."

Adeline gave him a pointed look. "What exactly did you expect, Godwyn? Until we know who we can trust, we have to hide the wand. Otherwise, it'll fall directly into the hands of the Order."

Olivia agreed, but there was still an uneasy feeling swirling in her stomach. What Ryder expected of them . . . She didn't know if they could do it.

Godwyn heaved a frustrated sigh, running a hand over his slicked back hair. "I *know*," he growled. "It's just . . . We're not thieves."

Adeline grinned at him then. She patted the back of his hand. "There's a first time for everything."

Ryder reached into his coat and spread out a map of Romania on the table. "Once we get to Brașov, we should jump straight into another train and put as much distance between us and the Institute as possible," he instructed them. "We'll need somewhere safe to hide, but with easy exits in case they find us. The wand can't travel through Portals, so we'll be limited to the traditional methods."

"Why not somewhere in the countryside?" Cornelius suggested. "Easy enough to disappear."

Adeline immediately shook her head. "Easier to stay hidden, maybe. But if they find us, they can block our exits and box us in. You need a place big enough to have so many ways out, they can't cut them all. Besides, we'll need specialised supplies to work on the containment cage, we'll need a city. A big one, preferably." She ran her eyes over Ryder's map. "How about Brăila? It's a port city, looks big enough to have all the supplies we might need, and it's close to the Black Sea and the border with Moldova if we need to run."

Ryder was staring at her, a brow arched. "You would have made a fine hunter, Adeline."

She raised her teacup with a very smug smile and clinked it with Ryder's coffee mug.

As the two hunters put their heads together and considered their options, Cornelius and Godwyn shared a bemused look, the latter muttering something along the lines of *"What have we done..."*

"I think you may be right," Ryder said, rubbing his stubbled jaw. "But to muddy our tracks, we should take another train to Bucharest. The capital is so big, it'll be almost impossible for them to pick up our trail. From there we can travel to the port of Călăraşi, board a ship and follow the Danube all the way to Brăila."

Adeline's fingers drummed on the wooden table as she considered Ryder's plan. "How about we make it even worse? We could..."

Olivia stopped listening, their excited voices fading into the background.

Godwyn had been right earlier. They weren't thieves, even if Adeline had unsurprisingly turned into a proper criminal mastermind. They would have Ryder's police contact on their side, but an investigation of this calibre could take weeks, *months*.

And she couldn't build a permanent cage for the wand, in case they had to move without notice. She needed to find a way to make a temporary hold, strong and durable enough for long-term containment.

A pulsing began behind her temples. She didn't regret her decision last night to take on this mission. But she was beginning to realise just how difficult, if not impossible, it really was.

Her hand shook slightly, causing her teacup to rattle against the saucer. All of a sudden, the air seemed to have gone out of this lounge.

She rose from her seat and muttered something she vaguely hoped was an *"excuse me"*, before making her way out of the stifling car.

She was fine, she just needed some peace and quiet. A chance to breathe, to think.

She staggered along the corridor, using her hand against the wood panel to guide her. She willed her body to pull itself together, but it felt as if a white veil had wrapped around her mind. Her thoughts were sluggish, slow to surface. She might have walked through a door. She definitely bumped into someone.

"Order!"

Olivia squeezed her eyes shut and cupped her hands over her ears. She just needed to get to her compartment.

"Order! I demand order!"

Everything around her was blurry now, as if she'd taken off her glasses.

The judge kept shouting, his face outraged and his lips twisted.

She stifled a moan. She didn't want anyone to see her like this. Compartment. Alone.

Bang!

Something grabbed her arm. She cried out.

"You killed her!"

"Olivia!"

A hand caught her elbow and she startled so abruptly she almost tripped and fell. "Olivia! What's wrong?"

She recognised Ryder's deep voice, but it sounded miles away. What was she doing here? Where was the judge?

Olivia shook her head, trying desperately to concentrate. What was happening?

Hands reached out to wrap around her shoulders.

"I . . . I don't know," she murmured. The words felt foreign on her tongue, somehow wrong. "I don't feel so good."

She tried to pull away, still longing for privacy. But Ryder refused to let go, wrapping an arm around her waist instead. "Come. Let's get you some air."

Olivia let him lead, not bothering to look where he was taking her. All she knew was that after only a few more ragged breaths, she finally felt sweet, *sweet* air.

She closed her eyes in bliss, pressing her face against the side of the window. She was already much more alert, the cold glass against her fevered brow awakening her mind.

Her vision began to clear as well. She saw Ryder standing on the other side of the open window, a hand still on her waist.

"I didn't feel so great either," he said. "It's stifling in there."

Indeed, he looked as exhausted as she felt. The light tan on his skin was gone, and his hair was even more dishevelled than usual.

Olivia raised a hand and ran the tip of a finger gently over the dark circles underneath his eyes. "You're exhausted," she said, her voice no more than a whisper. "Nightmares, again?"

Ryder met her gaze and nodded. Didn't shy away from her question.

It was then that Olivia realised she hadn't even thought, or cared, about *him* seeing her like this when she'd run out of the lounge.

Ryder turned his head to press against her hand. She hadn't even noticed that she'd started to stroke his temple. His soft beard caressed the inside of her wrist.

"It's been going on for weeks now," he said. "I can only get a few hours here and there. But I'm used to it."

"You are?"

"Former hunter, remember? Artifacts have this really annoying tendency to be most active at night. Like vampires. Or bats."

Olivia hummed quietly. "That's actually due to the effects of the astro—"

Ryder's chuckle stopped her. "How did I know you'd be able to explain it?"

Olivia felt her own lips tilt upwards in the faintest of smiles, the familiar cadence of his voice helping to soothe her frazzled nerves.

"Must be this mission," he whispered with a frown. "All this stress is making me remember . . ."

A terrible realisation suddenly hit Olivia and she gasped, her eyes wide. "It's not the mission, it's the *wand*!"

Ryder grabbed her hand and they sprinted across the corridor, flinging open the doors to the lounge. Adeline and Godwyn were still sitting where they'd left them, Adeline's head resting on her crossed arms. Olivia immediately noticed that her messenger bag was open on her seat.

"Where's the wand?" Ryder demanded.

"Cornelius took the cage to check on it." Adeline indicated behind her to where Cornelius was standing frozen, hovering next to the other compartment door. He was clutching the cage to his chest.

Ryder took a few slow steps towards him, his hand outstretched. "Give us the wand, Cornelius."

But panic seized his face and he clutched it tighter, shaking his head. "You don't understand . . ."

Olivia also inched her way to him, trying to appear as non-threatening as possible. Adrenaline was making her heart beat faster and focused her mind, even though she began to feel the white veil clouding her vision again. "Everything's going to be all right, Cornelius. It's the wand, it's controlling you. Just give it back to us."

"Please, don't come any closer!" Cornelius cried out. His warm eyes were frantic, his fingers trembling.

"Cornelius, look at me." Olivia put a hand on Ryder's arm so she could sneak in front of him. "You trust me, don't you?" she coaxed.

Cornelius took a few steps back but nodded at her. "I'm sorry, I didn't mean to do it!"

She was almost to him now, Ryder close behind. She concentrated solely on Cornelius, hoping to distract him long enough for the Warden to snatch the wand from his hands. She knew how fast he could be.

"I swear I didn't!" Cornelius' usual honeyed voice was so hoarse, so anguished. "But *it* made me. I'm so sorry!"

"We know it wasn't you, Cornelius. We forgive you." Olivia tried to keep her tone as gentle as possible, even through the terrible pulsing in her head. "What did it make you do?"

With an unsteady hand he reached into a pocket and pulled out a very familiar glass bottle filled with a milky liquid. "I swear I didn't put too much in! I thought it would help you! Make you stronger . . ."

Tears of Valeria.

Good gods . . .

The powerful extract usually resided in the small apothecary cabinet in her office, under lock and key, and was strictly reserved for emergencies. Olivia used it on very rare occasions when people who had come into contact with strong curses needed to be sedated.

Which meant that the wand had already taken control of Cornelius, before he'd even left Edinburgh. Damn it all to hells!

When Olivia's outstretched fingers touched the thin vial, Cornelius locked eyes with her and Ryder sprang into action.

He uncoiled from his position behind her and wrenched the wand from Cornelius's grasp. She saw him hand it to Godwyn next. It was all over in a matter of seconds.

As soon as the wand was taken from him, all strength seemed to leave Cornelius and he collapsed. Olivia helped him to the nearest chair.

He was still muttering how sorry he was when she gently cupped his cheek. "It's all right, nobody blames you," she said soothingly. "Tell me how much you gave us."

It took four drops to render a person under the influence of a curse completely unconscious, and the extract worked in minutes. Judging by how dizzy she was beginning to feel, Olivia knew they didn't have much time.

Adeline came closer and sank to her knees beside them. Her movements were shaky, lacking her usual feline grace. "No one's hurt, Cornelius. All is well. Just tell us how much."

Olivia felt a warm hand on her shoulder. She looked up at Ryder hovering somewhere above her. "What's that? Do you need the first aid kit?"

She shook her head, immediately regretting it when spots appeared at the edges of her vision. "Sedative. No, I just need to know how much."

Cornelius was clutching Adeline's fingers in a death grip, but his gaze was unfocused, eyes darting everywhere. His pupils were blown wide as if drugged, his brown skin now pale and clammy. Olivia wasn't sure if he could hear them at all.

"I don't understand . . . how I could have done this," he muttered. "I—It's like I wasn't myself any more."

"Because you weren't. The wand tried to take control of you but you resisted, you fought." Olivia realised she'd let go of him when her left hand slapped her thigh as it went completely limp.

Using the last of her dwindling strength, she raised the other one to grip his shoulder. It felt like trying to lift a dead weight. "Now, *focus*. Tell me how much of the Tears you used."

That seemed to get through to him as his wild gaze latched onto hers, not letting go. Still, it took him three tries to get the words out, his voice slurring. "Ten drops in the tea, three . . . three in . . . Ryder's coffee."

Olivia swore.

No wonder they all felt like death. They didn't have much time, in a few minutes they would be unconscious and the wand would be exposed.

Ryder's hand on her shoulder tightened. "What do you need?"

His voice was strong, calm. Like an anchor in the middle of rough seas. She let it centre her, keep her afloat.

But it was so hard to think. Olivia scrunched her eyes shut. The white fog was closing in on her.

What countered the effect of the Tears of Valeria ? There was something, she knew. What was it? She couldn't remember . . .

What did she even have with her? Her curse-breaking supplies, snacks, Ryder's first aid kit, his venom kit . . .

Then a thought struck her. They were falling asleep. Maybe she just needed to *wake* them up.

"Ryder, my bag. It's in . . . my compartment." Her voice came out so small, it was a wonder he heard her at all.

But heard her he did. No sooner had the words left her lips than there was a whoosh of air as he ran out of the lounge. With his hand no longer on her shoulder, supporting her, Olivia felt herself sway.

The others weren't faring much better. Godwyn seemed to be the only thing keeping Adeline upright as he knelt behind her, her head resting on his shoulder. His green eyes were staring straight ahead, but seemed glassy and unfocused.

Cornelius was leaning forward in his chair and would have toppled over if Olivia hadn't grabbed a hold of his shirt and pushed him back. She opened her mouth to speak but nothing came out. She had to clear her throat a few times, blinking furiously. "Everyone, stay awake. Don't fall asleep."

When no one answered, she wondered if they were already unconscious or if she had imagined saying the words.

Rustling sounds came from far away. Something was shaking her. She blinked again and saw Ryder standing over her.

He was speaking, his mouth moving, but she couldn't make out a single word. She tried to tell him. Her mouth refused to obey.

He grabbed her arm and pulled until she sat up. Strange, she didn't remember falling down . . . She was shaken again, mercilessly.

Infuriating man. Couldn't he see that she was trying to sleep?

Cold slapped her. She gasped.

"Olivia, wake up! Tell me what to do!"

She raised a trembling hand to her face, wiped some water from it.

Tears of Valeria. Cornelius, the wand. *Wake up*.

Olivia gripped Ryder's strong forearms. She forced herself to look at him, commanding her mind to bloody *focus*.

Another shake. "Olivia!"

She finally managed to make her mouth work long enough to mutter, "V . . . V-32."

The next thing she knew, someone was tilting her head back and a strong-smelling liquid was flowing into her mouth.

She had no idea what was happening, but the hands on her face felt familiar, so she didn't resist.

After only a few swallows, Olivia felt the confusion around her mind begin to lift. Her vision returned. She nodded, whispering something that vaguely resembled "I'm fine."

As the Vitalis Vigor worked its wonders, she became more and more alert. It was something she sometimes used to perk herself up after a particularly exhausting case, or during tax season. Much stronger than caffeine, she swore a few vials of the stuff could raise the dead.

She heard groans and muffled curses as Ryder helped the others to their senses. By the time he'd tended to everyone, Olivia noticed that his eyes were closing on their own and he looked ready to fall face first onto the floor. She hurried to grab the vial from his slack hands before it fell and shattered.

Now it was her turn to help him. She shifted until she was sitting beside him on the carpeted floor of the train, her bent leg supporting his back. She raised the small bottle to his lips.

As he drank, Olivia couldn't help the way her eyes roamed over his face. They were so close that she could count the light freckles dotting his cheekbones, which she'd never noticed before.

Too soon, the vial was empty. Ryder pushed her hand away but didn't release her wrist, his thumb drawing circles around her knuckles. His hand was so big compared to hers, the skin rough and calloused. Yet the touch of his fingers was light, gentle.

A slight blush rose to her cheeks, but Olivia couldn't tear her eyes away, almost mesmerised. He smelled good. A little like the forest, a little smoky. She could feel the steely strength and warmth of his body through her jumper.

A shiver ran through her. A wary thrill, part alarm and part . . . something else.

He was so strong. And he'd saved them all. She might have instructed him to get the V-32 but if it hadn't been for him, they'd all be passed down on the floor of this train right now. Infuriating, reckless, loyal, *brave* Viking.

A mysterious smile played at the corners of his mouth, as if he knew what she'd just called him in her mind. The slow graze of his calloused fingers against her wrist sent shivers up her arm.

She felt safe with him. She'd never had that before, it was . . . *nice*.

More grunts and uncoordinated movement behind them broke the spell they seemed to be under.

Olivia shifted away immediately.

"How's everyone feeling?" she asked as soon as she got to her feet. "Cornelius? Adeline? You still with us?"

Cornelius didn't reply. He was hunched over, one hand holding his bent head. But he raised the other in a thumbs up.

Adeline answered with a harsh sigh, fingers rubbing her temple. "That stuff is no joke."

An explosion of Swedish erupted.

Olivia whirled around in time to see Ryder slap the table he was leaning against, hard enough to make the teacups rattle.

"Ryder! What's wrong?"

He raked a furious hand through his hair and growled, "The wand's gone."

Olivia's mouth dropped open in shock. "Wh-what?"

She could only stare at him as he added, "And so is Godwyn."

CHAPTER TWENTY-SEVEN

"Cornelius was just a diversion," Ryder claimed as he tossed his bag into a corner of the room. "It wanted Godwyn from the start."

"But why?" Adeline asked, shrugging off her hat and coat in big, frustrated movements. "I don't understand why it's behaving like this. I mean, we're doing what it wants, aren't we? We're taking it to Romania. Why fight us?"

As soon as they'd discovered Godwyn was missing, they'd searched everywhere for him, combed the entire train. When it had grounded to a halt at the next station, Cluj-Napoca, they'd got off immediately, hoping to catch him.

But he and the wand had disappeared without a trace.

With no leads and no idea where the wand might take him, they'd decided to find a hotel room and figure out their next move.

Olivia shook her head as she smoothed out the creases of the map Ryder had laid out on the nearest bed. "It doesn't *just* want to get back home. The wand seeks power, it desires its freedom. It must know that we're bringing it back to Romania, only to be locked away again."

"You said cursed artifacts were like wild beasts, right?" Ryder pointed out. "So now that the wand has control of Godwyn, it'll want to get back to familiar territory."

Ryder was right. Most cursed artifacts tended to show only primal behaviour. Fight or flight. They fought for power and avoided danger, that was about it. But this wand was particularly cunning. It showed a far greater complexity of thought than any other artifact she had ever encountered.

They had to start treating it like an intelligent animal. Or better yet, a *person*.

And that thought did not just raise the tiny hairs on the back of her neck.

"What would it consider to be familiar territory?" Adeline asked. "Its home? Where the general lived?"

"No, the wand is much older than that," Cornelius disagreed. "If the legend is true, it was created by the Erdőelve king from the sap of the Whispering Tree. I think the wand is trying to get back to that forest."

Olivia rubbed her brow. "What I don't understand is why the wand would try to hide. It's certainly never been shy before. I think we should focus more on what it *wants*."

"And what exactly would that be?" Adeline stressed. "More people under its command?"

"Perhaps it wants to hunt down ophite stones," Cornelius suggested. "Bloat itself with power."

Ryder held up a hand to stop everyone. His voice was grimmer than Olivia had ever heard it. "Theories are useless here, we need to be certain. We've only got one chance. We need a way to locate him."

"Right now" went unsaid.

Because the cage would not last much longer. And once the containment broke, the wand would absorb all the energy inside the Serpenthyst crystals, making it even more powerful than it was now.

They all fell silent. Cornelius ran a hand over his face, thinking hard. Ryder began to pace, fists clenching and loosening at his sides.

"Liv . . . What will it do to him?" Adeline's voice was small, strained. "Will the wand drive him mad?"

Olivia forced her voice to sound reassuring. "For now, it needs him. It won't attack him if it doesn't have to, it's only interested in its own survival."

Ryder shared a dark look with her.

She hadn't lied to Adeline, but she hadn't told her the whole truth, either. She hadn't told her that if they didn't find Godwyn in the next few hours, the wand would take absolute control of him and there would be nothing remaining of their friend.

And if that happened, they would have no choice but to fight the wand head on to recapture it. Which meant fighting Godwyn.

Olivia gritted her teeth. They still had a few hours. She wasn't going to let that artifact consume her friend. She was a curse-breaker. Containing curses was her job, so she *would* contain that wand.

Determined, she pivoted to Cornelius. He was hunched over in the nearest chair, his head between his hands. Some colour had returned to his cheeks, but he was clearly exhausted, still reeling from the wand's compulsion.

"How did it control you?" she asked him. "Did it show you visions? Did it talk to you?"

"No, it wasn't like that. It was . . . as if I was in a dream. I had forgotten why we were here, what our mission was." He paused, trying to find the right words. "All I knew was what I could feel. I was terrified of the wand, of what it might do to all of you." Cornelius lifted his head from his hands, but avoided her gaze, turning to stare out the window instead. "Somehow, I became convinced that the Tears of Valeria would make you immune. Because if you slept, the wand couldn't hurt you. I felt it was the only way to protect you. To keep you safe."

"Oh, Cornelius . . ." Adeline murmured.

Ryder resumed his fast pacing, hands clapped behind his back. Olivia followed his movements with her eyes, mulling over Cornelius' words. "So the wand didn't really force you to act against your will," she said. "It just put you in a dream-like state, where your own thoughts and decisions would lead it where it wanted to go."

She felt dread settle in the pit of her stomach. Such intelligence . . . What the hells kind of magic was this?

She turned to Ryder, the chill in her voice easy to hear. "Do you realise what this means? That wand can control absolutely anyone, no matter how strong their mind. Because it uses your own motivations to get what it wants, it could turn anyone into its puppet."

Brute force, she would have understood. Even if the thought of an object capable of controlling your mind sounded properly terrifying. But it would have made sense. A battle of wills.

Except that wasn't what this wand was doing at all. It had somehow found a way to use people's own desires against them. It manipulated them in such a way that it made it seem as if they were still acting of their own accord.

Holmes voice came back to her. *"This wand can creep into your mind and draw out your deepest fears. It will use them against you in ways you could never have predicted."* He'd been more than right.

Olivia felt a shudder run through her. She knew that cursed artifacts had the ability to adapt and react to threats. This . . . this was as close to life itself as it could get.

"I've seen things," came a small voice.

Olivia closed her eyes on a sigh.

They all turned to Adeline. She was perched on the windowsill, head bent, shoulders slumped, staring at the joined hands on her lap. "Ever since you came back from the Museum, but especially on the train. I've had terrible nightmares," she forced out, her voice barely more than a whisper. "Hallucinations. They're actually memories, things I hadn't thought about in years. Things I had tried to forget. But more than that, I've felt sort of . . . detached from reality. Not just at night, but during the day too. I thought it was the stress, the fatigue. As if I was . . . As if I was stuck in a dream."

Ryder froze. He swore.

Olivia took in his pressed lips, his tense shoulders, and she understood. He had felt the same.

It looked like the wand had been toying with them all, trying to decide who it would enthral. Who might help it the most.

"But how could that be?" Cornelius frowned. "How could the wand have broken out of the Behr-Walde manoeuvre without us knowing?"

"I think some of its magic is able to slip through it."

"That's impossible. No artifact has ever cheated the manoeuvre."

Olivia shook her head, as lost as he was. But the better question was: assuming they got the wand back, how were they going to contain it?

And she had a growing fear that maybe, there wasn't anything in existence powerful enough to do that . . .

"Let's just focus on finding it, yes?" Ryder cut in.

Olivia had furrowed her brow, something bothering her. "Why did it choose to take Godwyn's mind? Why not mine?"

"Perhaps it ran out of energy from controlling the rest of us?" Cornelius suggested.

"But I would be the most obvious choice, wouldn't I? I could easily disarm the cage, since I'm the one who built it. Controlling Godwyn only helps it escape, I could set it free." She tilted her head to the side, fingers playing absent-mindedly with the edge of the map. "And if the wand had the ability to control us from the start, why didn't it?"

Ryder ran a hand over his beard. "You're right. It doesn't make sense."

"Maybe it couldn't, somehow," Adeline proposed. "Maybe you're immune to it."

"If anything, I should be the most affected. I handled it the most, I created the cage with my own magic. I even touched it when we were in the Cellars . . ." Her voice trailed off.

"What is it?"

"I think I might know what happened." Olivia felt her heart speed up in her chest. "When I transferred it to the cage, it fought me at first. And we didn't have any bait, so I . . . sort of appealed to it."

Ryder's gaze sharpened. "What do you mean *appealed*?"

"I let down the shields around my magic so that it could try to reach me."

"So you used *yourself* as bait!"

Olivia winced. "When you put it like that . . . But I really didn't have much of a choice! And it all worked out in the end."

The Warden opened his mouth again to argue, but Cornelius cut him off. "How does that explain why it hasn't been targeting you?"

Olivia's eyes glinted, a wild kind of hope rising with each word. "I think some of its magic got into me, latched onto mine. So the wand can't use its abilities against me because it would feel like attacking itself." Her voice grew more agitated as she looked at all of them in turn. "If I'm right, maybe

I could channel that piece of its magic. Maybe I could get a glimpse of where it is right now, or what it's doing."

"Do you really think it could work?" Cornelius sounded sceptical.

"I don't know. But it's definitely worth a shot."

Not waisting any time, they stood and cleared a space in the middle of the room, pushing chairs and beds aside. Olivia decided to draw a simple augmenting circle, hoping it would focus her magic onto herself. If that piece of the wand's magic really existed inside her, it would be buried deep and almost out of reach.

When Adeline and Cornelius returned after hunting down some candles, Ryder helped arrange them around the arcane circle she'd just traced. Olivia stood and dusted the chalk off her fingers.

Ryder came over. He didn't look happy as he ran a hand through his messy hair and whispered, "Are you sure it's safe? You're trying to connect with an artifact that likes to mess with people's minds . . ."

Olivia kept her voice low so the others wouldn't hear. "I know. But I don't have any other ideas. Ryder, I . . ." The words died in her throat. She tried not to let him see the fear gnawing at her. But he still saw it.

His face hardened. "You can do this, Olivia," he told her, his voice ringing with conviction. "I've never seen anyone with as much control over their magic as you. You'll find him."

Her eyes closed and her lips parted to let out a slow exhale. Then she nodded.

Ryder offered her a hand to help her kneel in the centre of the circle.

"Ryder, would you mind?" Before she could even finish her question, all the candles around her ignited.

Show-off.

Olivia took another steadying breath and closed her eyes, letting her power shot through the circle. The chalk lines ignited with a bright copper light, sending puffs of amber dust into the air, the colour of her magic.

It moved through the circle before flowing back to her, clear and pure. Olivia offered more power to the circle. Once, twice. Steadily, like water lapping on the beach with each wave, each burst of power came back to her stronger, sharper. It slipped into her body, twice as potent as before.

CHAPTER 27

When she felt her hands start to tremble, she stopped. Any more and she wouldn't be able to control that much energy.

The first step was done. Now it was time for the hard part.

Olivia concentrated on calming her mind. She took another breath, and fell deep within herself.

She spiralled down into her aura, as if plummeting from a great height. All the while concentrating on her memory of that night, when they'd taken the wand from the Cellars. She recalled the icy cold coming off the thick stone walls. Remembered the shouts of the guards echoing around her. She began to smell the damp air, still salty from the sea outside.

Olivia fell deeper.

Behind her eyes, the wand was resting on a stone pedestal, almost hidden in shadows. Except for the green crystals, locked inside the twists of the wood, which shone brightly.

She reached a mental hand towards the wand. Took one step closer, then another. Until the tips of her fingers made contact with the black wood.

And just like that, she wasn't in the Cellars any more.

Flashes of colour and sound assaulted her senses.

Green, brown. A cold breeze on her face. The rustling of leaves.

Olivia tried to make sense of what she was seeing, feeling. But the visions kept shifting and twisting at the speed of light. Too fast for her to make out. She fought desperately to grab onto anything that might help, anything specific.

A vision of roots, sticking out of the ground. The smell of moss and damp earth.

Everything was all jumbled together. Just a whirlwind of images.

And above it all, she felt a terrible sorrow invade her, tearing at her insides. Her throat tightened. She felt so *alone*. Adrift.

She longed for home, anything to fill this awful emptiness. Yes, such a yawning void that had grown and grown until it consumed her.

Wait, there was something there . . .

At the edges of her mind, something lurked in the shadows, watching. Fear gripped her by the throat. Squeezed.

Olivia tried to turn away, she tried to go back. But it was too late. It had seen her, it had *sensed* her. Oh, gods . . .

She shouldn't be here. She didn't belong here.

The Darkness slithered its way to her. A lethal serpent, its scales shimmering where there was no light.

Her blood went cold. This Darkness was a living, malevolent thing. It wanted to bite and tear into her with those sharp fangs. She was in its territory now, she was prey.

She had to get out . . .

The serpent came closer, ready to strike, ready to clamp her in its grip.

She had to get out . . . She had to get out, now!

Olivia came back to herself with a cry. Gasping, she sank to the floor and sucked in sharp, desperate breaths.

She could still *feel* it. That horrifying darkness lunging for her, ready to devour her. It was all things evil and terrible in this world. It had wanted to destroy her.

From very far away, Olivia heard people frantically calling her name.

The room was spinning. She squeezed her eyes shut. Her heart was hammering so hard in her chest that she thought she might pass out.

The Darkness isn't there any more, she told herself. It hadn't devoured her, she was safe.

She made it out. She was safe.

One breath. Another.

Safe. Safe.

Olivia clenched her fists, forcing herself to get some air into her lungs.

A large hand was rubbing circles on her back. The contact and warmth spread through her body, soothing her out of her shock.

She was cold, so *cold*. Her entire body ached from it, her skin like ice. A shudder racked her.

"I'm fine," she croaked out. "Just . . . give me a minute."

She whimpered in protest when the big hands disappeared from her back, but they were replaced by strong arms that lifted her. She was deposited in a soft armchair, right next to a fireplace. Olivia let out a sigh of relief. Delicious heat filled her, bringing her slowly back to life.

CHAPTER 27

Her vision was still blurred but the room had stopped spinning. She could feel them hovering around her, anxious tension in the air.

Smaller hands pressed something into hers. A teacup, steaming.

"Here, drink this," someone said, their voice shaking. Adeline.

Olivia kept hold of her friend's hand when she tried to pull away. "I'm all right, Addie. Promise." She took a sip of tea with trembling hands as her vision finally cleared. "Well . . . That went well."

Her attempt to lighten the mood was met with silence. Only Cornelius cracked the tiniest smile. Ryder, on the other hand, was leaning against the mantelpiece, his jaw clenched so tightly that he might break all his teeth.

"What happened?" Adeline asked.

Olivia took another sip, chuckled. There was whisky in that tea. "I managed to connect with the wand, so it did leave something behind in me. I saw visions . . . They were more like glimpses, really. All jumbled together. It all happened so fast, I had trouble keeping up. I think I could also feel what it was feeling. It was so sad. Alone."

She let the warmth from the roaring fire kiss her frozen cheeks. "But there was this . . . *thing* at the edges of my mind. I knew it wanted to hurt me. It tried to grab me, so I pushed with everything I had to get back here. It was a little chaotic."

A muscle in Ryder's arm jerked. His gaze was sharp on her, a dangerous light flaring in his blue eyes. Of course he knew she was downplaying what had happened, trying not to scare them. She imagined they would have private words about this later.

"And what did it show you?" Adeline asked her, her eyes brimming with emotion. "Did you see Godwyn?"

"No, but I saw flashes of where they are." Olivia's brow furrowed in concentration. "There was moss, leaves. Roots. I think it was a forest. Really dark, misty. All the trees were crooked and wrong. They looked like . . . The branches looked like skeleton fingers pointing in all directions."

Ryder came over and handed her the packet of mystic moons biscuits from her bag, practically shoving it into her hand when she was too slow to react. "Eat," he said gruffly.

"The wand is definitely looking for the Whispering Tree, then," Cornelius declared. "It wants more crystals."

Mouth full, Olivia simply nodded. The biscuit tasted like ash on her tongue and her jaw didn't want to work, but she forced herself to eat it all. "Yes . . . I felt it," she said at last. "It knew where it was going. It was like it was missing something. It wasn't whole."

"Do you think you could do a tracking spell?" Ryder asked her.

Before Olivia could answer, Cornelius suddenly sat up. "I know where it is!"

"What?"

"The Hoia forest!" he exclaimed, his voice becoming increasingly animated. "It's by far the most haunted place in Romania! The entire woods are believed to drive people to madness. There are reports of travellers wandering in, and only coming back years later with no memory of what happened to them!" He gestured for Adeline to hand him the map. "This *has* to be the place! At the very centre of the forest, there's an area in the shape of a perfect circle where nothing grows. No grass, no bush, nothing. It's called the Clearing."

Olivia could feel the excitement rising in her. "You're right, I've heard about this! They've done countless analyses of the soil, but could never explain why nothing grows."

Cornelius hovered his finger over the map. "There! Legend has it that nothing can survive in the Clearing because it was once the home of a great evil, before it was swallowed back into Hells."

Ryder sighed as he studied the map.

"How lovely," Adeline muttered dryly. "Why does it always have to be a graveyard or a creepy forest that swallows people? Where's my fairytale castle in the mountains?"

Cornelius lowered his voice, as if telling her a secret of the utmost importance. "There are even some who say there's a lake inside the forest infested with giant poisonous eels."

Olivia covered her mouth when Ryder whipped his head up.

He pointed a menacing finger in Cornelius' direction and growled, "You better not take us anywhere near that lake."

CHAPTER TWENTY-EIGHT

An eerie silence engulfed them as soon as they set foot inside the dark woods. No birds chirping away, no squirrels rustling the fallen leaves for food.

The trees they passed were dark and gnarled. They resembled skeletal figures, twisting and spiralling around them. So much so that the dried twigs they stepped on soon began to sound like bones crunching beneath their feet.

"Be careful, everyone," Olivia cautioned them, her voice dark. "The wand will want to mess with our heads, but not everything you see here will be an illusion. There are real things that dwell in these woods . . ."

Strangely, Cornelius had remained silent as they ventured in.

"What?" Ryder exclaimed softly, his voice almost disappointed. "No regaling us with everything you know that goes bump in the night here?"

"There is a time and place, Norseman," was Cornelius' solemn reply. "A time and a place."

A thick layer of mist appeared on the ground, swirling around them until it reached their knees. It was so heavy that they soon lost sight of the fallen leaves on the ground. All they could hear was the snapping of invisible bones and the occasional wind, making the crooked branches scratch against each other.

After about half an hour of wandering deeper into the woods, Ryder stopped abruptly. "Shh, there's something here."

He kept his legs planted firmly on the ground and his shoulders straight, ready to conjure up his magic.

No one dared move or so much as breathe as they strained to hear the faint sound floating on the breeze, distant one moment, but seemingly coming from right behind them the next.

Olivia followed it to her right, towards a dense group of warped trees, their spindly branches all intertwined. A pale figure emerged, then another.

It was a woman with long, cascading auburn hair, her gauzy white dress billowing around her. She was laughing, her silver eyes twinkling, and holding hands with a man dressed in a dark suit. The woman's movements were ethereal, like a beautiful woodland fairy. As she rested her hand on a low branch to pass underneath it, a ray of sunlight caught the wedding band shining on her finger.

The couple didn't seem to hear or see them. They slow danced among the trees, smiling at each other, the groom twirling his young bride.

Olivia held her breath, but the young couple simply continued on their way, towards another group of nasty trees.

When they were out of sight, she turned to the real Adeline, who stood frozen in shock, her face white as death. Her anguished eyes were still glued to the spot where the couple had vanished.

"Adeline . . ." Olivia reached for her hand. "Addie, it's just an illusion. It's the wand."

Her friend's hand was icy. She'd never told her she had been married. And it was clear from her tortured expression that whatever had happened had ended in tragedy.

Olivia squeezed her bloodless fingers.

Adeline finally let out a shuddering breath and met her gaze. "I'm fine. We . . . we should go."

"Are you sure?"

Adeline nodded. She was trembling, but her mouth was set in a determined line. "We need to hurry. Godwyn's still out there with that . . . that *thing*."

There were no paths in this forest, but finding the direction to the centre of it proved easy. They hadn't even needed Ryder's compass.

The trees grew progressively darker and nastier. The moss became more humid, the fog at their feet thicker. There was also a heavy sense of wrongness in the air, of something old and ancient that should not be there.

Olivia frowned as she watched Ryder, at the head of their group, lead them to the right and the others follow him without question. "Where are you all going?" She pointed to the opposite direction. "It's that way."

Cornelius's brows rose as he turned to face her. "What do you mean, boss? There's no path over there."

"Ahh . . ." Olivia cocked her head quizzically. "What do *you* mean there's no path there? There's no path anywhere."

He stared at her, apparently as perplexed as she was. "I can clearly see a path leading that way. Don't you?"

Ryder approached them. "Describe what you see."

Olivia hesitated, taken aback by his command. "Well, I don't know what you're talking about with that path. I haven't seen one since we entered the forest . . . Anyway, there's a thick group of trees where you're going, with an undergrowth full of thorns. Lots of those lovely roots sticking out of the ground we keep tripping over. It's also even gloomier this way than where we came from, if you can believe that, and there's one *very* peculiar-looking piece of moss hanging from the branch of that tree . . ."

She finally caught on when Ryder's face got progressively darker as she spoke. "You don't see the same thing, do you?"

Adeline let out a disdainful huff. "What we see is a nice little path made of soft grass and crushed leaves. There's even a quaint ray of sunshine to light the way. I wouldn't be surprised if a squirrel descended from a tree to beckon us further with its little paw. Subtle, this wand is not."

"A bit over the top, to be honest," Cornelius agreed.

Ryder gestured for Olivia to replace him at the head of their group. "You'll have to lead the way. Looks like this wand has a few tricks up its sleeve."

She set off at a brisk pace, or, she *tried,* seeing as Ryder easily matched her pace with about half as many steps, thanks to his ridiculously long legs.

The others also picked up speed without comment. They all felt the ugliness that permeated the air. It had settled on their skin, like an ugly sheen that felt so vile, so unnatural, your only instinct was to turn around and run.

Out of the corner of her eye, Olivia saw Ryder suddenly falter.

She turned just in time to see him stumble and brace himself against a nearby tree. Immediately alarmed, she rushed to his side. "Ryder! What's wrong?"

But he didn't seem to hear her. His head was bent, his eyes closed and he was drawing fast, shallow breaths.

As Adeline and Cornelius rushed to them, she warned, "I think there's something wrong with Ry—"

Olivia startled badly when his head snapped to her. The words died in her throat.

Ryder's eyes were open now, and fixed on her. They glowed with magic, just as they had when they'd been attacked on the ship. Only it wasn't the usual silvery blue of his power.

They were bright green.

Olivia held her breath. She took a few steps back, holding up a hand to stop Cornelius and Adeline from coming any closer. "Ryder? Can you hear me?" She kept her voice low, not wanting to spook him.

Waves of energy radiated from him, splaying out like an invisible but violent current. Where he'd been panting just a few moments ago, his breaths were now deep and even, focused. A dangerous expression claimed his face. He straightened slowly, letting go of the branch.

"Ryder?" Olivia tried again.

He didn't take his eyes off her. She took another step back, an icy feeling coming over her. The menace rolling off him was terrifying.

"Ryder, the wand is trying to control you," she said calmly. "Do you hear me? The wand wants to get inside your head, you have to fight."

Her next step back snapped a dead twig lying on the forest floor, breaking the uneasy silence around them. She froze, her eyes wide.

Olivia didn't know if it was because of the sound or her sudden gasp, but in the next instant, he lunged.

Bam!

She summoned a shield in the nick of time. It stopped his fist from connecting with her face, but the shockwave rattled her.

Just then, a yell broke out from behind her.

She dared turn her head to see Cornelius running full speed into the forest, towards an area so dense with trees that no light passed through. Adeline had tried to stop him, grabbing his arm in a tight grip, but he'd pushed her away roughly and in a few seconds, he was gone.

Bam! Bam!

Ryder hadn't stopped his attack. He swung his powerful fist at her shield a second time. And then again.

"Addie!" Olivia yelled. "The wand's controlling him too, you have to go after him!"

Adeline hesitated, torn. "What about you?"

"I've got it! Go!"

Adeline took off into the trees.

The next blow from Ryder sent Olivia reeling and she almost lost her grip on her shield. "Ryder!" she forced out, her jaw clenched. "You have to fight it!"

There was no recognition on his face, no sign that he'd heard her.

Fear gripped her. This was bad, very, very bad. How was she going to break the compulsion?

She wanted to use her magic to push him back, or swing a thick branch at his head to knock him out. Anything to make him stop, but she couldn't shift her focus, and he continued to swing relentlessly at her shield.

Soon her arms were shaking from the effort, she could feel her whole body trembling. Olivia gritted her teeth and planted her feet in the ground, determined to stay upright. But his next blow was so strong that it sent her stumbling backwards.

She cried out as she lost her balance. She hit the ground, *hard*, and almost let go of the shield. "Ryder!" she screamed. "Ryder! Please, I don't want to hurt you!" Her voice trembled with barely controlled emotion. Her eyes filled with tears.

The wand was going to make him kill her.

Panic gripped her, making it hard to breathe, to think. All she knew was that she would not last long. But she couldn't use her magic against him, she couldn't hurt him.

That was when she noticed the way his brows were knitted together. And another realisation made her eyes widen. Ryder wasn't using his powerful magic to fight her, and certainly not the gladius strapped to his back.

He was still in there. He was fighting it.

Because if he ever drew that weapon, or even used one of his powerful blast of magic she'd witnessed on the ship, Olivia knew without a doubt that it would cut through her shield, and then her body, like butter.

She was now on her knees on the forest floor, roots digging into her flesh, hiding behind a shield that was getting harder and harder to maintain. Ryder kept his relentless assault, pounding on it with both hands. Each impact reverberated up her arm, shaking her jaw. She didn't have much time.

"Please, Ryder," she tried again, her voice close to a sob. "Wake up!"

The barest hint of something passed over his face. Like a fine tremor. But then his eyes flashed bright green again, and his fist landed on her shield with a crushing force.

Bam!

Olivia allowed a frustrated cry to pass her lips. But then her eyes narrowed. Damn that gods-forsaken wand! If Ryder was still fighting, then so would she.

And if he couldn't break the compulsion on his own, she would have to do it for him.

She wasn't gifted with mental magic, but she had inherited a flicker from her mother. And that flicker was damn well going to help her now. She was going to slip inside Ryder's mind, and kick the wand out of there before he had a chance to swing his terrible fist in her unprotected face. Because for her plan to work, she had to let go of her shield first.

Olivia took a long, deep breath. She set her jaw, her eyes fierce.

The wand couldn't have the infuriating Viking. He was hers.

"All right, Isaksson," she muttered. "Here I come."

And she let go.

Her shield disintegrated instantly. At the same time, she projected herself onto him.

Time seemed to slow down . . .

The barrier that should have protected his aura had been blown apart. She slipped in easily and witnessed the wand's handiwork: a thick green fog surrounded his mind, completely obscuring him from view.

Olivia turned her magic into talons, into clawed hands that ripped through the dense mist. Huge chunks went flying.

She could feel the wand's surprise, how it hadn't expected her to do that. So it hadn't put up any defences in Ryder's mind, had left itself completely exposed.

Olivia didn't slow down, didn't stop as she tore it all off and away from him. As soon as a large enough section had been cleared, she felt it all shatter at the same time. Felt Ryder's mind pulverise it from the inside out.

The Viking was back.

Olivia retreated from his mind at once. Her eyes snapped open and she saw his huge fist dive towards her face. There was no time to duck, no time to do anything. She braced herself.

Only the impact never came. She felt a gush of wind across her face and then a huge body slammed into her, taking her to the ground.

For a moment, she just lay there. Just breathed. Didn't try to think, didn't move.

Her mind had snapped back into her body so quickly, *too* quickly. Black dots danced in her vision. She wasn't in pain exactly, but . . . shaken.

However, at that precise moment, her body felt safe, so she just allowed herself to rest a little, tried to get her bearings back.

After a little while, the dots disappeared, her heart began to slow down and she became aware of a frantic voice calling out to her. Something warm and soft was touching her cheeks. It felt nice.

"Olivia, Olivia," the desperate voice said. "I'm so sorry, Olivia. Come back."

Ryder.

He was caressing her face, coaxing her back.

"I'm here," she breathed. "I'm all right."

She felt the shudder rack his body. He murmured something in Swedish and pressed her closer to his chest, leaning in until his forehead rested against hers.

"I'm sorry," the barest whisper escaped him.

Olivia lifted a hand and placed it on his cheek, his beard soft under her fingertips. "I'm fine, you didn't hurt me. It's over."

They didn't move away from one another and calmed their ragged breaths together. Even though he'd been forced to attack her bare seconds ago, Olivia felt safe in his arms. For just a moment, she was warm and protected. She didn't want to let go.

Ryder flexed one of his hands slightly, and that's when she noticed the poor state they were in.

"Ryder!" she gasped. "Your hands . . ."

She took one of them in hers, as gently as she could. His swollen knuckles were bleeding and bruised, and he had trouble closing his fist.

"It's nothing," he said quietly. "Don't worry about it."

"Another mosquito bite for your collection?"

There was the slightest tilt to his mouth.

Olivia pushed away from his chest so she could grab the strap of her bag with her foot and bring it close. She reached inside for a clean handkerchief and tied it gently around his bloody knuckles.

Then she gathered both of his damaged hand in her lap and laid her own over them. Her eyes fluttering shut, she called to a distant corner of her magic.

It took a few moments, but finally, she felt cold radiating from her palms. It wasn't a lot, only as much of the Ice Element as she was capable of summoning, but it would do.

Opening her eyes, she saw the small smile that stretched his lips. "You, Ms Knight, have been keeping things from me." Ryder's breath grazed the shell of her ear.

"I can't reveal all my secrets now, can I?" she whispered back.

The sound of running footsteps broke their moment. They reluctantly drew apart as Cornelius and Adeline burst in.

"Liv! Are you all right? What was that?" Adeline's voice was frantic.

Ryder got to his feet, pulling Olivia up with him. After all that had happened, her legs didn't feel that sturdy underneath her. She allowed herself to rest lightly against his strong frame, and felt an arm sneak around her waist, anchoring her firmly to his side.

From her position, she felt rather than heard the rumbling in his chest as he growled, "That *jävla* of a wand got into my head. Forced me to attack Olivia."

"So I went into his mind and helped him break the compulsion," she finished. She pushed the heavy glasses over the bridge of her nose and frowned slightly. They were covered in water droplets and desperately needed to be cleaned, but rummaging through her bag was beyond her.

Ryder offered her a dry spot on his shirt. Olivia took it, the backs of her knuckles grazing his stomach.

"What about you?" she asked the others after clearing her throat. "What happened?"

Cornelius grimaced. A hand went to massage his jaw. "It was just like on the train," he said. "I wasn't thinking straight. I thought you were in danger and I had to find you, so I ran. But then Adeline caught up with me and . . . well."

"I punched him," Adeline finished. Then she shrugged. "Worked great."

Cornelius gave her a look. "You could have tried to get inside my mind like she did."

Indeed, Olivia noticed the beginning of what promised to become a spectacular bruise on his cheek. Looked like Adeline hadn't come to play.

"We have to hurry," Ryder declared. "If the wand is attacking us like this, it means we're close."

Olivia raised her head to look at him, her eyes steady as she held his. "Let's go."

CHAPTER TWENTY-NINE

THE ATTACK TOOK THEM all by surprise. Not even Ryder sensed it coming.

They had been going deeper and deeper into the woods, where the trees grew heavy with strings of moss and the ground muddy. The mist had risen to their mid-section now, twining around their legs. It made it difficult to move forward as they kept tripping over invisible logs and roots.

One second, everything around them was eerily quiet.

The next, shadows were attacking from all sides.

Cries and shouts ensued as everyone dropped to the ground. A horrendous sound filled the forest, ear-splitting and terrible.

Olivia felt the *whoosh* of wind all around her. Something grazed her cheek and she jerked back.

But as quickly as they had attacked, the shadows vanished and deafening silence filled the woods once more. Everyone stood still for a few moments, hands slowly lowering from where they'd been pressed to their ears.

"What was that?" Cornelius' whisper sounded as loud as a yell.

Ryder held up a hand to silence him. He unfolded from his crouch, half on top of Olivia and Adeline. One arm lifted to unsheathe the short sword at his back. He stood as if ready to repel an assault, legs splayed shoulder width apart, head held high, muscular frame solid.

Everyone could feel the tension in the air, the calm before the storm. Whatever those shadows were, they were coming back.

"Do you hear that?" Adeline whispered.

Olivia strained her ears but couldn't make anything out over the hammering of her own heart. Then she caught it. It was faint, steady. Almost rhythmic.

She frowned. *What was that?*

She got her answer when chaos broke out once again: the flapping of wings.

"Take cover!" Ryder bellowed.

The roar of wings was everywhere. The creatures flew in circles around them, coming so close that Olivia's hair lifted in the wind. Dozens of them. Accompanied by a terrible, high-pitched squeaking that was almost unbearable.

With each pass, half would swoop down in a wave, and it was all they could do to avoid the angry beaks and sharp talons seeking blood. Olivia found a huge branch and waved it around, trying to swing at the creatures. But every time she managed to hit one, another beast would immediately take its place.

Beside her, Ryder wielded his sword in a deadly arc. Adeline was hitting them with palm-sized balls of fire, while Cornelius threw black salt grenades at clusters of them. The creatures weren't cursed, but judging by their wails, the grenades were inflicting some damage.

That's when a terrified scream erupted.

Olivia whirled around and watched in horror as Adeline was lifted into the air, two beasts holding on to her arms. She was carried away, kicking and screaming. Cornelius leapt to her and wrapped his arms around her midsection. Fire burst from Adeline's hands, but she was shaken too violently to aim right.

Olivia looked around for something, *anything*. She saw a beast lying nearby, one of Ryder's knives protruding from its back. She ran to it, crouched down to wrench the blade out, and with a flick of her wrist, sent it flying again.

It embedded itself in the scaly face of one of the creatures gripping Adeline and sent them all careening toward the ground, the other beast not strong enough to carry her on its own. Cornelius caught her just in time and they landed in a heap.

The second creature also collapsed, a mass of twisting black wings and raging howls. But its thick claws found purchase on the forest floor. Olivia's breath caught in her throat as it righted itself, pivoted towards her. Stared.

Olivia noted the milky, soulless eyes, the pointed black scales and the jaws hiding rows of sharp fangs.

The beast flexed its legs, but before it could lunge at her, she'd picked up her trusty branch and swung it like a club with every ounce of strength in her body. The creature flew through the air to crash against a tree, dropping dead.

Olivia turned. Adeline was kneeling on the ground, her shirt covered in blood. Cornelius had lit a novelium flare and was standing guard over her, pushing back any monster wanting to try its luck. Ryder was still swinging his bloody sword, cutting them down one by one. He had dozens of angry scrapes on his face, his arms.

They wouldn't win that way. There were just too many of them.

Olivia narrowed her eyes, a plan forming in her mind. "Adeline!" she called. "Get ready to use your fire! Cornelius, shield her until my signal!" Then she ran the few steps to Ryder, dodging the furious strikes of his sword. "Ryder, I'll cover you! On my mark, set it all on fire!"

In the midst of another mighty swing, she saw the battle grin he sent her. It was wild, feral.

Olivia conjured up her shield, the bright copper light arching over them both, stopping the angry talons from tearing into their flesh. Ryder knelt and both of his hands burst into ice blue flame. He closed his eyes, his magic flared. The icy fire grew and grew, yet he sank even more power into it. It spilled out of him until he was holding a small supernova between his palms and his arms were shaking with the effort.

Olivia could feel it from there, a cold so powerful it *burned*. Ryder lifted his head to nod at her. From the corner of her eye, she saw answering ruby flames. "Ready?" she shouted. "Three. Two. One!"

She dropped at the same time as Cornelius, letting go of her shield, and above them, the world exploded into flames.

Deafening shrieks split the air. Olivia cupped her hands over her ears and crouched even lower. A frenzy of wings and thrashes erupted as the creatures sought to escape the icy blue and dark red inferno. Some managed to fly away, others fell writhing to the ground.

When it was finally over, Olivia's ears were ringing. She opened her eyes mere slits. Her hand fumbled somewhere behind her, grabbed onto a thick forearm, squeezed. Ryder's hand closed around her own, squeezing back.

In front of her, Adeline and Cornelius were huddled together. They looked a little worse for wear, with cuts and scratches covering their arms, blood on Adeline's shoulders, but they were alive. Olivia released a shuddering breath.

Her gaze fell on the monster she'd skewered with Ryder's blade. She walked over to it on not-so-steady legs. She wasn't an expert on creatures, but she had a few notions, and she was positive she'd never seen anything like it before.

They resembled giant bats with leathery wings, powerful legs that ended in long, wicked talons, and a massive jaw filled with rows of razor-sharp teeth that shouldn't exist anywhere in the real world, but belonged to some monster of lore.

Her lips curled into a disgusted grimace as she braced one foot on the monster's wing to pull out the dagger.

"I wouldn't expect a curse-breaker to be so good with blades," a deep voice rumbled.

Olivia lifted her head to look at him, staring up into those impossibly blue eyes. "I have a wall of weapons in my house, you know."

"I'll keep that in mind," he replied in a low, intimate tone that sent a shiver down her spine.

Ryder held out his hand. As she placed the blade in his palm, her fingertips danced over his rough skin.

"Cornelius!" An exasperated voice rang behind them. "You can't possibly be thinking of bringing that back with us!"

"Why not?" he replied. "He's sad and lonely."

"But . . . you don't even know *what* it is!" Adeline countered. She stood up with a huff, hands on her hips.

Olivia scowled as she walked over to them. "What is going on here—" she started, but froze as soon as she saw him. "Oh."

Adeline rolled her eyes. "Not you too," she muttered.

Cornelius was kneeling on the ground next to a fallen log and patiently trying to coax a . . . *something* . . . closer.

The strange lizard-dragon creature alternated between taking a few steps towards his open palm, then immediately scurrying away again. Slightly bigger than regular lizards, it had four legs and a tail, all covered in shiny green scales, and a frill around its neck that looked velvety soft. The little beast was flattened against the bark of the log, alarmed yet intrigued, its back and forth movements so fast they were hard to follow. Its large golden eyes, however, were fixed on Cornelius's hand, shining with uncontrollable curiosity despite its fear.

Olivia knelt beside them. "Who is this little beauty?" she crooned.

At first, the little creature puffed out its frill with a hiss, trying to scare her away. But when it heard Olivia's voice, it stopped and stared intensely at her instead.

"He was afraid of the winged monsters, too," Cornelius whispered. "I saw him hiding in that log, poor *bebette*. It's all right, now," he said softly. "They're all gone."

Finally, the strange lizard decided that they were safe. As Cornelius' fingers began to scratch the scales on its head, it let out a rumble so loud, Olivia couldn't believe it was coming from a creature that size. She ran the tip of a finger along its frill. It was incredibly soft, as if covered by a layer of fuzz. The creature didn't waste any time and came to perch itself on Cornelius' shoulder like a bat, hanging upside down, tail wrapped around his shoulder.

"All right, everyone. Break's over," Ryder ordered. "Olivia, which way is it?"

After one last caress, she got to her feet, stifling a groan of pain. She looked around with a frown. She hadn't had any trouble finding the way to the centre of the forest before, but now couldn't tell any more. "I . . . I'm not sure. I can't sense anything."

"Guess we'll just have to use the good old methods, then," Ryder replied. He reached into his pocket and pulled out his compass, placing it in the palm of his hand. Very soon, he was spinning around in a circle, scowling.

"I know I'm no expert in compasses, but I'm pretty sure they're not supposed to do that," Adeline said sarcastically.

Indeed, the needle was swinging erratically, not stopping in any direction for more than a few seconds. Ryder tried to find north again, going around slowly this time. His scowl graduated to a full-blown grimace.

Olivia put her hand on his arm to stop him, her voice resigned. "Don't bother. It's either the wand's doing or the forest, but either way it won't work."

After mumbling something in Swedish, Ryder closed the compass with an audible snap. "Explain to me why cursed things *have* to mess with physics," he growled.

Cornelius chose this moment to look up from petting his new companion. "What's going on?"

"We're lost, that's what's going on," Adeline replied, attempting to pick the twigs and crushed leaves out of her hair.

Olivia corrected her, "We're not lost, we're just dealing with a temporary equipment failure."

Adeline snorted.

Pacing, Ryder ran a hand through his hair, no doubt considering their options. "Could we cast a locator spell?"

"We could try to locate the crystals inside the wand," Cornelius suggested.

Olivia shook her head. "I don't have any left, they're all in the containment cage."

"What about something that just came in contact with the wand?" Adeline asked. "Would that work?"

Olivia hesitated, "I don't know if I have anything . . . Let me check." She reached for the leather satchel at her hip and rummaged through its contents. The thing wasn't very big, but it was *packed*. "I have the scarf I wrapped around the cage when we were on the ship." She pulled out a woollen shawl she'd stuffed at the very bottom. "I doubt it has enough residual energy for a spell, but we can always try."

"I say it's worth a shot," Ryder said. "Why don't we set up—"

A flash of movement cut him off. Olivia let out a strangled yelp as the little lizard-dragon charged at her.

"Wait!" Cornelius shouted, spreading his arms to freeze everyone.

His outcry stopped Ryder just in time, whose hand had been ready to send the creature on Olivia fly away.

The tiny beast had flattened itself on her shoulder, claws digging into her clothing, spooked by their reaction. When no one else made any sudden moves, it warily stood up again and descended the length of her arm. When it reached her hand and, more specifically, the scarf Olivia was holding, it pressed its scaly nose against the fabric and took a deep sniff.

Everyone held their breath, waiting to see what it would do.

"Is it *smelling* the wand?" Adeline wondered softly.

After a few seconds, the scaly little lizard was gone. They stared as it bolted towards the trees, leaping over fallen logs as if they weren't there and scaling tree trunks at incredible speed, only to bounce off the branches and do it all over again.

When it realised they hadn't followed, the small creature came back. In a flash, it had climbed up a tree, becoming a blur, before hanging itself upside down from one of its spindly branches.

Cornelius stood gaping at it, his jaw slack.

"We're not going to follow this strange lizard-creature through the woods, are we?" Ryder snickered, obviously finding the idea ridiculous.

"Did you see him move?" Olivia breathed. She shared a look with Cornelius, who had the same awe-struck expression on his face.

"He's *tracking* it," he whispered.

Adeline turned to Ryder with a resigned sigh. "I'm afraid we are."

He might have objected again at the thought of blindly following an unknown creature, but after only a few steps it became clear that they were on the right track.

The sense of otherness in the air intensified until they could almost taste it, until it coated their tongues, made it hard to breathe. No other sound could be heard beside their laboured breathing and the cracking of the twigs beneath their feet.

Even though they were surrounded by huge trees with thick ropes of moss hanging from their branches, Olivia felt completely exposed. As if countless *things* lay around them, hidden in the shadows, watching. Ryder kept his sword at the ready, battle awareness pouring out of him.

Finally, they reached the heart of the forest.

Just as the stories had described, a perfect circle opened up before them, devoid of any vegetation. There were no trees, not even grass. The ground was solid dirt, covered with a thick layer of something that looked surprisingly like ash. And they had a perfect view of the ground, for the dense fog that had enveloped them as soon as they'd set foot in these woods was gone. It had halted right at the edge of the circle.

But what caught Olivia's undivided attention was what resided in the middle of this disturbing place.

A tree. Huge. With a thick trunk and twisted branches. Pointed leaves of green and copper. And most importantly, lines of glowing emerald running through its bark.

The Whispering Tree.

Cornelius murmured to no one in particular, "It's supposed to be empty here . . ."

Olivia was about to agree when another thought struck her, one that felt far too right. "I don't think it was ever empty . . . I think people just couldn't *see*."

Then they saw a familiar figure emerge from the other side of the clearing. And in his hand, the wand glowed with a bright green light.

Out of its containment.

"Godwyn!" Adeline cried, and took off running before Ryder could stop her.

They all followed. Ryder reached her first, grabbing her wrist to keep her from getting any closer.

Godwyn didn't raise the wand towards them, but he held it tightly. He stood still, calm. Yet there was an edge to his posture, as if his movements weren't entirely his own. And his normally emerald eyes had acquired an unnatural sheen.

"Godwyn," Adeline breathed, relief and fear mixing in her voice. "Please, Godwyn. Give us the wand."

He was only looking at her. His lips curved into a sad smile. "I can't."

"Yes. Yes, you can." Her voice was so soft, soothing. "You trust me, don't you?"

He didn't answer, instead taking a step back, towards the tree.

Olivia could feel the tension gripping Ryder. His gaze was fixed on every move Godwyn made.

Just as she'd done when Ryder had been forced to attack her, Olivia kept her voice low and calm. "Godwyn, this is the wand controlling you. It's making you do things you don't want to do. You have to trust us."

He shook his head and took another step back. "No! No, you don't understand." His voice grew agitated. Desperate, even. "It's not controlling me, it's showing me the truth!"

Olivia went motionless. "What truth?"

"They're coming. They're on their way here right now. To get the wand. I have to stop them."

Adeline tried to go to him, but Ryder held her back. "Who's *they*? Who's coming?"

Godwyn's face contorted in anger. "The thieves, the traitors," he spat. "They want the wand for themselves, to rule over everything."

"And we will stop them, Godwyn," Olivia declared. "We will defend it. That's what we've been doing since the beginning, isn't it?"

"You can trust us," Adeline added, her voice breaking. "I swear it."

"I know," Godwyn replied softly. His unnatural eyes roamed over her face, over the tears rolling down her cheeks. Then they hardened. "But we cannot protect it. Not like this."

Olivia's breath caught in her throat. "What do you mean?"

"We have to use it." His grip on the wand tightened until his knuckles turned white.

Adeline gasped. "No . . ."

"We have to! It's the only way to make sure they never get it!" Godwyn sounded imploring, as if begging them to understand, to agree. "Addie . . . they will kill us!"

They will kill you, his eyes screamed.

Gods . . .

Olivia knew if Godwyn used the wand, it would consume him. He would fall completely under its control . . .

Ryder's sudden tenseness beside her told Olivia he'd figured out the same terrible truth. If they couldn't stop him, they would have no choice but to fight him.

Panic gripped her. Godwyn was here because of her. She'd insisted on this mission, she'd done this. *No, no, no.* It couldn't be her fault again.

Desperate now, Olivia pleaded, "Look at me, Godwyn." Her voice shook with barely controlled emotion. "We've known each other for years. Please, you have to believe me, this isn't right. Don't do this."

Godwyn shifted his gaze from Adeline to look at her. She dared to hope that her words had finally got through to him.

But then he shook his head. "I'm sorry, Liv," he said, and raised the wand.

Everyone started yelling and begging him to stop.

Adeline used the distraction to wrench her wrist from Ryder's grip and run the last few steps until she was standing directly in front of Godwyn.

Olivia gasped in fright. She gripped the back of Ryder's shirt as he hissed, "Adeline, get back!"

But there was no hesitation in Adeline's voice, no fear as she stood straight. "This isn't you. This is the wand speaking. I know you're still in there, I can feel it. You need to *fight*."

Godwyn's lips parted.

Adeline kept her eyes on his, even as her chest made contact with the tip of the wand. "You have to believe us, Godwyn. We're trying to help you." Her voice was so calm, so soft, barely more than a whisper amid the other's desperate cries. "Please."

An agonised expression filled his face. "I'm doing this for you, Addie. To keep you safe."

Adeline didn't answer. She met his glowing green gaze with her silvery one.

"Get out of the way," Godwyn begged her again, his entire frame shaking.

"No." She radiated pure calm. "No, I won't move. You'll have to kill me."

He shuddered. His hand lowered a fraction.

Then Olivia watched in horror as his eyes instantly turned an even brighter green. The wand was fighting him.

That's when Ryder began to push her away from him. Alarm shot through her, for she knew what he was preparing to do. She tried to protest, grabbing his shirt with both hands to stop him.

But then Godwyn suddenly whipped his head towards him. His eyes were drowning in acid green. "Do it."

The words were barely past his lips before he was thrown backwards and flew towards the tree. His head connected with the trunk with a terrible crack and he crumpled to the ground.

"No!" Adeline's anguished scream echoed as she rushed to his still form.

Olivia started to run, but Ryder held her back. "We've got him!" he yelled. "Take care of the wand!"

She only hesitated for a moment before hurrying to the fallen wand.

It was angry at being denied. Furious.

A dark, churning cloud had wrapped around it like a nest of writhing serpents. Black, streaked with flashes of pure green. Phantom fangs snapped at her, trying to tear into her aura, spill her magic as if it were blood.

Olivia fell to her knees, noticing the empty containment cage on the ground nearby.

Power radiated from the wand, piercing her senses. So much magic . . . She nearly recoiled. It felt a hundred times worse than in the Cellars.

To get it back into the containment, Olivia would have to reach through the raging storm that surrounded it. But it was pure black magic and would likely rip her apart. She needed something to protect herself, something to shield her.

Olivia tried to tear her eyes away from the wand, to look behind her, but found she couldn't. Blood roared in her ears and her chest heaved up and down in short, shallow breaths.

"Corne . . ." Her voice came out as a choked gasp. "Cornelius . . . Feylin."

The Darkness had just made its presence known. She felt it from deep within her bones. An awareness as primal as it was violent. It screamed at her to flee, to escape the malevolent thing that watched her.

"I've been waiting for you."

The Darkness hadn't forgotten her. It was . . . *pleased*.

Someone grabbed her hand, thrust something cold into her palm. Olivia tried to uncork the bottle, but her fingers were shaking too badly. Panic tightened around her throat, trapping her in an icy vice.

Oh, gods. She couldn't do this . . .

Long fingers uncorked the bottle for her. They wrapped around her chilled ones. Olivia clung to that warmth, that touch.

"Breathe, Liv," a voice said. "Breathe."

She did as the voice commanded.

"You're all right. You can do this."

The voice was warm, soothing. With a tilt to it that felt like warm honey. *Cornelius.*

Olivia took a deep breath and nodded.

Chanting under her breath, she sprinkled the contents of the vial onto her right hand, then her left. Relief instantly filled her. An older experiment, the feylin compound dripped down her fingers as it coated her skin, creating a silver glove that would shield her from the black magic.

But it was so incredibly strong, she would only have a moment. One tiny instant to reach into the dark and raging cloud, and wrench the wand back.

Olivia braced herself. This was going to hurt.

The energy coiled around the wand was so potent that reaching in felt like sticking her hands into a live wire. It lashed out at her, snapping and tearing at everything it touched.

The pain ripped a gasp out of her, but she gritted her teeth and reached even deeper.

Wails assaulted her. Horrible, agonising cries. The clash of swords. The ground shook beneath her. So much death, she could smell it. Could taste the iron on her tongue. It was everywhere around her, blocking out her other senses.

But then, above the screams, she heard something else.

"You killed her!"

Olivia would have crumbled to the ground if she wasn't already on her knees. She only ever heard his voice in her nightmares.

"You killed my girl!"

A whimper escaped her. No, no, no. That was the wand. It was trying to use her demons against her, it wanted to control her. She couldn't let it, she had to push back.

I'm sorry...

She clawed at the angry storm with renewed fury, gouging out chunks. A burst of agony exploded in her hands, but she didn't stop.

I'm so sorry. I swear I tried.

The Darkness fought her with all its might. It buckled and strained. The cries around her grew even louder, blood filled her mouth. Her eyes were still closed, but she knew it was on her hands as well, she could feel it dripping down her fingers.

Just as *her* blood had done when the curse had broken. She'd been so small, so delicate. Olivia had seen her standing in the gardens, watching her argue with her father. Satin ribbon blowing in the breeze.

Olivia raged. This wand would *not* win. She would not let it!

She gathered all her magic, every tendril of it, and shaped it into an arrow, making the point so wickedly sharp. It whistled as it tore through the mist and pierced the Darkness right at its core.

The roar was deafening. Olivia had hurt it and it wailed in pain.

At that precise moment, she spotted an opening. A sliver of light at the centre of the furious mist. She didn't think, merely acted. Reaching through the gap, she pulled the wand out.

Before it had time to wrestle itself free, she flung it into the cage and wound her entire magic around it. In a heartbeat, she'd spread it around like vines, like chains. Growing and growing, encasing the cage so tightly it couldn't escape.

Olivia slowly came back to herself.

She'd done it. It was over.

She opened her eyes, but her vision wavered. Her blood was rushing through her veins, her heart pounding too loud and too fast. Yet a smile lifted the corner of her lips. *She'd done it.*

Everything looked so peaceful now. The seething cloud had dissipated, the cage lay on her lap, placid, the wand suspended inside. The only thing that had changed were the thin bronze chains that now encircled it.

Lifting her gaze, she sought Ryder. His blue eyes were already locked on her. She nodded her head slightly.

A grin spread across his face. He looked unbearably pleased with himself. No doubt the Warden was congratulating himself on having chosen her for this mission. Arrogant Viking.

He helped Godwyn to his feet. The other man was unsteady, his face no more than a pale mask, but he was alive, he was whole. Olivia's trembling fingers went to her brow. It really was over.

Still, her eyes darted uneasily to the massive tree behind her. This was the passage that led to where this Darkness resided. And the wand had led them straight to it . . .

Exhausted and injured, the journey back took them twice as long, but when they spotted the rays of sunlight streaming behind the twisted branches, they collectively drew in what felt like their first full breath in hours.

They'd made it out of this gods-forsaken forest . . . To fall right into another welcoming party.

CHAPTER THIRTY

A MAN STEPPED FORWARD. Stern, with small, cold eyes and lips pressed tightly together, he regarded them with barely disguised contempt.

"My name is Sergeant Nicolae. High Commissioner Mitrea sent us. We are here for the Dark Wand."

Olivia kept her face carefully blank, glancing at Ryder out of the corner of her eye. She was waiting to see how he would react. Right now, he was watching their greeting party intently, taking in their tension, their weapons, their numbers.

Finally, his shoulders relaxed and he approached the sergeant eagerly, one hand outstretched. "Sergeant! It's *very* nice to meet you! I'm Ryder Isaksson, Warden of the Cellars, and this is Olivia Knight, the curse-breaker on this job, as well as her team."

A flash of disdain crossed the sergeant's face, but he reluctantly shook the offered hand.

Olivia tried to match Ryder's nonchalant, amicable demeanour. "I must say, Sergeant, it's a relief to see some friendly faces after trekking through these woods. As you can probably tell, we met some of the locals."

Ryder cringed and raised his arms to show the multitude of cuts there. "These little buggers were not happy to see us! What even are they, anyway?"

The sergeant shrugged, obviously lying through his teeth. "No idea. But they never venture out of the forest, and they keep people from going into the woods, so we let them be. How far in did you go? Did you reach the Clearing?"

"How far in?" Ryder frowned. "I don't know . . . It didn't feel like much."

He turned to Olivia with his brows raised. She shook her head, her best innocent expression on her face. "It didn't feel like we got very deep inside," she agreed. "What's the Clearing?"

The sergeant dismissed her question with a wave of his hand. "Nothing of importance. We're just glad you're all back safe and sound," he said.

The falseness of his concern almost made Olivia snort, but she controlled herself just in time. He really could do with some acting lessons.

Ryder laughed. He, on the other hand, was an extremely good actor. She would have to remember that.

"Believe me, we're glad too!" he exclaimed. "By the way, how did you even find us here?" After his insouciant act, the sergeant didn't even notice the intent glint in the Warden's eyes.

"The Hoia Forest is very dangerous," he replied. "As you've learned. The perimeter is heavily warded, so we knew the second you entered."

Ryder nodded as if his explanation made perfect sense. But it was a lie. Olivia would have sensed it if the forest had been warded. Ryder, too. The sergeant probably had them followed from the moment they set foot on Romanian soil. Only, something didn't quite add up . . .

"Now." The sergeant clapped his hand together. "If you could hand over the Dark Wand, please."

As soon as the words left his lips, Olivia saw each policeman behind him inch his hand a fraction closer to his weapon. The sergeant, too, tried — and failed — to hide the dangerous edge in his eyes.

"I'm afraid that's not a good idea, Sergeant," Ryder said. His voice remained easy and laid back, but he allowed a flicker of authority to pass through. "Only an experienced curse-breaker can handle this artifact. I can tell you from experience that it is extremely volatile. Ms Knight, here, will be able to safely contain the wand until we personally deliver it to the High Commissioner."

The sergeant's face hardened. "I am acting on his direct orders, Warden. He has instructed me to retrieve the artifact on his behalf, as he is quite preoccupied with tonight's event."

Ryder turned his head slightly towards her, and Olivia read the message in his eyes clearly: *Do your worst.*

She took a step forward and cleared her throat. "The transport contract I signed unquestionably states that I must relinquish the cursed artifact directly to the High Commissioner, Sergeant Nicolae. I am afraid that any deviation from these instructions would be considered a breach of contract and bring forth much unpleasantness for both of us."

As he listened, the scowl on the sergeant's face darkened.

"Furthermore, section three of the Dark Substances Act stipulates that only a recognised and accredited curse-breaking expert is allowed to handle dark artifacts of level three and above, or those that pose a significant threat to life and property. I understand that we currently stand on Romanian soil and not in the United Kingdom, however, the cooperation agreement that your country signed with mine considers the transfer of such an artifact to be a diplomatic mission. Which in effect means that the artifact and the team assigned to guard it will be subject to the law of the country from which the delegation originates, until such time as the object is safely handed over to the receiving state." Olivia put even more steel into her tone. "In addition, one of the most fundamental rules of this act of cooperation is that the agents who make up the diplomatic team are inviolable. They cannot be detained or arrested, and they enjoy complete immunity from criminal prosecution in the receiving state for actions performed in their official capacity. Of course, far be it from me to imply that what you are doing now is a violation of diplomatic law . . ."

Nicolae sputtered.

"But I feel as though you might have needed a reminder of the legal limitations of your powers and authority. And finally, Mr Isaksson here wasn't exaggerating when he explained that only an expert curse-breaker could manipulate that wand. It is a very unstable, very delicate artifact. I wouldn't want to put you or your men in a dangerous situation that you're not equipped to handle." She offered him a sickly sweet smile. "You understand, of course."

Sergeant Nicolae was now staring daggers at her. His lips had all but disappeared during her lecture, having pinched them so tightly, and his face had turned a lovely shade of red that was immensely satisfying.

"Then we will escort you to the Institute at once," he finally managed to pass through his clenched jaw.

Not before she had a chance to talk to Ryder and formulate a plan first, he would not.

Olivia waved a dismissive hand, like he'd done before. "There's no hurry. If you could escort us to our hotel so we can get ready for the evening, that would be much appreciated. You said so yourself, the High Commissioner is rather busy at the moment. We wouldn't want to disturb him." And then she added smoothly, "I'm sure my Ministry will be most appreciative of all the help you've offered after our difficult ordeal."

The sergeant eyed them all in turn, no doubt weighing the benefits of turning their verbal stand-off into an all-out fight. Behind her, she could feel Ryder squaring his shoulders. He stood still but ready, his magic hovering atop his skin.

Time for the finishing blow.

Olivia drew back to her full height, her voice rising in indignation. "I sincerely hope you're not insisting that we hand over the wand because you suspect us of criminal intent. That would be a very serious accusation, indeed." *And one that she would certainly make him pay for,* were the words she didn't say, but hung between them.

There was a long pause.

Finally, sergeant Nicolae gave a curt nod. "Of course not, *Domnișoară*." He'd almost spat out the words.

He glanced over his shoulder at one of the policemen, who immediately approached. "Andrei. Please take your men and escort them to their hotel in Brașov so they can tend to their wounded. You will stay there as their security until they're ready for the auction. Understood?"

Subtle, he was not. It was clear that these men weren't going to act as their security, but as their jailers.

Adeline and Cornelius each grabbed one of Godwyn's arms as they made their way to the cars.

When they were out of the Romanians' earshot, their escort following a few paces behind, Ryder leaned in to whisper to Olivia, "Didn't you say that after the General's death, the wand might have ended up with a secret order?"

"Yes, the Order of the Dragon," she whispered back. "Why?"

Ryder's voice held warning. "The sergeant wears a very shiny signet ring on his last finger. With a dragon on it."

After a few hours' journey, Godwyn staggered into their hotel room before promptly collapsing into an armchair, a wince and a bitten off curse escaping him. His face was still far too pale for Olivia's liking, and he'd obviously had trouble keeping his legs steady under him, but he seemed much more alert than before.

Olivia came over to kneel beside his chair, also wincing. Her arms felt like they weighed three hundred pounds each, and all the various cuts she'd accumulated during their journey through the forest burned, but she pushed the pain aside.

"How do you feel?" she asked him gently, placing a hand on his shoulder.

"Like I've gone three rounds with a giant troll," he groaned. "That bloody tree's like steel." Then he put his own hand atop hers and squeezed. "I'm fine, Liv."

His eyes fell on her silver fingers. The feylin compound had coated her hands as if she'd dipped them in molten metal. "Guess that worked, huh?"

Olivia nodded with a small smile. But then she heaved a deep sigh, suddenly feeling so exhausted she didn't know how she was going to get up from her crouch. "Don't you do that again."

A tart voice replied, "Don't worry. His skull is so thick, that tree didn't stand a chance."

Godwyn let out a weary laugh.

Sharp words, but Olivia noticed the way Adeline's steel eyes kept darting back to him, as if reassuring herself that he was still there. She hovered nearby, wrapping some ice she'd asked the reception for in a cloth.

Godwyn's eyes followed her as well, his expression softening into something Olivia had never witnessed before. It was soft, tender, when they'd always seemed so at odds. But there was also a weight there, some hidden knowledge she wasn't privy to.

Turning away, Olivia picked up some of the remaining ice and wrapped it in another napkin before noticing Ryder's bag in a corner. She gave it a suspicious look.

For all she knew, it was crammed full of bombs and other incendiary devices. But she managed to extract the first aid kit without blowing the room to bits and handed Ryder a tube of ointment along with the icy bundle.

He stood in front of the window, muscular arms crossed over his chest, staring at the streets below. His blue eyes were hard.

"We have no choice," Olivia told him. Indeed, they had run out of those.

He heaved a deep sigh.

From behind them, Cornelius called out in disbelief, "Wait. Are we really giving it to them? After everything that's happened?"

Olivia took off her glasses to massage her brow. "We have no choice," she repeated. "Right now, there are five policemen outside who won't hesitate to shoot if we don't follow their orders to the letter. We were already outnumbered, but now some of us are injured. And even if we could find our way out of this hotel, where would we go? We can't take on the entire Romanian police force. We need a plan. We need resources, backup."

Ending up in some miserable Romanian dungeon wasn't high on her list of thrilling adventures. She wanted to study curses, not all the different types of ghosts that inhabited some forgotten, horrid underground cell.

Beside her, Ryder remained silent, but his anger was evident as he began to pace the room, brows drawn tight together.

"We're certain, then," Cornelius said grimly. "The Romanian police are not to be trusted."

Olivia winced. "I wouldn't say we're certain, but . . . it seems that way, yes."

She'd only agreed to help Isaksson with the fate of this wand the night before, mere hours ago. And now it looked like they'd failed their mission before it even had a chance to begin.

"So we're letting the High Commissioner get the wand. And then what?" Godwyn asked. He still looked rather pale and flinched now and again, but his mouth was set in a determined line.

He hadn't moved from the armchair and was now leaning forward, his elbows on his knees. One hand held the ice firmly against the back of his skull, and with the other, he ate some biscuits Adeline placed in his palm. Olivia had seen her snatch a tray from the concierge's desk when his back was turned, in retaliation for taking so long to bring the ice.

"Isaksson's inspector friend is on his way, he'll help us," Olivia declared. "Until then, we're not wasting our time. We'll go to the auction and try to gather as much information as we can. Maybe follow the High Commissioner to see what he actually does with the wand. So that when Isaksson's mysterious contact arrives, we can formulate a new plan."

A wicked gleam appeared in the Viking's eyes as he paused his pacing to survey her. "Listen to yourself, you've turned into a proper spy."

She snorted. "Hardly."

"Hmm. Yes, I can see it. Ms Knight, perfectly respectable, curse-breaking expert, guardian of the laws and protector of the artifacts by day, sneaky thief by night."

"You're mistaken. Hunting and spying are much more your area of expertise. I thought we'd agreed that I'm the half of this partnership that speaks reason, and you're the impulsive, reckless half."

He barked out a laugh. "Ah! That would have been true if it weren't for the wandering hands. Did you know she stole an artifact from the Cellars?"

Olivia squawked in indignation. Ryder simply gave her a pointed look, daring her to correct him.

The others all gaped at her. Then there was a flurry of exclamations and demands for details as Adeline applauded. Olivia felt a blush creep up her cheeks.

A small but rumbling sound interrupted them as their newest companion poked his scaly head out of her messenger bag and yawned.

Olivia immediately dropped to her knees, a grin on her face. The little creature didn't hesitate and leapt straight into her open palms, arching its back like a kitten and yawning again, revealing rows of tiny, but deadly sharp teeth.

"What the bloody hell is that?"

The tiny beast screeched and spread its frill angrily.

Olivia glanced back at Godwyn, who was staring, mouth agape and something akin to horror on his face. A laugh escaped her. "Looks like he doesn't like you very much." She scratched under his chin. "Clever beastie."

Cornelius came to join her on the floor, running a finger along the ridges of his frill. "Do you think he's hungry? What does he eat anyway?"

"Small mammals, I imagine," Olivia mused. "Mice, birds, that sort of thing."

"Hmm. I'm afraid there's no juicy mouse on the hotel menu." He still dug through the assortment Adeline had stolen. "How about this?" he asked, pointing to a small packet containing two round, fluffy crumpets, a British staple. Looked like the hotel catered to an international clientele.

Curious, the little lizard watched Cornelius place the treat on the floor. He came closer to investigate, claws clinking against the polished floor, and sniffed the strange offering. Finding it to his liking, he sank his sharp little teeth and tore off a large chunk, all the while growling like a tiny demonic beast. Soon, he had devoured the whole thing and was nudging Olivia's hand.

"Look at him, he loved it!" Cornelius cooed as he scratched the scales along his back.

"Who's a good beastie?" Olivia whispered affectionately as she offered him the other crumpet, which he wolfed down as quickly as the first.

"Did those two really use my near-death experience to pick up a weird creature from the woods?" Godwyn's lips had curled in disgust.

"What?" Olivia replied. "He's cute."

She and Cornelius both stared, as proud as first-time parents, as the little creature settled onto Cornelius' lap to doze off, after releasing what could only be described as a tiny dragon burp.

Olivia tucked the last wisp of raven hair into the elegant updo Adeline had taught her and secured it in place with another pin, hoping she'd put in enough to hold the mass of dark curls in place for the entire evening.

After having helped apply some of Ryder's miraculous ointment to everyone's scratches and scrapes, all she had left to do was to change into her deep red and emerald sari, and loop the heavy gold earrings through her ears.

Instead, she rubbed a palm over her right arm, deep in thoughts. For the millionth time, it seemed, she wondered if the part of her that rejoiced at this unexpected hurdle in their plan made her a terrible person.

She'd told Ryder on the train that she was ready to take on this mission with him and see it through to the end. She'd meant it, really. But now that they found themselves with no tricks up their sleeves, no choice but to hand over the wand, all she could feel was relief.

She could still hear the sound of Godwyn's back hitting the tree, the crack of his head. Could still see the terror on Adeline's face, the utter hopelessness in her eyes.

And more than that . . . She was still reeling from her contact with the Darkness. The pain she'd felt was still in her bones, the wails still ringing in her ears. It had come so close to swallowing her whole. To plunge her into an abyss so deep that Olivia would never have been able to find her way back.

Did wanting to avoid it all again really make her a coward?

A soft knock jolted her from her bleak thoughts.

Olivia quickly pulled on her dressing gown and opened the door, thinking it was Adeline coming to borrow something, but Ryder stood on the other side.

She froze, her hand gripping the edge of the wood. She might have been afraid he could somehow hear the treacherous thoughts swirling in her head, but that wasn't why her eyes widened and a blush crept up her neck.

His wild, unruly hair was brushed back. His beard even looked as if it had been trimmed, giving him an air of rugged elegance. He was only partially dressed, wearing black dress trousers and a white shirt that was still open, showing off the hard planes of his chest.

The only spot of colour on him came from the crimson tie that hung loosely around his neck, embroidered with gold thread. And of course, the eyes that were fixed on her. So arresting, so blue.

They took in everything, roaming over her body, from the darkened eyelids that she knew showed off her hazel eyes, to the slender column of her neck. Then down to the tie of the silk dressing gown at her waist, and the bronze legs visible beneath it. And then back up again, to her lips, parted in a breathy exhale.

Olivia suddenly realised how long they'd been standing there, staring at each other, and the blush on her face deepened. She clutched the panels of her dressing gown tighter together, which seemed to break the intensity of the moment.

Ryder cleared his throat. "Sorry to bother you. I just . . . Hmm . . . I was hoping you could help me. My shoulder."

Concern immediately snapped her into action. She moved to let him into the room, her voice worried. "Are you in pain?"

"No, no," he quickly reassured her. "I just can't tie this dressing as neatly as you did and it keeps falling down." He made a face and raised a hand to rub the back of his neck. "Also, it tickles."

Smiling, Olivia closed the door. She waited until he'd stretched out on a chair and shrugged off his shirt. The sight of his pathetic excuse for a bandage kept her eyes from wandering over the bare expense of skin.

"Is your mosquito bite giving you trouble?" she couldn't resist teasing him.

He only shot her a narrow-eyed look in response.

Concentrating solely on her task, she unravelled everything, deftly removing the knots he'd made. The smell of ginger from the Mendix kit enveloped them.

Far too soon, she'd wrapped his shoulder back and let her hands drop. "How does that feel?"

Ryder blinked. He twisted his arm, testing the snugness of the wrapping. "Perfect. Thank you," he said, but his voice sounded distant, pensive.

"What's going on?"

He shrugged his shirt back on, but didn't touch the tie around his neck. His brows were furrowed. "Something's been bothering me."

"What is it?" Olivia asked as she rose and picked up the heavy velvet sari draped over the back of a chair.

"I've been thinking about how the wand suddenly became so unstable..." Ryder had absent-mindedly followed her movements with his gaze, but then his voice trailed off.

A hand rose to scratch the back of his neck. Olivia knew now that it meant he was feeling uncomfortable.

"Ah... Maybe I should go. Let you get dressed."

Olivia waved him off. She took a few steps and disappeared behind a wooden partition on the other side of the room. "It's fine. Tell me."

She shrugged out of her dressing gown and laid it over the top of the partition. Then she slipped into her underskirt and her crimson embroidered blouse.

After a few moments of silence, during which she imagined him scratching his nape again, Ryder continued. His voice was rougher than before, though. "That wand has been hell to handle for years, but in the last few weeks, there was no containing it. It *had* to go."

Olivia nodded. "Ah, I see. You're wondering if someone didn't have a hand in that. If they didn't provoke the wand in order to force the Ministry into trying another transfer."

"They sure would have needed the nudge, after the disaster that was the one. Is that even possible? To push the wand to react?"

"I suppose, yes," Olivia replied around the pin in her mouth. She was in the process of creating the pleats at the front of her sari and tucking it into her underskirt, then pinning everything in place. "But it would have to have come from inside the Cellars."

"Hmm."

"So either one of your guards," she pointed out, "or another curse-breaker."

"You're thinking of Crowley," Ryder declared.

"He certainly has it in him," Olivia admitted. Crowley had been power-hungry for as long as she'd known him, craving fame and success. He had always considered it as his due.

Still, there was one piece of the puzzle that bothered her. "But if Crowley is part of this," she thought aloud, "wouldn't he prefer to distance himself from the case? I mean, he called to threaten me into dropping it. That doesn't make any sense. It's the same with Skelton, really. If they were the ones transporting the wand and it went missing, everyone would automatically think they were . . ."

Silence.

"Guilty," Ryder finished for her, his voice ice-cold.

A terrible certainty settled over Olivia. It all made sense now . . . To steal something, you didn't just have to get away with it. You also needed to know what to tell the police when they came knocking on your door.

And what better way to sink her and her business than to accuse her of stealing the very artifact she was sworn to protect?

"We're being framed," Olivia whispered.

She heard a thud and then Ryder cursing in Swedish. "Of course we are! *Alltså,* I used to be a treasure hunter!" His voice turned bitter. "That's why I was really hired."

He swore again.

Olivia couldn't believe this. She'd insisted on taking this case to save her business, and now it looked like she'd doomed it instead. The night Crowley had called her, he'd been right. She really wouldn't like the consequences of getting involved with that wretched wand.

"We still have to return it tonight," Olivia finally said. Her voice was strained as frustration gripped her, right alongside fear. "Nothing's changed."

"I know," Ryder conceded with a harsh sigh. "Everything inside me is screaming that we shouldn't give it back, and it's killing me to ignore it. My instincts have saved my life more times than I can count."

Olivia willed her hands to move and finish creating the pleats in her skirt. The crackling of the fire was the only thing that broke the quiet.

Yet, she didn't feel as hopeless as perhaps she should have. Ryder's presence comforted her. She wasn't alone, there was a hunk of Swedish foolishness currently pacing in front of the fireplace that would put all his devious brain into getting them out of this mess. She trusted him.

"That inspector contact of yours . . ." she began, "Cillian Blackwood. Are you sure we can trust him? Because it looks more and more like we've stumbled right in the middle of a bloody conspiracy."

"Yes," he replied simply, but with absolute certainty.

Olivia didn't ask anything more. She didn't question him further, or remind him that whatever intrigue was at play here, the detective could very well be a part of it. No, she knew Ryder well enough now to know that when he believed in someone, they were good.

"Do you really think he'll be able to find out more about what's going on?"

Ryder huffed out a laugh. "That, I have no doubt. He's from one of the oldest Houses in Scotland, so mystery is his middle name. If there's any secret to be known, he'll find it. He's one sneaky bastard."

Olivia hummed softly as she put the last pin in, securing the pallu, or the loose part of her sari, to her shoulder. She sneaked a peek behind the partition.

Ryder had added a black waistcoat to his ensemble, with gold buttons to match his tie. However, said tie still hung loosely around his neck.

He'd stopped pacing and was standing near the fireplace, one clenched hand braced on the mantelpiece. Tension radiated off his frame, frustrated magic dancing atop his skin like a very faint shimmer.

Olivia knew he was doubting his decisions, worrying about their safety.

But she trusted him. She wouldn't have agreed to this mission if she hadn't. Even though she'd only known him a short while and still ignored a lot about him, she trusted him in ways she couldn't explain. She opened her mouth to tell him so, but the words caught in her throat.

He needed to know, though. He had to know that she would never have gone this far with anyone else.

"You said that following your instincts has saved your life many times," Olivia said softly. "Well, you're doing it again right now. By not jumping blindly into this fight. You're doing the right thing."

"Maybe," he replied. "But you were right, on the train. This is a lot more than what you signed up for, and it is not your fight. Maybe I shouldn't have dragged you into this."

Olivia stepped out from behind the partition, heavy embroidered velvet rustling as she moved. The flickering light from the fire illuminated the deep furrow between Ryder's brows, the lines bracketing his mouth.

She shook her head, smiling. "I wanted adventure, a crazy case . . . I've still got a competition to win, you know. Besides, you said you needed my help. What would you do without me?"

Her teasing words seemed to ease some of the strain on his face. He turned to her fully, an emotion in his stare she couldn't name.

Olivia took another small step towards him. She was so close now that she could smell his woody, masculine scent. She could see the flecks of gold hiding in his gorgeous eyes, the tiny freckles that dusted his cheekbones.

Her hands moved without her conscious control. They reached for the loose tie at his neck and the dark silk danced across her fingers as she tied it into place. "We're in this together now, Warden. No running away."

She kept her eyes on his tie, unwilling to bear the heavy weight of his gaze, but she could *feel* it.

One of his hands lifted. He rubbed his knuckles against the bare skin of her arm, leaving a shiver in their wake. Up and up they went, until they reached her fingers, still tangled in the silk of his tie.

Olivia's heart beat faster. His skin was warm, his hand so much larger and rougher as it covered her more delicate one. She inhaled sharply.

She dared raise her head to look at him, staring up into those impossibly blue eyes. Right now, they were stormy and wild. Not the deep blue of an ocean, but rather the colour of a raging tempest.

His gaze roamed over her body once more. Inspected the heavy crimson fabric spilling over her right shoulder, snagged on the sliver of bronze skin that showed at her waist. "Olivia . . ."

The deep timbre of his voice enveloped her, intimate and warm. She swore even his magic curled around her, as if it too didn't want to let go.

"I could never do this without you," he continued, his Nordic accent stronger. "I hope you know that."

She opened her mouth to utter something, though she didn't know what, but never got the chance because there was a sudden and harsh knock on the door, followed by Godwyn's solemn voice.

"It's time."

CHAPTER THIRTY-ONE

Olivia groaned as she stumbled again. There must have been a rain shower while they were getting ready because the stone path leading up to the castle was wet and slippery.

In front of her, Adeline balanced flawlessly on top of her high heels, without a care in the world, looking the perfect picture of a Parisian femme fatale.

She had to be using magic to do that. Had to.

Her long gown flowed and danced like water with every step. A very warm silver colour, it reminded Olivia of ancient Corinthian bronze. In contrast to the ethereal ripples of the silk, she wore a heavy velvet cape of midnight blue, adorned with silver thread. With her hair pinned elaborately on her head to reveal her slender neck and the arresting colour of her eyes, she looked breathtaking. Both regal and otherworldly, like a Fae queen from another time.

Her hand rested lightly on Godwyn's arm, who hadn't stopped sneaking glances at her ever since they'd left the hotel. Adeline had ignored them all, of course. But from her vantage point behind the couple, Olivia noticed how she sometimes looked back when he would finally manage to tear his gaze away.

Cornelius had spotted it, too, and flashed Olivia a knowing smile every single time.

Ryder slowed his steps to match hers, hooking her arm around his. "Shall I just throw you over my shoulder and carry you there, *Älva*?"

"You shall throw me anywhere and die."

The Viking laughed, but then Olivia's smile faded as she became aware of her glove-covered hand, casually draped over his arm. Of what she was hiding from him.

When Ryder found out, he would *not* be happy.

"So, I have to ask you something." Ryder's serious whisper gave her pause. *Had he noticed?*

"Yes?" she answered carefully.

"Adeline and Godwyn. Is there something there?"

"Ah . . ."

She'd seen her two employees yell at each other, bicker like an old couple, or furiously try to win whatever competition existed between them. But she'd also noted the fleeting glances, the loaded silences and, most recently, Adeline's terror when Godwyn had been under the wand's influence.

There was something there, all right. The question was what.

"They won't say and I don't ask," she replied simply. "All I can tell you is that they're both the most stubborn people I know. So they're well matched."

There was another bend in the path and Peleș Castle finally emerged from behind tall trees, taking Olivia's breath away.

The moon had risen fully, illuminating an enchanting construction of rounded turrets and conical spires, timber-framed facades, massive arched doorways edged with gold. Torches dotted the exterior and were scattered throughout the gardens, bathing the entire castle in a warm glow. Around them, fountains played and water cascaded into pools below. The air felt like a decadent summer's night and carried the smell of smoke and rich night blooms.

It was a fairytale palace, whose imposing sight was only heightened by the dramatic backdrop of the Carpathian Mountains behind it.

Yet, mist had risen from the trees around the castle, and even though heavy braziers burned throughout the gardens, darkness clung in corners, heavy and thick with secrets. Whispers of dark magic pervaded the air and glided over their skin.

CHAPTER 31

As they climbed the monumental marble staircase, flanked on either side by guarding lion statues, Ryder pulled out their invitations and they were allowed to pass through the great oak doors into the Honour Hall.

Three stories of intricate woodwork unfolded before them, with spiral staircases and alabaster sculptures. Dark walls rose high, proudly decorated with long banners embroidered with coats of arms: the Drašković family's feather and golden arrow, the House of Ambrózy with its raven holding a cross, the famous Humboldt family's tree of knowledge, all of them patrons of the Institute of Dark Arts.

Far above, crystal chandeliers hid among the panes of stained glass and glittered, reflecting a soft and dazzling light onto the crowd below. Laughter floated, diamonds shone. Guests in dark tuxedos and bright dresses glided through the room, strolled, conversed. Waiters whispered their way through it all, carrying trays of delicacies and wine.

Godwyn and Adeline gave them subtle nods before heading upstairs. People looked at them as they passed, staring at the stunning woman and the handsome man beside her with the emerald eyes and the high cheekbones.

The Baron and the Spy.

Olivia wondered if the two of them would have this whole case solved before the night was through.

Cornelius had already set off on his own quest with a parting wink and a smile, their new lizard-dragon content to snooze in a tiny ball tucked into the satchel at his side.

Olivia's hand reached out and patted her own bag, as if to reassure herself that the wand was still there and hadn't vanished in a puff of smoke. A habit she'd developed since the beginning of this case.

"*Scuzați-mă?* Excuse me?"

Tearing her eyes away from the stunning sights around her, Olivia turned to a severe looking man with long limbs and lips pinched in annoyance. He was flanked on either side by two security guards who eyed her with open suspicion. "*Domnișoară* Knight, *Domnule* Isaksson?"

"That would be us," Ryder replied, his gaze assessing.

"The High Commissioner sends his apologies. There's been an incident with a guest and he is otherwise indisposed. He asks that you please wait for him in the main hall and he will be with you shortly."

Ryder nodded. "Of course."

Once they were gone, Olivia smoothed a hand down her velvet skirt, then took a deep breath. "Shall we?"

No sooner had they taken two steps inside the hall to examine the many artifacts on display than her skin started tingling. The cursed energy was so strong that it flowed all around them, permeating the room. Dark magic pooled in the alcoves and burrows, stretched forth in search of power, mingling with the expensive gowns and the glittering jewels.

The Gauntlet of Gustav the Accursed, whispered to grant its wearer the ability to drain the life force from enemies, as the warlord once did. The Candelabra of Spirits, whose flickering flames emitted ghostly murmurs, each candle a soul bound to its curse. Each of these relics encased in a glass dome with a small card underneath bearing the lot number, like so many little presents for the avid collectors and the practitioners of the forbidden arts.

"Can you believe they found a Scroll of Power? This one was made by Tycho Brahe. There are only five still in existence to this day. I simply *must* have this."

Olivia's lips thinned at the excited chatter that floated over to her.

Her eyes rose to the stern, forbidding portraits of ancient figures suspended on the walls, that stared down at the crowd sauntering past. She couldn't help but feel that they were silently judging them all, not content to witness what their palace had come to.

"*Jäklar*," Ryder swore under his breath. "I don't hear anyone speaking English."

"I know it's all been quite the whirlwind, but . . . you do realise we're not in England any more, don't you?"

Ryder pinched her arm where it was draped over his, then asked, "Do you understand what they're saying?"

CHAPTER 31

Guests had come from all over the world for the chance to win a dark relic tonight, so all around them was a mixture of Romanian, English, some French, some Russian.

"I can understand a little Romanian here and there, but there are so many different languages going on at once, it's confusing," she whispered. "However, Adeline is fluent so she might have better luck."

"That assistant of yours was a spy in a previous life."

Olivia hummed. "You don't know how fervently I agree."

Ryder threw her a brief look as they walked on, concern on his face. "Are you all right, Olivia? You seem . . . unsteady."

She kept her face carefully blank, wondering again how long she could hope to hide the truth from him. "More than usual, you mean?" She gave him a reassuring smile. "I'm fine, just tired. I'm not used to adventures, remember?"

Ryder eyed her suspiciously for a moment, but then leaned closer to her so that his words wouldn't carry to other guests. "I know you hate all this," he whispered, "but I see the way you've been staring at that parchment."

Olivia smiled in spite of herself at the deviousness she heard in his tone.

"What in Odin's name is this absolute monstrosity?" Ryder's sudden exclamation startled her so badly that she almost dropped the glass of champagne she'd just accepted from a waiter.

"Will you tone it down!" she hissed. "People came here to buy those, you know."

He huffed, but lowered his voice. "No one in their right mind would buy that one, that's for sure."

Exasperated, Olivia rolled her eyes and turned to look at whatever had disgusted him so. "What do you even find so repulsive . . . Oh."

Ryder only sighed when he spotted the expression on her face.

A delicately detailed, anatomical heart made of stone rested on a small velvet cushion. What resembled grey marble was riddled with tiny cracks where moss and dirt had gathered. It looked like a well-made, if strange, sculpture but there was an inexplicable sense of *something* coming off it, even through the glass dome it was encased in. It made the small hairs on the back of Olivia's neck rise.

She tried to lean closer, but Ryder caught her arm. "I have no idea what this is," she said softly. "I've never seen anything like it before . . ."

"Try not to sound *too* excited about that," Ryder muttered.

"I studied the catalogue before we came here, and I'm sure it wasn't on it," Olivia continued, ignoring him. "Perhaps it was a last-minute acquisition? But that seems unlikely . . ."

"Alright, we're going now." Ryder tried to tug her away.

"Wait, I want to look at it some more—Did you see that?"

Ryder froze and his hand tightened on her arm. "What do you mean, did you see that? What did you see?"

Olivia kept her eyes glued to the stone heart. "I'm pretty sure I saw it . . . *beat*."

Ryder gave up on trying to convince her to move and simply pulled her away with a firm grip on her elbow and a hand on the small of her back. "We're going. Right now. No arguments."

Olivia's lips twitched as they left the disturbing stone heart behind. Then they passed a massive, intricately carved door and she had to force herself to keep walking instead of stopping mid-step to gape.

The room she'd glimpsed was packed with various swords and sabres, shields, armour, ceremonial weapons . . . The soft glow of the hanging chandeliers made the polished metals, the etched runes down the blades and the precious stone inlays in the hilts sparkle.

The Armoury.

Another glance made her eyes widen. What could be better than a room full of antique weaponry? *Cursed* ones.

Ryder caught her staring. "Why don't we go in there? Looks less crowded, maybe you'll hear something interesting."

Olivia winced, shook her head. "We can't."

"Yes, we can. Look, there are guests coming out of it—"

"All right, let me rephrase that. *I* can't."

At his quizzical expression, Olivia heaved a deep sigh. "That's the Great Armoury of Peleş Castle. It already contained the finest collection of weapons and armour in Europe, and now it even has cursed and enchanted ones. There are pieces in there dating back to the 14th century. If I go in, I am never coming out, and we have things to do."

Ignoring the chuckles beside her, Olivia spotted a waiter nearby and raised her hand to deposit her empty glass on his tray.

Only her arm refused to obey and instead flailed aimlessly, colliding with Ryder's chest.

"Olivia." His previously amused expression had vanished. Now his blue eyes bored into hers. "What is happening to you? You've gone pale."

It was all blurring together. Ryder's words, the clinking of champagne glasses, the light from the candles reflecting off the glass cages ... It took every ounce of strength she had to keep her face impassive, even as icy shivers ran down her spine.

There were just too many people here, too much magic coming from everywhere all at once. From the guests, seeping out of the artifacts, from the very walls of the castle.

"Ladies and gentlemen!" An attendant came out of a door on their left. "The Books and Manuscripts auction is about to begin. We invite all guests to please join us in the Florentine Room."

Everyone around them converged at once in the direction he'd indicated, but something out of the corner of her eye made Olivia jump.

Lord Hadley stood among the guests, his unblinking gaze full of rage fixed on her.

She took an involuntary step back, almost colliding with a statue, but Ryder caught her arm just in time.

Her blood had frozen in her veins as everything around her stilled into deafening silence. The hushed conversations and laughter, the sound of heels clicking on the marble floor, the attendant's tenor voice leading everyone to the auction room ... All replaced by a vast nothing as her eyes never once wavered from Lord Hadley's murderous glare.

He had wanted to kill her that day in court. Had wanted to wrap his hands around her throat. Maybe he would have done so if others hadn't restrained him, his face so twisted with rage that it had become unrecognisable. Perhaps now he might get his wish ...

That was surely why the fates had brought her here. Not because she had a mission to fulfil, but because she had to pay for her crimes—

"Olivia!"

She came to as Ryder shook her none-too-gently. He'd manoeuvred her into a somewhat secluded corner behind an elegant marble bust.

What she'd thought was Lord Hadley turned out to be just another guest who cast her a curious look before disappearing into the Florentine room with the others.

A shaky breath escaped her lips. "I'm fine, I'm all right," she ground out as calmly as she could. "I just need some air."

Ryder immediately took her hand, his large shoulders easily clearing a path through the densely packed crowd.

Olivia closed her eyes in bliss as soon as they left the stifling interior of the castle behind. It felt as if she'd been drowning in smoke, the dark magic turning the air heavy and thick, and it was only now that she was able to take a full breath.

She picked up the hem of her sari as they descended the few steps from the stone patio to the courtyard. Her mind was already clearer, her eyes sharper.

Somewhere to her right, a man hurried across the edge of the gardens, looking suspicious. He wore a carefully blank expression on his face, but his hands kept clenching nervously at his side and he was failing to hide his hurry.

But before Olivia could point any of this out to Ryder, she saw another form materialise from behind the marble statue of a forest nymph and head towards him. They met as far away from the row of torches illuminating the night as possible, and joined in a passionate embrace.

One that quickly made her eyes widen and a blush spread across her cheeks.

She felt Ryder laugh softly beside her. He led them to a small white bench, vines wrapped around the base, and sat her down.

He lowered his head until he could whisper directly into her ear. "I don't think they're here for the wand."

Olivia should have retorted some snappy remark, but she felt his chuckle directly against her neck and it was all she could do to stop the shivers racing down her back, that, this time, had nothing to do with black magic.

"Is that your professional opinion?" she managed to murmur.

"Hmm hmm." The grin that blossomed on his face looked positively wicked.

But all too soon, his expression darkened. "What was that back there? What's happening to you?"

She couldn't tell him what she was hiding underneath her velvet gloves. Not yet. So she decided to give him another truth instead, buy herself some time. "This curse, Ryder, it's... It's nothing I've ever felt before."

She let her eyes wander over the beautiful garden, breathed in the scent of jasmine. Everything to ignore the knot forming in her stomach. "When we tried to locate Godwyn and I connected with the wand, I told you there was something else there... Something that tried to get to me, hurt me. I felt it again in the forest."

"What was it?"

"Darkness," she replied, past the tightness in her throat. "Pure black magic. But it was more than that, it was... *sentient*. It thinks, it feels. It was..." Her voice dropped to a whisper. "Glad to see me again."

Olivia risked a glance at Ryder. His face was filled with menace. "What do you think the curse wants with you? Your power?"

She swallowed heavily. "You misunderstand me. Whatever that thing is, it's not the curse."

His eyes widened in surprise. "What? Are you sure?"

"I'm certain. I felt the curse inside the wand, my magic recognised it. It's dark and powerful like nothing else, but I know what it is. That hungry thing around it, however, I... This is something else."

"Holmes did imply that the wand was part of something much bigger than we realised. Walker too."

Olivia ignored the ice spreading through her veins... What nightmares the Order would conjure if they managed to channel this Darkness... Not to mention, if the wand really was connected to a Gate, as they thought, then there was a place somewhere that had birthed it, and was surely brimming with other horrors just like it.

And they were the ones who had to make sure none of this ever happened. The weight of that task came down so hard on her shoulders that it stole her breath.

Or perhaps it was the black magic seeping deeper and deeper into her.

"Well, if it isn't my rogue Warden and his . . . *expert,*" someone behind them drawled.

Ryder sighed. "Speak of the troll," he muttered.

Olivia shared a pained look with him. "And he shall appear."

The Head of the Dark Artifacts Department in person, Artemus Lionel Skelton, stood behind them, an indignant expression on his face and Edmund Crowley flanking him.

Two trolls, actually.

Looking dapper in a sleek navy suit, he had dark skin, glossy with an ebony sheen, and black hair streaked with grey. His features were well-defined but elegant, with a patrician nose, a broad forehead and hazel eyes under forceful eyebrows. In his right hand, he held a long black cane, topped with a gleaming silver dragon's head. An aura of wealth and prestige radiated from him, like a thin layer over his appearance. He resembled many of the guests here this evening: rich, cultured, worldly, a little conceited. Yet, Olivia knew all that to be a front for a bloodthirsty shark.

He was smiling, even through his glower, and she stiffened.

Meanwhile, Crowley had a deep sneer on his face, as if he'd just chewed on something terribly sour or noticed a bug crushed underneath his gleaming shoe. His slightly deep-set eyes peered at Olivia, at once triumphant and outraged. His black hair was in its usual slicked-back state, showing sharp cheekbones and a square, clean-shaven jaw.

"What you both did was completely unprofessional," the Head of Department snapped, his voice iced over. "Undeserving of the respect your professions demand. I'm greatly disappointed in you."

Olivia's lips twitched, she couldn't help it.

Beside her, Ryder drawled, "And what exactly is this in reference to?"

Skelton's voice turned even more frigid, and he spoke each word very distinctly. "This is about you leaving me the transfer of a forgery, while you abscond with the real artifact, without my knowledge or consent."

Ryder crossed his arms, biceps straining the sleeves of his jacket. "Do I need to remind you that the wand has been at risk for months because of a leak in your Department? If I hadn't hidden the real transfer, it would never have made it to Romania."

Skelton scoffed, "You cannot possibly blame my Department. The leak originated from your people, Warden. Nevertheless, you are deliberately missing the point. You kept the real details of the transfer from *me*."

Ah. There it was.

"I am your superior," he ground out. "You are under my command, under my jurisdiction. Keeping things from me, means keeping them from the Ministry itself."

Olivia pressed her lips together. How about from the King himself, while he was at it?

"I can promise you there will be an inquiry, mark my words. And you . . ." Skelton turned his affronted face her way, his eyes narrowing into slits. "I can't say I was surprised to learn that you played a part in this. Following the rules has always been a challenge for you."

Ryder choked back a laugh and had to clear his throat a few times.

"I've let it slide in the past as a courtesy, but this time, I'm going to make sure you reap the consequences of your recklessness. It is past time you learned your place, Knight. And that you cannot disregard the rules when they don't suit you." An ugly grimace skewed Skelton's features. The civilised mask had slipped from his face. "I would have believed, after what happened the last time you defied orders, that you would have learned your lesson."

Olivia's entire body froze. Everything ground to a halt.

"Do you have any idea what that trial cost us?" Skelton continued. "The Minister himself had to intervene when the papers got hold of the story. They accused us of murdering that child, that Ann—"

Olivia's hand slashed the air. "Don't."

At her side, Ryder stiffened.

"Don't you *dare* say her name," she hissed, not even recognising her own voice.

If she hadn't kept her magic in a leash, one so tight it might as well have been a chokehold, she would have attacked the Head of Department, right there in the middle of those fancy gardens.

One deep breath. Another.

"A child *died* because you wouldn't listen to me, Skelton. You may pretend otherwise, you may lie to yourself so you can sleep at night, but I know the truth. We both do."

Olivia took a step forward. Ryder's hand seized her forearm.

"Go ahead," she spat. "Launch that internal review, report us to the Ministry, I dare you. I welcome it, even. But mark *my* words: I promise I'll make it hurt when I drag you through the mud, where you belong."

While Crowley spluttered, his face going red with indignation, Skelton's glare gained a dangerous edge. His flat voice would have made her take a step back if Olivia hadn't been so irate.

"You forget yourself." The polished, sophisticated scholar was well and truly gone, now only the shark remained. "I have more power and authority than you could ever dream of. Do you really think the word of a broke, small-scale agency owner about to have her licence revoked is stronger than one of the most prominent men in the community? Remember what happened the last time we crossed paths. And who won."

He jabbed the head of his dragon cane in her direction. "Everyone will soon see you for what you truly are: nothing more than an attention seeker. I know you only took this case in the foolish hope of winning that pitiful competition. As if it would ever have saved you." He sneered. "As if I would have *let it*."

So he was the reason her business was failing.

And he would make sure to sink her this time. So even if she pulled off this impossible mission, even if she returned to York triumphant, with an astonishing story of how she had contained the most dangerous artifact in recent curse-breaking memory, it still wouldn't be enough.

And yet, she couldn't find it in herself to care.

"You forget, Skelton, that I worked in your Department for years. I saw what really went on in there. Little secrets you tried to hide, bribes you took, mistakes you let pass... You're taking away my agency? My licence? All the things I care about? Then I'll make sure to take everything of *yours* down with me."

Skelton's face was terrible. His mouth was a narrow, straight slash. He regarded her like he wanted to strangle her.

Olivia would have loved nothing more at this precise moment than to get into a brawl right there in this courtyard, but an attendant materialised behind their group. Oblivious to the tension in the air, he came close to whisper something in Skelton's ear that made him nod sharply.

"Watch yourself, Knight," he warned before pivoting on his heels, Crowley in tow.

As soon as they were out of earshot, Olivia turned to Ryder. "We need to follow them."

He startled. "What? Why?"

"That man just told Skelton that the mage wanted a word." Olivia quickly gathered her sari and went after them, keeping to the shadows of the tall hedges.

She heard Ryder mutter to himself as he followed her, "And she can even read lips."

Skelton's cane hit the stone pavement like the striking of a bell as he made his way to the farthest corner of the gardens, where there weren't as many torches and no guest wandering about. He stopped beside a large fountain, a statue of a Greek mythology figure in the centre.

Olivia and Ryder hid behind a half-wall a few paces away, the Viking having to crouch and almost kneel on the gravel, he was so ridiculously tall. They could see through the gaps in the marble balustrade, but were too far away to hear anything, and the dim light made it impossible for Olivia to read their lips. She could tell, however, that Skelton and Crowley were having a rather heated discussion, all furious low tones and sweeping hands.

"Ryder, how could this have happened?" Olivia whispered. "You forgot you were under Skelton's orders? Such an oversight seems beyond belief."

The joke felt ashy on her tongue, but she needed the distraction, else she was going to hurl the decorative urn beside her at Skelton's inflated head.

"A momentary lapse in judgement," Ryder replied. "It was good of him to remind me."

"Hmm hmm. So gracious is our Skelton, so generous."

"The best boss I could ever have wished for." His gaze stayed glued to the two men, sharp and focused. "Now I understand why Adeline calls Crowley your nemesis. I don't think his face will ever recover from that sneer."

"Right? Loved that little twitch in his eyelid when I mentioned the Department's secrets. Did I ever tell you that I was one level above him in the hierarchy? He was only a level three technician, while I was a fully accredited curse-breaker."

The corner of Ryder's lips quirked upwards. "Good for you."

Silence stretched, heavy and tense.

"Are you all right?"

Olivia didn't try to lie. It would have been pointless anyway, he could read her mind. "No."

Ryder slanted a look at her, then. It was dark and stormy. "You're really going after him?"

She'd let it go before. Instead, she'd chosen to flee, attempted to salvage whatever was left of her career, her reputation.

She regretted it now. Oh, how she regretted it.

"Him and everyone else involved. I'll take them all down."

He nodded slowly, the promise of a Viking in his midnight blue eyes. "Count me in."

Suddenly, Ryder's entire frame tensed beside her. And for a hunk of muscle such as him, it was saying something.

He didn't move, and no emotion showed on his face, but from one moment to the next, he'd gone battle ready.

Words were unnecessary. Olivia kept quiet and simply waited for whatever it was he'd sensed.

Soon enough, she *felt* it.

CHAPTER 31

A figure was hurrying along the stone wall at the edge of the garden. He tried to keep to the shadows, but every pool of light he approached illuminated parts of his features.

And the sight raised every hair on Olivia's arms.

The man wore a blood-red robe, edged with gold, that covered him completely. A pitch-black mask covered his features, from the top of his cheekbones to his hairline. A black so deep and true that it appeared almost flat, making his face look as if half was missing. Even his eyelids had been painted black. Only his eyes showed, and what eyes he had. Milky white irises with dark pupils.

But the worst part was how his presence *felt*.

The effect was so unsettling, so unnerving, that Olivia had to grit her teeth and force herself not to take off running. "What . . . What *is* that?" she dared whisper.

Ryder glanced over at her. His jaw was as hard as a block of granite. "A Furtum mage. And I can guarantee you, he's not on the guest list."

A Furtum mage . . .

An extremely rare type of magic, arcanists with this talent had the power to absorb arcane energy from inanimate objects. But stories went that they could also absorb it from *people*.

The Guard had spent centuries hunting and imprisoning them. If any still lived, they were kept locked away in rehabilitation facilities, where all those with what was considered unnatural magic inevitably ended up.

It was where Adeline would end up if her magic ever became known. Among other inmates just like him, whose mere presence felt like sandpaper rubbing against her aura.

And as for what they might do to her with this particular branch of magic . . . She couldn't even think about it.

Olivia craned her neck to catch any words showing on their lips, but to no avail. The Furtum mage had a brief conversation with Skelton, Crowley keeping quiet beside him, and then it was all over. The mage went back the way he'd come, hurried footsteps making his blood-red robe sway before he slunk back into the shadows. Skelton bit out a few harsh words and then left, too.

Damn it.

Olivia's brow furrowed in frustration. What had they talked about? What did the mage want with them? She was about to suggest that they get back to the reception before the High Commissioner sent a group of security guards to track them down, but that was when she spotted Crowley hurrying towards them.

Ryder hadn't noticed because he couldn't see the other man from his vantage point, but in a heartbeat they would all come face to face.

Olivia didn't stop to think. Grabbing the lapels of Ryder's jacket with both hands, she pulled him to her and crushed her lips against his.

She made sure to turn around so that her back would rest against the half-wall, and Ryder's dark clothes would cover her sari. Crowley walked right past them, completely oblivious, and continued on to the other side of the gardens. She nonetheless kept him in her sight until he'd disappeared behind a tall hedge.

That was when Olivia's brain finally caught up with her.

In her eagerness to hide the sight of her clothes, she'd plastered Ryder against her, so much so that not an inch of space remained between their bodies. She could feel his heart beating against her chest, the warmth of his legs next to her velvet covered ones.

His lips were surprisingly soft. And his beard wasn't rough at all, but felt silky against her cheeks, her chin.

She'd kissed Isaksson.

Actually, no. She *was* kissing Isaksson.

The thought blazed through her mind with the force of a lightening strike. Her eyes went wide as furious heat spread across her face.

She leaned her head back, but couldn't move any further than that, trapped between the hard rock at her back and the equally hard surface of Ryder's chest.

His eyebrows had risen to his hairline, his mouth slightly agape. One forearm was braced against the stones above her head, the other hand resting on Olivia's waist, covering the slight expanse of bare skin at her midriff.

His surprise faded and she watched as a grin slowly spread across his face. His gaze traced her kiss-swollen lips, the flaming blush that had erupted on her cheeks, all the way down to her neck. His eyes were so blue, so captivating.

He bent his head to whisper in her ear, "Can't say I'm too familiar with this evasive technique, *Älva*. But I approve."

The warmth of his breath tingled against her skin, making her heart beat faster inside her chest. Her hands were still gripping the lapels of his jacket, completely frozen, unsure whether to push him away or draw him closer.

But all at once, the moment shattered.

The heat drained from his face, replaced with thunder. His eyes hardened, his hand tightened on her waist.

Oh oh. He'd finally figured it out.

Olivia's lips parted. She tried to think of something to say, but couldn't.

Ryder's hands moved to encircle her forearms. They didn't hurt, but his grip was firm. He lifted them from the lapels of his jacket, piercing eyes falling on the crimson gloves masking her fingers.

"You lied to me," he all but growled.

Olivia winced. "I'm sorr—"

She was saved from Ryder's wrath when someone behind them cleared their throat loudly. "If you would please follow me, High Commissioner Mitrea is ready to see you now."

CHAPTER THIRTY-TWO

They were escorted up a lavish, red-carpeted staircase by no less than three security guards, their expressions impassive. From the corner of her eye, Olivia caught a glimpse of a familiar cascade of bronze fluttering across a room, leaving a trail of dazed men in its wake.

Their silent escort led them to the very end of the corridor. Unlocking a door, they made sure the room was empty before posting themselves outside, their arms crossed.

As Ryder and Olivia stepped over the threshold, they were enveloped by the scent of aged books, mingled with the faint aroma of the cedar wood burning in the fireplace.

Carved bookcases, their mahogany surfaces polished to a lustrous sheen, stood sentinel along the walls, bearing the weight of countless tomes, their spines adorned with faded titles and gilded accents.

A crackling fire swirled in the hearth, casting a warm glow across the library and contrasting with the tall, stained glass windows on the other side that sent colourful patterns dancing across the smooth hardwood floor.

Here and there, a few artifacts were displayed under the same glass cases, but these ones gave off distinct threads of magic that told Olivia they were the more unique pieces.

"Do you know what those are?" she heard Ryder ask from behind her. "They're everywhere."

He was examining an antique lantern perched on a white pedestal in the corner of the room, one of many scattered around the castle. All gold metal with delicate carvings, the lantern contained a small and simple candle.

But that wasn't what had caught Ryder's attention. The entire lantern seemed to be surrounded by twisting shadows, dark shapes that slithered all around it. And where the candle should have cast a golden light around itself, the flame was black and there was only deeper darkness.

"Beautiful, isn't it? I think I could stare at it for hours," Olivia said as she approached. "I wouldn't touch it, though, if I were you," she added, just as Ryder had raised a hand to run it through the winding shapes.

"What are those . . . *things?*"

"Trapped residual curses. Whenever you deal with a cursed artifact, some of it always gets released into the air. Like dust particles, floating away. Except curses, unlike ordinary dust, like to mess with your head. So this little beauty here, traps them." Olivia pointed to the inconspicuous candle inside. "This candle is not made of ordinary wax, but of a particular substance curses that can't get enough of. To them, it's like catnip. So they try desperately to get inside the lantern, but can't penetrate the glass panels. And as soon as they see the candle, they become sort of entranced and don't ever leave."

"Like a snake charmer."

Olivia laughed. "I guess you could say that, yes. They can't get in, but they can't leave either, and as long as the candle still burns inside the lantern, they'll keep on dancing."

Ryder's eyes followed the twisting shadows for a long moment.

Olivia smiled inwardly. Turned out the enchantment worked on more than just curses.

"What would happen if I touched them?"

"I think they would get a taste of curious Viking flesh and latch on to you. I would have to . . . *purge* them out." Olivia smiled as he grimaced. "I can't tell you how much one of those lanterns would change my life at the office," she continued. "I have to do a complete cleansing every week to get rid of the residual curses in the air. With this, I could just sit in my chair and sip a glass of wine while watching all the little buggers fight to get in. Holmes sells them in his shop, but unfortunately this fancy contraption costs an arm and a leg and he refuses to grant me a family discount. But make no mistake, as soon as I get the funds, I'm getting one."

When Ryder began pacing the length of the room, hands clasped behind his back, Olivia went to examine the row of auction items.

There was a tall and very thin glass vial, dusty with age, encased in gold chains. The liquid inside was a purplish red, like thick wine, with an emerald sheen that swirled and danced within. The ivory card underneath read "Vial of Chimera Blood. Cerca 1840. Black Forest, Germany."

"How strong are those, as containments?" Ryder pointed a finger at the glass domes covering all the artifacts. "I can feel some magic escaping."

"I'm afraid that's unavoidable with objects of this magnitude and age," Olivia replied. "This is arcane treated glass. Very finely crafted, very expensive." She'd recognised it immediately by its slight opalescent glimmer. This type of glass was infused with warding runes as it was blown, and retained a faint trace of them when viewed from a certain angle.

"Why didn't we use one of these domes for the transfer?"

"In a way, we did. The sides of the cage were made of the same kind of glass. But we couldn't have used one of those domes as it is. The arcane treatment given to the glass is very strong, but only lasts for about forty-eight hours. After that, it starts to break down and becomes vulnerable to the artifact's magic."

Ryder hummed quietly.

"Want to know a secret?"

A gleam immediately appeared in the Warden's eyes. He came over to her.

"This containment is almost impenetrable," Olivia whispered. "At least for the forty-eight hours. The arcane treatment makes the molecular structure of the glass align, in such a way that it starts to resonate harmoniously. That resonance is what makes it so strong. But it has one weakness." She pointed to a particular spot with the tip of her finger. "You see this edge here? Right at the junction with the wooden base. That section is structurally unique. Because of the difference in material, there is a slight misalignment in their magical resonances. And this creates a tiny, almost imperceptible, dissonance in the frequencies. So, if you were to take a very thin object, wrap it in a null shield, and give a firm press right *there*, you could temporarily destabilise the harmonic resonance. You could create a very small window in which the dome's containment is weakened, allowing you to pry the entire case from its base without triggering any alarm. That's why it's always recommended to put a few extra wards around the entire building."

"I'll just have to add potential museum thief to your repertoire of qualifications, Ms Knight."

Olivia shook her head as her eyes slid to the next artifact. The shadowed funeral crown of Karl IX of Norway rested on a bed of velvet, its darkened gems seeming to absorb the very light around it. She was about to get closer, curious about the writing that seemed to be etched into the gold, but Ryder's voice stopped her.

"Do you remember the path we took to get here?" he asked, his deep voice quiet. "Would you be able to make it back to the courtyard?"

Olivia looked at him in surprise. His face had taken on a sombre expression. "I think so . . . Why?"

"I have a feeling something's about to happen. I don't like the way the guards have been watching us ever since we got here."

"They know we have the wand, they're probably worried it'll influence all the other artifacts."

Ryder shook his head. "No, it's more than that. I know a man who's seizing me up for a fight when I see one. I have a strong suspicion we're going to need a diversion to get out of here."

Olivia's eyes darted to the closed door, behind which she knew the guards were waiting. "Can't you use one of your Night-Night balls?"

Ryder stared her down. His brows rose. "My . . . what?"

"Your Night-Night balls," she repeated. "You know, your little gadget? Cloud of black mist, a hundred grams of . . . something obscure?"

"You mean my tactical, highly efficient, low-impact, targeted black dispersion cloud bomb."

"Sure. Yes. That."

"I left it in my bag."

"What?" Olivia snapped.

"Oh, I'm sorry." Ryder crossed his arms over his chest. "I thought carrying a bomb on my person was *'irresponsible and dangerous and an accident waiting to happen.'*"

Olivia huffed. "And you chose this moment to finally listen to what I tell you?"

She began looking around with interest. Well, desperate times . . .

Ryder noticed the way she was eyeing the auction displays. "I can't believe you'd lecture me about my plans when you're about to steal another artifact!" he muttered. "You're unbelievable!"

Olivia pulled a hair pin out of her complicated updo. "And you're hallucinating. It's all that champagne," she replied. "Now, keep quiet and cover me."

Ryder came to stand behind her, as if to examine the vial of Chimera blood more closely, his broad back completely hiding her from view.

Exactly as she'd explained before, she twisted a strand of magic around the pin, as if she'd wrapped the metal in a thin, gossamer-like veil. She carefully positioned the tip right at the base of the glass case, holding her breath. A sharp push and the whole thing snapped out.

No alarm shrieked, no guard came rushing into the room, guns blazing. With an all too satisfied smile, Olivia grabbed the vial, grimacing at the feeling of crusty dust around it.

Immediately, visions of flames and heat wavered before her.

Burn it all . . .

She slammed her mental shields up, locking the curse out of her mind. *Let's not.*

She quickly slipped the vial into a pocket of Ryder's jacket and seconds later, the mahogany door of the library swung open.

Making sure to hide the now empty dome at their backs, they turned to watch a man stride in, a warm and relieved expression on his face.

Olivia couldn't help the sudden shiver of excitement that ran through her. She was about to meet the man who had undoubtedly shaped the direction of her career.

Although, he wouldn't be all that impressed when he found out she'd stolen one of his artifacts. Oh well . . . She'd stolen one of Ryder's. Fair was fair.

Tall and lean, with olive skin and a wealth of wavy, coal-black hair that didn't show the slightest hint of silver, the High Commissioner's features were bold and handsome. The eyes looking back at them through thin-framed glasses were at once kind and brimming with intelligence. He radiated wisdom the way some men exuded strength, as if he were some old, knowledgeable wizard who had suddenly materialised on their path to help them in their quest.

He raised his arms. "Ms Knight! Mr Isaksson! You have no idea how glad I am to see you." His thick Romanian accent only added to his charisma. "I was afraid they would get to you before you had a chance to arrive."

Olivia glanced at Ryder. *"They?"*

"Right, yes. We have much to talk about. But first things first, please tell me you have the Dark Wand."

Olivia's eyes met Ryder's again. He was considering the High Commissioner with a kind of fierce, shrill suspicion. His face might look calm, focused, but she'd noticed the half-step he'd taken to put himself in front of her, shielding her from Mitrea.

"We have it," she replied cautiously.

Mitrea let out a long breath. "What a relief."

"Who's *they*?" Ryder asked again.

The High Commissioner's face hardened. "I am sure you've already guessed. The Order of the Dragon is very much alive, has been for centuries. They are now embedded in every single institution in this country. Nowhere is safe."

He walked around the room, not quite pacing but instead fluttering from one place to the next. Olivia discreetly repositioned herself to keep the empty dome out of his sight.

"You have no idea how difficult it has been to keep these artifacts safe when I cannot trust a soul. I only have a few contacts that I know beyond a shadow of a doubt to be loyal, but the rest ... any one of them could turn out to be a Dragon Knight."

The lassitude and frustration were clear in his voice. But also the steel, the anger. Olivia thought she would have sounded just like that in his place.

Mitrea raised a hand to brush back his hair, revealing a fresh, inflamed scar on his temple. "I narrowly escaped an attempt on my life yesterday. That was when I decided to send you the telegram, Ms Knight. I had to warn you."

"You don't trust the Romanian police department?" Ryder prodded.

The High Commissioner's gaze met his squarely. "No. And I suspect you do not either, if what I overheard of your conversation with the sergeant is anything to go by."

"Who else?"

Mitrea's lips curled upwards. Wariness was pouring out of Ryder in waves, but he didn't seem put off by it. "Ah, I believe this is a *'show me yours and I'll show you mine'* situation, as the Americans would say?" He raised his hands placatingly. "I understand. You have endured a harrowing journey to bring the Dark Wand back to Romania, and you have no reason to trust me."

He hadn't said this with any resentment, instead he sounded as if he approved.

"Believe me when I say, listing all the people I suspect would take me until dawn. Sergeant Nicolae's family in particular has a long history of deep ties to the Order. I don't believe he is a full fledged member yet, but he undoubtedly helps their cause. I am afraid many high-ranking police officers or members of the government are such friends of the Order."

Mitrea took a few steps to stand in front of the stained glass windows, his hands clasped behind his back. His gaze lost itself on the lush gardens outside, lit only by a few braziers and the silver glow of the moon. "Your Head of Department, on the other hand ... I have reason to believe Mr Skelton is deeply embedded within the Order. The man has an insatiable appetite for power, it would not surprise me if he was striving to become a true Knight."

Oh yes, Olivia could believe it. If there was a higher step on the ladder of power available to him, he would do anything to get it.

"If you know all this, and no one here can be trusted, why insist on having the wand at all?" Ryder pointed out. There was an edge to his voice as he added, "You've put it, and us, in great danger."

"You are quite right, Warden. And I would not have done so had I been given any other choice. But I heard the Order was planning something major. They were furious that their previous attempts had all failed, and were ready to steal that wand from your Cellars. Once and for all."

Olivia could only see his profile from the way he was turned, but she saw his lips twist in a grim line.

"They had hired mercenaries before. Guildless thieves, petty criminals and the like. But this time, they'd bartered for the services of a serious crew behind some of the most high-profile, high-value robberies. Professionals. The two break-ins they'd finally managed to pull off in your Cellars . . . I would bet they were not mere attempts to steal the Dark Wand."

Olivia's face paled while Ryder swore harshly. "They were casing it. Figuring out the layout, planting things." He raked a hand through his hair. "I'm gonna have to inspect every inch of that place."

Mitrea turned from the windows. "You would be very wise to do so."

"How did you discover all this?"

Something like a chuckle escaped the High Commissioner. "Being in a constant state of paranoia has its advantages. Just as the Order has spies in my Institute, I too have spies in the Order."

He walked to a row of artifacts on the other side of the room, straightening labels and picking lint from a velvet drape. "When this became known to me, I knew I had to act swiftly. I came up with this transfer plan so the Dark Wand could be brought to the auction tonight, and I could ship it somewhere the Order would never find."

"With all due respect, sir, that's one hell of a risky plan," Olivia couldn't help but point out, her voice hardening. "If it hadn't been for the Warden, the wand would have been transported under Skelton's direct orders."

The High Commissioner acted as if it had all been some sort of master plan of his, when only Ryder's persistence had prevented a catastrophic disaster—

"I chose you both personally."

Olivia's eyes widened in surprise. "What?"

Not one to stay still for long, the High Commissioner moved to the bookshelves, running his finger along the aged leather spines. "When I started working on this transfer plan, I did so knowing who the new Warden would be."

He picked up one of the volumes and flipped through the pages. Ryder watched him carefully.

"Ryder Isaksson," the High Commissioner began, still looking down at his book. "Former treasure hunter with an impressive track record. You were later recruited to work exclusively for the Swedish Ministry, where you hunted all manner of things throughout the Lapland wilderness with one of the finest success rates in your division. You were then transferred to Scotland to fill the newly vacant position of Warden of the Cellars, based on the glowing recommendation of Inspector Cillian Blackwood, a highly decorated Scottish detective you'd met on a gnarly mission a few years back." He put the book back, selected another. "I knew you would never be foolish enough to trust anyone with that wand, that you would keep it safe and out of sight. I also knew you would need an experienced curse-breaker, and not the one your Head of Department would undoubtedly pressure you to use. You would be looking for someone highly competent, someone you could trust, which meant it had to be somebody not connected to the Ministry. By word of mouth, you came across the Knight Agency. There you would find a curse-breaker who put the welfare of the public and the protection of the artifacts above all else, as evidenced by her utter disgust at this whole auctioning event . . ."

Mitrea closed his book with a snap and turned to them. His eyes locked on Olivia, the nearby light from the fireplace glinting off the edge of his silver spectacles. "*I chose you*, Ms Knight."

Olivia's mouth opened, but nothing came out.

"I have followed your career for a long time," he continued. "Finding curse-breakers who share my particular views is . . . rather difficult. So when someone makes waves in the community as you have, I notice."

He knew who she was. He knew what she did.

"What happened with the Hadleys . . ." He shook his head, his face filled with kindness, with compassion. But there was also outrage there. "It was a terrible tragedy. Mr Skelton, and your entire Ministry, acted with disgrace. You deserved nothing of what you had to endure. But I have to admit, your actions that day are the reason why I knew I could trust you with the Dark Wand."

Olivia's mind was blank. She could only stare at him, caution, relief and pride swirling and fighting inside her.

Mitrea winced. "I know your business has been struggling of late. The work of your Head of Department, I presume. When all this nonsense with the Dark Wand is over, and if you ever decide you need a change, I would be honoured to have you on my team, Ms Knight. I could do with more people like you. People who understand the responsibility of caring for these dark artifacts. Where some would only see relics of power or old, worthless antiques, what we see are . . . fragments of our history." His lips curled into a self-deprecating grin. "Please forgive me. We find ourselves in the midst of a dire situation and I use the opportunity to try and recruit you."

Olivia could only manage a tight smile.

"How exactly do you plan on keeping the wand safe?" Ryder cut in. "And out of reach of the Order?"

"One night, as I was finishing work in my office, I had an unexpected visit from Inspector Blackwood." Mitrea's smile was devious. "I don't need to tell you that my wards were up, the door to my office was locked and I had an entire security team monitoring the building."

This certainly sounded like the infamous Scottish detective.

"He reiterated that I should trust no one, that both my Ministry and his had been corrupted by the Order," he continued. "He also told me of his connection to a secret branch of special forces. People he knew were the only ones capable of protecting the Dark Wand. After some lengthy discussions, I finally agreed to their help."

Ryder slanted a dark look at Olivia. She hoped the High Commissioner wasn't talking about Black Knights, because there was no way in all the hells they were getting their hands on that wand, Blackwood-endorsed or not.

But Mitrea lowered his voice and leaned forward conspiratorially. "Between you and me, I think I was dealing with a special division of the Guard. I did try to ask questions, but was firmly rebuffed."

"You said they would help you get the wand out of here. What did you mean by that?" Olivia asked.

The High Commissioner's brows rose. "Don't you know? This is a trap."

"A *trap*?"

"I'll give it to them, they're being discreet. But this is *my* event, I know everything that goes on here. There are at least four security guards who shouldn't be here, and two of my staff are unaccounted for. I was looking for them when you arrived. I've been followed ever since the auction started, so they know I'm meeting with you. I would wager that they are waiting for us to make the transfer before they break into this room."

He'd known exactly what was going on, and had played along with it instead of resisting, giving him the element of surprise and a welcomed edge. It was clever, and something Ryder would have done.

"Their plan is most likely to storm this very library, kill me and then use the wand on the both of you. That would make it seem like you'd gone rogue and murdered me for it."

Judging by the tightening of Ryder's jaw, he was thinking the same thing.

"However, Blackwood and I came up with a plan. There are tunnels underneath this castle. King Carol the First had them built so he could avoid unpleasant conversations with his ministers. Blackwood is waiting for you there to escort you out of the city."

"What about the wand?"

"I will take it to the secret vault I had installed. It's warded with the strongest containments I know, it'll be safe there for tonight. I will return to the auction as if nothing had happened. The Order will think you're the ones running away with the wand, so they won't bother me. As soon as the auction is over, I'll retrieve it and Blackwood's secret agents will help me smuggle it out of the country."

Olivia studied Ryder's tense shoulders, the arms crossed over his chest, the harsh line of his lips. He considered Mitrea's words for a long moment, then finally turned to her. She read his thoughts clearly in his stormy blue eyes. It was as good a plan as was possible under the circumstances, would certainly take the focus off the wand and onto them, even if all his hunter instincts were screaming at him.

Olivia turned to face Mitrea fully. "High Commissioner, I have to warn you, this wand... It has a will of its own. I have never seen anything like it."

There was a solemnity in his eyes as he replied, "I promise you, Olivia. I will not underestimate this foe."

The chest rattled the table when the High Commissioner set it down. Strong and sturdy, with thick walls of gleaming silverstone and protective runes etched into the sides, it looked as if it had been used to hold all manner of dangerous artifacts, judging by the *weight* emanating from it.

Mitrea opened it to reveal the fake wand, powerful threads of dark energy still swirling around it.

Olivia placed the containment cage beside it. A fierce green light poured out of the glass panels, bathing the entire library in an emerald glow.

The High Commissioner met her eyes, nodded.

The bronze chains fell, then the cage opened with a metallic click. The verdant light grew even stronger, blinding them.

When it was done, the High Commissioner slipped a crudely drawn map into Ryder's hands and showed them the spiralling staircase hidden behind one of the library's bookcases.

Olivia didn't stop to question herself as Ryder stooped to enter the secret passage and they went down, and down. She had just done the most reckless thing of her entire career...

She simply hoped she hadn't made a terrible mistake.

CHAPTER THIRTY-THREE

Every one of Olivia's senses was on alert, trying to discern any sound, any magic coming their way, any sign of attack.

Which was why when Ryder stopped abruptly, she smacked right into his back.

"Hmph!" She took a step back, rubbing her forehead. "What are you doing?"

He was examining the piece of paper in his hands, where the High Commissioner had scribbled directions to get out of these never-ending tunnels. Then he raised his head, his gaze fixed on the dark corridor to their left.

Olivia stepped in front of him, frowning as she snatched the paper from his hands. "Are you lost? I think it's that way." She gestured to their right, where the curved corridor led deeper underground, and had to stifle a grimace. *Were those gods-damned tunnels spanning the entire country?*

A salty air seemed to emanate from there, as if coming from the ocean. *How strange,* Olivia thought. Although, she had to admit it was a nice change from the otherwise stale and musty smell.

"Do you see that?" Ryder whispered to her.

"See what?"

Ryder extended a hand and pointed a finger at a symbol etched into the stones wall. It was a dragon, its wings spread wide, two tiny rubies serving as the creature's eyes.

"And what of it . . ."

Ryder slowly turned towards her. He grinned — that reckless, *wicked* grin that preceded crazy flights through thunderstorms and falls down endless wells. "You know, my people have a saying . . . All ways are good, except for the bad ones."

With a sigh, Olivia peered at the passage to their left, the map in her hand, and then Ryder's knowing smirk.

"You wanted to learn more about what really goes on here, right?" he insisted.

Resignation settled over her features. Hazard pay, she reminded herself. Really big hazard pay.

"Lead the way, Warden."

The sounds hit them first.

Through the thick stone walls, a steady pounding reached their ears. Like drums. But as they emerged from their tunnel and staggered into a gigantic cave, Olivia realised it was chanting.

Around them, a crowd of hooded Order members were uttering harsh and guttural sounds, the words twisted. Olivia didn't try to make out what they were chanting, the magic emanating from them enough to tell her those were words of power. The incantation echoed off the stone walls, flowed down from the high ceiling, seemingly coming from everywhere all at once.

She jerked when something touched her shoulders, but it was only Ryder, enveloping her in a crimson robe he'd found gods knew where. Her skin prickled as it settled around her small frame heavily, much like the weight and unease currently swirling in her stomach. He grabbed her hand and pulled her off to the side.

Inside the cavernous chamber, tall braziers provided plenty of light, illuminating carved steps leading down to an empty platform below, like an arena, but they failed to banish the gloom entirely. Shadows gathered in the corners and along the walls, the darkness not quite . . . *empty*.

The scent of candle wax and dark magic hung heavy in the air. Almost like a thin powder, settling over their skin, getting into their lungs.

A figure emerged from a tunnel at the far end of the stone chamber and a torrent of power filled the cave, so potent, it glided over Olivia's skin like a physical touch.

Gasps and cries of joy echoed through the crowd, an elated wave as the man descended the steps to the arena. When he lowered his hood, reverent whispers floated inside the cavern, two words repeated over and over.

Grand Meister. Grand Meister . . .

Beside her, Ryder tensed in a way she'd never felt before. His hand squeezed hers. In shock, but also in warning not to utter a single sound, not to react in any way.

For the man who now faced the rowdy crowd, dark power wafting from his fingertips, held features she knew very well.

The aquiline nose, the sharp jaw. The golden eyes that glowed in the dimness of the cave like two shiny coins. Even the dramatic strand of white hair amid the black.

Holmes . . .

But another version, younger. Without the scars, the lines at the corners of the eyes or the downward tilt to the lips. Yet he had the same magic, dark tendrils of shadows curling around his body like a moving cape.

A few paces behind him, more figures appeared. First the Furtum mage, making Olivia's skin crawl at the sight. Then a short man, with hair turning steadily grey and a kind face that looked more like a professor than a high-ranking member of a secret society. The last one, however . . . His sneer reaching new levels of arrogance and pretentiousness, he surveyed the crowd like a king atop his throne, clasping his dragon-headed cane in front of him.

Skelton.

That lying snake.

The professor was handed a flaming sceptre, burning with an intense purple flame, which he then passed to the Grand Meister, bowing at the waist.

The man raised his arms. The sound of his voice slapped at the outer reaches of the stone chamber like a wave crashing against the shore. Even from afar, Olivia could see his golden eyes were smouldering, as if born of a fire not from this world.

"Brothers! Sisters! You have joined me this night as we unveil a new chapter in our history, the dawn of a new era!"

A murmur of excitement rippled through the assembly. It was hungry, eager. A fervour bordering on the fanatical. Olivia wrapped her arms around herself.

"After countless years of uncertainty, of obscurity, we have finally reclaimed what is rightfully ours! A weapon, from a realm beyond our own, that can bend the fabric of reality to our will, expand the boundaries of magic itself."

Cries and applause followed his words. The man resembling Holmes continued, his rich voice echoing off the stones. "Brothers, sisters. Let me show you our new destiny. For the time of the Order of the Dragon is nigh!"

As if summoned by his words, the air in the cave shifted. It grew colder, thicker. The Grand Meister made a gesture with his shadowed hand, waving it over the sceptre. The bright purple flame turned into an unearthly green Olivia recognized very well, pulsating with a light that seemed to swallow the darkness.

Beside her, Ryder radiated fury.

Then the chamber held its breath when behind the Grand Meister, shadows swirled and undulated, before taking the form of two nightmarish creatures. Eyes glowed molten silver, fangs elongated, vicious claws sheathed powerful paws.

The assembly gasped alongside Olivia.

They smelled of death. There was no other way to put it. Shaped by the darkness of rotting things, of decay. There was power, yes. A lot of power. But it was what lingered after things had passed on to the eternal beyond. It was the echoes off the stones from ruins, the whispers carried by the wind through graveyards, the fragments of incantations heard when wandering near a relic. A thousand times worse.

These creatures were not of this world.

They should not be *in* this world.

And the magic flowing out of them...

It had whispered in Olivia's ears, reached inside her mind to draw out her deepest fears. She felt it settle against her skin, around her. Like a shroud.

Whatever these creatures were, wherever they came from . . . They and the Darkness were the same.

It took every single ounce of her strength to stay still, every shred of will to keep from screaming in horror.

The Grand Meister spoke again, his words flowing like dark waters. "But such ambitions cannot be realised on a weak foundation. Only strength can usher in the new world order we have dreamed of. Power and an undiluted will. Sacrifices will be required, brothers and sisters. Hard choices will have to be made, and above all else . . . *Loyalty*."

On this final word, he turned to his left. Towards Skelton.

From her position, Olivia clearly saw his brown eyes widen in shock. Then there was confusion, denial. And finally, terror.

He staggered backwards, but two hooded men grabbed him. They kicked his knee until he crumpled to the ground, cane clattering against the stones. His aristocratic face contorted, hasty pleas escaping his lips.

But the Grand Meister simply turned his back and walked out of the arena, shadows swirling in his wake, the green sceptre still in his hand. A flick of his fingers and a black circle ignited, trapping Skelton inside.

With the creatures.

A hushed silence fell over the assembly. A mixture of fear and exhilaration.

The monsters made of shadows prowled the periphery of their cage, inspecting it, *testing* it, their forms flickering like flames in a draft. Talons scratched the stones with a high-pitched sound. Lazily, unhurriedly. They knew their prey had no hope of escape.

They looked like wraiths, neither fully in this world nor out of it. Their wicked forms shrouded in perpetual darkness, only their eyes, glowing like burning silver, were visible. The rest came and went as the shadows parted to reveal a powerful hind leg, the edge of a talon.

Skelton let out another cry begging for help, floundering on his knees. When none answered, he scrambled to his feet. One hand raised in preparation to conjure his magic, while the other brandished his black cane in front of him, gripping it with all his might.

The two creatures hissed. Olivia's blood ran cold at the sound.

Skelton let out a terrified whimper, his entire body shaking. His left hand ignited with a pale yellow energy that he sent scurrying towards the nearest beast.

The monster turned its head to survey its prey, the movement idle, the bolt passing through its shadowy body with no effect.

Skelton gasped. He released another sphere of energy. Then another, then another. Bolt after bolt, the yellow orbs did nothing more than illuminate the hideous creatures skulking within the circle.

Finally he stopped, gasping for breath.

Olivia could swear the creatures bared their teeth in a horrifying grin as they crept slowly closer.

Begging and screaming, Skelton conjured a thick shield of the same citrine light around himself. It made the creature's silver eyes ignite.

Ryder's hand gripped her arm. "We need to go. Right now."

Without waiting for an answer, he pulled Olivia back towards the tunnel they'd come from. She didn't struggle, but couldn't tear her gaze away from the hunting shadows.

They left, just as the screaming began.

Olivia's mind was churning as they raced through the tunnels, her heart firmly lodged in her throat. She tried to push it all away, but thoughts and images kept assaulting her. Holmes' twin, the terror on Skelton's face, the echo of his screams still filling her ears. And that light, that eerie, sickly green light that seemed to haunt her . . .

A man stepped into their path.

His face was masked, only two soulless eyes showing against a backdrop of darkness. The Furtum mage.

"I've been waiting for you."

Olivia felt the blood drain from her face. Those words . . . The same words the Darkness had whispered in her ears.

Ryder immediately stepped in front of her and drew his sword.

"I knew I'd sensed something," the mage continued. "Something that should not be there."

His white eyes settled on her and Olivia took an involuntary step back. His presence felt so unnatural, so utterly *wrong*, that it grated against her senses.

He angled his head, the movement not entirely human, but that of a predator. "Did you enjoy our show? Such beautiful creatures, they are. Such power..."

Olivia had been hidden behind Ryder's broad back, but when he shifted slightly and the mage caught a glimpse of what she carried at her side, his white eyes flared.

"What have you done?" he snarled.

Horror shot through Olivia. He knew... His eyes were fixed on the satchel at her hip. He knew what it really contained, he knew what she had done.

Tired of waiting, Ryder sent a bolt of thundering power down the corridor, heading straight for the mage, who only raised a hand.

The bolt vanished as if it had never been there.

Olivia's eyes widened and Ryder swore. She'd felt the force of that blow, it had nearly singed the stone walls and yet, the mage had destroyed it as if it'd been a mere flick.

It was his turn now. Dark magic boiled, drowning out his side of the corridor. It flowed from him like an invisible octopus, spreading its tentacles in search of prey.

Ryder drew in a harsh breath.

The next moment, he was doubling over, moaning in agony.

"Ryder!" Olivia caught him as he crumpled to his knees, tremor after tremor rippling through his body.

Her horrified gaze swung to the mage. What had he done to him?

She reached out, feeling for the power, trying to stop him — but at the first brush of her magic, recoiled with a strangled gasp.

The mage smiled at her from within his seething darkness. He spoke a single harsh word and his inhuman eyes grew into two bottomless pits. Commanding, sucking her into their terrible depths, promising death.

His power slammed into them, hungry for blood.

Ryder moaned, an anguished sound that tore at her heart. Olivia's chest shuddered, tears wetting her cheeks. She tried to grab hold of her magic, but it slipped through her fingers, as if not her own any more. *Gods, no, no, no!* What was happening?

The darkness pounced. The agony ripped a cry out of her.

Ryder tried to rise, but slumped back against her, his body ice-cold, his lungs heaving.

The mage's power welled around them like a tornado, distorting sounds, their thoughts, overwhelming them until nothing else existed but his will. Pain slammed into Olivia, wave after wave, threatening to sweep her under.

A hoarse yell escaped her lips.

Her hands fisted against Ryder's jacket, desperate for anyone, anything to help them.

Please, please, she begged.

Her sight faded completely. She was so scared, everything around her was dark and cold. She couldn't feel her body any more, as if it no longer existed. Couldn't feel Ryder under her hands. Where had he gone?

Blind and deaf, she was falling. Falling into nothing, falling into the dark void . . .

Something burned her fingertips. It was hard and scolding hot, as if carrying the wrath of a thousand fires.

Burn it all . . .

With a roar, Olivia threw the vial of Chimera blood at the mage.

Glass shattered, unleashing the curse.

A pool of dark blood spread across the dirty stone floor. It moved and undulated with each passing second, its emerald sheen swirling.

Hurry, Olivia pleaded. *Let's burn it, come on.*

She threw herself back when flames filled her vision, howls erupting like an enraged animal. Olivia saw sweeping wings of fire, churning with violent reds and yellows, roaring towards the mage. The Chimera lashed out at him, its power a blasting wave.

For a moment, Olivia couldn't breathe as fire battled shadows.

The mage uttered a harsh cry. He smashed his power out and the seething darkness pounced on the roaring creature, making the walls of the tunnel rumble.

The other members of the Order would have surely heard them, they had to be coming. And they would bring the shadow creatures with them...

They had to leave those tunnels... They had to leave those tunnels *NOW*.

The thought blasted through Olivia's mind with the force of a sledgehammer. She crawled to Ryder and shook him. His head was lolling, his skin white as death, but his eyes gleamed.

Clumsy fingers went to his shoulders, his cheeks. "Get up, Ryder, please," she begged him. "Get up!"

She roughly gathered her skirt and tried to push on her weak, trembling legs. Ryder braced a hand on the stone wall, but jerked away with a hiss at the scorching heat. Olivia pulled on his jacket and together they managed to stagger up.

That was when running footsteps sounded behind them. Ryder pushed her away again, wavering on his feet, but his sword was raised and his teeth bared.

A man with the palest eyes Olivia had ever seen tumbled into the corridor.

"Blackwood," Ryder murmured, lowering his sword.

The detective took everything in with a single glance, threw Ryder's arm around his shoulder and barked, "Out. Now!"

With fire raging behind them, they ran.

Olivia leaned against a tree, a hand pressed to her forehead. It was the only thing keeping her upright.

Next to her, Ryder paced. He'd regained his strength as soon as they'd left the tunnels, whatever terrible magic the mage had directed at him dissipating.

Blackwood had abandoned them at a crossroads, saying he would find the others and bring them to the rendezvous point, so they hadn't stopped running since they'd emerged from the underground tunnels, and Olivia was ready to keel over from exhaustion.

Said rendezvous point was a small clearing tucked away from the main forest path leading to the castle. There had been a small burning torch waiting for them, as well as the pile of luggage they'd left at their hotel next to a stone bench.

As he paced, Ryder wrestled out of his evening jacket and waistcoat, leaving only his white shirt, then put the leather harness that held his sword over it.

He fished out his flask from the forgotten garments, then thought better of it, and tucked it back into his jacket before resuming his pacing. Olivia was about to tell the Viking to stop his endless back and forth as he was making her nausea worse, but the back of her neck suddenly prickled with the eerie sensation of eyes boring into her.

She turned her head to peer through the large pine trees beyond their clearing, just as there was the sound of soft padding. Olivia squinted. When her sight finally accustomed itself to the dark, what awaited her were two glowing eyes staring straight at her. She froze.

"I don't want to alarm you," she said softly, her voice barely above a whisper. "But there's a wolf over there."

"Hmm."

"I'm serious, Ryder. It's staring at us like it wants to swallow us whole."

Ryder didn't even look as he chuckled. "I assure you, he's not going to eat you. Have you seen the size of him? You're not too much in the way of meals, *Älva*. Maybe a snack . . ."

Olivia didn't dare take her eyes off the huge beast prowling over on silent paws. Oh, she had seen its size, all right. And she wished she hadn't.

"Ryder, what . . ." she started to murmur, but he stopped her with a hand on her shoulder.

"I should have warned you. Blackwood has a familiar."

Her mouth dropped open in surprise. "A *familiar?*"

"Indeed, I do."

The detective emerged from behind the trees, like a shadow gaining the appearance of a man. He moved without making a sound, almost gliding across the ground. Deadly, like an assassin. The white wolf immediately padded to his side, its head almost reaching the man's chest, and the same piercing, icy blue gaze.

So this was the infamous Inspector Blackwood Ryder had called for backup. Olivia studied him. There was no mistaking the coolness beneath his easy tone of voice, or the dangerous intent in his eyes that said he was capable of just about anything. Both were as clear to Olivia as a curse surrounding an artifact.

"Liv!"

Godwyn burst into the clearing, Adeline close behind, her dress billowing behind her. She ran to Olivia and immediately reached out to grab her hands, squeezing them tightly. "Are you both all right? Are you hurt?"

Olivia shook her head, but immediately regretted it as spots danced around the edges of her vision. "We're fine. We're all right. Why . . ." She finally noticed her friend's pale face, the haunting look in her silver eyes. "What happened to you two? Where have you been?"

"We were there."

It was Godwyn who'd spoken. He was bent over, hands clasped to his knees as he tried to catch his breath, but his face was sombre when he lifted his head. "We were there during the gathering. We saw those . . . *things*. What they did to Skelton."

"I still can't believe it . . ." Adeline said, her voice growing increasingly strained between her labouring pants. "The creatures tore him to shreds. They all watched, and-and his magic did *nothing*."

Olivia swallowed past the lump in her throat. "Where's Cornelius? Did you see him?"

The detective answered her. "I saw him. He went to retrieve something, he'll be here."

Olivia's attention shifted back to her friend. "How . . . How did you even end up there? Did you take the secret passage in the library?"

The Baron straightened from his crouch as Adeline waved a slender hand. "Long story. Bad guys. Baby creature in distress. Godwyn fought some members of the Order. You know, the usual."

Olivia couldn't help the warning look she slid her assistant. She had a pretty good idea how they were able to infiltrate those tunnels...

Ryder resumed his furious pacing. "What happened in there, Blackwood? How did the Order get the wand?"

"What do you mean?"

"The Grand Meister," Adeline replied, "his sceptre turned bright green, and he said they finally got their weapon back. It's clear he has the wand now."

"And how exactly is that my doing?"

At the incredulity in the detective's voice, Ryder's entire frame froze. So much so that the tiny hairs on the back of Olivia's neck stood up.

He slowly pivoted towards him. His voice grew cold, wary, as he enunciated every word with precision. "Did you not arrange with the High Commissioner to take the wand to a safe place?"

Blackwood didn't have to answer, the white lines that bracketed his mouth spoke for him.

A volley of Swedish curses erupted as Ryder slammed a hand against the nearest tree trunk. His expression was terrible.

"I can't believe I fell for it!" His voice cracked like a whip.

"Wait, wait." Godwyn's face was slack with shock. "You're saying that the High Commissioner is part of the Order too? Then why wasn't he at the gathering?"

"Who cares?" Adeline said, her scarlet lips a straight line and her gunmetal eyes hard. "What's important is that they have the wand now."

Olivia should have felt something. The man she'd idolised for years had just been exposed as nothing more than a liar, a traitor... But all she felt was numb.

She let go of Adeline to rest a hand on the stone bench beside her. She opened her mouth, but a sudden wave of nausea forced her to take a few deep breaths instead.

"I'll kill him," Ryder declared, his voice vibrating with fury.

He began to march towards Peleș castle, but the detective barred his path. "Isaksson! Where do you think you're going?"

"Out of my way, Blackwood."

The detective's jaw tightened. "You're not thinking straight, this is suicide. The wand is gone, there's no point."

"That's why we have to get it back, *right now*. This is our last chance. If they leave with it, that's it. It's over. We'll never find it again."

Godwyn threw up his hands. "So you want to go back there, in the middle of dozens of members of the Order, and retrieve the very artifact they've spent months hunting? This is madness!"

Ryder's face had turned into a thunderstorm. "And what exactly are you suggesting, Baron? You were there, you heard what they said. You know what they intend to do with it."

"They won't be expecting us," Adeline pointed out. "We'll have the element of surprise."

But the detective shook his head. "Mitrea will be waiting for you, Isaksson. He knew I'd find you eventually and reveal everything. You'll be dead before you even get through the gates."

Yet the Warden had clearly had enough of reason and common sense.

"Then I guess I'll just have to find another way in." He smiled, something utterly wicked that blazed with ridiculous determination. "Wouldn't be the first time I managed to get in and out of a trap."

Olivia felt an overwhelming urge to strangle him.

Godwyn seemed to feel the same way as he sneered with contempt, "You're even crazier than I thought."

"I'm in," Adeline declared, completely ignoring him. She returned Ryder's grin with an arrogant smile of her own. With her chin held high and her eyes blazing, she looked just like a warrior queen, about to charge into battle. "Trust me, Norseman, you're going to need my help."

Godwyn's head whipped towards her. "Stop playing games, Adeline!"

Her whole body went tight with fury as she spat, "Don't you talk to me like that!"

Isaksson bent down to retrieve his sticks of dynamite from his bag. "Enough! I'm going in. Whoever wants to join me, now's the time. The rest of you can wait here until we return."

His declaration sparked a flurry of indignant responses as tempers flared.

Once more, Olivia tried to speak but nothing came out, blood pounding in her ears.

Blackwood took a warning step, going toe-to-toe with the Warden. He was clearly nearing the end of his patience. "What exactly was the point of bringing me here if you're happy to jump into danger without a shred of a plan, knowing they're waiting for you?"

Ryder stared back at him. A dangerous intensity crept into his voice. "Get out of my way, Blackwood. I won't ask twice."

Beside them, the detective's familiar let out a menacing growl. His lips peeled back to reveal razor-sharp canines.

Olivia rolled her eyes. For gods' sakes, she couldn't have a *single* moment of peace. "Enough," she rasped. "Stop it."

Ryder didn't even glance at her, the idiot. If he carried on like this, he was going to get himself mauled by the huge white wolf with violence in its eyes.

Olivia straightened to her full height with a bitten-off curse. "For the love of ... I have it. I have the wand."

They'd all gone back to arguing among themselves but at her words, turned to stare at her.

Good. Olivia hadn't even been sure they would hear her over their absurd bickering.

"I know the High Commissioner said all the right things," she began, "and he seemed so sincere. He even offered me a job at the Institute, or at the very least implied that he could save our agency from utter ruin, but I couldn't shake this feeling ... Also, there was a pale band on his finger, as if he'd taken off a ring. I don't have to tell you what that made me think and—"

"You have the wand?" Ryder interrupted her.

She nodded. "I only pretended to switch them."

An incredulous silence filled the clearing.

Then Ryder threw his head back and laughed. He laughed, mumbled something in Swedish, then laughed some more until his eyes welled up with tears. Everyone else gaped at her, speechless.

Only Blackwood was eyeing her with open curiosity, something in his gaze telling her he was evaluating her in a new light. "Ms Knight, if you ever decide on a career change," he told her. "Come see me."

That stopped Ryder's laughter and he turned to scowl at the detective.

Olivia noticed tiny dots drifting before her eyes. A grimace escaped her. They might be relieved now, but they would *not* be happy for long. "There's just one problem."

She reached into a hidden fold of her sari and pulled out the wand.

Free. Without any containment in sight.

Olivia heard gasps of shock and horror. She tried to reassure them, but that's when her vision turned completely black.

The wand slipped from her limp fingers and she felt herself crumble, the ground rushing up to meet her.

CHAPTER THIRTY-FOUR

WHEN OLIVIA CAME TO, she was lying on something hard. She winced, ran the back of her hand over the surface. It was the bench, made from a block of stone and uncomfortable, but someone had slipped what felt like a rolled-up coat under her head.

She peeled her eyes open with difficulty. The first thing she saw was Adeline's face, etched with worry.

"She's awake."

Careful hands helped her sit up. Olivia managed what she hoped was a reassuring smile. "I'm fine, just dizzy."

Judging by the closed off faces of everyone around her, her tone must not have been too convincing.

"What happened to you, Liv?" Adeline asked. "Was it the wand?"

Olivia's eyes immediately searched for it. She remembered it slipping through her weak fingers before she fainted.

"It's all right," her friend reassured her. She nodded to her left, where the wand was bundled up in a scarf. "We put it over there."

"What are we supposed to do with it now?" Godwyn asked. He stood a few feet away, arms crossed. He was eying the wand as if it might sprout fangs and claws at any moment. "And I still don't understand how you can bear to touch it, Olivia. Why is it not attacking you?"

"I think it's because of this connection between us," she replied, carefully avoiding Ryder's eyes as he loomed against a nearby tree. "I'm pretty sure the wand sees me as part of itself." She ran a weary hand over her face. It almost felt like lifting the stone bench she was sitting on. "So as long as I don't do anything against it, it won't attack me."

"We should go," Adeline declared. She straightened up, a fierce and determined look on her face. "If the wand isn't a threat to you, we can still follow our original plan to get to Brăila. That would give us time to contact the Ministry, work out a long-term plan."

"We can't," a deep voice cut in.

Olivia couldn't avoid it any longer, she looked up at Ryder. His jaw was clenched hard, his mouth set in a straight line. His eyes pinned her to the spot, the edge of a storm brewing in their depths. He was *really* angry with her.

"Why not?" Godwyn pressed.

Ryder pushed away from the tree he'd been leaning against, temper evident in every rigid line of his body. He raised a brow at her, his voice sharp enough to cut. "You want to tell them, or shall I?"

Olivia sighed. She peeled off her gloves with trembling fingers, until everyone could see the darkness that had taken hold of her hands, spreading in thin, black veins and covering up the silver of the feylin.

"Is that . . ." Godwyn began. "The dark magic is poisoning you."

Olivia nodded.

"How long?"

"Since the Hoia forest, when I had to wrap my magic around the containment cage to keep it shut."

"All this time?" Adeline exclaimed. "Why didn't you say anything?"

Olivia winced at the hurt in her friend's voice. Her eyes darted to the hunk of angry energy brooding a few paces away. She really shouldn't have kept it from them, from *him*. "I'm sorry, I know I should have but . . ."

Ryder cut her apology off with a slash of his hand. Oh, the Viking was *mad*.

"We can't hide," he declared firmly. "She can't. We have to do something tonight to end this. Once and for all." He jerked his chin to the side. "Blackwood."

The detective followed him a short distance away, where they began debating furiously. Soon, Godwyn joined them. Olivia heard enough to guess that they were arguing about a new makeshift containment plan, one that would hopefully buy them a few days.

CHAPTER 34

She shut her eyes and let out a long, shaky breath. She could have told them right then and there that it wouldn't do any good, but one look at the scowl hardening Ryder's features and she'd realised the Warden needed a few moments to calm down.

Her hand went to her ears and she removed the heavy gold loops with a sigh of relief. Her hair pins were next, Adeline helping her with the ones at the back, until her long raven hair fell over her shoulders.

Her eyes wandered over the dense woods that surrounded their little clearing, and something stirred in her mind.

"Ryder." Her voice broke his intense conversation. "How did the sergeant find us in the forest?"

His brows rose at the specific question. "They must have put someone on the train to follow us."

"Maybe... But they just stayed at the edge of the woods, waiting for us. They didn't even try to get inside. And didn't we come in from the north side? I think they were waiting for us at the west exit..."

"What are you saying? You don't think they followed us?" Ryder passed a hand over the beard sheathing his jaw, frowning.

"No," she clarified. "I think they've been *tracking* us."

Ryder's face hardened instantly. Beside him, the detective examined her words in that calculating way of his.

"Could they be tracking the wand instead?" Godwyn suggested. "It's such a rare magic, they might be able to isolate it on a map."

"I don't think that's possible, the wand gives off too much energy. Whatever they tried to use would have been overwhelmed." She met Ryder's eyes and saw the storm rolling through the blue.

"They're not tracking *us*," he growled. "They're tracking *me*."

"How?" Blackwood asked.

"When we went to pick up the wand, I got a telegram. Remember?"

Olivia nodded. "It was to tell you that Crowley and the Head of Department were on their way..." Her voice trailed off.

"When I touched the paper, I felt something."

Adeline declared at once, "White Wolf Powder."

Because of the magic always coursing through their veins, there weren't many ways to track arcanists. Usually, it was done with an enchanted object, given to someone, that could give away their location. But White Wolf Powder was one of the rare substances that could bond with someone's essence.

"What's that?" Godwyn asked.

"It's odourless, colourless, and feels inert to your magical senses" Olivia explained, her finger absent-mindedly drawing patterns on the stone bench. "But if touched, it will bind itself to you for up to a few weeks. It comes in two parts, much like a magnet. One part you put on someone, the other you spread out on a map. It will show where that person is within a radius of about ten miles, if you've got the good stuff. It's very expensive and there's a lot of counterfeit out there, but you can find some if you know where to look."

When she'd finished her explanation, Olivia looked up to see Ryder and Blackwood staring at her warily.

"How do you know so much about White Wolf Powder?" Ryder asked.

"Ah . . . because Adeline taught me?"

"And how did she learn about it?"

"I also would very much like to know." Blackwood's tone was edgy.

Both men turned to Adeline. Her assistant only replied with a sweet smile and a wink.

"So that means," Godwyn interjected, "they'll be able to know wherever we are."

No one replied, but Ryder let out an impressive string of curses under his breath.

"Then you're lucky I've arrived," a raspy voice announced from behind them.

Olivia gasped.

They whirled around to discover a figure half hidden in a mass of rolling shadows. The moon illuminated the angular features of his face, the dramatic slash across his cheek.

Only Blackwood hadn't stirred, the detective's familiar obviously having sensed the newcomer.

Cornelius appeared next, and Olivia breathed a huge sigh of relief. One trembling hand rose to her brow.

"Cornelius!" Godwyn went to clap him on the back, but noticed the lizard-dragon hanging from his shoulder and decided against it. "Where have you been, mate?"

Cornelius grimaced. "That's a long story."

Holmes made a beeline for Olivia. As always, he was a collection of hard lines and sharp edges — honed jaw, lean build, expensive black suit. A cravat pin, in the shape of a dagger, pierced his crimson silk tie, the only colour he wore. On his way, he threw something which Ryder caught in mid-air.

When he reached her, Olivia ignored the angry shadows swirling around him, the piercing gold eyes, and leaned forward to kiss him on the cheek. "I'm glad to see you," she whispered.

His face remained as emotionless as ever, but she felt his fingers caress her hair for a fleeting second. Then he reached for her hands and his expression hardened into a furious mask.

Olivia noticed how Adeline kept staring at him and shot her a look. Now was *not* the right time to ask the Purveyor why the Grand Meister of the Order of the Dragon looked exactly like him.

"Do you make a lot of handcrafted runic limiters in your shop?" Ryder asked dryly. He was turning a large metal bracelet between his hands, wide and textured, with indentations where the hammer had struck. Runes had been etched all around it in sharp, rough strokes.

"Only for special occasions," was Holmes' retort.

Runic limiters were used to create a sort of bubble from which no magic could escape. They were mostly employed by authorities as magical shackles to prevent prisoners from using their power, but Olivia guessed that this one had been modified to only stop the tracking of magic. Still, they were highly controlled devices that he shouldn't have access to, let alone be able to craft one from scratch.

Cornelius' voice cut through the tension. "Walker's here."

Olivia sucked in a breath.

"What?" Adeline exclaimed.

"I saw him," he continued. "With his hulking colleague. But . . . There's more. The mines underneath Peleș castle are set to blow."

There was a moment of silence as everyone tried to process Cornelius' words.

From seemingly far away, Olivia heard Adeline gasp. "Wh-What? But who . . ."

"The Black Knights," Cornelius replied. "The Black Knights have come to fight the Order, and they're willing to kill dozens of innocents to do so."

"This isn't a fight," Olivia whispered as her stomach fell. "This is a massacre."

A cold wind cut right through her clothes and made her shiver. Fatigue wrapped itself around her, pulling her down to the ground like an anchor. Olivia felt like she didn't have anything left. No more magic reserves, no more energy.

She'd sunk it all into this doomed mission and now . . . Now she didn't know what to do.

A scaly head peered from behind Cornelius' shoulder. The lizard-dragon's back arched in a sinuous stretch, dark emerald scales shimmering in the dim light. Fast as quicksilver, he descended from his perch and raced to her, its paws gripping the hem of her sari.

Olivia gently untangled his claws. He stepped onto her arm and climbed up until he could rest on her shoulder. Like a demonic kitten, he turned around a few times to find a good spot, then settled down and wrapped his tail around her neck to anchor himself. He was poking her, scratching her skin, and a few strands of her hair had caught in his scales, but Olivia let him be.

Raising her head, she became aware that the others were talking among themselves, but that Ryder's eyes were fixed on her. "Give us a minute?" he asked.

After everyone had moved a few steps away, Ryder knelt down in front of her bench. He didn't look angry any more, but his expression was determined. She should have known that meant trouble.

"All right, let's hear it," he said.

"Hmm?"

"I'm sure you think I'm just a brute, but I've learnt how you work. You, Ms Knight, have a plan."

Olivia blew out a breath. She knew it was pointless to try to deny it, but she still refused to say anything for a long time, turning her face away. Ryder merely waited.

"Godwyn's wrong," she said at last. "Another containment won't work."

"Why not?"

"The wand has been fighting to get here for so long. Now that it is, it won't let us cage it again. Besides, the containment I created back home was the strongest I could make it, and the wand still found a way to compel Godwyn and Cornelius. No amount of runes and moonstone powder can chain it."

No. The wand was simply too wild, too *alive,* for anything like that to work. There was only one thing that could.

Once again, she shouldn't be surprised that Ryder managed to figure out exactly what she hadn't said out loud.

He caught her chin between two fingers, ignoring the warning growl from the lizard wrapped around her neck, and tipped it up until she could no longer avoid meeting his stern gaze.

"No." His voice was unyielding.

Olivia sighed. "Yes. It's the only way. Only an arcanist is strong enough to contain it. And it's not just that. This wand is after power. It knows where the rest of the Serpenthyst crystals are, it can find the tree. A bait won't work. But the magic of an arcanist . . . that might."

His blue eyes were blazing as he repeated, "No."

"It has to be me, Ryder. No one else can handle the wand without being compelled. Only I can, because of this strange connection we share."

His gaze dropped to the hands resting on her lap, the silver slowly turning black. "You can't handle it either," he growled. "I can tell it's getting worse. You're in pain."

Damn him and his ability to read her mind.

"It wouldn't be forever, Ryder. Just a few days. Enough for you and Blackwood to figure something else out."

Those few days would be agony. The dark magic would slowly seep into her, corrupting her own. She could very well go mad or become one of the Warped. Already, she felt the black veins gaining strength, climbing towards her heart.

But the other way . . . It wasn't an option. Between risking everyone's lives on a mad idea, or just her own on a much safer plan, she didn't even have to think about it.

"No," he protested. "Why don't you tell me about your *real* plan instead?" A fleeting smile curled his lips. "You've been nothing less than recklessly clever ever since I met you. Don't be shy now."

Olivia stifled a frustrated groan. "I already told you. Recklessness is *your* speciality. I'm a saint."

"We'll just have to agree to disagree, Saint Olivia of the Wandering Hands."

Ryder's face turned serious again. "If you fall . . . we fall together." His eyes were so blue, so calm. "You're not alone."

Such simple words, she thought. And yet she believed him with everything she had. But that wasn't what compelled her to silence now. She trusted him. She just didn't trust herself.

Ryder cupped her chin again when she would have looked away. "You're one of the most brilliant people I know," he said, his voice firm. "You think outside the box. Your idea isn't crazy. I trust you, we all do. We're willing to bet our lives on it."

"And what if it doesn't work?" Her voice was barely above a whisper.

Ryder's callous fingers tucked a loose wisp of raven hair behind her ear, grazing her cheek in the process. "Then at least we would've tried."

"Just like that?"

How could he be so nonchalant? How could he not be afraid? The regret and guilt and fear were crushing her. It was squeezing her throat, weighing her down. She felt like she was drowning in it.

CHAPTER 34

She never should have insisted they take this case. She never should have allowed her team to follow her into this madness. She should have realised how powerful and dangerous that wand really was. She should have...

All these thoughts kept swirling around her mind like an angry tornado. She'd sworn to herself that she would never take such risks again. And yet she'd done it, and worse.

Ryder took her blackened hands in his. It still surprised her how broad they were compared to hers. The fingers large, the skin rough and covered with countless tiny scratches. His thumb drew small circles around her knuckles.

"Olivia. You can pretend that you have chosen a quiet life for yourself, without danger or risks. But you'd be lying. You could have kept your job at the Ministry, done what they expected of you, but instead you chose to fight. You keep chasing the craziest cases, the most impressive ones. You invent experimental concoctions that could explode at any moment. You swap stories with Cornelius about the nastiest, darkest curses, and you both get that hungry look in your eyes, like a wolf seeing a group of nice, tasty sheep.

"The truth is, you crave the thrill of adventure, the feeling that what you do *matters*. That is who you are. You're not the kind of person who hides behind others, behind rules. You break them."

"You're wrong. I love my rules."

"You love stealing things more."

Olivia sighed. She wanted to protest. Just out of principle, and also because she liked to think of herself as a stickler for reliable and prudent enterprises. But the maddening Warden was unfortunately right in every way.

Her fear of failure was suffocating her. And in retrospect, that was a failure in and of itself. Because the thing she kept forgetting was that her plan might fail, yes. But it also might just *work*.

She'd allowed herself to become a creature crippled by doubt. The kind of person who would prefer certain doom over the possibility of success.

No more.

Ryder got to his feet in one strong motion and helped her up. Not happy at being jostled, the lizard-dragon unfurled his tail from around her neck and scattered.

Olivia took a deep breath and announced in the strongest voice she could muster, "I have a plan. But I warn you all, it's a crazy one."

"We're all ears," Cornelius replied immediately.

Adeline grinned. "Where do I sign?"

When she turned to him, Godwyn crossed his arms over his chest and frowned. "Exactly how crazy are we talking here?"

Olivia couldn't help the smile that escaped her. How she loved her team.

"Do you remember the hidden text on the Legendarium page? The one Cornelius translated," she asked. Her gaze darted first to a silent Holmes, who inclined his head a fraction, which she took as acquiescence, then to the detective, his pale, *pale* blue eyes suspiciously bland.

Adeline answered her, "The strange poem about the Gate, yes."

"I certainly remember how some reacted to it," Ryder muttered. Then he blew out a breath, understanding blooming in his voice. "The tree... You said no one could see it, but it must have always been there. You think the tree *is* the Gate."

"Yes. And every time I came in contact with the wand, I felt something else..." Olivia's chest tightened. "Lurking. Waiting for its opportunity."

I've been waiting for you...

She fought against the tension in her muscles as she recalled those memories. "A living Darkness. Something not of this world, but from another place. Wherever this Gate leads to."

"That's why the sergeant asked us if we'd reached the Clearing," Cornelius added. "He wanted to know if we'd seen it."

"I felt it a second time," Olivia went on. "Down in that cave with those creatures made of shadows... Their magic was the same." She took a deep breath. "I think that's the real reason why the Order is after the wand. Not for the curse or its abilities. But for the Serpenthyst crystals inside, for what they can do."

A dangerous silence greeted her words.

CHAPTER 34

"So if the Order is trying to reopen the Gate..." Godwyn began.

Adeline quickly added, "And access whatever's lurking on the other side."

Godwyn blinked. "I'll pretend I didn't hear that for now. What exactly is your plan, Liv? You can't take the crystals out of the wand, the curse won't let you. It's the source of its power, it'll never let them go."

"I agree," Olivia declared. "Which is why we need to get rid of the curse first."

"That's impossible," he replied. "Curses cannot be destroyed, that's the very first thing you taught me."

"Yes. But they can be moved."

Godwyn's brows knitted together, his doubt evident. "You want the curse to give up the wand? What do you have that could possibly be powerful enough to motivate it... *You*. You'll be the bait. You want the curse to seep into you."

That gave Ryder pause. He turned to glare at her, his eyes narrowing into slits. If he'd thought her real plan was less dangerous than the first, he'd been wrong.

"*Crazy* doesn't even come close, Liv." Godwyn's deep sigh held so much dismay that she felt sorry for him.

"I'm going to draw the Shrine circle around us," Olivia explained. "It will slow down the curse, giving me enough time to remove the crystals before it can reach me. Once they're safe, I'll sever our connection. The curse will have no choice but to return to the wand. Then we disappear with the Serpenthyst, and all we'll leave behind is a very cursed piece of wood."

Cornelius walked across the clearing to where their bags were gathered, and began rummaging through his own. Curious, the lizard-dragon came to perch on his head, surveying everything.

"Letting that curse loose is far too dangerous, Olivia," Holmes rasped. "If it escapes your control..."

"Which is why I'll need to do this somewhere special," she replied. "Somewhere that can contain it if things go wrong."

Godwyn clicked his fingers. "A salt mine! Romania's famous for them, and salt can seriously blunt curses, right?"

When Adeline turned to gape at him, he shrugged defensively, a slight pink tinge blossoming on his cheekbones. "What? I know things too."

"Yes, salt mines are perfect," Olivia agreed. And here came the worst part of her plan. "There's just one problem . . ."

Godwyn muttered, "Why am I not surprised?"

Not one to pull punches, Blackwood drawled, "The closest one happens to be located right here, underneath Peleş Castle."

Ryder sighed — or was it a frustrated growl? — and raked a hand through his hair. Olivia had the sudden thought that he should be careful, or he wouldn't have any hair left when this was all over.

He turned to Blackwood and Holmes. "Do you know how to disarm them?"

Both men looked thoughtful before Blackwood said, "Perhaps. But the hardest part will be to find them."

"The demonic lizard can do it."

Godwyn held up a hand, his eyes darting to Cornelius. "Wait, wait. Hold on. You mean the mines full of explosives? Those ones?"

"We have to do something, Godwyn!" Adeline snapped. "We can't abandon those people to their fate!"

"Pardon me, let me rephrase. So you want to go down into mines that are not only crammed with explosives, but also full of members of the Order who would like nothing better than to kill us in order to get their hands on the real wand?" Godwyn threw up his arms and continued, exasperated, "And how are we even supposed to reach them? Have you forgotten that there is a horde of Dragon Knights between us and those mines? Are you preparing for an *actual* war, Cornelius?"

The young man looked up, his arms holding a bundle of salt grenades, spectral bangs and all manner of curse-battling artillery.

"Did you leave anything behind?" Adeline added. "Or you took it all?"

"It doesn't hurt to be prepared, *cher*. It doesn't hurt," he said, and went back to his inventory of supplies.

Ryder had been watching him with rapt interest, and when he spotted a familiar belt, came over immediately. "I'll take that."

Cornelius handed him the string of black salt bombs with a knowing smile.

Gods help them.

"Olivia, do you feel strong enough for this ritual?" Holmes asked her.

She steeled her spine and took a deep breath before nodding. There was only one way to find out.

"This is ridiculous! There are mines all over this bloody country!" Godwyn protested. "Why are you fixated on going to the only one that has the potential to blow us to smithereens?"

"The biggest one, Salina Turda, isn't too far from here," Cornelius supplied, his arms brimming with multicoloured flares. Novelium, mandrake root, even Greatwood bark... *Where had he got all these?* "If we leave now, I'd reckon we could be there by midnight."

"Perfect." Godwyn clapped his hands. "Let's go."

But Olivia shook her head. "We can't."

"Why not?" he pressed. "You heard Cornelius, it's the biggest one. Surely, it'll work."

"That's not it." She raised both hands in front of her, and they all saw that the black veins had reached her elbows now, with no trace of the feylin's silver any more. "I won't last until midnight."

Godwyn scrubbed a hand over his face and started pacing a few steps away. "What about the Black Knights?"

Something cold and stark passed over Holmes' features. "Don't worry about them."

They were no doubt tied up somewhere in those woods, inside a circle made of roiling shadows.

Godwyn stepped forward again, his mouth a straight, hard line. "That does not change the fact that we'll never get to this mine. They have a Furtum mage, Olivia. And those shadow monsters."

"I can help with that."

Olivia's eyes widened immediately. "Addie..." she began, glancing at the detective.

He stood straight, hands in the pockets of his dark coat, watching them with that unblinking gaze of his. His familiar seemed to have vanished, but a tingle at the base of her spine told Olivia he wasn't far. "It's too dangerous. We don't know anything about him."

Godwyn finally caught up. His face darkened. "*Adeline* . . ."

Blackwood remained silent, but a brow had crept up in interest.

Adeline waved a dismissive hand, ignoring their objections. "I trust Isaksson," she declared in a strong voice. "He won't let anything happen to me. If he trusts him, so do I."

Godwyn's mouth opened, but Adeline hissed, "I suggest you choose your next words carefully, Baron."

Ryder pivoted to face Adeline, his voice grave and solemn. "I trust Blackwood."

And Olivia trusted *him* implicitly. But still, she hesitated.

If they were wrong, the consequences for Adeline would be terrible. This went beyond the immediate dangers of this mission. If her abilities became known, it could ruin her life.

Her eyes flickered to Griffin, who immediately scoffed, "Please, Olivia. You insult me."

And she understood at once that he wasn't talking about betraying Adeline to the authorities, but the fact that she thought he might not already know about her powers.

"Is anyone ready to tell me what's going on?" Blackwood asked.

Before anyone had another chance to object, Adeline declared, "I have Illusion magic."

"Illusion magic?" the detective repeated, incredulity clear in his voice.

The very next moment, he gaped in astonishment as the face that looked back at him was that of High Commissioner Mitrea.

Ducking his head, Cornelius coughed into his hand. "Show-off."

Mitrea turned to him. "What was that?"

"I said 'My darling Adeline, even after all this time, your priceless abilities still manage to take my breath away.'"

"Hmm. I thought so."

Blackwood chuckled softly, shaking his head. Despite the seriousness of the situation, Olivia felt mighty proud to have caught the unflappable detective off guard.

"Well, now," he rasped. "You lot are certainly full of surprises."

CHAPTER THIRTY-FIVE

THE TEMPLE OF STARS was a constellation nestled in the far east of the northern hemisphere, shaped like an arched doorway. It was named after a fabled temple, which centuries ago, young gifted arcanists had to enter as a rite of passage. They would step inside the labyrinth at its centre and seek the truth of their power, reach enlightenment. Only then would they be allowed to leave.

At that moment, Olivia felt very much like one of those young arcanists, about to test the strength of her magic against the almighty maze.

Named after that constellation, the Shrine circle she'd drawn on the small wooden platform was one of those circles that was purely theoretical, studied by academics as nothing more than an interesting research tidbit. No one in their right mind would attempt to draw one, let alone devote as much magic to it as she was about to. Not unless they were desperate, that is.

Olivia lifted her head and took a moment to dry her sweaty palms on her trousers, rub the crick in her neck.

After they'd changed out of their finery, they'd set off for the salt mine to prepare for the ritual. Adeline had used her powers of illusion to help them cross the still ongoing auction and avoid all its security guards, all the way to the small library on the first floor and its secret passage leading underground.

Olivia had held her breath the entire time, sure they were about to come face-to-face with the Furtum mage again, but they'd followed the salty air through the dark tunnels, silent as ghosts, and emerged into the mine.

CHAPTER 35

A breathtaking sight had unfolded before them, a gigantic underground cathedral whose sheer size had made goosebumps arose on her arms.

The ceiling soared hundreds of feet above, disappearing into darkness, stalactites of pure salt hanging down like the ridges of a slumbering beast. Striated rock walls in intricate patterns encased them, glistening with a crystalline sheen. The light from luminescent veins of metal running through the rugged surface cast a surreal glow as it reflected on the dark lake below.

At the centre of the lake stood an island pavilion, while suspended over the water, a labyrinthine network of wooden bridges and platforms formed a complex web.

Olivia had stepped onto one of the smaller floating platforms and begun drawing her highly technical circle, while the others set off on their assigned missions, or their "important hunter business", as Adeline had put it. Olivia didn't know exactly what that entailed, only that Cornelius' supplies had apparently been put to good use and that Ryder had had a long talk with her assistant, their heads close together, both of them grinning. The word *trap* had been used quite often.

So now all around her was ghostly silence, thick and heavy. The kind she'd only ever encountered deep within a crypt. This place felt *alive*, as if the walls themselves were breathing with the memories of centuries gone by. But that didn't frighten her. Instead, the taste of salt on her tongue was strangely refreshing, the glow coming from the metals inside the walls soothing. The lake around her made no sound, there were no waves, its surface was simply a perfect blackness, as if she were floating in space.

A flash of green to her right made her smile. The newest member of their team was clearly hard at work. But her amusement faded as she glanced at the ever-growing mountain on the other floating platform: all the bombs they'd managed to find stuffed into the cracks and crevices of these mines. Such destruction . . . She didn't even dare look at them too long, in case the devices exploded from the intensity of her gaze alone.

Instead, she reached for the dagger she'd stolen from Ryder and raised her left hand, which had now turned completely black. Between one blink and the next, however, her wrist was caught in an unbreakable grip.

"What do you think you're doing?" A deep voice growled from behind her.

Ryder. She hadn't even heard him cross the plank bridge.

"I need blood to draw the runes."

"Blood?" Ryder looked down at the paper in front of her, where she'd scribbled the circle design. "There are far too many runes for that." He still hadn't released her wrist.

"It'll be fine, Ryder," she tried to reassure him.

He let go of her hand, only to crouch down and lift his sleeve past Holmes' runic limiter to bare his own forearm. "Take mine."

Olivia stared at him. His strong jaw was set, his posture solid, ready. He radiated calm and alertness. A soldier ready for war. But his blue eyes betrayed him, a flicker of fear and unease in their depths.

Before she could think better of it, her hand snaked its way to his cheek. "I can't take your blood, Ryder. It has to be mine. But it's all right. It'll work," she promised.

If she wanted the curse to take her bait and flow through the circle, she had to make it sizzle with power, turn it irresistible. That wouldn't be a problem with a smaller circle, but this one was a maze. Dense, complicated, filled with lines and glyphs. She would need to sink more magic into it than she'd ever attempted before. More magic than was safe.

So she'd slightly modified the traditional shape of the Shrine to turn it into a hybrid augmenting circle. Each time she poured magic into it, it would spread through the labyrinth and then loop back to her more potent. Just like a traditional augmenting circle, except she wouldn't stop after one or two waves, but would keep going. And if that still wasn't enough . . .

Olivia didn't tell him any of this. She wasn't really lying, he knew how dangerous her plan was. She was just pretending, trying to gather her courage for what was to come. She knew he understood because he didn't question her any further, instead resting his cheek against the palm of her hand.

Too soon, she let go. Taking a deep breath to steel herself, she dragged the edge of the blade against her skin.

Gods. That hurt more than she thought it would. Wincing and biting off curses, she clenched her fist tightly while she added blood to key points of her circle.

"How's it going out there? And where is everybody?" she asked to distract herself, a strain in her voice she did her best to hide. She began drawing the runes, trying to get the symbols as precise as she could.

"Cornelius and his demonic pet are making a final sweep to make sure we got all the bombs. The activation device is keyed to Walker's magic, so it's useless to us. Blackwood has been trying to disarm them, but according to him they're extremely unstable. He says it's highly restricted military equipment." Isaksson's voice turned to a furious rumble. "Walker likes to play with dangerous magic."

"Then what do we d-do?"

"That godfather of yours spread a protective shield around them. He's almost certain it'll be enough to absorb the blast if they go off."

"Al-almost certain doesn't seem very . . . reassuring," Olivia said. Her voice came out as a wavering stutter.

"That's all we can do for now," was Isaksson's straight reply. "Adeline and Godwyn are finishing setting up some warning flares. We'll know when the Order comes."

When, not *if.*

Olivia winced, gritting her teeth. Only three more runes to go. Ryder had been right, it *was* a lot of blood. She was starting to feel light-headed. "Speaking o-of . . ." *Deep breaths, focus on the lines.* "Holmes. How do you think he f-found us? And why is he . . . here?"

Ryder didn't answer. He'd torn a strip from the bottom of his shirt and was waiting for her to finish, his eyes glued to her bloodied hand.

Finally, it was done. Olivia let out a shaky breath and he immediately wrapped the white strip around her palm to stop the bleeding. She had to bite her lip when he tightened the makeshift bandage.

"All right?" he asked her gruffly.

"Yes." Then she gave him a questioning look. "So?"

Ryder grasped her wrist and lifted her hand higher. His fingertip tapped the skin of her forearm. It only showed smooth brown skin at the moment, but a flicker of her power and it would reveal the twisting lines of copper that formed the mark of her arcane Pact.

"Ah. The Warden doesn't appear as clueless as I'd previously thought."

Olivia smothered an exasperated sigh at Holmes' sardonic rasp. Predictably, Ryder's eyes iced over as he helped her to her feet. They left her circle, careful not to disturb her chalk lines, and walked up the bridge to the main platform.

"You still haven't told us what it is you're doing here," Ryder said as he crossed his arms, biceps rolling under the raised sleeves of his shirt.

Instead of answering, Holmes craned his neck to study Olivia's lines. His brows rose. Tawny eyes snapped to hers, and his jaw turned into a block of ice, but Olivia gave him a warning look. It was too late to change plans now.

"Same as you, I suppose," Griffin finally said. "Making sure the wand is safe."

"But why didn't you tell us you were coming?" Olivia insisted. "Why hide?"

"There were already too many people tracking your every move. You needed someone to watch your backs from the shadows."

"Great. More riddles." Ryder's voice was sharp. "I'm getting tired of the enigmas and the vague answers. Why are you really here, Purveyor?"

Holmes took a menacing step forward. The area of the cave directly behind him suddenly grew a shade darker. "Are you calling me a liar?"

"You knew a whole lot more about what was going on than you told us. You've deliberately kept us in the dark!"

Cornelius chose this moment to come towards them, the sleeves of his white shirt rolled up to his elbows and sweat on his brow. His lizard-dragon was hanging upside down from his shoulder, glowing amber eyes not missing anything around him.

Without a word, he moved to Olivia's side and wrapped his long fingers around her wrists.

"I chose not to disclose certain information in order to protect you both!" Holmes snapped. "Knowing about the Order would have put you directly in their path."

"As if we haven't been there since the very beginning," Ryder countered dryly.

Olivia was about to interject when a pleasant tingling sensation went up her arms. She looked down to see the black veins on her palms lighten, allowing some of the feylin's silver to show through. Immediately, she felt her breathing settle, some warmth return to her body.

"Still working?" Cornelius asked, his voice quiet.

Olivia nodded as another wave of energy washed over her, bringing with it a contented sigh. Cornelius was sharing his magic with her, reviving the failing feylin. He'd done it twice already: once when they'd still been in the clearing, then as soon as they'd arrived inside the mines, before he'd set off on his bomb-gathering mission.

She could almost *taste* his magic. It was something she'd never told anyone she could do. Her own little secret, for her own private enjoyment. Cornelius was like warm spices and cognac, the smell of leather and the feel of the Louisiana sun on a late summer's day. A few months ago and after a particularly nasty case, Adeline had used her magic to lift a stubborn curse off Olivia. It had tasted like sharp wine and stormy nights, fiery temper and an unbending will.

She wondered what Ryder's magic tasted like. Pine and sandalwood, perhaps. A hint of smoke for a dragon racer. She glanced at him. Right now, it would probably taste like a raging storm at sea, all icy, biting wind and deafening howls.

"Thank you, Cornelius," Olivia whispered gratefully.

The silver on her fingers was bright and shiny now, swirling around like a lake of molten metal. The warmth had spread up her arms, all the way to her chest. Sadly, she knew it wouldn't last. Every time he'd done this, the veins had reappeared, perhaps even stronger and faster than before. But she didn't tell him any of that.

Cornelius winked at her, a dazzling grin on his face that made the corners of his eyes crinkle. "At your service, boss."

Ryder and Griffin stopped arguing when Blackwood strode in, followed by Godwyn and Adeline, streaks of dirt marring their cheeks, their clothes. Tendrils of hair had escaped Adeline's bun and framed her face. Olivia realised this might be the first time she'd ever seen her assistant looking so casual, in no-nonsense trousers, suspenders and sturdy boots.

"All the defences are in place," Blackwood declared.

Ryder turned to Adeline. "The cursed lanterns?"

Her assistant smiled, a wicked gleam in her silver eyes. "Curious Dragon Knights are in for a nice little surprise."

Ah, so that's why Ryder had made them steal all the lanterns on their way through the auction. Sneaky hunter.

"Excellent." Ryder pivoted towards Godwyn next. "The flares?"

"Armed and ready to go."

Ryder finally spun to Olivia, his face set. "We're ready."

Olivia started for the floating platform that contained her circle, but Griffin suddenly materialised in her path, stopping her with a hand on her wrist. "Be careful."

Nodding, she wobbled down the bridge to where her chalk lines awaited, inert and strangely beautiful. A complicated array of geometric shapes and runes, pure white against the dark wood.

Only this circle was the most complex design she'd ever attempted, and if she couldn't control it, if she sunk too much magic or lost her grip, she would become Warped. Her power would rush out of her in one fell swoop, leaving her a husk of her former self, her mind probably scorched by the onslaught of magic. She would spend the rest of her days in an asylum, her eyes blown white, her face haggard and her articulations distorted.

Dread settled in the pit of her stomach. Her heart began to pound in her chest, her hands shook.

Deep breaths. In and out.

Olivia reached her floating platform and turned around. Ryder was crouched on the edge of the main structure, the rope to the plank bridge she'd just crossed between his hands. He was staring at her with steel in his eyes.

"Let's do this, boss," Cornelius said as he came up behind him.

They'd agreed that the circle was too much for one person to handle, and he'd immediately volunteered to do the ritual with her. He, too, was willing to risk his life for her plan. Such a crazy plan, it was. So many things could go wrong . . .

Olivia watched as Cornelius went to step onto the bridge.

He was such a bright light in her life. Full of swagger and charming smiles, mischief and so many morbid tales. He was the heart of their little makeshift family.

She smiled as he threw her a wink.

His foot never touched the planks.

Olivia sent a pulse of magic that made him stumble back, made the rope fly out of Ryder's hands. The floating platform she stood on drifted away, surrounded by the salt waters of the mine.

"Olivia!"

She ignored Ryder's cry. Instead, she carefully placed the wand at the furthest point of the circle, and poured the ophite stones that had been in the containment cage next to her.

Then she raised her arms and concentrated. A bright amber glow ran through the chalk lines, igniting them. It raced through the entire design, then rushed back to Olivia, infinitely more powerful.

"Olivia!" they shouted again, begging her to stop.

"I'm sorry, Cornelius," she whispered, knowing they wouldn't hear her. "I can't let you risk your life for me."

She would do this alone. She *had* to do this alone.

When the power had smashed back against her, it had done so with the force of a crushing wave. But it wasn't enough.

She did it a second time, gritting her teeth as the magic struck back. The wave had doubled in strength. It hurt now.

The circle around her began to spin, puffs of dust flying into the air. A wall of amber light rose from the lines. Still not enough.

She sank more magic into the circle, and when it reached her, it wasn't a wave any more. It was a tsunami.

Her jaw locked tight to strangle her screams. She fought to breathe, couldn't. So much magic, it felt like trying to grab a bolt of lightning with her bare hands, hold on to it.

Olivia reeled, trying desperately to absorb it all. But it was too strong. She'd poured so much magic. A whimper escaped her, it hurt so much.

From far away, she heard anxious voices. What might have been her name. Yes, people were yelling her name.

But she couldn't stop, not now. Her arms jerked, her whole body shook with the strain. She took a wavering breath, another. She could feel tears running down her face, her skin buzzing with excess energy.

It still wasn't enough.

She needed more.

Her head turned to the side and the voices calling her name grew even more desperate. She made the platform drift closer, the one stacked high with a mountain of bombs. She shredded the shield of darkness that Holmes had spread over it. It took only a flicker of her infinite power.

And then she blew it up.

The energy from the bombs lashed into her circle in a torrent so powerful, so violent, it was a geyser of pure magic. It flashed through the lines, so bright it illuminated the entire cave, blinding her.

For a split second, time stood still. As if Olivia had leapt through the air and was now at the top of the arc, floating, weightless.

But then it started again and she fell. The magic barrelled towards her, a terrible avalanche of power that slammed into her body.

A burst of agony exploded in her mind. Magic surged through her veins, streaming fire. She screamed.

The world swayed. She was drowning.

She had to control this power or it would kill her, turn her into a mindless skeleton. She had to complete the ritual or the wand would be lost.

Olivia clung desperately to consciousness as the fire raged inside her. Coppery lines appeared on her skin. Too much magic. It was crushing her, the pressure so intense that she felt as if it might explode out of her. The world turned scalding white, her heart raced. She was going to die.

No.

It was *her* magic, *her* own power. And she would. Control. It!

Olivia let out a roar full of pain, of terror. She strangled the avalanche of magic rolling through her veins. It raged, clashing with her will, but she clamped it in a deadly grip and refused to let go.

Sweat dripped down her back. Her heart pounded madly in her chest, blood roaring in her ears. She held on. *Squeezed*.

Then, she finally felt it. The last note of the crescendo, the highest peak.

The pressure slowly began to recede. Breathing became easier, her vision cleared. Her trembling arms fell to her sides.

"Liv! Liv! Are you all right?" Cornelius was calling to her, his voice frantic.

Olivia raised her head and nodded. She didn't have the strength to do much more.

She'd managed to control the power and now, the circle around her radiated pure magic. The light emanating from it was so bright it hurt her eyes. She'd never seen anything like it before.

She squinted as she looked to the farthest point, where the wand rested. If the curse didn't take the bait and poured itself into the circle, leaving it behind, it would all have been for nothing.

Olivia held her breath, teary eyes glued to the lines.

Something shifted.

She wiped her face with her sleeve. Had it been a trick of the light or . . .

No, it did it again. The line closest to the wand was slowly changing from a coppery glow to a sickly green.

Yes!

Olivia let out a shuddering breath. Wisps of mist spread out from the wand, travelling across the surface of the lake. It was working.

Behind her, the others cheered.

That was when a bright purple light appeared, coming from deep within a neighbouring tunnel. Olivia's smile froze.

The warning flare.

"They're coming," Ryder shouted. "Everyone to their posts!"

He went to take up a defensive position at the entrance to the cave with Blackwood, behind piles of heavy crates they'd stacked high. Ryder unsheathed his gladius and made a few circles to loosen his wrist. He looked like some sort of avenging warrior, with the angry look on his face and his gleaming sword.

Holmes' magic splayed out, a focused blanket of darkness that wrapped around him like a mantle. It flashed orange and ruby, as if licked by fire. The griffin had just spread its wings.

He planted himself behind the two men, ready to catch anyone who managed to slip inside the cave.

Adeline and Godwyn waited behind another makeshift barricade. Their expressions were focused, sharp. Adeline's hands sparkled with crimson as she stood ready to unleash her fire.

Gods, this was it. They were about to be attacked.

Olivia's mouth went dry, her palms wet. She watched helplessly as Cornelius ran to where Ryder was pointing, his hands reaching for the black salt grenades and flares strapped across his chest.

Please, Cornelius, be safe. All of you.

She was powerless to help. The Shrine circle was so powerful that it had generated a null field around it. Until she dropped it, the barrier would repel any magic coming in or out. All she could do was stare at the battle raging around her.

Not that she would have been much help anyway. She was barely holding on. After the initial shock, the pain had subsided to a dull ache coming from deep within her, from her organs, her bones.

The sounds coming from outside were strangely muffled, distorted. That was why it took her a long moment to realise that the battle had already begun.

Flashes of magic erupted in every direction.

She heard screams, wolf snarls.

A black explosion shook one corner of the cave.

Olivia clenched her fists. *Come on*, she urged the curse. *Come on, you know you want to.*

The green glow was picking up speed now. Its tentacles spread out, taking over more of the lines. It flooded about a third of the design, but more was still pouring out of the wand.

Olivia stifled a cry of frustration. *Good gods, how big was this curse?*

She needed it to lose itself in the maze, leave the wand behind, so she could get the crystals out of it. But if the curse got to her before then, it was all over.

The green light reached the centre of the circle.

A knot formed in her stomach. It was still not done, more nasty green pouring out of it endlessly.

It had now consumed two thirds of the design.

Olivia held her breath, fear turning to dread.

What had she done . . . Her plan wasn't going to work. The curse was endless, it was going to reach her any minute now. She'd underestimated it. The Shrine had almost killed her and it was still not enough . . .

The curse was almost upon her now, barely a foot away from her kneeling form.

Tears streamed down her face. From the searing light or the anguish consuming her, Olivia didn't know.

The curse would drive her mad. It would make her attack her friends, attack Ryder. *No, no, no . . .*

Suddenly, she saw it. A flicker of amber at the edge of the circle, closest to the wand. The curse was finally out. This was it.

Olivia didn't even think, her magic *leapt* to the unprotected wand and ripped it open. She felt the Serpenthyst crystals inside, felt the Darkness too, but paid it no heed. She couldn't be afraid, she didn't have time.

She only thought of the way she'd felt every time she had come into contact with them. This emptiness, this void. The terrible yearning to be complete.

She wrapped herself in that desolate feeling, fell headlong into the loneliness, the grief.

You could become one, she whispered to the crystals. *You could finally be whole again.*

They'd been torn from where they belonged. The separation an aching, bleeding wound that could never heal.

Get out. Join the others. Become one.

Another push of her magic, stronger this time. She was beyond coaxing.

Be one! she yelled.

Olivia's eyes flew open. The wand lay inert at the edge of the circle, empty. Just a simple piece of wood. And next to it, a large chunk of crystal rested on the ground, radiating light from within.

Her eyes dropped just as the curse reached her and green tentacles wrapped around her hands, her wrists.

Power detonated from the circle. It shattered.

Olivia screamed.

A dark, churning cloud exploded from it, encasing her in utter darkness.

CHAPTER THIRTY-SIX

FEAR SLAMMED INTO HER. She couldn't see, couldn't hear over the roar of her blood in her ears, her ragged breaths. There was pressure all over her body, a huge weight pressing down on her, and yet she felt empty inside, floating.

If she hadn't been breathing, Olivia would have sworn she'd fallen to the bottom of the lake.

The black mist around her shifted, twisted. Phantom serpents took shape. Sliding over one another as if emerging from a huge, angry nest, flashing their fangs at her.

Olivia's magic flared, but her hands were still viciously bound, green shackles that bit into her skin and *burned*.

Like a deadly cobra, the black mist retreated slightly and then snapped out, clamping her in its grip. Olivia screamed.

It hurt. Gods, it hurt so much.

A sob wrenched itself out of her. What had she done? How could she have been so stupid? The curse was going to drain every last bit of arcane energy from her body, leaving nothing but a desiccated husk behind. And all the while, the Order would crush her friends, kill them one by one. They would never leave those gods-forsaken mines.

She could see them already.

Cornelius' golden-brown skin had turned ashen and pale where he slowly vanished beneath the black waters. Adeline's delicate hands were dripping with blood as she clutched Godwyn's form, his broken body sprawled lifeless on the dirty ground. And Ryder . . . He was on his knees, covered in wounds. His beautiful face burned down one side, his eyes milky white, unseeing.

His gladius slipped from his fingers. The sound of metal hitting stone echoed around her, again and again. It felt like heresy. His sword shouldn't be lying on the ground, forgotten. It should be in his hand, wielded against his enemies, along with Viking battle cries.

No! she screamed. *Pick it up! Fight!*

But he didn't move, didn't rise. His head hung low.

The smell of blood was everywhere now, saturating the air.

It was all her fault. They had followed her here, trusted her. And she had failed them. She squeezed her eyes shut. *No. No, no, no. This isn't real.*

"You've condemned them."

Olivia's eyes flew open. A whimper escaped her lips.

"You've condemned them all."

She was in her home, flames roaring in the fireplace beside her, yet she only felt cold and numb. It was raining outside. The clouds were tinted pink as the last rays of the sun vanished beyond York's rooftops. It was her favourite time of day.

Her father sat in his chair, a stack of books to his right and parts of a pocket watch spread out on the desk before him. His glasses were perched on the tip of his nose, his focus on the tiny gears and minuscule screws. "It is your fault, Olivia." He slowly raised his head and placed the parts back on the table.

"I'm sorry, Father. I . . . I tried."

"Did you?" He took off his glasses and folded them neatly before depositing them on the pile of books. "Is there not a part of you, buried deep inside, that is glad they're gone?"

Olivia's mouth fell. She took a step back. "No! They're my friends, Father. I would never do anything to hurt them!"

"Is that not why you brought them here with you? Because you wanted to succeed. No matter the cost."

"No, I swear that's not true, Father! I tried to make them leave, I didn't want them to get hurt!"

"But they were nothing but weights, weren't they, Olivia?" he insisted. "Weak. Useless. And now dead."

Olivia stumbled backwards, colliding with an armchair. "No! No, please. I love them!"

"Don't you love success more? That's why you stood there and did nothing, isn't it, Olivia? Just like with her."

A little girl appeared from behind his high-backed chair, a familiar, blood-soaked ribbon in her hair.

A sob caught in Olivia's throat. "No, no. Please, you must believe me! It was an accident!"

Her father stood and gently took the little girl's bloody hand in his own. "Now, now, Olivia. I told you never to lie," he scolded her. "Is that not why you feel such guilt all the time? Why you cannot even bear to say her name?"

"You killed her! You killed my Annabel!"

The angry yell reverberated through the silent office, rattling the windows. Olivia tried to cover her ears, but Lord Hadley's voice echoed inside her mind.

"Murderer!"

"No, no. Please, Father!" Olivia begged him. "I would do anything, please don't let them die!"

He sighed. "You know what you must do, my dear Olivia. The question is, do you really love them enough?"

"Yes, yes!" Her heart leapt beneath her chest as a heartbreaking hope filled her. "Whatever it is, please tell me, I will do it."

"The Order wants to hurt them. Kill them. Anything to get the wand."

Olivia's hands clenched into fists. She would destroy them all. Yes, she was going to eradicate that wretched Order. Once and for all. They were a scourge, a relic of the past. They did not deserve the wand. They were beneath it, unworthy of its power.

"You killed Annabel, but you could still save your friends," her father said softly as he walked to her. "You know what you must do. The only thing left to do."

Olivia's eyes dropped to the wand clutched in her hand.

"It's the only way to save them."

Yes. Yes, she had to save them, whatever the cost—She couldn't control the wand. No one could.

"No!" her father howled. "You've damned them all!"

It was cursed. Dangerous. It had to be locked away and contained. Olivia's fingers opened and the wand slipped out.

Power splayed out as it hit the ground, and a wail of pure rage sliced the air.

Olivia moaned in pain. She clamped her hands tight around her head. Her fingers clawed at her temples, trying to dampen the appalling shrill.

No! It shrieked again, louder. *No!*

It was all around her, coming from every direction at once, echoing inside her mind. Each scream was painful, like repeated blows, but it was the psychic power it carried that made it so unbearable. It didn't feel like anger, it felt like wrath. It made her throat rise and her head split. It was the sound of pure madness, pure fury. Drawn out indefinitely.

You killed her! You are a murderer! You deserve this!

The dark, churning cloud erupted again, a nest of writhing serpents. Fangs ripped through the air, ready to rip into her flesh.

Horror gripped Olivia. Every fibre of her being begged her to flee.

Standing in the midst of that seething cloud, her father smiled at her. A terrible, gentle smile. He raised his hands to her face. They were drenched in blood.

Olivia gasped, choking on her tears. She tried to back away but the serpents held her captive.

"It's all right, my Olivia," her father whispered. "That is why I'm here. You can let go, now." His cold fingers brushed over her cheeks, drying her tears.

Olivia sobbed. Her guilt and her pain were so heavy that it was making it hard to breathe, like a rock wedged firmly inside her chest. She could only suck in increasingly shallow gasps of air. "I'm s-orry, Father. I'm so sorry."

"I know, Olivia. It's all right."

Darkness crept into the edges of her vision. All she could see was her father's face, illuminated by the flickering light from the fireplace. His eyes were so kind, so loving. She hadn't even realised she'd fallen, but was now lying on the floor in his arms.

"That is why I'm here, my dear, dear Olivia . . ." Soft as a feather, his long fingers stroked her face.

The pain had receded behind a wall of numbness. Her eyelids fluttered. She felt herself tilt sideways . . .

Olivia's eyes snapped open. She couldn't *breathe*!

Her hands unclasped from around her throat and broke her fall when she landed in a heap on the damp wood of the platform. She sucked in terrible, ragged gasps as sweet air finally filled her lungs.

"That . . . didn't work, you . . . spineless . . . cursed bastard!" Desperate coughs wrecked her body, along with horrible inhales.

That bloody wand had tried to make her choke *herself* to death. Oh, Olivia had already known that curse was cunning, but this was really a low blow.

"Come and . . . fight me like a man!"

All at once, the black veil around her vanished. Suddenly, she was kneeling right in the middle of a battlefield.

It didn't take long for the crimson-robed members of the Order to notice the lump of Serpenthyst lying in the centre of the now depleted circle. It glowed a bright green and would catch the light every time a spell careened past. But even if it hadn't, there was no mistaking the *power* radiating from it. Like a siren song, it tugged at something deep within.

Olivia scrambled to pick it up and get to her feet, barely avoiding a black arrow made of pure magic.

"Liv!"

"Olivia!"

Cornelius ran up the plank bridge towards her and grabbed her shoulders, his face frantic. Griffin, too, looked over her body with unrestrained worry. He protected them from attacks by conjuring a wall full of writhing shadows.

"Are you all right?" Cornelius' hold was warm, solid.

A soft smile fell over her lips and she nodded, which made him exhale a deep sigh of relief. Her left hand was clutching the chunk of Serpenthyst, while the other fell to her side.

Cornelius turned his head, his eyes scanning the area around them, searching for a way out. He shouted something to Griffin. It sounded like a plan, a strategy.

For an arcanist, using his magic was like breathing. Like a heart beating. It was instinct, hardly requiring any thought. So when a dagger of pure ice appeared in Olivia's palm and she raised it to plunge it into Cornelius' heart, she didn't even notice at first.

Time froze.

The horror that gripped her was unlike anything she'd ever felt before. She saw the reflection of the light on the dagger's deadly edge, felt the cold seep into her fingers, noticed how Cornelius' warm eyes widened in shock.

Her blood had frozen in her veins too, as the dagger raced towards his chest.

But there was a flash of black, a searing pain, and it shot to the side instead.

Cornelius jerked back, his mouth agape, too stunned to speak. Holmes grasped his shoulder and shoved him back roughly, putting himself in front.

Olivia's singed hand filled with ice again. Not a dagger this time, but bright, silvery flames, bursting with power. Pure Ice Element.

She'd never been able to summon those before.

Amidst the roaring in her mind, it was the only thought that made sense. But then she began to scream. *What is happening? Somebody help me, I can't make it stop!*

But her lips didn't move, her tears didn't fall. The current of ice shot out of her hand, headed straight for Griffin. So did the next, and the one after that. She didn't stop, not for a second.

Holmes summoned his shadows to protect him, the shifting wall of black absorbing her rush of power. But her magic was so strong after the Shrine circle. She was glutted with it. And he was also protecting them from all the Order members trying to get to the glowing crystals still in her hand.

His tawny eyes blazed with the strain. "Olivia . . ." he growled. "Snap out of it!" He yelled at Cornelius to do something, to find a way to break the compulsion.

Yes! she screamed inside. *Do something, please, help me!*

Her magic whipped inside her, bucking and straining to break free.

Cornelius tried to knock her out with a powerful blast, but Olivia swatted at his magic with barely a flick of her wrist. She attacked *him* in return, and his face paled with the force of her blow. He combined his magic with Griffin's.

Her ice fire battered against their combined shields. Spots appeared in places, as if the magic had been stretched too thin and snapped. Cornelius took a step back.

Please hold. Please.

The sight of the silvery flames bursting from her hands brought a wave of nausea. They were not the right colour.

At the heart of the white flames, where her magic should have shone with a rich bronze, vibrant and bright, there was only a hideous green. The green of Godwyn's eyes when he'd crashed into that tree, the green of the hands that had slithered out of the walls of the Cellars, the green that had spilled out of a keyhole and under a door . . . Gods, how she *loathed* that green.

The revulsion she felt as that terrible, bastard magic poured out of her and attacked her loved ones was more than she could bear. Her mind began to drift elsewhere, hovering above the body it no longer commanded. She was turning mad.

Ever since that terrible day, that fateful moment that had altered everything, she'd carried her guilt in her chest, in her heart, wrapped around her throat. It was an anchor, banded tight around her soul.

For days, she'd agonised that her friends would get hurt because of her choices, because of her foolish desire for fame. For her selfishness. The wand had shown her hellish visions of their deaths at the hands of the Order. She'd thought the sight of their broken and twisted bodies lying on the floor of that gods-dammed mine had hurt, well . . . In the end, the Order wouldn't kill them. Not the curse, not the Darkness.

She would.

Griffin had been right, that wand was the most terrible thing she'd ever encountered.

They were yelling at her now. Trying to tell her something, get her attention. But Olivia was deaf.

Everything was a haze, tinged with sickly green. Her mind wavered, thoughts colliding with one another, there one moment, vanished the next. She didn't hear the chaos of the battle still raging around her. Didn't see the colourful blasts as they whizzed by. She felt lost at sea, untethered. Adrift.

Griffin's figure swam before her eyes. His austere and sharp face. His straight posture. Always in control, always a power, no matter the situation. There was panic in him now, dread.

Cornelius' arms were shaking. Every terrible blow of her magic nearly made him crumble, his legs barely holding him up. But he would straighten back up every time, try to meet her gaze, scream at her.

A broad figure that was all too familiar was running at full speed up the main platform, Griffin's wall of shadows parting to let him pass. Her magic instantly erupted to collide with his. White tinged with green against icy blue.

"Olivia, you can break this."

She didn't know how, but his deep voice carried to her ears when she couldn't hear anything else around her.

"You helped me break the compulsion once, remember? Let me help you now."

His clear blue eyes were focused on her, unwavering. He was so calm, so sure. He looked at her as if she were the only thing that mattered.

It was all right, she felt the same way.

In the end, it wasn't really a choice.

There was too much magic coursing through her after the circle. She was already warping, she could feel it. Like a million bees trapped inside her, buzzing in unison, trying to break free. Nothing she did now would change that fate.

Olivia's resolve hardened. In her mind, she bared her teeth. The curse had engaged in a battle of wills with her, trying to crush her spirit, using her worst nightmares against her. Well . . . She was a curse-breaker. And she would be damned if she didn't break that curse.

Olivia's fingers opened and the chunk of Serpenthyst fell to the ground.

Then she reached deep within herself, plummeted all the way to the core of her arcane powers. The curse was using her magic to attack them. So there was only one thing left to do.

Loose the magic.

Olivia bundled it all up and let it explode out. It tore out of her, a blinding flood of light. She took everything, every flicker, every shred, leaving nothing behind. She ripped it all from the curse's grip.

Her arms rose to the ceiling, the torrent that punched out of her that of a tornado. It rippled and billowed, colliding with the thick, rock walls of the mine.

The entire cave shook.

The column of blinding white roared, seeping into the cracks of the rock walls as the salts that had imbued it over many, many years struggled to absorb it all.

Ryder must have seen something in her eyes, some clue that gave her away, as he'd always done. Horror gripped his face, his voice hoarse when he yelled at her.

He tried to get to her, but her spear of power was too strong. He recoiled, raising his arms to shield his face. Still, he didn't back down. He wrapped icy blue magic around his figure like armour and tried to wade through her torrent of magic.

He hissed, he cursed. He pounded his fists against it.

Everything around Olivia was cold, bitterly cold. The kind that burned. And yet the geyser of power moved like flames. White flames with a heart of slithering green.

This was not her magic. This was the wand's. But the fire still raged and raged, draining everything from her.

Olivia didn't know how much time passed, it had slipped from her grasp. A coppery tang flooded her mouth. Her mind had restricted itself to one thing, that feeling of blessed *relief* she felt as the magic left her body.

She'd kept that power coiled inside her by sheer force of will, but it had been unnatural, the strain terrible. It had nearly killed her.

So the cooling emptiness that filled her now brought tears of joy to her eyes. As if she'd turned back into a normal body again, into *herself* again, and not a vessel of terrible power for the curse to feed on.

Slowly, the tornado of her release faded, the deadly wave turning into a violent current, then an angry stream. As the last of her blinding fire disappeared through the stone, Olivia fell to her knees.

From somewhere far away, she heard a cry. "Olivia! Get down!"

The words didn't make sense for far too long. By the time they did, she knew it was too late. She only had enough strength to look up, so she saw the blast coming straight for her.

There was no time to be afraid. The only thought that crossed her mind was that this would be a better way to go, in the end.

A huge force slammed into her chest and the next thing she knew, she was flying through the air.

Another impact drove all the air out of her lungs and everything turned to black.

CHAPTER THIRTY-SEVEN

Cold encased her body like sharp claws. Her mouth filled with salt water, needles going down her throat and into her lungs. Her mind emptied of all thoughts except *out*. She had to get out. But the water was so dark around her, she couldn't tell which way was up any more.

Olivia forced her weak body into action, struggling to move. Her clothes weighed her down, her mind struggling to make sense of it all.

What was she doing here? Why was it so dark?

She whirled around desperately, kicking her arms and legs. Her lungs were burning now, everything felt like it was on fire, and yet her limbs had gone numb.

A loud ringing began to echo in her ears. She shouted at her body to respond, to use the last dregs of its energy. Yelled at her legs to push her to the surface, to *fight*.

Something closed around her wrist like a vise.

Olivia screamed. More icy water immediately rushed into her mouth, her throat. The nightmares lurking in the water had finally reached her. Their phantom hands would shred her flesh mercilessly, tear her apart. She tried to fight them, thrashing against their hold with everything she had, but it was no use. The corpses dragged her down, down into the abyss.

When her head broke out of the water, she let out a gasp but still couldn't breathe, as if her lungs had completely frozen in her chest. She threw her fist blindly, her other hand still trapped in that merciless grip. All she knew was that she didn't want to be pushed down again. She tried to hit it again, and this time her fist connected with something hard, eliciting a grunt from above.

She punched, kicked, buckled. Her vision came back in indecipherable flashes. Booms of sound erupted around her above the ringing in her ears. Her body was wrecked with sharp gasps of air that *burned* all the way down her chest, making the water rise up in her throat.

"Olivia! Olivia, stop. It's me, stop!"

The familiar voice finally registered in her confused brain. The deep timbre, the Nordic lilt. *Ryder.*

The wave of relief that washed over her was so overwhelming that her entire body went limp. Ryder immediately shook her hard, yelling in between his own ragged breaths. "Olivia, stay with me! Stay awake!"

His solid arm was wrapped around her torso, his hand still encircling her wrist like a brand, clutching her to him. He pressed her too tightly, making it difficult for her to cough and purge the water from her lungs. Her icy skin felt like it was made of needles and every contact brought gasps of pain, but she gripped him with the same ferocity, her hold on his arm desperate.

She didn't try to help, couldn't have even if she'd wanted to. She let her head rest in the crook of his neck instead, trusting him to support them both and concentrating on calming the spasms ravaging her body, desperate to draw air into her deprived lungs. It was so cold that it hurt to think. The world swayed.

She vaguely registered twists and strange movements, Ryder shifting his hold on her and then she was tossed out of the water. Olivia collapsed in a heap, trembling and chocking on salt water. But her cheek was resting on strong, solid wood, so the most ridiculous laugh wheezed out of her.

Alive. She was still alive.

Ryder must have mistaken her relief for hysteria because he tried to soothe her, his hands gentle as he brushed the hair from her face, inspected her for injuries. "You're all right, Olivia. It's all right. You're safe now, *älskling.*"

Yet, she wasn't all right. She was warping, right there in his arms.

Her entire body hurt. Her skin, her tendons, her bones. The fire radiating from her right leg told her that her joints were beginning to crack, to distort.

But even though the pain was unlike anything she'd ever experienced before, it was nothing compared to the way she felt inside. The earlier overwhelming relief was gone, now there was only emptiness. Empty space where there shouldn't be any, utter nothingness. It was so *wrong*, so unnatural, that she wanted to scream, to beat her fists against her face. She would have done anything to make it stop.

"Did the magic hit you?" a voice asked urgently.

Ryder took her face between his hands, blue eyes boring into hers. Olivia's vision was blurry, swinging wildly from clear to flashes of colour. She'd lost her glasses in the lake, or maybe it was just her, she didn't know.

But she saw it nonetheless. Ryder's face was drenched in blood.

"Ryder," she gasped. She gripped the labels of his shirt with white knuckles. "Your face . . . You're h-hurt."

He gripped her chin in his fingers. "Olivia! Answer me! Did the magic hit you?"

"No," she managed to say. "No, just . . . cold. Empty. Ryder, my ma-magic, it's . . . gone."

A flurry of curses erupted from him. He shook her when her eyes drifted shut. "You stay with me, you hear me! You stay with me!"

The last of the numbness was slowly leaving her, only pain followed. Her whole body burned. From the inside out.

How could Ryder bear to touch her? She had to be engulfed in flames. Olivia whimpered, her voice breaking. "Hurts . . ."

Ryder cursed again, gathered her against his chest. "I know, *älskling*, I know."

A flow of magic poured out of him. Of course, it would taste even better than she'd imagined. Wild and free, just like him. With his cockiness, his mischief and his incredible bravery.

It should have been a balm to her heart, but instead his magic *stabbed* her.

Tears streamed down her cheeks, mixing with the salty water. It felt like razor blades slicing across her skin. The pain tore a sob from her. Her weak arms tried to push him away. "No . . . please, don't. It hurts. It hurts so much."

"I'm sorry, I'm so sorry. It'll make you feel better, I promise. Just stay with me. Please."

Her body was starved of magic, but like a dry patch of earth desperate for rain, it wouldn't absorb it. His arcane energy only rolled around inside her, highlighting every wound, every gash, all the damage she had done by ripping out her own magic so violently.

A distant voice cried out. Then a black figure appeared beside them, its eyes two chunks of arctic ice. "You have to go now!" It shouted. "Get her out of here!"

Olivia willed her mind to work again. She squinted, tried to make sense of what was happening around them. Loud explosions and screams kept ringing in her ears. There were flashes of light and colours that assaulted her senses.

At first she'd thought they were hallucinations, a creation of her crazed, pain-filled brain, but as her mind cleared, she realised they were very real. Ryder was crouched protectively around her on a corner of the floating platform, Blackwood standing guard nearby, sword at the ready.

And all around them . . . *War*.

The gigantic cave was filled with people. Olivia could see members of the Order of the Dragon in their recognisable red robes, but there were others dressed entirely in black. Some wore hoods obscuring their faces, some didn't, and they fought among themselves.

In one strong movement, Ryder gathered her to his chest and took off. The agony it brought her almost made her pass out.

Deadly spells continued to fly everywhere, whizzing past them, but Ryder stormed through, darting left and right, as nimble as a cat. For someone as tall and broad as him, not to mention how he was also carrying her, it was damn impressive. Out of the corner of her eye, she spied Blackwood's huge white wolf leap over fallen debris to charge a group of red-wearing men. Screams ensued.

As he ran, Ryder continued to feed her more of his magic. She tried to beg him to stop, but her mouth wouldn't form words. She was so tired, so cold, but her heart was racing and she couldn't get it under control.

Olivia wanted to tell him that it was too late, that there was nothing anyone could do. Not even a strong, reckless Viking who was the most honourable person she'd ever met.

He'd come for her. He'd found her. He'd dived headfirst into the frozen lake and fished her out, even when his face was dripping with blood and she could feel his whole body shaking uncontrollably.

But there was no way anyone could survive a loss of magic so complete, so violent. And now he was about to kill himself trying to save her.

Cornelius had shared some of his magic with her before. But it hadn't been more than a drop. What Ryder was pouring into her . . . it was an ocean.

It would kill him. Or at the very least, warp him too.

She couldn't let that happen. Not when she'd sacrificed herself to save *him*.

So she gathered the last of her strength and pushed it all away. Pushed away the scent of moss-covered earth and ocean's breeze, the feeling of warmth and flying embers. She closed herself off.

Only Ryder tensed and an even greater rush of magic flooded past her feeble defences, overwhelming them instantly. He stumbled and they barely avoided falling face first onto the stone floor. "Stop it!" he hissed.

"And you stop . . . giving it . . . to me," Olivia gasped. "You'll . . . warp too."

"No." Ryder's voice rumbled against her chest with the force of his growl. "If you don't want that to happen, I suggest you let me in!"

Impossible, arrogant, reckless man.

Olivia tried to resist, she really did. But there was nothing left in her body any more. So as her breath turned jagged, her heart pounding even faster inside her chest, she lost herself in the taste of whisky and pine needles.

They were still running, but Ryder was panting now, he'd slowed down. And Olivia knew that the wetness seeping into her clothes wasn't just lake water.

A wave of pain washed over her as every nerve in her arm snapped, frayed with agony. Her bone cracked. Then her wrist. Her eyes fell to her left arm lying on her stomach, twisted in all the wrong places. The sight would have repulsed her if her mind hadn't already been floating away. But Ryder saw and immediately cursed long and hard, a tone of desperation entering his voice.

"The crys-crystals . . ." Olivia stuttered weakly.

Please, let it have worked. Let it not all have been for nothing . . .

Olivia hadn't even spoken loud enough to hear herself, but somehow, Ryder did. "Holmes has them!"

"Cornelius . . . The others . . ."

"I saw them, they're all fine! We'll meet them at the tunnel entrance!"

She'd done it. It had worked. It was finally over . . .

"Don't close your eyes, Olivia!" Ryder begged. He couldn't hide the raw fear in his voice, the desperation. "We're almost there! Talk to me!"

A crack reverberated through her entire body. A rib.

She spoke around the coppery tang filling her mouth. "You used . . . one of your . . . Night-Night balls."

"Took out four bad guys with it, too." His own voice was a wet rasp. "Did you see?"

Olivia's lips stretched into the faintest of smiles. "I saw . . ."

Her vision blurred again. Relief, agony and fear twisted together in her heart, her bones, her breath. Every step he took while carrying her, every leap, every jolt to avoid enemy strikes, it broke her body anew. Never ending, merciless.

But all would be well. Her friends would live, the crystals would be safe. There would be no more phantom serpents, no more sickly green, no more Darkness slithering into people's minds.

She'd saved them.

At last.

She had the vague sense of someone yelling beside her. Others too. The voices sounded familiar. Olivia caught a few words here and there, floating in the haze.

Rejecting. Wrong power. *Dying.*

Something stirred in her mind. Olivia blinked. Swallowed.

She tried to squeeze Ryder's shoulder to get his attention, but her fingers had completely hardened, turning into twisted claws. She had to tell him something. She didn't know why, but she had to.

"Grif . . ." *Come on, you can do it.* She swallowed again. Her breath felt like shards of glass in her throat. "Griff . . . Griffin . . ."

She thought she'd been too quiet, but then there was a mighty bellow. "Somebody get Holmes!"

Another wave of magic flooded her parched soul. Bitter, sharp, *piercing*. The pain was unbearable now.

Her breathing turned shallow. Olivia heard the sound of stone rasping against stone. The air changed. Lights danced around her.

Then the world went quiet.

The pain in her body faded to nothing and she fell into blessed oblivion.

EPILOGUE

OLIVIA LIMPED UP THE last few steps, thankful that no one had witnessed the string of curses she'd uttered along the way. For the first time in a long time, she neared a bustling office, the clacking of typewriters, the bubbling of potions and the furious ringing of the telephone all audible through the heavy wooden door.

Her hand clenched on the doorknob, a familiar pit in her stomach. It had only been four months since she'd last set foot in this building, yet it felt like a lifetime ago. And if she was being honest with herself, Olivia knew that the reason she hadn't been back for so long wasn't just because she was recovering. The truth was she'd been avoiding it.

Her pulse quickened.

Maybe coming here hadn't been such a good idea, maybe it was too soon. She wasn't ready yet . . .

"Liv! You're back!"

The door burst open from the inside to reveal Adeline, her arms full of folders and a pen tucked beside her ear. There was even a smudge of ink on the top of her left cheekbone.

Olivia forced a smile as she stepped inside. "I don't know about *back* yet. I just came to pick up a few things." She looked around the office in surprise. "Where is everybody? Where's Crumpet?"

"Cornelius took that demonic beast with him into the field. You haven't seen how crazy he's become about its training."

"And Godwyn?"

"Still at the Cellars. Apparently, it's a huge job that's going to take way more than two weeks." Adeline sent her a sharp look. "You know, the Warden often asks about you . . ."

She was interrupted by the sound of shattering glass coming from their inventory room, just as the telephone on her desk started to ring, followed by the other one on Godwyn's desk.

Olivia raised her brows. "It *still* hasn't stopped?"

Adeline rolled her eyes as she blew out a frustrated breath. "I'm not sure it ever will."

Chuckling, Olivia took off her coat and scarf but left her gloves on, before saying, "Go, I don't want to disturb you. Come by my office when you have a minute, yes? I'll make you a nice cup of tea."

Her lips still pressed in an annoyed line, Adeline pointed at her with her pen. "Don't go anywhere!" Then she ran to the telephone and wedged the receiver in the crook of her neck, furiously scribbling on the nearest piece of paper.

Even though she'd been dreading it, Olivia smiled when she stepped into her private office at the back. Perhaps she was ready to come back after all. Perhaps.

She still gave her Wall of Doom a wide berth as she approached her desk, piled high with letters and other papers Adeline had set aside for her. She started to rummage through them, then frowned.

She poked her head round the door and called out, "Adeline, you haven't seen my notebook, have you?"

She'd looked for that notebook absolutely *everywhere,* had been sure it was hiding somewhere on her desk.

Her friend's brow furrowed in thought, the receiver still clenched against her cheek. "Did you check your coat? Or maybe you left it at the hospital?"

"Hmm . . . Let me see."

A few moments later, she indeed fished it out of the coat lying on her sofa and yelled, "Found it!"

She quickly flipped through the pages, which were covered in tiny notes and scribbled sketches. She'd been thinking about the vanadium again, but couldn't remember what she'd mixed it with to create her energy enhancer. She'd wondered if adding some . . .

A piece of paper was stuffed inside.

Olivia pulled it out. Written in black ink, the note was short and direct. As she read, it became difficult to breathe.

With trembling fingers, Olivia leafed through the rest of the notebook, and what she saw almost made her drop it on the floor. Of the pages where she'd copied the Gate prophecy, only a sliver of torn paper remained.

Congratulations on not letting the Serpenthyst fall into the wrong hands. It seems we have indeed underestimated you. As guardians of dark artifacts, we applaud your efforts.

We'll be coming by to collect it very soon.

- Black Knights

ACKNOWLEDGEMENTS

Writing a novel is a hard journey. Anyone who tells you different is either lying, only in the blissful beginning stages, or in fully-conscious denial in order to finish the damn thing. It's also a very lonely quest, full of teeth-gritted focus, late-night hours and many, *many* doubts, punctuated by a few short bursts of blistering genius.

But now that Olivia's story is complete, I know that I was never truly alone, and I couldn't have done it without the support of my incredible family.

To my parents, thank you for always believing in me. Your unwavering love and support means the world to me, and I think it's safe to say that this book wouldn't exist without you.

So thank you for taking me to storytelling shows when I was a little girl, for reading with me or falling asleep next to me as I listened to audio cassettes on my bed. Thank you for buying me more books than I could ever want, and for getting up early to queue at the store so you could buy me the latest one on release day.

And most of all, thank you for making me fall in love with stories — you've given me a gift more precious than you'll ever know.

To Virginie, you're my partner in crime, keeper of all the secrets, coach *extraordinaire*, comedic sidekick, voice of reason and devil on my shoulder, all rolled into one.

You've been with me since the very beginning of this journey, when I first got the idea for Olivia's story while walking in circles in the garden, and this book was supposed to be nothing more than a quick novella.

Thank you for always listening to me when I was stuck, for trying to fix my plot holes, for encouraging me to keep going, and for crying when you finished reading the manuscript for the first time.

I can't imagine my life without you.

To my three musketeers, thank you for all your help, your advice, your hard work and your encouragement as I wrote this novel. It's been a labour of love, full of ups and downs as life threw wrenches into our carefully laid plans, but I couldn't have wished for a better team by my side. I'm proud to have been able to create Olivia's story with you.

Here's to many more books.

Mist & Magic

Explore our Arcane world...

Mist and Magic is an online magical shop filled with replicas taken directly from our world. There, you can find artifacts, prints, homeware products and so much more...

Ever wondered what the Castle Wynd street in Edinburgh looks like? Wished you could find a pamphlet explaining how the Dragonling Postal Service works? Wanted to see old wand designs from Wardlaw Wands?

Look no further! Come delve inside the Mist & Magic store for a spellbinding collection of products and replicas that will make you feel like a real Arcanist.

www.mistandmagic.com

Curse Breaker Box

To celebrate the release of A Study in Curses, we've created an entire collection of replicas taken directly from Olivia's story.

Experience her curse-breaking journey through Romania as if it were your own with the Curse Breaker Box.

Will you be brave enough to enter the world of Curses, Dark Artifacts, and become a true Curse-Breaker?

mistandmagic.com/collections/curse-breaker